Proles

Proles

A novel about 2084

Joel E. Lorentzen

This is a work of fiction. All of the characters, organizations, and events portrayed in this novel are either products of the author's imagination or are used fictitiously.

Cover art by Evernight Designs

To Mom
Who always wanted me to try

Table of Contents

Acknowledgements..vii

Julianna 1

Eric Brunson, somewhere in what used to be Ohio.............................. 8

Complexities 25

This is what it looks like for real 34

I was in your dream last night... 41

Behavior is what matters 49

Junior Brunson, somewhere in what used to be Ohio 55

Junior Brunson, somewhere in what used to be Ohio 59

Kelly, somewhere in what used to be Ohio 68

The Founders' Canon 74

I wonder why I don't go more 79

Keaton, somewhere in what used to be Ohio 84

How can it be wrong? 95

Kelly, somewhere in what used to be Ohio 103

A closer look.. 112

The cosmos doesn't need a language... 119

Abby and Keaton, somewhere in what used to be Ohio..................... 127

Science can't explain them 133

Should I ask?.. 142

It's good that you know the truth... 146

Doing important work.. 155

Falsehoods are the guideposts 163

Meghan and Chad 168

Kelly 174

It's just a normal transition 186

Doesn't seem very equal to me.. 190

It has to change 198

They only damage themselves... 207

What good had he done? 213

I am who I am.. 218

You might not be aware that you are ill 224

Never to lapse again 233

She already knew them.. 240

But not necessarily standard work.................................. 247

We'll be good parents.. 253

Until now 257

You've been very helpful 262

Can you go back? 265

Not very believable... 270

Scientists need to do that 275

I think I know how.. 280

Can't we just ignore them?... 289

These were her people 294

Acknowledgements

Many authors, artists, and associates contributed to this novel, either by critique or encouragement. Chris Rayburn, a photographer (www.chrisrayburn.photos), reviewed my earliest work and didn't wrinkle his nose too badly, which I took as a rousing endorsement. Paul Lewellan, a seasoned author of short stories, served as an infinitely patient writing coach. After three full critiques and innumerable phone calls and zoom meetings, I had to call it. I doubt he was done. I still owe him a bottle of Writer's Tears. Sophia Elaine Hanson (www.sophiaelainehanson.com) was already such an accomplished author of novels and poetry that she shouldn't have taken me seriously. But she did. *Proles* is much better for her content editing. LaVina Vanorny-Barcus, an author of novels and children's books (but especially cookbooks!), spent some miraculously productive time helping me figure out what to do with the manuscript. Elle J. Rossi of Evernight Designs (www.evernightdesigns.com) translated my clumsy, adjective-rich description of a cover idea flawlessly and quickly. Callie Heiderscheit, the latest arrival to the effort, interrupted her Australian adventure to perform the final proof-read and nurtured the backflap description into maturity. If it pops, it's because of Callie.

In addition to listening to me whine, my cousin Tony Lorentzen bothered to read it in a state of semi-completion. He and Fred (Rip) Engle, a friend since college who probably didn't read it but who trusted that I would try to do good work, encouraged me to continue, even when I was ready to throw away the most recent draft.

I'm not certain if it is politically correct to say this anymore, but I've been blessed with the support of strong women throughout my life. My wife, Ann, took over for my mother, Marilyn, nearly 40 years ago. They made this work possible by expressing faith and encouragement in unquantifiable and sensible ways. I know it goes well beyond the food! Thank you.

-1-
Julianna

2084

Protocol. Nobody touched. The crowded lift was quiet. Julianna-119 was riding from her apartment to the lower floors in the building where she worked. Soap-and-fabric-softener smells filled the space. To Julianna, everything was both familiar and oddly out of place. Seeing her reflection in the spotless, mirror-finish stainless steel of the walls, Julianna forced her face to a mask of obscurity.

Doesn't death matter to anybody but me?

The lift glided to a stop. No one spoke, but there was a bustle of motion as Julianna exited with several others. She spied her two co-workers – Ashley-071 and Tim-127. They stood on the NetSurface where they met each morning. There were always challenges to discuss with Julianna's test results, the group's next game, or results from the last one.

"Greetings, Ashley, Tim," she said.

"Greetings, Julianna. I'm glad to see you back." Undertones from Ashley didn't match the word "glad." Something was up. Ashley was the Game Coordinator who managed computational resources for the group's upcoming games. There was continuous professional tension between the two of them. Julianna often ran her tests right up to the last moment. This meant that Ashley might need to work extra hours, sometimes urgently, to adjust and secure the right resources for the next game.

Ashley's petite build and Asian features made her appear younger than her approaching fifty years. She was crisp and businesslike as usual, but there was no acknowledgement that Julianna's father had just died. *How could that be?* It had only been three days.

1

But all of Julianna's experiences since had been distracting. Work seemed extraneous to a new reality, and she was barely able to concentrate.

"Thank you," Julianna responded guardedly. "I hope my absence didn't put us behind."

"It hasn't been a problem," Ashley averted her eyes to Tim. "We weren't certain when you would be back, so we sent our recommendation yesterday based on your test series sixteen. It won't be necessary to run any more tests for this game, so we can start researching the next project."

Ah, that's it. Julianna had not been satisfied with any of the tests thus far. Results tended to improve with every iteration. She usually ran well over twenty tests before recommending. There were several weeks before the game started, and she hoped that her planned tests would be more promising. Ashley's decision seemed arbitrary. But at just twenty-nine years old, Julianna was reluctant to challenge her. She was caught between the triumvirate forces of her high spirit, loyalty to the Best Society, and just recently – a hint of self-concern. She acknowledged Ashley's message with a resigned nod.

Tim watched their interaction with a good-natured smirk. Ashley, Tim, and Julianna worked in a Thelite group that developed and tested remediation hypotheses for extra-terrestrial bodies that threatened Earth. To do this, they played an interminable series of "games" inside a gigantic, universal, virtual model. The games modeled the overall threat to Earth after remediating targets using technologies both current and emerging. These included applying rocket force after interception by a probe, nuclear explosions in the vicinity of the body (or of another body that may affect the trajectory of the threatening body), electromagnetic pulses directed from space stations, and others. The model predicted the incredibly complex compounded effects of these nudges on all identified bodies in the holistic system. The goal of the games was to continually diminish the future threat to Earth.

Julianna was responsible for pre-testing remediation techniques for bodies within a certain zone, establishing the first, second, and third order effects of its use in the current game environment. Her recommendation would then be applied to the next game. It was a big effort to run a whole game, generally

2

taking several months. These hypothetical actions all took place many years in the future as the bodies came into closer proximity to the planet and more reachable with the remediation methods.

There were many groups like Julianna's with responsibilities for other bodies in other zones, employing tens of thousands of Thelites for this model alone. Each game was coordinated with all the other groups to ensure the model included all currently adopted remediations as starting conditions and anticipated all other groups' new recommendations. At the end of the game, the optimum combination of recommendations was adopted as Best Society policy. Those policies were then included in the environment for all future games.

"So," Tim said, "you'll have some time on your hands. Maybe you can help me with the boson-cannon and give it a try on the next project?"

Really? He's making a joke? The "boson-cannon" was an idea based on recent discoveries in particle physics. It offered a dramatic, new mechanism to extend the reach of remediation methodologies. But so far mathematics were insufficient to describe it – much less deploy it to practical purpose. Tim and his counterparts worked doggedly, but an applicable model was elusive. It had become a common jest among the testing community to jibe with developers, "if we only had a boson-cannon…"

"I still have plenty of prep work and research to occupy my time until then," she said in a frostier tone than she intended. She was disappointed that even Tim didn't seem to understand, but she certainly didn't want to alienate him. She forced a smile and he seemed unfazed, still pleasant.

After reviewing their project-related issues, Ashley changed the subject. "It is absolutely critical that we make better use of our CosmoPods. They use a lot of energy, and the Bureau has many demands for them." Looking directly at Julianna, she continued, "So maybe we can dial back some of the testing iterations." Then turning to Tim, "And we need to start seeing some results from development."

Tim responded with his usual frivolity. "I've already reduced my usage by twenty percent. Any less and I might as well spend my whole day at the

Center! Any takers?" He glanced at Ashley, then flashed Julianna a mischievous grin.

Really? Another joke? Even among Thelites, Julianna's appearance commanded more attention than most. Tall and willowy with auburn hair, she had an alluring, airy look, earthy-hued skin, freckles, striking facial features, and luminous green eyes. Many Thelite men pestered Julianna to join them at the Center for Reproductive Liberty, but none more than Tim. She had agreed on several occasions.

Wasn't anyone concerned that my father just died? But this was typical Tim. He continually added levity and sexual innuendo into their conversations. A few years older than Julianna, Tim wore his South Eastern European features, olive skin, and jet-black hair with a charming, comic arrogance.

Ignoring him, Ashley reinforced her point. "Let's just pay attention to CosmoPod utility and more precise scheduling, shall we?"

They paid cursory attention to the topic, but Julianna thought Ashley was off base. Running the models was important. If their work needed to be done, they needed to use the CosmoPods. But she said nothing. When the resources, structure, and policies at the Bureau of Scientific Truth (for whom they worked) were discussed, the topic was treated with delicacy. The Bureau was a massive organization, the largest in the Best Society and in the history of humanity. It adjudicated factual truth on everything. Firm regimentation was required. The Bureau's leadership encouraged informal discussions, but protocols for addressing challenges were rigid. Subordination of the Bureau's mission or leadership was unacceptable. The consequences were well understood. Your trajectory into higher accountabilities and the subsequent improvement in your living situation would be compromised.

The NetSurface where they stood was an electronic floor continuously displaying NetGrams. NetGrams are the mass publications and archives of Thelites. They employed many visual, audio, and physical effects to optimize the conveyance of information, like news articles created in a highly-animated, motion-picture studio. The NetSystem would automatically select

NetGram productions that were interesting to the parties immediately present on the NetSurface.

As their conversation closed, the NetGram was a chronology of how the current model for extra-terrestrial threats had improved over time. Early in the century, significantly simpler models were run by several organizations whose efforts were not coordinated. Thelites were alarmed when a sizable asteroid unknown to any model was discovered in near-Earth proximity. Fortunately, the asteroid flew by harmlessly. But the near-miss event made it clear that those models did not do their job. This meant that other threatening bodies might have been missed as well, a serious safety deficiency. So, the division was consolidated, and the new, singular model was created in a massive undertaking requiring many years of effort from the most brilliant theoreticians in the world.

This NetGram reported it was 99.999992% likely that anything that would threaten the Earth in the next one-hundred years had been identified and remediated. The mission of the division was to continuously improve that probability by remediating the most likely threat candidates. The probability was revalidated by running new games several times per year. This was part of the Best Society's effort to guarantee safety. The NetGram highlighted the infinitesimally-small-yet-positive gains their groups' work had accumulated.

Their conversation lightened to social topics. "There is a new spirit formulation being introduced," Tim observed. "It extends sleep effectiveness. Supposedly, six hours of this sleep refreshes you as if you had seven hours. Sounds amazing and I can't wait to try it!"

"I know, Tim," said Ashley. "So many benefits! The Best Society just continues to move forward in so many ways!" Julianna, too, was always amazed at the unimaginable pace of improvements in the Best Society.

The three of them were friends to the extent that Thelites have friends. They addressed each other only by their first names. Tim's full name is Tim 113050127. Julianna's full name is Julianna 082154119. For efficiency and as part of dissembling disruptive family associations, the Best Society had replaced last names with unique identifiers. First names were kept so that people were addressable without the identifying numbers because numbers were impersonal. In friendly conversations, first names were used and the identifiers were ignored. In formal conversations, the last three digits of the identifier were tagged onto the first name. Ashley's full name is Ashley 071834071, so, in formal settings, or for clarity in a group, she was called Ashley-071.

As the meeting wound down, they discussed new dining opportunities, community events, and other friends. But neither Ashley nor Tim said anything to Julianna about her father. *These are some of my closest associates in the world. Shouldn't they care? Shouldn't they say something?* She did her best to engage in their conversation, but it all felt wrong.

They broke up shortly after and went to their CosmoPods. Beyond the NetSurfaces, this floor of Julianna's building was dedicated to row after row of CosmoPods for use by the buildings' occupants. CosmoPods were recognizable by a circle of light on the floor and a concentric circle on the ceiling creating a cylindrical zone. Julianna approached the first idle one and stepped onto the circle on the floor. She used her BioGram to signal her intent to engage. Immediately she felt the sensation of floating. She was immersed in an active plasma, like a warm gel, that enveloped her whole body and provided continuous support, resistance, massage, comfort, temperature, and freedom of motion. She was also inside a hologram. She could use visual cues, physical motion, or BioGram commands to navigate the innumerable functions of research and analysis available through the NetSystem. She could be engaged in the CosmoPod for many hours with minimum fatigue and perfect levels of low-impact exercise while performing largely intellectual work. CosmoPods greatly magnified the productivity and happiness of any user.

Once engaged, for privacy's sake, she was invisible to passersby. Yet she could be identified by her signature pattern that cloaked the outside of the CosmoPod cylinder. Julianna's signature was a likeness of herself acrobatically flitting between stellar objects, jumping from galaxy to galaxy, using them like stepping stones.

While idle in a CosmoPod, the Centering Production of the Founder's Canon was presented in dynamic, swirling motion. Julianna focused hypnotically on the slogan visuals. Three big words – Safety, Equality,

Science – were changing color, growing and shrinking, circling her, chasing each other, zooming by and sometimes through her, only to appear again in a different spot in her field of vision. These principles were established based on historic consensus documented in the Canon that human happiness was optimized by eliminating human distress. Even in her depressed state, Julianna marveled at how elegant the principles were. *Happiness and scientific truth – how simple! Eliminate insecurity. Eliminate jealousy. Eliminate non-scientific beliefs.* This was revolutionary thinking earlier in the century, and the fortitude of the Founders to make it real was awe-inspiring. Thelites revered their Founders and their successors in the High Council. Humankind had never known such glorious benefits as were offered in the Best Society.

Julianna used her BioGram to initiate inquiries on the next game from the NetSystem. Like all Thelites, Julianna was equipped with a BioGram to facilitate all types of thought transmission, both to other Thelites and to the myriad of automated devices that populate Thelite communities. BioGrams were micro-devices implanted in the brains of Thelites soon after birth. A person's BioGram continuously identified them to the NetSystem with their unique identifier wherever they were so their profile and preferences were known to every device they used. A person could use or not use their BioGram by simply deciding to do so. It buffered incoming thoughts from others and stored "draft" thoughts that you might care to transmit in the future.

She really did have a lot of research to do, but it wasn't related to the next game or even in service of the Bureau. It troubled her that neither Ashley nor Tim had acknowledged her father's death. Her experiences in the last few days niggled at the edges of her confidence. Things she had never questioned were now uncertain.

How do I learn things I don't know how to learn? What do I really know about my father who raised me, Jacob 051729024, Ph.D.? Who can I even ask?

Proles. I need to know more about proles! Julianna turned to the task and began her journey.

7

-2 –
Eric Brunson, somewhere in what used to be Ohio

2060

Everybody knew how it would end. But nobody knew how it would happen.

Eric Brunson jumped out of his electric cart after a brief inspection of the various production areas of his foundry. He was a large man, but he moved quickly toward the stately brick house that his company had refurbished to use as a corporate office.

He could tell the workers were distracted today and he knew why.

"Kelly!" He addressed his production manager over his shoulder who followed close on his heels. With his booming voice, he had no problem being heard over the clanks and pulsing rumbles of heavy equipment emanating from the factory below. "Are we going to get anything done today, or should we just bag it – send them home?"

Kelly looked at her tablet and scrolled through several pages of production data. She shook her head. "We need to pour at least sixty metric tons if we're going to keep our deliveries next month. The castings for Best Society Services Mining and Energy groups are especially important right now. They're in deep shit already, again. If we stop, we run the risk of getting backed up on molding, but we can catch that up next week assuming we have a full crew – maybe some overtime. What are you thinking, Eric?"

Kelly always had that level of precise information at the ready. Eric appreciated it. "Give me a few minutes," he growled as she followed him into the building.

They charged bullishly into an oak-paneled hallway that served as the lobby. They interrupted Steve, the dedicated corporate secretary, and Junior, Eric's 17-year-old son. Steve was instructing Junior in foundry practices. Junior's enthusiasm to learn the business consumed every extra minute Steve had. They looked up at the intrusion.

"OK. Kelly, Junior, Steve, let's get this figured out," Eric called as he strode past Junior into his office. Steve and Junior jumped to their feet and followed. A wide window looked out over the foundry to the river. Sunlight filtered through the ancient leaded glass in distorted patterns, like the surface ripples of clear water. Eric had preserved that feature of the old building, along with the window seat in front of it that Junior now occupied. Eric sat at an antique table that served as his desk, with Kelly and Steve seated opposite.

"Steve, what's going on downtown?" Eric asked pointedly.

"The conscription is supposed to start officially at eleven o'clock this morning," Steve answered, referring to his tablet. "The Public Safety arm of Best Society Services has been positioning around the community for weeks. It all looks like typical conscription prep. Thelite advisors have been in and out – all over the place. Protesters from both sides have gathered all around the public buildings. Probably thousands of them."

"Some of our folks are there, Eric, and a lot of their family members," Kelly interjected.

Eric closed his eyes. "Shit."

"Temporary service trailers are already in the square along with some demo and construction equipment," Steve continued grimly. "They've already razed two blocks in every direction from the city center, not including what they did to the road."

Eric did a quick calculation. "Over twenty blocks?"

"Yup," said Kelly. "And you know they're not done."

The conscription of their community into the Best Society had been anticipated for months. Eric took his dreams seriously, and they had been

9

ominous. All the signs were there. There was the demolition of commercial buildings and homes around the city center to make room for Hub buildings. The main roads to and from the town center had been modified to accommodate exclusively driverless vehicles. This meant that the roads were no longer accessible to the local citizenry – the proles – whose lives and livelihoods were being reordered right under their noses. Local media blitzed information on the advantages of Hub services as well as the timing and the process of its establishment. Today was the day it became official.

Conscriptions were occurring more frequently around the world – sometimes several per month. The communities were divided between support and defiance. It was never accurately reported, but violence and death were open secrets to most proles, including Eric. Eric's biggest concern was that none of the foundry's employees would experience an undue hazard or hardship, and that the foundry could continue to run, doing its important work.

Steve nodded to Eric, "You know, you are expected to attend the ceremony at ten-thirty. All the community leaders should be there. It's been on your schedule for weeks."

Eric grunted under his breath. That was the last thing on his mind. Productivity in the foundry was sure to drop – but it wasn't the workers' fault. He was most worried about how to be fair with them, given all the anxiety.

"How many of our people didn't show up today?" he asked.

Kelly checked her tablet. "About thirty. But I'll bet there's at least a hundred or more who would prefer to leave." With her head bowed to read her tablet, she raised her eyes and looked at Eric from under her brow, an expression that always conveyed serious intent between them. "Those with family involved downtown."

Eric caught her message. Decisive as usual, he concluded, "OK, Kelly. Let's ask for volunteers to pour today – pay double to everyone who steps up. Everyone else is free to leave if they want or to stay and do their regular jobs. We'll see what happens in molding and make it up next week if we get behind. Does that work?"

"Got it, boss," she affirmed. Kelly was hawkish and small of stature. She had dirty-blond hair cut short, with a pixie face that could be described as pretty with premature crow's feet; or, it could just as easily be described as well-preserved for her age. Eric knew she was about thirty and lived a hard-scrabble life. She was gay, single, and drank to excess on occasion (Eric had bailed her out of jail three times). He didn't care.

She was smart and dutiful – the only person who beat him to work virtually every day, often before daybreak – and nearly capable of reading Eric's mind. They both already knew who would volunteer, who would stay, who would leave, and that the production requirements would be met. She jotted his directions onto her tablet and left the office to inform the production crews.

"Anything else?" Eric asked Steve.

"Nothing we can't handle. But I recommend that you get downtown early. It could be hard to get around," Steve answered.

Eric grumbled to himself again. He looked at Junior, and his gaze went to the window. The placid river, viewed through the bent light of the paned glass, usually brought him tranquillity. Instead, today it presaged a sense of ruin. *So, this is it. How will this day end?* He looked back at Junior. *What will it mean for him?* Junior watched him expectantly, but Eric had no intention of taking him downtown. *No reason to tempt fate.*

"OK," he resigned. "Give me a couple minutes, and I'll get going. You guys do what you can to keep things moving out here." They stood and left – leaving Eric a moment with his thoughts. He leaned back in his chair and put his feet on the table, closing his eyes.

Eric breathed in slowly to collect his thoughts. He loved the leather and steel smell of his office building. It was a notable old house that sat on the bluff above the foundry that had been abandoned before he bought it. *Who wanted to live next to a foundry?*

Eric's family started and grew the foundry over several generations. They were proud of their reputation for making the most difficult castings in the

11

world for the most complex applications. But they always respected the well-being of the workers and their community.

He remembered arguing with his father nearly fifteen years ago, as he took the reins of the company and decided immediately to make the investment in the building.

"Something can be both useful and beautiful!" he had reasoned.

His father had countered, "What will the workers think? It's wasteful and showy. Don't you think they'll resent it?"

"I think they'll love it!" Eric had proclaimed.

And he was right.

In truth, they mostly loved it because they loved Eric. Big and gregarious, Eric sported shirtsleeves and jeans with a hail-fellow-well-met personality and a razor-sharp memory. He knew their names. He knew their jobs. He knew his foundry. He paid fairly and was generous to his community. They trusted him. "He's a rich guy, but he's our rich guy. Everybody should have one!" He treasured their trust.

Eric had the advantage of being a skilled dreamer. But his dreams had been dark. People in his community were suffering through the conscription. He needed to keep them safe.

Back to the present. He forced himself out of his reverie. *The only way through it is through it. All I can do is my best. Time to get going."*

The foundry was on the outskirts of town, and the drive in took half an hour. As he approached downtown in his luxury car, protestors were evident on every street. They were divided into camps; their views were made obvious not only by their signs, but by their age, dress, and demeanor. The pro-conscription camps were younger, generally better dressed (some already in Best Society uniforms), and intensely joyful. Eric recognized very few of them, which was unusual because he had lived his entire life in this community. The anti-conscription camps were more diverse in age, but included much more middle-age participation. They were a more rag-tag bunch, carrying hand-painted signs of protest. Everybody slapped his car as

12

he crept by, the "pro's" flashing him thumbs-up gestures while the "con's" defiance was evident on their sour faces. He recognized many of the foundry workers among the con's. Block after block, the same images repeated themselves with growing passion as he approached the city center.

Eric was aghast at the new nakedness of the area. So many splendid homes, trees, and buildings that characterized the city had been replaced with rubble. Crowds of unruly demonstrators had staked claims on and around the rubble, stabbing it with ugly signs of protest. There were ramshackle tents and lean-tos, as if some had been there for days.

When he finally made it to the city center, he parked on a side street that was cordoned off by Public Safety and walked to the front steps of City Hall. The whole of the street in front was filled with euphoric pro demonstrators, while across the square a crowd of con demonstrators attempted to meet their enthusiasm with equal venom. Public Safety officers were guarding the doors of City Hall and the streets around it.

Eric entered through a security scanner and joined dozens of familiar businesspeople and elected officials. The community room was ornate with two rows of crystal chandeliers gracing the high ceiling, twinkling with light reflected from a row of side windows that overlooked the city square and what remained of the downtown buildings. They milled around their seats until officious-looking people gathered at the dais on a stage in front, doing sound checks and scanning their notes.

Eventually, a young man approached the lectern and stood quietly. Tightly curled black hair and closely cropped sideburns framed his ebony face. His clothing was casual-plus but of obvious high-quality fabrics. They fit perfectly over a body that was just taller than average, shoulder-y, and with an innuendo of muscle. Gleaming dark eyes pierced wherever they looked, and his comportment was such that whoever he looked at responded to him. The expression on his face conveyed *unapproachable*. Just his presence at the lectern commanded attention.

Over the next few minutes, people took their seats and the humdrum diminished steadily until it was totally quiet. He watched his communicator for a full minute, until exactly 10:30. Then he raised his eyes to the audience.

13

"Greetings," he said. "My name is Franklyn-008. I am the Director for the new Thelite Hub that will be established here over the next few months, beginning at eleven o'clock today – thirty minutes from now."

Several people in the audience cheered, but their enthusiasm didn't infect the group. Their cheers dissipated in a matter of seconds.

"Thank you, but please allow me to speak without interruption," he continued. "I have been in this community for the past several weeks preparing to establish the Hub. Precisely at eleven o'clock an armory will escort a group of several hundred Thelite specialists to this facility. They are experts at enlisting and training proles into the ranks of Best Society Services to construct and operate this Hub. Materials are being provided to assemble the new centers as soon as the work forces are established. You are expected to encourage everyone to register for participation in a Best Society Service. Our models indicate that the centers will be established within eight weeks."

Franklyn paused. Eric glanced at the people sitting next to him, trying to gage their reactions. There were several murmurs around the room, but Eric couldn't assess whether they were supportive or not.

Franklyn continued, "These establishments are often resisted by disordered community members. There is a possibility of violence. The main purpose of this meeting is to minimize the resistance. As community leaders, the Best Society is calling on you to influence your neighbors to accept the Hub and its many services.

"Once the Hub is established and the violence is quelled, the living condition of everyone in this community will improve. People will be happier. They will have less anxiety and fear. Thelites have a lot of experience with this. This is the four-hundred-and-seventy-first conscription into the Best Society."

Franklyn's dark eyes flashed with excitement as he said this. He beamed, as if expecting the audience to applaud. There was no response other than a few brief claps. But the hair was up on the back of Eric's neck at the mention of violence. *What did Franklyn mean, exactly? And what, exactly, was he supposed to do?* Eric didn't see the need for the Hub himself, but his preference was to simply ignore it – to not fight anyone.

Franklyn continued. "I have time for a couple of questions before things get rolling. Any questions?"

Eric shook his head in disgust as Mayor Ball stood. The two had never been friendly. They didn't see eye to eye on most community issues. Eric had been known to refer to him as Mayor Puff Ball to the delight of his audience – usually the foundry workers.

"Greetings, Franklyn. I am Mayor Ball. On behalf of this community, I welcome you and your staff. This conscription will generate great economic benefits for our citizens. Thank you." The mayor bowed his head in respect before continuing. "I'm curious, though. How is community governance expected to interact with the Hub once it is established? I'm the Mayor. What role will the Mayor have in Hub operations? And how will the Hub affect future elections?"

"Thank you for the insightful questions, Mayor Ball," Franklyn answered. "Nothing will change in regard to your office. The only difference will be that the mayor will report to the Director – for the time being, me – as part of the leadership council."

Mayor Ball looked quizzical for a moment. "But I'm elected by the citizens. I'm supposed to report to them."

Franklyn was unperturbed. "As I said, there will be no difference. You and the next mayor will be part of my staff. Thank you, Mayor Ball. Anyone else?"

Mayor Ball sat without changing his confused expression. Eric had not wanted to be in this assembly to begin with, but now he couldn't stop himself from asking about the subject he feared most – the violence. He stood.

"If you suspect there will be violence, isn't there some way you could avoid it?"

"Thank you, Mr. Brunson." Eric wasn't happy that Franklyn knew his name. "Our behavioral models confirm that disordered proles will do disorderly things. Predicting specifically who, when, and where is elusive. It's not practical to *avoid* the violence. There are protocols to address the violence that will be followed by Public Safety, and that will minimize its impact on the schedule."

Eric looked around the room, hoping that his peers might help with his argument. Seeing none, he reacted, "Couldn't you just slow down, meet with people, or offer them something? Someone could get hurt or killed. Isn't anything better than that?"

Franklyn was not flustered. "Mr. Brunson, you are wrong on many points. No, we can't just slow down. Slowing down will just delay Best Society's benefits longer from the vast prole population on Earth. It's rather selfish of you to think only about your community, Mr. Brunson. It takes a lot of Thelite resources to get this done, so the quicker we can get it done, the better. If anything, we would like to speed up. There's absolutely no reason to slow down to accommodate the disordered.

"Furthermore, it is not true that *anything* is better than somebody getting killed. Until the Best Society was founded, the only thing certain in life was death. Now, under Best Society principles, people can be certain of happiness and an anxiety-free life until their death. That is absolutely worth the deaths of a few disordered proles who can't know happiness anyway."

Franklyn finished, talking paternalistically to the entire group. "I understand that you have no way to know these things. That's why it is up to Thelites to make it happen."

Eric felt the insult. He was tempted to press on, but he realized that he would have no influence on what was to come. He sat down without saying a word, now anxious to leave as soon as he could manage.

There were a few more superficial questions, all of which were similarly dismissed. One of Franklyn's aides then stepped up to the lectern and whispered in his ear. He looked at his communicator to verify the time.

He lifted a gavel and held it aloft for several seconds, eyes on his communicator. At exactly 11:00, he pounded the gavel and announced, "Congratulations! Welcome to the newly-established People's Village four-hundred-seventy-one."

16

The lack of response was surreal. Nobody spoke. After a minute, a rumble of equipment outside drew everybody from their seats to look out the window. Trucks, buses, and military vehicles were parading through the streets around the square. The pro-conscription throng was ecstatic and swarmed them in welcome. There were dozens of public safety officers in full riot gear interspersed in the crowd, protecting the Thelite specialists exiting the buses. The contra-conscription crowd jeered at them from across the square.

Eric headed immediately for his car. If he could prevent any of his people from getting hurt, he wanted to warn them. But in just the few minutes that it took him to get outside of City Hall, the con crowd had become much more threatening. Eric couldn't stop himself from watching it unfold.

Several con members raced into the pros and flailed at them randomly before quickly retreating into their own defensive numbers. They would get knocked down by the pro crowd and dragged back to safety by their own throng. First one at a time; then two; then three would move forward to strike their blows. Pros started to follow them back, kicking at them as they were dragged away. The din of the crowd had given way to the shouts, swear words, slaps, and sounds of struggle of each new fight.

Signs bobbed above the con crowd like corks on a wave, the words "Thelites" and "Hub" with big, bold, red X's drawn through them, along with other contra-slogans. The swell accelerated unrelentingly.

Then, as if a general command had been called, the con crowd started pushing from the rear and advancing en masse – menacing. The pro crowd retreated, and public safety officers stepped forward to face the cons. The cons launched a series of rocks and bottles at the officers. The officers calmly raised their firearms. Two shots were fired harmlessly into the air, three seconds apart. The muzzle blasts echoed eerily from the various buildings around the square. The cons recoiled.

Let that be it.

Suddenly, a rock flew from the middle of the con assembly and struck one of the pro protestors directly in the head. She fell to the ground. Then, the public safety officers again raised their firearms and began to shoot. Not randomly. Not riotously. But with deadly precision, each officer would take aim and shoot a con protestor to death. Boom. Three seconds. Boom. Three seconds. Boom. And another.

"Holy shit," Eric shouted, petrified into inaction. He watched as people got shot and fell dead. Too many already and it wasn't stopping. The con crowd was trying to retreat, but those in the rear were in the way, and the carnage was invisible to them. As they pushed back, people tried to drag the bodies of the fallen with them, but then would abandon them as the disciplined shots continued. People were slipping on the bloody pavement.

Eric forced himself away from the scene and ran to his car. The streets behind City Hall had been cordoned off, so he was able to wind his way out of the city center. But then he was slowed by protestors assembled further away from the square. They were all looking curiously toward the gunshots, but otherwise still standing off against each other. He yelled from his window to people he recognized.

"Don't fight, Claude – go home. Mason, don't fight. Get out of here. They're killing people up there. C'mon guys – it ain't worth it!" Inching along in his car through the crowd, he repeated variations of his warning to anyone he recognized on either side of the street. Some people heeded him and started moving away from the fray. Others didn't and raced toward the gunshots, or stood in place taunting the other side.

Then, in his rear-view mirror, one of the con demonstrators produced a shotgun—something proles were strictly forbidden from owning—and fired it indiscriminately into the pro crowd. The whole street erupted. Several people tackled the shooter, but everyone else ran helter-skelter away from the scene.

Eric abandoned any thought of assisting or changing the course of events and at the first opportunity to avoid the crowd, he gunned his car toward the most direct route back to his foundry. There, he believed, he could reason with people and try to keep them from getting involved; he could keep as many safe as he could. He drove with abandon, running through traffic control signals and jumping curbs if he had to, avoiding the discarded detritus of the fleeing mobs. He witnessed several bodies lying unattended at one street corner and almost wept.

Once he left the city center, Eric noticed an eerie calm. Nobody was outside. The streets were vacant, as if everyone had been sucked into the downtown melee like a black hole, leaving the rest of the community abandoned. Eric urged his car at breakneck pace through the clear roads, fearing what he would find when he arrived.

Eric braked hard and skidded to a stop in front of the foundry office. He stepped out of the car, finally noticing his own breathlessness, and almost shook with relief. Everything was fine. The hums and bangs emanating from the foundry were just as he would have expected. The river below the bluff reflected a gentle blue sky with puffy clouds moving about lazily with the light afternoon breeze. As he slowed to try and catch his breath, he even noticed birds singing and insects buzzing in the verdant landscape surrounding the office.

The only thing out of place was a sedan parked in the lot. It carried the slogan of Best Society Services – "Safely Serving the Best Society" – along each side. Services' factories were some of Eric's largest customers, so it wasn't unusual for them to visit. Eric recognized the car was from one of those clients, but no appointments were expected today. He sensed trouble.

He allowed himself to catch his breath before walking with a deliberate, measured stride through the office door. Steve and Junior were in their spots chatting about something on Steve's tablet. Kelly was looking over their shoulders. All normal. They raised their eyes in greeting.

"Hey, Eric," Steve said. "I wasn't sure when you'd be back. How'd things go?"

"Haven't you heard?" Eric asked, incredulous. "It's a disaster downtown! People are getting killed!"

All three of them looked horrified. "What?!" Steve exclaimed. He started poking frantically at his tablet looking for reports. "There's nothing about that on the public news service! Shit! Are any of our people hurt?"

"I don't know," Eric replied honestly. "I saw some of them, and they weren't in the middle of it. But I have no idea what's happened since I left." Eric glanced around the entry hall. "But we have visitors somewhere? A really bad day for that."

"Yes, it's the Best Society Mining Equipment folks. Not sure what they want. I told them I wasn't sure when you'd be back, but they decided to wait. I set them up in your office."

"Just what we need today. Some new quality issue or something?" Eric asked hopefully.

"They didn't say. They just said they needed to speak with you at the earliest opportunity. I left you a message, but you must not have checked your communicator," Steve answered.

Eric hadn't. He had been too distracted. "Well, let's go see what they want," he said darkly as he walked into his office. Steve, Kelly, and Junior filed in after him and took chairs against the wall, leaving Eric with three visitors seated at his table.

Eric knew two of them. Magid and Hector were administrators at the Best Society Services Mining Equipment manufacturing plant. They had met on several occasions as they calculated the upcoming demands for mining equipment and the castings that would be required. Magid and Hector were always very precise in their forecasts, but nearly always had to change things at the last minute. Managing those changes was one of the biggest headaches Eric dealt with in operating his foundry.

The third visitor was new. Middle Eastern skin tone and hair, large brown eyes, and high cheek bones sat atop a fit body of medium height. She was businesslike, meeting Eric's gaze directly as he took in the group.

"Magid, Hector, nice to see you. Sorry I wasn't here to greet you, but it's a tough day for our community," Eric said. Then he turned to the third visitor and said, "Greetings. I'm Eric Brunson," and he held out his hand. He knew it was not Thelite protocol, but Eric always offered a handshake. It was how he knew to be friendly.

20

The woman did not take his hand, but stood and nodded. "Greetings, Mr. Brunson. I am Pria-144," she said. They continued standing for a moment until Eric took his seat and she sat as well.

Looking at Magid, whom he knew the best, Eric opened, "I hope I didn't miss a meeting scheduled today, but if so, I'm sorry. What can I do for you?"

Pria answered, causing Eric to turn in her direction. "Mr. Brunson, I am from the Best Society's Department of Optimum Allocation. We are here to start the process of integrating this foundry into the department's allocation models. The resources available to this foundry are not optimally deployed, and production protocols are loosely administered. The Department of Optimum Allocation has models to optimize this, which will improve the foundry's performance for Mining Equipment – and all other clients that you serve. This is an opportunity to use your skills to improve the happiness of all society from now forward, while securing premium allocations of staples and luxury goods for you and your family."

Eric's dark expectation was happening, and he didn't know how to react. His visitors looked at him with frank and happy expressions, as if expecting him to respond with joy at the tremendous good news. To Eric, it just seemed like a nightmarish demand from his most antagonistic client. He sensed it was futile, but he had to resist.

"I'm sorry, Ms. Pria, but I'm not certain how that is going to help my other customers. If it is the same system used at Mining Equipment, then in my opinion it's not that good. I think Magid and Hector will agree that we end up doing a lot of scrambling to adjust to unforeseen changes."

"It is true that you do a lot of scrambling," Magid replied. "We at Mining appreciate the effort. But it is not the fault of our production models. Our models indicate that your foundry should be more inherently flexible. It shouldn't be so difficult to accommodate us. This is the case with many prole factories. That's why we are here with Pria. Once your foundry has been integrated into the allocation models, you will scramble less! It will be better for us and for your foundry."

"I don't know what it means to be 'integrated into an allocation model,'" Eric deflected. "Honestly, this is a really bad day to be talking about this.

21

There is a lot of violence in town right now, and many of our workers have concerns for their families. Can this wait?"

Hector poked at his tablet for a moment, then offered a report. "According to the NetSystem, the conscription is proceeding according to expectation. There is violence, but it is being addressed per protocol. They expect to be easily within the point two five percent casualty target, mostly disordered proles with some collateral." He addressed the group, "Nothing that should affect the foundry, Mr. Brunson. I'm not sure what you're worried about."

Pria spoke again. "Mr. Brunson, you can be forgiven for not understanding – proles do not have the mechanism or inclination to consider these things. This foundry is too critical to be left to the vagaries of purely prole administration. Integrating it will be a benefit to all society. Hector, Magid, and I will oversee that integration.

"Your role will not change. Your family will be allocated goods appropriate to your on-going contributions, which will provide you a premium lifestyle. You should be happy for this opportunity. But the foundry will be operated within the framework of the optimum allocation model. Work schedules, allocations to workers' families, sourcing decisions, and production schedules will be developed by the model and complied with. We expect your constructive participation beginning immediately.

"We didn't think it would be necessary to include a public safety representative in this meeting. I hope we don't need to contact them," she finished.

Eric looked at his hands which were folded on the table. He didn't know if he was angry or just sad. In the further recesses of his mind, he had expected something like this, but now that it was here, he didn't know how to act. "Can you excuse me for a few minutes while I use my office to confer with my staff and my son?" he asked.

Pria answered, "Yes – but your office is now over in the factory. This building will house the Thelites administering the integration of your foundry. This building is also an example of an extravagance that wasn't serving the foundry's direct needs – so it needs to be reallocated in any event. You may go. We will wait for you here."

Eric, Steve, Kelly, and Junior stood. They walked out of the office door into the hallway and proceeded outside. Not wanting to go all the way to the factory, they stood around Eric's car.

The world seemed muted to Eric. Numb. The sky wasn't bright blue; it was transparent blue-gray. The noise from the foundry was a hum, as if he had cotton in his ears. He seemed to float above his footfalls. He called on his faith, seeking the right words for the moment. It was hard to be noble when it seemed like surrender. But his first concern was to stay peaceful. He put his sentences together slowly and carefully, talking more to himself than the others.

"This factory is being conscripted," he started. "Nothing I can do can change that." He looked wistfully toward the factory.

Turning back to his staff, he continued, "I've made it a practice my whole life to always seek best outcomes, whatever the situation. In this case, the best outcome includes nobody getting hurt." He paused. Everyone waited.

"We are a great foundry," he continued. "So, we should keep on being a great foundry to the best of our ability."

"Other than that, I don't know what to say. But I think our lives are going to be very different from now forward. We should continue doing our best work regardless. Good luck to us all."

"Thanks, Dad," said Junior, whose life had just been redirected in ways that he was too innocent to understand. "I'll help however I can."

Eric looked at him earnestly. He already saw a different person. This morning, Junior had been preparing ravenously for the future's bounteous buffet: curious, expressive, and adventurous. Now, he looked resigned to a future of whatever – succor for his discouraged father – but chin-up, noble, and committed. Eric felt he was betraying him.

"Thanks to you, son. I'll need your help," Eric said. He turned slowly and walked back toward the building and stopped. Then he said back over his shoulder, "Just remember – we've always been dreamers. We need to keep dreaming."

Steve stared at the ground. Kelly flashed him a look of disgust. He ignored her. Then he went back inside.

-3-
Complexities

2084

The events that disrupted Julianna's life forever occurred over a very short time.

Her father Jacob 051729024 turned 55 the previous week. Thelites were required to report to the local Center for Health Solutions within a week of every fifth birthday. He was a stickler for compliance, so he went immediately. He didn't come home. She received a BioGram from him informing her that "...complexities were discovered during a routine examination..." The treatments were supposed to take about a week.

Julianna had never spent that many evenings without seeing him. Not knowing what else to do, she went to her CosmoPod each day as usual and worked later than normal. She received his BioGrams describing test results and diagnostic steps that were being performed, but they made little sense to her. Her father was always dutiful to his health and was still young. *What could be wrong?* She was anxious for the week to be over and to speak with him about the complexities.

On the third day, the BioGrams stopped. The lack of contact unnerved her almost to a panic. She was relieved to find Mark 030633057 at her apartment door. She greeted him and they went in together.

Mark was a co-worker and reliable confidante for her father – the sober complement to her father's energy and wit. He was of medium height with dark hair, unreadable dark eyes, and an expressionless face. Unflappable, careful with his words, and always perfectly groomed, Mark had always seemed to Julianna the picture-perfect middle-manager-with-a-future. She respected him.

For as long as she could remember, the three of them spent evenings sharing spirits. Her father and Mark pored over technical ideas, structures, and efficiency at the Bureau of Optimum Allocation where they both worked. Her father animated with voice and body while Mark demurred with soft-spoken responses. Julianna never knew how the ideas developed, but these sessions dominated her social life. Mark was always there.

Mark's attention to her father seemed sycophantic. In more recent years, as Julianna participated more materially, she started to understand why. She found her father's intelligence and reason almost intoxicating. She didn't have a deep understanding of the subject matter, but he was overwhelmingly articulate and intellectually fearless.

After entering her apartment with Mark, her relief quickly disappeared.

"Have you been getting his BioGrams?" Mark asked.

"Yes, but nothing since early this morning."

"I need to tell you something unpleasant," he said in a level tone that seemed forced. Julianna stiffened. "As a Director at the Bureau, I received a notice today. Your father has been admitted to the Center for Transition Management. He no longer has BioGram capability, and the Bureau needs to begin his replacement process."

"Transition Management!?!" Julianna couldn't believe her ears. "But he was fine when he went in!"

"We had no reason to think otherwise," Mark responded, letting his gaze shrink away. "I suspected how you might feel. That's why I came. They have Transition Guidance at the Center, and hopefully they can explain things. I thought you would be more comfortable if I went along."

Julianna almost choked. Her worst fear was being confirmed by the person she trusted most other than her father. She barely remembered gathering her things, following Mark, hailing the driverless, and traveling to the Center.

The Transition Management Center was positioned between the Center for Health Solutions and the Behavioral Science Research Center. The low-profile structure was separated from other buildings by tall hedges, trimmed to perfection and shaded by tall trees. The entry path wound through a sculpted garden with sequestered areas for meditation. Each area was appointed with decorative benches, water features, bonsai trees, and artistic renditions of "infinity" to draw the eye. As was the case with all things in the Best Society, the design was perfect for its intent: to reduce the anxiety of transition.

An official met them in the lobby and introduced himself. Charles-013, she remembered. Somewhere in his thirties, he was nearly a duplicate of a younger Mark, crisp and officious. Julianna had expected a somber setting, but he wore a medical gown and checked his communicator frequently, as if between appointments. He took them to a private meeting room – one of several – a few steps down a hallway.

As soon as they were seated, Charles spoke in a prescriptive manner. "A complexity in his organic function was terminal. Bio-economic algorithms stipulated that the most aggressive course of treatment be initiated immediately," he said. "If the complexity reacted to the treatment, his life could be extended cost-effectively, but it didn't work. This is an unfortunate, but not entirely unexpected outcome. The algorithms also indicate that the cost of sustaining his life with the complexity will exceed his value. A coincidence, really. He just crossed over this week, mostly due to side effects from the treatment."

"But father's BioGram said that he would be out within a week," Julianna interrupted.

The official checked his log, then responded with smug officiality. "No. We told him that '…outcomes would be definitive within a week…'" He continued his explanation. "He's still alive, but in a managed coma. It will take time to systematically shut down his body, because we need to sustain certain organs during the process. The Organ Exchange Center may call at any time, so we need to keep enough inventory mid-transition. His final transition will occur when his organs are demanded, or when the transition queue has adequate capacity – first in, first out. This usually takes four or five days. So, within the week, your father's outcome will be certain. His transition will be completed."

27

Visibly distraught, Julianna interrogated him loudly, "You're killing him? Deliberately? And what do you mean about his organs?"

Her outburst caught both Mark and Charles off guard, and they glanced at each other in confusion. Mark cautioned her, gently, "Julianna, please. We all know this protocol, and you know your father supports it."

Julianna caught his tone of caution. She felt impotent and wanted to scream, but with deliberate resolve, she slowed her breathing and softened her facial expression to what she hoped was sad resignation.

"I'm sorry," she said. "Please continue."

"Thank you," Charles continued. "To your question, we may or may not harvest his organs. In fact, it is unlikely. Some of the most critical organs have been rendered unacceptable for the Exchange due to damage from his treatments. So, he has only a few available, and those would only be used as a last resort. We need to keep a certain supply excess, just in case, so we have to keep his organs available for harvest until someone else comes in to replace him."

"I see," Julianna replied. "So, what am I supposed to do?" she asked, her fear and confusion obvious despite her efforts. Again, the official and Mark exchanged a glance.

"There's really nothing for you to do. It's all very convenient." Charles spoke now with a little pride showing through. "We will complete his transition in due course according to protocol. His final event will be scheduled immediately. Since you are a close associate, we will inform you via BioGram of certain protocols to address your anxiety. This will help you manage your own best psychological outcomes. There are requirements, of course, but most activities are voluntary."

Julianna was reeling. She would never see her father again. But ironically there would be a "best outcome" for her since she was a "close associate." She had never been to a final event, and just the thought left her dazed and directionless – like some very important steps of an intricate process were being completely overlooked.

She lived the next several days in a state of slow-motion expectancy. Waking in the morning from spirit-induced sleep to the beckon of a BioGram alarm; dutifully performing physical measurements and personal hygiene to Thelite standards; gathering her things and travelling from her apartment to her CosmoPod; morning break; lunch break; afternoon break; and returning to the apartment each evening. Nutrition; no visitors; some BioGrams (mostly Mark); some spirits; and sleep again. And repeat.

She received the BioGram upon waking on the fourth morning. A NetGram had been published overnight announcing the final event for Jacob 051729024, Ph.D., distinguished Thelite, that afternoon. Attendees were asked to confirm and to expect a half hour program – longer than normal – due to his notable contributions to the Best Society.

Julianna felt vacant. A week ago, her father was alive and part of her life. Yesterday, he was in a coma, but still sort of in her life. Today, he was dead and was not a part of anything except her memories. But all the atoms and energy that make up the universe were still there. *Is anything really different? Everything that made him still exists.* No answers. Just the confusion of grief.

Mark joined her at the apartment. They exchanged pleasantries, but didn't speak about anything significant. They hailed a driverless and left together. Julianna sensed that Mark was performing his duties, staying aloof and attending to an agenda as he guided her through the steps. *I guess it's good that he can stay so strong.*

They arrived at the Center and were directed to a wing dedicated to final events. The lobby was lined with stained-glass windows along a long exterior wall and a series of double-doors along the opposite wall. The doors opened to about a dozen event rooms.

There were small groups gathering in front of each set of doors. The crowd for her father was large by comparison, maybe thirty in all. Attendees stood in uncomfortable silence, waiting for the event room to open.

An imposing woman entered and approached her. "Greetings, Julianna. I am Marlo-286. It is an honor to represent the Behavioral Science Group at this event for your father. We worked closely on the intersectional aspects of behavior and allocation models. I have great respect for his work." Her piercing eyes met Julianna's briefly before she turned to join the crowd.

Mark watched her walk away, covetously, then whispered to Julianna, "She's trustee level! For a scientist, your father sure got a lot of attention!" Julianna blinked. *What did he mean by 'for a scientist'?*

Through the other doors, they heard faint cheers and the muted bass rumbles of applause. One by one, each door went quiet. Within several minutes that door opened and the crowd would file in. To Julianna, it all seemed inappropriately systematic, too sanitary for something so morbid. Soon, she heard the finale behind their door. After several minutes it opened for them to enter.

The room was bare except for a semi-circular stage on the far side. Always with respectful distance from each other, the crowd jumbled into position to view the stage and mumbled restlessly until the entry door closed. Then everyone went uncomfortably quiet for about thirty seconds. The stage door opened, and a Center official stepped out.

"Welcome," he said, "to the final event for Dr. Jacob 051729024. The celebration of his life and recognition of his contributions to the Best Society."

He stepped back through the door. The lights in the room dimmed until the stage was the only thing visible. The air above the stage glowed like a luminous cloud. Soon, the cloud formed into a holographic likeness of Julianna's father as a young man, talking to someone offstage…

"Professor, let me elaborate. The Best Society cannot allow the inequity of outcomes to continue. We know that in any contest of strength, the strongest win. We know that in any contest of speed, the fastest win. We know that in any contest of wills, the most stubborn win. In accepting opportunity as a constraint to equality, we are ensuring that life's bounty will flow to the strongest, the fastest, or the most stubborn. But what of the weak, the slow, and the compliant? In the Best Society, shouldn't they share in life's bounty equally? For what is known of strength without weakness to compare?"

Julianna choked a little at the sound of his youthful voice. The hologram went still and faded back into a cloud. She sniffed back a tear as he disappeared. She recalled many discussions with her father on this theme. Until the Best Society, so many resources of the world were concentrated on so few of its people, and there was so much human distress. Improving that condition was her father's true passion. How far they had come based on these common-sense principles!

After several moments, a new image appeared with another likeness of her father, somewhat older than the first, again talking to someone off stage…

"Your Honors and fellow Thelites, I submit for your consideration this project to refine the optimum allocation model. The current model was developed early in the century. It was constrained by computational power and limitations in the practical embodiment of physical, political, and behavioral science in effect at the time. That science is now settled. Computational power is virtually unlimited. What remains is to establish the practical embodiments of political and behavioral structures as outputs of the model as opposed to constraints. My colleagues and I have tested a skeletal theory against historic data. We have the data, the science, and the means to consolidate these refinements. We propose that the Bureau should serve the Best Society by completing this incredibly complex project, which will improve living conditions for all humankind…"

Again, the hologram went still and faded away. She wiped her eyes and glanced at Mark to see how he was reacting. "I was there," he whispered. "That's when I was assigned to him at the Bureau. Your father was brilliant at constructing virtual-behavior models." Mark's words seemed a little off to her, but Julianna didn't analyze why.

More holograms of her father's work were viewed progressing through his career. There were technical subjects, confrontations, challenges, staff changes, and ultimatums – presented and led by her father's passionate conviction to perfect the Bureau's model. There were audible approvals from the crowd after each holograph, starting as just a murmur and building to applause for especially inspiring words.

In the final hologram, her father's likeness was much more recent – just several years ago.

"Your Honors and fellow Thelites," he began. "It is with great pleasure and humility that I submit to you now, the refinements to the optimum allocation model are ready for full implementation. This model is the way forward for the Best Society. Its predictive benefits have been demonstrated with generations of historic data. This Bureau will maintain the model, continue its improvement, and use it to measure the effectiveness of the implementation. But implementation is beyond the scope of this single Bureau. I call on the High Council to lead this effort to the benefit of all humankind!"

The hologram went still, but instead of fading into a cloud, it exploded into a scattering of points of light spreading through the whole room and illuminating it, then concentrating over several seconds into a point so bright that it was hard to focus on – and then it went out. In the darkness, the crowd erupted into applause. Only then did Julianna realize how involved these people were with her father's work. It was their work, too. The applause was genuine, and Julianna noted with wonder that they and Mark seemed truly joyful, not deeply grieved like she felt. Dismissing it, she did her best to mimic them, sensing that she wasn't successful.

The tribute sustained until the lights started to come up. A door in back of the room opened, and the crowd exited into a hallway that delivered them to the building exit. Once outside, people bid their goodbyes, distracted by new demands from their BioGrams, and dispersed.

Julianna and Mark returned to her apartment. Mark was unusually attentive, offering repeatedly to perform some service or attend to some issue. But Julianna was exhausted and in no mood for company or spirits. Not wanting to offend, she looked him squarely in the face and donned a gentle expression.

"Mark, you've been a wonderful friend to Father and me. Thank you. But I'm OK being alone. I will ask for your help if needed. Could I please be alone? I just want this day to end."

Mark studied her face. "I'm concerned, Julianna. You seem unusually emotive about your father. You should have some spirits. I hope you will follow the protocol for your best outcomes."

"Yes, yes, yes," she responded impatiently. "I'll do whatever. I just want to be alone and sleep." They stepped apart and Mark slipped out the door.

Julianna was troubled in a way that she knew Mark couldn't appease. They seemed to be in different places. Julianna *was* emotive. That seemed *right*. But Mark was stoic and dutiful. That also seemed right. *But what had he said during the event? "I was assigned to him?" Was he also assigned to her?* Julianna was tired and she was confusing herself. She looked to the spirit dispenser, decided against it, and went straight to bed.

-4-

This is what it looks like for real

2084

Julianna awoke the next morning from a restless sleep. Cloudy sensations hung around her consciousness – like a memory was getting away. She opened her eyes slightly to dim light spilling through photochromatic window shades. As her half-lidded vision focused on real things, her sensations started to solidify, and she slowly recognized that her memories of the last days were more than impressions. They were reality.

Now fully awake, but still in bed, Julianna willed her sorrow and confusion aside long enough to unpack her BioGrams. Other than the routine, she had a new BioGram for transition recovery protocol recommending that she not go to her CosmoPod today. Among other things, she was to gather her father's personal items from his apartment and discard them appropriately. Items that could be repurposed should be sent to a People's Distribution Center for the proles.

She arose and quickly dispensed with physical measurement and hygiene – anxious to touch her father's things for one last time. Julianna had lived with her father while she grew up. She knew this was unusual, but it was his preference and it was sanctioned by the Bureau. Though rare, these situations provided evidence to improve behavioral models. Throughout her childhood Julianna was tested, interviewed, and evaluated by educators and psychologists for her social and educational progress. She'd had several opportunities to voluntarily change to a more common situation offered by the Best Society – but she declined. When she turned twenty, Julianna adopted the conventional lifestyle – a modest private apartment in this same building – but on a much lower floor.

When she arrived at her father's apartment, she was depressed by how few "personal" items there actually were. Hygiene kits, obsolete electronic

34

gadgetry, awards and sundry objects, uniforms, and a few items of fine clothing. She discarded everything except the hygiene kits and clothing, which she packed affectionately in a hamper for delivery to a People's Distribution Center.

She was done. In less than an hour, she had removed all visible remnants of her father from his apartment.

Her protocol included a few other steps to adjust allocations for certain items that they had shared, re-registering some shared services, and validating official data about her specific relationship with her father. These were also done quickly. But one voluntary instruction for her best outcome was a behavioral activity, "…to spend time outside among unknown people in recreation or casual settings. Smile frequently. Try to converse pleasantly…" The day was sunny and pleasant. With that in mind and little else to do, she decided to deliver the hamper herself.

Like every building in the regional capital where she lived, Julianna's building was equipped with the most efficient amenities, including automatic systems for parcel pickups and deliveries. She could have just carried the hamper to the shipping port at the end of her hall and sent a BioGram with delivery instructions. But somehow, she felt a stubborn compulsion to go personally. On any normal day, this would have been highly unusual, and her spot decision to go came with a weird sense of anticipation. She carried the hamper from the building and hailed a driverless, directing it to the nearest People's Village about a half an hour away.

While leaving the city, her driverless passed the Centers for Health Solutions, Transition Management, and Behavioral Science Research. All very orderly. Julianna noted the recent expansions in the complex of buildings. The Behavioral Science Research Center was the butt of many dark jokes among Thelites because it was so large and mysterious – almost a self-contained city within a city. It was set back unusually far from the streets and its access points were hidden from view. It was reputed to employ many brilliant Thelites, yet the people who worked there rarely interacted with the rest of the community. Just past that complex of buildings was the city's edge and the landscape beyond was largely undeveloped.

Within the metroplex of the regional capital were several People's Villages. Driverless vehicles hummed between them delivering goods and people with frictionless efficiency. Her destination was People's Village #179. It was closest to the capital and relatively old, so its Hub was well developed. Once conscripted, Hubs were established in People's Villages to provide amenities similar to Thelite communities. The Hubs were comfortable for Thelite visitors and served as an interface point between Thelites and the proletariat citizenry of the Best Society – or "proles," as they were commonly referred to. The People's Distribution Center was on the fringe of the Hub, so Julianna could get there and back without getting very far afield.

As she watched the countryside go by, Julianna felt tingles of expectancy. Thelites were free to travel to the People's Villages only after demonstrating proficiency and allegiance to the principles of the Canon. Like all Thelites, Julianna had received the Canon through Social Awareness Training beginning shortly after birth and lasting until early adulthood. Julianna's sole visit to a People's Village was to #179 during this training.

But it was still a People's Village, and outside the Hub it was markedly different than a Thelite community. Social Awareness Training taught Thelites to be cautious outside the Hub. Simply moving around could be hazardous. The buildings in prole communities are near relics with little or no automation. Driverless access was rare, and any number of obscure transportation devices navigated the nonsensical community layouts. Proles also acted unpredictably. Unregulated interaction with proles was discouraged as a safety protocol.

Yet the health and well-being of proles was a source of virtue for Thelites' work and a key goal of her father's optimum allocation model. Initiatives to establish more People's Villages and improve their living conditions were continuous. Thelite research groups travelled to these villages, and even to the countryside, gathering information on prole behaviors and conditions in their disparate communities. Results were collected in deviation reports, which all Thelites were required to submit if they were off-grid for more than an hour, and published in NetGrams.

Julianna knew that most proles lived their lives passively inside their communities, benefitting from the developments, the planning, and the largess of Thelites. Despite this, NetGrams reported that some proles were hostile to Thelites. This was another reason for safety concerns while off-grid. Julianna was confused by this and had always been curious to understand more about proles – but she had never spent time in their communities. She brightened a little as she realized that today might be an opportunity.

Her driverless slowed as it entered People's Village #179 and made some gentle turns, completely stopping only when immediately in front of the People's Distribution Center. The square, concrete building stood on a half-block area with entry points through multiple glass doors along a street, facing away from the Hub. The street provided a stark dividing line between the Hub and the prole community. Julianna exited the driverless and entered the building through the nearest door. A line of kiosks with automated handling ports filled the whole front lobby. She set the hamper in the nearest port and BioGram'd the inventory to the kiosk. The port door closed and the hamper disappeared. She was done. The whole process took less than 45 seconds since entering the building.

She stepped away and looked up and down the line of kiosks. The crowd was modest, there were no lines, and things seemed to flow smoothly. People would step to the kiosks and poke at it with their fingers for several seconds. Then the port door would open, they would take the packages out, and leave. Nobody was dropping anything off as Julianna had. She was fascinated as she realized that these were all proles retrieving their allocations of products. She knew nothing about the inner workings of the Center, but it was satisfying to her to see how efficiently it served people.

As she stood there, a small, elderly man in disheveled clothing came to the kiosk she had just used. She watched as he poked at the kiosk with slow, insecure motions. He stared at the kiosk intently and mumbled to himself in exasperation. He poked at it some more and stared some more. After several minutes, he shrugged his shoulders, turned away, and looked hard at Julianna.

"Did you break it?" he demanded, his breath sour from even several feet away.

Julianna swallowed. "Excuse me? No! I just dropped something off."

"Why'd you touch it!" he screamed. "This is where I get mine, and it's the only one that works! Now you broke it!"

Several people glanced in his direction, shook their heads, and went about their business.

"I don't think I broke it. Is there some way I can help you?" Julianna asked.

He recoiled and raised his hands in fear. "No! No! I don't need no help! Just leave me alone!" Then he turned and ran out of the building. Julianna stared after him, flabbergasted.

She felt embarrassed and out of place. She was considering hailing a driverless to return home, when an elderly lady stepped away from another kiosk and walked toward her. "Don't let Winston scare you, miss. He's schizo and a drunk, but harmless, you know. I saw you make a donation. Thank you."

Despite her coarse words, Julianna felt drawn to the lady. Remembering the intent of her trip and the protocol, she smiled at her in return. "You're welcome. Repurposing usable items is required in the Best Society. I just felt like delivering it personally."

"How interesting." She scrutinized Julianna for several seconds, then smiled. "My name is Delores," she held out her hand to shake.

Julianna took her hand tentatively since it was offered, but she was not accustomed with the gesture. Thelites only touched each other in rare, defined circumstances. "Julianna," she replied. "Nice to meet you."

"And you," Delores said. Then, as if having made up her mind about something, she continued, "Julianna, you seem tense, but you seem like an interesting young lady. May I offer you some tea? I have a shop just a short walk from here."

Julianna was wary, recalling that beyond the Hub, her BioGram connection would be uncertain. BioGram implants were neural devices that

38

worked best in areas with high concentrations of other devices. The more neural connections in range of any BioGram device meant that all devices within that neural field would be more effective. For health reasons, the BioGram implants were very low power. Being outside of BioGram connection was highly discouraged. Julianna had been off-grid for only a few moments of her life, and that was a closely-monitored situation during Social Awareness Training.

But remembering her protocol and her hopefulness for adventure, she accepted. They walked side by side, idly chatting, getting farther away from the Hub with every step. After several minutes, Julianna's BioGram gave an off-grid warning. She felt no sense of danger.

Julianna was soon lost in the confusion of streets, residences, and non-descript establishments whose purposes were not obvious until Delores described them. She marveled at the eclectic shop fronts with shopkeepers bustling around – so obviously inefficient compared to Julianna's home community. In one shop a short, roly-poly man with a bald head and dark mustache, smeared white from baking flour, argued loudly with a woman shaped similarly but with bright red hair while they both worked. In another shop, a young lady with beads in her waist-length hair and colorful, wispy clothing that hid nothing, delicately hung macramé creations in a display window. They rounded a corner, and a middle-aged man with a skinny ponytail was sweeping the sidewalk in front of an entryway, complaining loudly in a squeaky voice and a language Julianna couldn't recognize. A tall man and a striking woman wearing dark, formal clothing and stern expressions of disapproval strode toward her and Delores, clearly expecting them to give way on the sidewalk, which they did, as the couple passed by them with no acknowledgement.

So interesting! Julianna was fascinated. She recalled that the Canon described the proles as varying widely in their base level intelligence and non-uniform educations. Their nutrition was highly variable, and their body metrics varied drastically. They used intoxicating substances with ancient formulations, which could produce unplanned affects, short-term distress or illness, and dependencies. *This is what it looks like for real?*

"Look out!" Delores tugged on Julianna's arm, pulling her to a stop just as two giggling, unruly children chased a kickball from an alley across their path. The ball went into the street, and the children stopped short as a car braked to avoid them. The driver swore as one of the children retrieved the ball and they retreated into the alley. *There must be no rules here!* Thelite children would never behave this way, unsupervised around obvious danger. The Canon described that prole communities nearly always had laws of some type, but there was little uniformity between communities. Beyond these laws, protocols that governed individual behaviors and well-being were virtually non-existent. Compared to Thelites, prole behaviors were unpredictable and erratic.

Eventually, they reached a small shop littered with cookware and household trinkets. "Here we are, dear. My little corner of the world." Delores led her inside through two sets of glass doors. A bell on the inner door tinkled, proclaiming their arrival.

Everything was clean and fresh smelling. *What were those pleasant aromas?* The clutter and imprecise room arrangement was foreign to Julianna. She couldn't imagine the function of the many objects that were strewn about on tables, hung on the walls, or stored in cabinets. So many things seemed breakable. She moved cautiously to avoid bumping into things as she followed Delores through the shop.

Behind the counter was a swinging door that led to a kitchenette. An enticing aroma flowed from there throughout the shop. Delores led Julianna to the door and stood aside for her to enter. "Please," she said in her welcoming way. Julianna stepped into the room curiously.

To her momentary alarm, a man was seated at a table looking expectantly in her direction. He was roughly the same age as her father and dressed as a prole would dress. His intense gaze caught her eye instantly. He had a disarming smile. He ticked with comfortable, nervous energy – but that didn't affect his gaze which held hers. They stared at each other wordlessly and Julianna visibly relaxed as she did so. He seemed so familiar. Finally, she said, "I know you, don't I?"

He answered enigmatically, "Yes, but I'll bet you don't know why."

-5-
I was in your dream last night

2084

"What do you mean?" Julianna asked. "Who are you?"

"I am your uncle," he answered.

What!? Julianna was startled.

Julianna appraised him. His clothing fit loosely and showed some wear. The fabrics were low-tech, nothing that would be worn by a Thelite. Controlled, nervous energy was apparent in his twitching muscles, but he met her eye directly and for a long time. Among Thelites, this was considered impolite.

Uncle? Prole? How can this be? Yet his features recalled her father's, and to some degree, her own. He was fit like her father, but lankier and more sinewy. He was slightly taller than Julianna, and he shared her rust-colored hair and green eyes. His face was noticeably asymmetric, but not enough to be obtrusive.

Julianna barely knew the word "uncle." Extended families had been dissembled in the Best Society. Family linkages like siblings, aunts, and uncles were obsolete. Genomic pairings were precisely managed based on models operated by the Center for Reproductive Liberty. Thelite babies were born from surrogate mothers whose bio-metrics were ideal for reproductive success. Even direct parental relationships were diluted with gene-editing of each embryo to assure its virtual perfection. As a result, the level of birth defects and the infant survival rates were the best of any time in history with a continuing trend of improvement. Each successive generation trended toward predictability and equality in physical acumen and mental dexterity, so their contributions to the Best Society were reliable.

Julianna was bewildered. *Was my father aware of a brother?* Julianna's situation was unusual – living with her father – but not unprecedented. She had never given thought to a sibling or any other type of blood relative. Thelites simply didn't care. *But why did he seem so familiar?*

"Excuse me? My uncle?" She sat down across from him at the table and leaned forward to study his face more closely. He engaged her with an open expression and bright, almost mirthful eyes. "Have we met before?" she asked.

"Yes," he explained. "I was in your dream last night."

Her head snapped up again in instant recollection. "You were," she said. "Is that what they call it – a *dream*? You were telling me things that I didn't understand." She reflected for a moment. "You told me to come here today."

"Yes, I did," he acknowledged. "But until now, I wasn't sure you heard me. Communicating that way is not a skill you've been trained in. In fact, you've probably been taught that it can't be done."

"That's true," she agreed. She recited what she knew in almost drunken relief to be speaking. "The Canon teaches that many proles have non-scientific beliefs. The existence of deities, a soul apart from the body, spiritualism – so many things outside of provable science. Many of the largest tragedies in human history are due to these beliefs and the differences in these beliefs among people. Society sustains best based on science. So Thelites do not share in these beliefs.

"And Social Awareness Training focuses on our safety. When in the company of proles, we should be aware that they may hold these beliefs. We are taught not to make offensive statements regarding these beliefs because proles may become violent to those who don't share their particular belief.

"Also," she continued with a new note of alarm in her voice, "we were taught that many proles are skilled at deceiving people that their beliefs might be truth. This is explained in great depth in the Canon, that historically proles can be receptive to the powers of fanatical suggestion. Many have been persuasive, and this may persist even now."

Julianna stopped. She was surprised at how much she had just said to this person, who up until several minutes ago she had never seen. Her shock was affecting her self-control. Suddenly cautious, she was concerned that she might be under a spell of some sort, that this man might be manipulating her mind in a dangerous way.

The man watched her intensely as her facial expressions broadcasted her various reactions. "So," he said, "according to what you've been taught, I might be either a violent zealot or a fanatic deceiver." He continued watching her thoughtfully. "Which do you think I am?"

Delores had been tinkering with some appliances out of their view. A hiss of steam overlapped briefly with gurgles of water being poured, a pleasantly strong aroma filled the alcove, and Delores carried in some steaming cups of a hot, light-colored beverage.

Distracted with the motion, Julianna deflected his question. "This isn't a spirit. What is it?"

"It's tea," Delores said. "It's just not something that Thelites would serve. There are hundreds of varieties of tea. Please, taste it. It's very good and it's safe."

The protocols taught in the Social Awareness Training discouraged consuming anything unless its nutritious or medicinal characteristics were qualified by the Center for Health Services. But without BioGram capability, there was no way to check. She couldn't recall being in a similar situation. But Delores was so gracious and the aromas so calming, she decided to take a sip. She was glad she did. She immediately felt more comfortable and maybe even a little more courageous. Her anxiety was wearing off and she was recovering her normal high spirit. She took another sip before answering the man.

"You don't *have* to be either," Julianna countered. "You just *might* be." She hesitated slightly before continuing. "For some reason, I don't think you are either."

"Be careful," he responded, with humorous irony lighting his eyes. "You might be counting on your *intuition*."

She relaxed a little and smiled tentatively at them. "Why am I here, then?"

"Your father was concerned about you. He fears you might need help."

"My father is dead," she told him, submitting again to her intense grief. "His final event was yesterday."

"I know," he said, letting his gaze drop, apparently managing grief of his own. He recovered his composure and continued explaining. "I also know that his BioGram implant was disabled when he was moved to the Center for Transition Management several days ago. He had no way to communicate with you then. While he was in his coma, he visited my dreams for the first time in many, many years. He was so delirious it was hard to understand him. But I knew him well enough to figure out what was going on. He was terrified for you. He wanted me to warn you – you may be in danger."

His explanation made no sense to Julianna. Her father communicating from a coma seemed like pure imagination. And fear didn't sound like her father at all. Her father had emphasized for years that the guarantee of personal safety and equality were the very underpinnings of the Best Society and lauded the fact that they were Thelites with all those benefits.

"Danger?" she asked. "That doesn't sound like father."

"He seemed concerned that someone influential might be corrupting some of the science. I couldn't figure out who, and maybe he didn't even know. He was confused and he was hard to interpret. But he was adamant that someone could deceive you in a way that puts your career at risk. Maybe even your safety," he explained.

"Safety and equality are absolutely guaranteed in my community," she recited. "Nothing can happen to anybody other than an accident, and those are very, very rare."

He nodded, as if resigning to her challenge. "I think your father wanted me to warn you, which is really all that I can do. Julianna, we have a lot that we could talk about, but we won't have time right now. You should be getting back. You don't want to have to file a deviation report."

Julianna was anxious to return as well, but her curiosity had been unleashed. "But...what's your name? Do you live here? Will I see you again? Can I contact you? How...?"

He held up a hand to restrain her questions. "All of these questions can be answered in time, if you want. But it's time to go, Julianna. Delores, can you see Julianna back to the Hub?"

They stood, and Delores and Julianna prepared to leave. He extended his hand to Julianna – that gesture again – and she took it. "It's nice to meet you, Julianna. You can call me Uncle David, for now. You shouldn't mention this meeting to anyone. But I'm your uncle. I care for you. If you want to see me again, it can be arranged."

Julianna and Delores left, walking at a brisk pace to make sure Julianna's BioGram reconnected in time. They reached the Hub, and Julianna was relieved when her BioGram signaled connection. She had been off-grid for only about forty minutes.

Julianna could have hailed a driverless and returned to her apartment at any moment. Instead, she relaxed and sat on a bench with Delores. There were many proles moving around the Hub, accessing services offered there from the various centers and inquiring about others. A lower concentration of Thelites moved among them, seeing to the orderly performance of the centers. It all seemed so civil and good.

Delores watched her quietly. Julianna sensed that Delores would be content to sit with her for hours. Finally, almost reluctantly, Julianna disrupted the reverie.

"How do you know my uncle?" Julianna asked.

"I've known your uncle and your father since they were very young," Delores explained. "Your grandparents took me in as a young lady. My parents sent me to the countryside to live with them during the conscription of our community."

Julianna digested the news quietly. "So, my father grew up in the countryside?" she asked.

"Yes," Delores answered.

"He wasn't born a Thelite?" she asked.

"No. He became a Thelite by choice. That is almost impossible to accomplish now, but it wasn't always. Your father and your uncle were brilliant. Your father was convinced of the correctness of Thelite ideas for the Best Society, and his work at the university caught the attention of some influential members in service of the High Council."

"How did you get to this People's Village?"

"I was born here, before it was conscripted. My parents died during the conscription. Soon after your father left to join the Thelites, his parents died. I moved back here to survive among people who knew my family. A prole can live in a People's Village pretty comfortably, and many of us have to. I live on subsistence rations because I don't work in a Best Society service. I just tend my shop."

"Why would you not work in a Best Society service?" Julianna asked, confused and curious. Social Awareness Training emphasized how the more people submitted to service, the more effective levels of equality and safety for all. This was a scientific truth and an underlying concept of the Best Society.

"The simple answer is that I prefer not to. I'm happy this way. There are a lot of people like me."

Delores' words were nonsensical to Julianna, and she had to concentrate hard not to respond dismissively. Happiness was known to be a direct extension of a sense of safety and equality and contribution of service. The idea that someone would have a living condition less than their neighbors, yet be happy, was contrathetical for the science of optimum allocations. Science had shown that jealousies between the haves and have-nots caused extreme unhappiness throughout human history. And yet, Delores was so warm and disarming – it was impossible not to take her at her word.

Julianna didn't know how to phrase her questions without being insulting. This simple lady had no apparent deficiency in mental capacity and nothing

46

but harmless intentions. In their brief time together, Julianna was becoming more aware of how arduous the process might be for Thelites to ensure that proles would benefit from the Best Society achievements. Delores watched Julianna's face with an amused expression, similar to the way her uncle had looked at her.

"You're thinking that I might not be qualified to make these decisions for myself," Delores observed, with no trace of animosity and a hint of matronly warmth.

"The Best Society has so very many things that could make you healthier, safer, and happier – just like Thelites. Why don't you want them?"

"You are clearly your father's daughter," said Delores. "He never understood me either, but I loved him anyway."

With her question unanswered, Julianna didn't know how to continue the conversation. So she was quiet, sharing nothing but a placid, teary smile with Delores, reflecting on the fact that her father knew them both. Eventually, Delores broke the ice.

"And frankly, having met you now, I love you, too. You are cerebral – like your father – but with a less obsessive nature. That's probably good. I'm glad you came here today."

Julianna wasn't sure how to respond, so she offered a tentative thank you. Delores used the word "love" so quickly and easily, and it felt so good to hear. She again wondered if she was under some type of spell. *Or perhaps it was the tea?* Comfort radiated from Delores like an aromatic fog, and the sensations it left in Julianna softened her grief for her father.

Eventually, Delores touched her hand. "I miss him, too, even though I haven't seen him in almost thirty years. But meeting you has brought me new joy. Thank you for coming." Then, she stood up as if to leave, and Julianna quickly followed suit.

"May I come again?" Julianna asked.

"You are certainly welcome to, but it might be dangerous for you," Delores replied.

Again, Julianna was nonplused by the reference to danger. She had felt anxious while her BioGram was not connected, but she had never felt unsafe during her entire experience. "How can I contact you?"

"For the time being, you can't," said Delores. "But I might be able to contact you." She looked Julianna full in the face, conspiratorially. "Here, please accept this gift." She held out an envelope. "Please don't open it until you get home. I don't want it to spill. Good-bye, Julianna." Delores surprised her with a tender kiss on the cheek and walked away.

-6-

Behavior is what matters

2084

Once inside the driverless, Julianna realized how stressed she had been. She was acclimated to the rigorously managed Thelite communities. Only Thelites with BioGram capability were allowed to reside there. The penalty for unauthorized proles to enter Thelite communities was imprisonment and acceleration into the Organ Exchange Center (otherwise known as the "Exchange"). Most Thelites never had direct contact with proles.

Her experience seemed surreal. Her uncle David and Delores obviously grieved her father's death. This was totally different from Mark and the other Thelites at his final event, but somehow it seemed more *right*.

She tried to make sense of her uncle's message, but to no avail. After a few moments, she doggedly unpacked her BioGrams. She ignored an inconsequential update from Ashley on their current game preparation. Another was from Mark. He was anxious to see her, and she agreed to meet him. She was unprepared to talk to him about her day, but she was still very sad and felt his company would be helpful. He was at her apartment when she arrived and he immediately noticed her distress.

"Oh, Julianna…" He let his voice trail as if disappointed. "Are you following the protocols?"

"Yes," she said, "I should return to my CosmoPod tomorrow. But there is nothing specific about tonight, other than to use spirits to ensure my rest." Suddenly, for the first time – surprising even herself – she cried openly. "I don't see how this is supposed to work. I miss my father, and I can't see how these protocols are going to make me miss him less!" She was standing, weeping, and facing Mark with respectful distance that neither did anything to close. She knew Mark better than she knew anyone else alive, but she still

49

felt an unnatural detachment. There should have been comfort, but she felt nothing other than a little embarrassment.

Mark was patient while she gathered herself. "Emotions can get the best of a person in these situations," he explained, "and the protocols have been designed to help. Without them, a person could become depressed or disillusioned – which would lead to extended unhappiness. That's why you should follow them to the best of your ability." He moved toward the spirit dispenser. "Here, let me get you some spirits, and I will join you."

Like all Thelite homes, Julianna's was equipped with a spirit dispenser. "Spirits" were beverages that created the perfect balance of a joyous alternate state-of-consciousness and mind-readiness while awake, and promoted deep and undisturbed sleep. There were no lingering effects. Spirits were invented in the early part of the century, and their uses and benefits continued to be refined. Spirits lowered stress levels and supported positive interpersonal relationships. They also delivered individualized formulations of nutritious and medicinal supplements for performance enhancement, as well as taste preferences. The dispensers automatically adjusted the formulation for each individual it served. Protocols stipulated regular use of spirits for health and well-being, and also as a social lubricant.

Mark brought their drinks and they sat at her little serving table. It felt odd to have Mark in her apartment and not have her father between them to facilitate a discussion. They struggled in silence. Julianna wanted conversation. She just wasn't sure what to share. She took several sips and soon she felt her muscles begin to soften and her mind relieved from the tension of grief.

"Don't you miss him?" she finally asked. "How come I feel like the only one who misses him?"

Mark took a long sip before responding. "Your situation is a little confusing to me. Yes, I have the separation anxiety that would normally be anticipated. But when you keep the society at the center of your life, and use the protocols that have been scientifically developed, these things are very manageable."

He paused for another sip before saying, "I'm concerned that your reactions seem extreme. Your father would encourage you to look at things more logically. People transition – but there is no pain. Transitions disrupt the society of survivors – but there is no threat to our well-being. It is fairly simple to minimize these disruptions with behavioral science. But the depth and duration of your reactions are out of place. I'm afraid they might get noticed."

"Noticed?" she asked curiously. "What do you mean by 'noticed'?"

"You know that everyone's work performance, communication patterns, and bio-metrics are quantified and systematically observed. The behavioral models are really good – maybe the best we have – and even subtle variations can be predictive. That is where destructive behavioral symptoms are usually identified," he explained. "When a Thelite acts in unpredictable or eccentric ways, they are monitored more closely. This is done mostly to help the Behavioral Science Research Center refine their models. It also helps to ensure that a person's actions aren't destructive in any way to the Best Society or the safety of any other Thelite. They may need some behavioral correction."

Julianna recoiled. She truly believed in Best Society's principles and had never viewed herself as acting outside of behavioral norms. "Correction? That's ridiculous! Are you suggesting I need to be fixed? My father just died!"

"But you're a special case. You were *raised* with your father. Family devotion can interfere with devotion to society. I doubt that anything is wrong with your work or living habits. You've always been disciplined. But people like the Transition Counselor the other day...or people you may have talked to today? The way you've been acting, they might report that you are overly sensitive to your father's death. You could get scrutiny you don't want."

The idea that her grief was not appropriate seemed dizzyingly off-balance. But the spirits were having their intended effect. She took several more sips and challenged, "Are you going to report me?"

"Of course not!" he said, maybe too quickly. "I think your behavior is edgy, but not out of bounds. If I thought you were a danger to yourself, to somebody else, or to society in some way, I would! But somebody else might, that's all."

"So, if I change my behavior, I won't get noticed, but what if I still have the same strong feelings of grief? Doesn't that mean that the protocols aren't working?"

"Behavior is what matters," he explained. "The protocols help us control our own behaviors. They work a little differently for each of us. We are expected to follow them and behave within an expected range. If an ambiguity remains internal, but our behaviors are acceptable, then the model is working. But if something is wrong with our behaviors, then we need to submit to corrective procedures."

Julianna didn't like the sound of *corrective procedures*, so she regrouped. "So as long as I can control my external behavior, my grief won't matter?"

"Sort of. Your behaviors also affect your grief. Some of the protocols suggest that you should do certain things to lower the intensity of your grief by focusing you on positive things. This is a virtuous cycle, because that will in turn give you more control of your behaviors. For example, my protocol suggests that sometime in the next few days, I should visit the Center for Reproductive Liberty. I might even go tonight. That will help to reattach me to the joys of the Best Society and help to diminish my anxiety."

The Centers for Reproductive Liberty were among the most important innovations of the Best Society. Among Thelites, sex for the purpose of reproduction was no longer a consideration. A Thelite female never experienced pregnancy or childbirth. Reproduction was performed exclusively by specialists, usually surrogate proles. Freedom from reproductive pressure provided Thelite women with the joy of lifelong productive service to society. Studies demonstrated that Thelite females contributed more and were happier than at any time in the entire history of humankind.

Sex was a pleasure choice, not a moral choice. As part of Social Awareness Training, Thelites were introduced to sexual enjoyment by professionals from the Centers. The Centers provided access to sexual expression in fully uninhibited, fantasy-filled, and most gratifying fashions.

The Centers provided the most attractive and skilled partners for whatever a member might seek, whenever they might seek it. In this way, society's members become passionately, emotionally, and sexually attached to the Best Society – not to a specific person.

Sexual relations between Thelites outside of the Centers were not prohibited, but were discouraged. There were consent, health, and anxiety concerns as well as unintended attachments could disrupt the orderly function of the Best Society. If these behaviors became evident, the Centers also assisted people to remedy their lapses. These undesirable events were less frequent each year – another positive trend in the Best Society. Julianna used the Centers exclusively and couldn't imagine why anyone would choose not to. One popular form of recreation for Thelite adults was attending the Centers as couples or groups and sharing the experiences in real-time using their BioGrams.

Mark was looking at Julianna expectantly, and she realized his comment might have been a veiled invitation to go with him. That seemed odd. Their relationship was always platonic and intellectual. The spirits were making a difference to her and, surprisingly, she momentarily considered it. She decided against it and to diffuse the situation.

"My protocol includes a visit to the Center sometime in the next few days as well, but I'm going to wait. Based on everything you are saying, I should focus on my behaviors before venturing too far."

"Good idea," he said without a trace of disappointment, making Julianna wonder if she had misjudged. "It will do you good."

They each had another spirit and chatted on neutral topics for several minutes – deliberately avoiding the mention of her father. Julianna began to feel more comfortable and a little sleepy. Mark took the hint and left with a promise to check on her soon.

As Julianna made ready for bed, she discovered an envelope in her pocket. She had forgotten that Delores had given it to her. She opened it. The envelope held what appeared to be crushed up leaves. The aroma was strong and slightly familiar. *Was it tea?*

She closed the envelope, set it in a drawer, and went to bed.

-7-

Junior Brunson, somewhere in what used to be Ohio

2067

Moments before he heard the explosion, a brief visual cue presaged the worst day of Junior Brunson's life.

Only those with the right protective gear were allowed in the pouring area of the foundry. This was a critical pour, and Junior's father, Eric, was one of three staff attending to it personally. Junior, Kelly, and other employees had cleared into the adjoining bay several hundred feet away to watch.

A ladle containing 20,000 pounds of viciously hot molten steel was suspended from a massive overhead crane. From where he stood, Junior could see his father using his walkie-talkie and hand signals to direct the crane operator, moving the ladle gently and precisely over the mold in preparation for the pour. Nothing could be heard over the artillery staccato of the electric-arc furnaces and the screeching of dozens of steel grinders.

This was important. The mold had been painstakingly prepared over the last three days. Eric, Junior, and Kelly had spent the entire time in the plant overseeing the incredible effort, napping in the breakroom as they could. Tons of special sand, chemicals, and custom pieces went into the construction of the incredibly intricate mold. Too many things could go wrong, too many details could be missed, any one of which could scrap the whole cast. And the Mining Equipment Group of Best Society Services had communicated its importance in forceful terms – they really needed it.

"Typical crap," Kelly shared with Junior on that second day. "Optimum production model my ass. We should've had materials for this mold weeks ago! Your dad never woulda let this happen if he was really in charge. What kind of an idiot would think we could make this mold in three days? And those cocky, Thelite dumbasses just keep actin' like we're just a bunch of idiots."

Like his father, Junior was circumspect. "Maybe this will open their eyes," he said. "I don't think they have any idea how much shit we go through when that model screws up. They have to know what's going on here, maybe we can finally talk to them about it."

Kelly just shook her head. Junior knew she thought he and Eric were patsies concerning Best Society Services. But there was no use talking to them. Best to just do what you could when shit hit the fan. Fill in the blanks and make it happen. That's what Eric had taught him. They seemed to do a lot of it.

Junior also knew that Kelly, like everyone else in the foundry, thought of him as just a younger knockoff of Eric. Eric and Junior shared their looks, build, voice, and demeanor. His name even implied it. It didn't offend him. He thought his father might be the smartest, most reasonable person in the world. His father had been tutoring him in foundry sciences since his earliest memories.

Eric had recently told Junior that he, Junior, might be the best mold-setter in the industry. It was a secret source of pride for Junior. But he would never upstage his father. Working with his father was a source of joy, and he only hoped to have the same relationship with his own son Chad, now a three-year-old.

Eric, Junior, and Kelly all knew how the extreme stress affected the workers. True to form, they wouldn't ask anything that they weren't prepared to deliver themselves. They took accountability for every tough decision and compromise that was required to keep things moving. Truly, they should have had ten days to make this mold. But it had all come together. It was late afternoon, and they looked forward to completing the pour, having a celebratory drink, and retiring early. Now was the moment.

After the last adjustment of the crane, the ladle swung slowly for a few moments and finally settled with its tap directly over the spout of the mold. Eric and the others in the pouring area signaled the crane operator to hold and positioned materials around the mold to initiate the pour. One of the workers

56

set up a stepladder to access the tapping wheel at the bottom of the ladle. Eric stood below, examining the last steps on his process sheet. When he was through, he backed up and nodded to the worker.

The worker spun the large wheel which opened the tap of the ladle. Junior had watched this thousands of times, but he always held his breath at this moment. From the bottom of the ladle, a white-orange glowing stream of molten metal started pouring into the spout on the top of the mold, thousands of pounds per minute. The intense heat caused fire to spit from vents in the top of the mold, and there were the typical burps and sparks that would splatter out and spread around the mold like so many roman candles.

This was all normal. After twenty or thirty seconds, Junior started to relax. It seemed to be going well.

And that's when he saw it.

In a fraction of an instant, Junior watched the world change. The top half of the mold – many tons of sand – suddenly shot up several inches. A red band appeared in the middle of the mold where the top had separated from the bottom. Smoke and metal streams squirted out of the sides of the mold. The last visible thing was the stepladder starting to topple; that worker started to fall while Eric and another worker began to turn away. Smoke and debris covered the scene, and at the same time a muffled *phoom* reached Juniors ears, forceful enough to shake the building and knock dust streamers from the beams above.

"Eric! Shit!" he heard Kelly yell. She started to run toward the explosion and Junior caught her arm and yanked her back, knocking her to the floor.

"Kelly! Don't go in there!" he shouted. "Shit!" he cried in futile panic. Workers from all over the foundry ran toward the accident to see what happened. Junior pulled Kelly up by the same arm he still held. "We've got to get these people out of here!"

They leapt into action and corralled as many people as they could, ordering them to the nearest exits. Kelly used her radio to announce a general evacuation and alert emergency teams. The fire and debris around the mold made it impossible to get anywhere close.

57

Only as they were escaping themselves, amid the buzzing of evacuation alarms, the sirens of emergency vehicles, and the crowds of workers, did the enormity of the accident hit Junior.

He tried not to think the worst. But he did anyway. *How could his Dad have survived? No – don't think that!* He pummeled himself again and again. But he knew. *Nobody had a chance of surviving the inferno!*

-8-
Junior Brunson, somewhere in what used to be Ohio

2067

Fifteen hours. That's how long it had been since his father and two co-workers had died. Now, Junior and Kelly were sitting in an emergency meeting with Pria-144 and her aides from the Department of Optimum Allocation. They were in Eric's beloved old office building which had been conscripted from the family years ago.

Junior hadn't slept. Focusing was hard. He had no idea what caused the explosion. He was certain that nothing in this meeting was going to help.

"Mr. Brunson," Pria started. "This department takes seriously the safety and welfare of everyone working in our service. As the Director in charge of this foundry, you need to know that these deaths and the subsequent disruption in supply to Mining Equipment are unacceptable. We are here today to begin the process of optimizing your staffing systems to prevent this from happening again, while simultaneously expediting the casting for Mining Equipment."

"I'm sorry," Junior said. "I'm not the Director here. That was my Dad, Eric. He died in the explosion."

Pria tapped on her tablet for a moment. "I should clarify, Mr. Brunson. Effective with this meeting, you are now the Director in charge of this foundry. And I reiterate, this performance is unacceptable."

Kelly muttered under her breath, to Junior's annoyance. Kelly was always so hostile around the Thelite administrators that she made it hard to stay constructive.

"Excuse me, ma'am, but I have no interest in being Director of this foundry. I am a master mold-setter and a foundry scientist. I am only twenty-four years old. I have no experience in the broader management of the business," Junior said.

Pria tapped on her tablet again and whispered with her aides. A moment later she continued, "Mr. Brunson, your age is of no consequence. We already have record of your capability in foundry science, which is superb, and which is all that is needed to direct the operation of this foundry. All aspects of order entry, supply, scheduling, employment terms, and general administrative concerns will continue to be provided by the allocation model. Your role as Director is to oversee the continuous improvement of the science within the targets set by the model. Those improvements have also been unacceptably slow."

Kelly inhaled sharply, but to Junior's relief, said nothing.

"Ma'am, again, I am very interested in advancing the science, but I have no interest in being the Director. Can we just get on with the investigation?"

"Mr. Brunson, there is no other employee here that would satisfy us as Director. The Best Society can provide a Director who is superbly educated in the allocation model, and we can bring in other scientists. But if we do, your family's allocations will be diminished dramatically. Is that what you are recommending?"

Junior saw immediately that the foundry's workers would be worse off under that leadership. Fewer allocations would be an additional penalty to his family, adding to the grief of losing his father. He was trapped. Kelly was watching him closely.

"No," he answered. "That's not what I'm recommending. OK. So, I'm the Director. What's next?"

Kelly rolled her eyes and shook her head but remained silent.

Pria proceeded with the assurance of natural authority. "We have actions for you to implement as quickly as possible. First, the allocation model has already expedited materials for the new mold. Those materials will begin arriving this afternoon. As soon as they do, you need to personally direct the assembly of that mold on the same aggressive time frame as the last one. That casting is even more critical now. Second, Best Society behavioral scientists will test your workers and assign them to jobs based on a best fit behavioral model. This counteracts the incompetence of whatever mistakes were made that caused your explosion. That work will start today, and you need to direct your workers to cooperate."

Junior was alarmed. "We don't even know what caused the explosion! Why would we build another mold?"

Pria was unfazed. "The allocation model has reduced the assembly of this and all other molds to standard work tasks. Obviously, one of those standard tasks was done incorrectly. This is explained by routine variations in prole behaviors. The best fit assignments will assure that only the most regimented workers are assigned to set that mold. Our models show that with a high level of certainty, there is not likely to be another explosion. There never has been before."

Junior's family had led the foundry for generations. Pria was right. There had never been an explosion. He couldn't rule out that there had been some mistake at assembly, but he strongly suspected that something else caused the explosion. They had checked every step of assembly.

He knew that arguing the point was worthless, at least until he had better information. Kelly was watching him intently. He had some work to do if he was going to protect the crew that poured the next casting. He needed time.

"OK," he said. "I understand."

Kelly crossed her arms and looked away sullenly.

Junior ignored her and continued. "But everyone is scared. My dad and those guys that died – they were all friends. I don't know who will even show up today. Can we meet later to firm things up?"

Pria whispered again with her associates. Several times they referenced their tablets and reanimated their conversation. Minutes later, Pria responded. "OK. We understand that some prole characteristics make this situation less predictable. We can give you some relief – hours, maybe up to a day. We suggest that you two should get some rest and we'll expect your results soon."

With that dismissal, Kelly and Junior rose and walked out. Once outside, Kelly launched into him. "Why do you let those jackasses push us around?" she fumed. "They don't know shit! I don't know what caused that explosion, but it sure as hell ain't that we didn't follow the process sheets! Safety, equality, blah, blah, blah! They don't know shit and someone else is gonna get killed! What's wrong with you?"

"Kelly, shut up!" Junior's fatigue finally broke through, and he lost his temper. "I'm gonna do what I gotta do to make sure that doesn't happen. But arguing with them gets us nowhere. Their models are their fuckin' religion! You can't convince them of anything sittin' in there. Let's just do our work and figure this out!"

"I'm just tired," Kelly admitted, perceiving that she had pushed him too far. She stood looking uncomfortably at Junior, sniffing back tears. "And Junior, I feel so bad for you and your family! I don't know how you're doin' it!"

Junior reached out and pulled his long-term associate into a bearhug, sharing his own grief. In a brief respite from anger, Kelly rocked contentedly in the embrace.

When they separated, she said, "Junior, I'm just so fuckin' mad! They don't give a rat's ass about Eric or the others. When is somebody gonna stand up to them?"

"Let's just remember what Dad always said. Work for best outcomes." Then Junior slumped in exhaustion. "Go home. Let's get some sleep. We've got a lot to do if we're going to prevent another disaster."

In his gut, Junior knew that there was no error in the assembly of the mold. Things had been too tight, too precise, for that type of an error. Before doing anything, he was going to seek out Dr. David Sanderson, an old family friend, and maybe the smartest person he knew in manufacturing science.

The Brunson and Sanderson families had been countryside neighbors for generations. Their parents and grandparents had socialized and thought highly of each other. Both families had taken in conscription refugees. Both families avoided the violent conflicts that they viewed as so destructive. Both families had good businesses and good reputations, though the Brunsons were much wealthier. The Sanderson's building company had refurbished the dilapidated mansion that Eric used as the foundry's office. When the Sanderson parents died, their countryside home was sold. The relationship between Junior and David had sputtered some since, just by lack of contact. But there was still mutual respect.

As a child, Junior idolized David and Jacob Sanderson. He knew they were brilliant. They were older and in high school when Junior was a child. Jacob was awarded some fellowship and left the area, but David stayed. David was very friendly. He treated Junior as an equal, despite the age difference, and regularly included Junior in his escapades and experiments.

The Brunsons and Sandersons were dreamers. Eric had always encouraged Junior to accept his dreams, but dreaming in that manner was becoming stigmatized, so Junior never fully embraced it. He was passive. Now, with Eric dead, and in dire need of help, Junior took his Dad's advice to heart.

So, when Junior went home, he made tea as he'd been taught, and then he slept. He sought and found David in his dream. There was no conversation or meeting. Junior was aware of David's presence while the enigma of the explosion surrounded them: swirling sequences and questions, no center point, impressions without words, amorphous scientific relationships that needed no diagrams – all just understood. No beginning and no conclusion, just immersion in shared experience and elusive, multi-dimensional logic. Together, they were able to focus the disparate know-how of the cosmos onto the very particular thing that Junior needed to know.

And when he awoke, Junior knew exactly where to look. *Core volatiles.*

In the making of a mold, separate elements called *cores* were used to create certain features in the casting. The cores were sand elements, like the rest of the mold, but they were smaller and made separately from the mold.

They were inserted late in the process of mold assembly. Since they were handled separately, they needed more structural rigidity than the rest of the mold, which required different chemicals. Manufacturing cores was part of the trade that Junior knew so well.

When Junior arrived again at the foundry, the workers were already positioning the materials and mixing the sand with the binding chemicals for the major cavities of the mold. He quickly checked the materials and workmanship, satisfied that the work crews were executing according to the process sheet.

He found Kelly and proceeded to the area where the cores were manufactured. "It's the core binder chemicals!" he said excitedly.

"What are the core binder chemicals? What're you talking about?" Kelly asked.

"That's what caused the explosion! There's something wrong with the chemicals binding the sand to form the cores. I'm sure of it!"

Kelly stopped, thoughtfully. "That makes sense!" she said. "The metal would have filled the mold up until it hit the first core!" Catching up to him, she said, "But we're not doing anything different to make the cores. Why would that happen in just that mold?"

"That's what we're going to find out," he said as he pushed open the door to the core manufacturing area. Workers were already laying out some of the new cores.

"Have they mixed any sand, yet?" he asked Kelly.

"Just getting ready to," she said. "Should we stop them?"

"Yes – I think so. Tell them to stop and meet me over by the chemical storage area."

Kelly did as she was instructed. When she arrived, Junior was holding a can of chemical binder and reading the label. "When did we start using this binder?" he asked as soon as she walked up.

"A couple months ago. This is what we get supplied from that optimum allocation model. It's identical to the stuff we've been buying for years, according to the label, but it's more available," she said.

"Have we run our own analysis?" he asked.

"No. We can't anymore. That lab equipment was deemed unnecessary. We're supposed to rely on the supplier's lab. But Junior, why would it make a difference only on this mold?"

"Because we're expediting it," he explained. "Normally, our cores cure five or six days before we insert them in a mold. This allows the volatile compounds in the binder to evaporate. But we're making everything in a couple of days. Those cores that are hitting metal have probably only cured for two days, maybe less. Those volatiles are still very active. That would cause an explosion in a heartbeat!"

"That does make sense," she said. "But this isn't the first mold we've expedited. Why wouldn't it have happened to others?"

"Because we weren't using this binder, yet. We were using our old binder. I'm betting these are not really identical. Do we have any of the old binder around?" he asked.

"Actually," she said cagily. "We were supposed to discard the old stuff when we switched. But I kept a pallet of it in the basement, just in case. You know how we sometimes need stuff in a pinch."

Junior closed his eyes to think. There was no way he was going to let them pour with cores using the new binder. He would shut the foundry down first. But he needed to confirm his suspicions about the new binder. And he also needed to keep the schedule if he was going to prevent a takeover of the foundry. "OK, Kelly. Tell them to make the cores with the old binder. Let's send some samples of both binders over to the trade college. They have a lab. I'll call David Sanderson and see if he can get over there and run some tests."

Kelly disappeared and did as she was told.

As he walked back to his office, Junior contacted David on his communicator. "Hey, David!"

"Junior," David said. "And...?"

"We're onto something, David," Junior said. "I'm sending samples of the old and new binder to the trade college lab. Anything you can do to expedite some tests?"

"I'm already there," David said. "It's a pretty simple test – takes a couple of hours. I'll get right on it."

"Thanks. Let me know as soon as you can."

"Will do," David said. "Junior, I want you to know how sorry I am about your father. He was a great man and an inspiration to me growing up. I don't know how you are pulling all of this together so soon. If there is anything more I can do, please ask."

"Thanks, David," Junior said. "I'm running on adrenaline right now, and we've got to get through this cast. But afterward, oooph. I don't know what I'm going to do."

"Take care, then. I'll be back with you as soon as I have something," David signed off.

Three days later, in the middle of the morning, Junior climbed the stepladder to turn the wheel and tap the ladle to pour the ever-so-critical casting for Best Society Services Mining Equipment. He was wearing a fire-retardant gown, gloves, and a face shield. The test results confirmed his suspicion. The new binder was more available because it used a faster manufacturing process that retained a higher level of volatile compounds. Those compounds needed time to evaporate. The labelling on the container correctly identified all the inputs to the binder – which were essentially the same as the old binder – but did not identify the difference in evaporation level.

The changes he demanded had taken extra time to finish. Everyone had been especially meticulous with the final process sheets. So, they were a few hours late of their target to pour. After the final checkoffs, Junior had all staff leave the pouring area. He trusted his insights, but not enough to gamble with someone else's life. He spun the wheel as quickly as he could to establish metal flow, adjusting as necessary to assure that it didn't overtop the spout. He watched the metal enter the spout and the expected fiery expulsions from the vents in the mold. It couldn't have gone more perfectly. Four minutes later, he closed off the tap. While he climbed down the ladder, the crane operator moved the ladle away to dispense with the overage of molten metal. He walked over to the group watching.

"Thanks to all of you," he said. "Extraordinary effort. Came off like clockwork."

They accepted humbly but without excitement. Given the casualties from the explosion so recently, they mostly just felt relief. Something had gone right. Junior watched them separate wistfully. He looked to Kelly for some encouragement, but she just turned and walked away with the others.

He went to his office and sent a message to Pria, along with the detail on the binder, relieved that the pour had been safe and successful. Minutes later, he received her message in reply.

"Objectively, Mr. Brunson, the performance on this casting has been completely unacceptable. It is at best hours late, even after relief was extended. If the Department of Behavioral Science had not stepped in, it is unlikely that it would be completed even yet. Many of the optimum allocation protocols for this foundry have been lax. We expect your support as we implement more fulsome changes."

Disheartened but not surprised, Junior chuckled bitterly to himself. He felt trapped. He thought about his three-year-old son, Chad, his lovechild from a too early affair. Abandoned by his mother, but loved by aunts, uncles, cousins and the household help they had been lucky enough to retain. Chad would never know his grandfather. For the first time, Junior realized that he would be the last generation of his family at the foundry.

-9-

Kelly, somewhere in what used to be Ohio

2067

"It's weird, sis. I'm so terribly sad, but, but…" Kelly was trying to explain to her younger sister, Sandy Brooks. "I loved working for Eric, but I've been mad as hell at him for years. And now he's gone – poof! – and Junior's gonna be in charge, if you can call it that."

Kelly's comfort place was Sandy's kitchen. Sandy always kept the kitchen bright with curtains tied open and colorful with placemats and tea towels. Fresh-bread aromas always seemed to be there, and cinnamon, even if she wasn't baking. Sandy was frequently up and down, her loose housedress swirling around her ankles as she attended to each new task of household and family care. The countertops usual clutter included a toaster, can-opener, bread basket, and blender, as well as, this afternoon, an ice-bucket and bottle of gin.

"But I thought you liked Junior," Sandy responded, trying to keep Kelly calm.

"I do!" Kelly exclaimed. "He's fine. But he's not Eric! And Eric wasn't really even runnin' the place!" She paused while she gulped back some of her drink. "Why was he such a pushover to those *Thelite jackasses*!" Kelly spat out the last words with punctuated emphasis. Anger was her best relief. She was now three gin and tonics into the late afternoon and not inclined to hold her tongue. "He'd still be alive!"

"But what choice did he really have?" Sandy asked.

"Just one word from him, and everyone would have walked out!" Kelly said. "He didn't even think about asking me! He just gave it away.

"None of us gave a shit about those pompous jerks! So self-righteous, screwing everything up and blaming everybody else. Then they come in and just take the foundry from Eric – just like that – and he just lets them."

"What does all this mean for you?" Sandy asked, concerned. "Are you going to be OK?"

"Oh, yeah, I'm sure I'll be fine. I have pretty good allocations. I just think work is going to suck even worse now. I mean, back in the day Eric and me – with the crew we had there, we could work miracles! But it's gone to hell with their stupid optimum allocation bullshit. Junior ain't gonna fight it either."

Kelly rattled her ice suggestively, and Sandy rose to freshen her drink. But she was interrupted by Abby – her three-year-old daughter – dragging her yellow blankie behind her into the kitchen with her thumb in her mouth. "Mommy – Aunt Kelly woke up Meghan. She's fushin' in there," she said, talking mushily around her thumb and pointing her eyes back through the door to an old-fashioned playpen in the living room. Sure enough, when Sandy looked, Meghan was standing up by holding onto the rail of the playpen, sniffling and red-eyed, and looking curiously after her sister.

Kelly and Sandy forgot about the drink. Sandy stepped into the living room to attend to Meghan. "Come here, sweetheart," Kelly said to Abby. Abby climbed into her lap, relying on Kelly's assistance so that she didn't need to remove her thumb from her mouth. Kelly hugged her hard for several seconds. She loved her nieces. She loved their smells, baby shampoo hair mixed with the scents of fruit juice spilled on their terrycloth bibs. Abby leaned against Aunt Kelly, sucking her thumb with relaxed and unfocused eyes, taking in the rest of the world.

Now in her late thirties and still single, Kelly had mixed emotions about her decision not to have a family. It had been easy for her at the time, she recalled. She was gay. She had never found a partner she could believe in, and she wondered now if she had ever really tried. She had loved her work and she loved the trappings of being well-off and single. Unbounded life appealed to her. She had never thought negatively about her drinking and promiscuity, either.

She admitted that Sandy's settled home and family plucked some muted heartstrings of jealousy. Kelly's life seemed ungrounded, she reflected. *First the conscription of the foundry; what was it – seven years ago?* Now the explosion and Eric's death. She could never have imagined such a purposeless future, as she now saw it. She liked Junior, but she had loved Eric, and she couldn't just will her loyalty to move. It felt like a sacrifice. *Was that really her only purpose? To do her best work with Junior for the thankless Best Society Services?*

She watched Sandy putter around the kitchen with Meghan slung in a baby-poncho over her shoulders. Sandy's life was settled. But it was not to Kelly's liking. Sandy's husband was a teacher in the Thelite college that had been established in the Hub. They had succumbed to the conscription without resentment, and they were satisfied with their allocations. Kelly suspected that they actually supported the conscription. They had never been vocal about it one way or another. And nothing had been taken from them. Not like Kelly, who – like most people from the foundry – wore her defiance proudly.

Sandy put Meghan in a highchair and sat down again to feed her with a plastic-tipped spoon. Sandy wheezed a little with the effort and coughed a wet, noisy cough. Something Kelly noticed she was doing more and more often. Meghan tried to grab the spoon from Sandy with uncoordinated hands. She blew bubbles with the food instead of swallowing. Kelly grinned to herself as Meghan's face and hands were coated with applesauce and pureed spinach. *Yes, she loved her nieces to death – but she was glad she didn't have to raise them.*

Sandy looked sidelong at Kelly. "Aunt Delores is coming to town this evening to see the girls. Do you want to hang around? I'll make you another drink."

"Nah," Kelly said. "I should get going."

Kelly stood up, lifting Abby with her. Abby took her thumb out of her mouth and gave Kelly her favorite hug – all limbs, arms, and legs wrapped tightly around Kelly's torso. Then she pecked Kelly on the lips with exaggerated kisses while saying, "Mwah, mwah, mwah," with pursed lips.

Another hug, and then she slipped to the floor and reset her thumb in her mouth.

"Bye-bye, Aunt Kelly," she said around her thumb.

"Bye, Sweetie," Kelly said. Abby turned and dragged her blankie back into the living room.

Sandy hacked another annoying, wet cough just as Kelly left.

Kelly didn't go home. She wandered the streets trying to tie up loose ends in her mind. Seeking someone to commiserate Eric's death with, she stopped at a bar that was frequented by the foundry workers. It was a place that didn't operate inside of Best Society Services protocols; it still only accepted coin payment. Here, she knew, she could be herself.

The conscription had been hard on the bar. The boisterous rowdiness of earlier years had been replaced with clusters of quiet, secretive conversations. There was a dustiness to the place that made it seem unkempt. Some of the lights didn't work, and the floor creaked under even her slight footfalls. As she stepped toward a line of high tables full of her co-workers, she noticed chips in the laminated tops and cuts in the fabric of the chairs. Cheap attempts to keep things minimally functional were obvious everywhere.

"Hey, guys," she greeted a group of co-workers as she pulled a stool up to join. A round of depressed, mumbled responses was the only reaction. They were largely quiet, distracting themselves by feigned interest in a match of darts taking place at the end of the bar.

Kelly had known everyone at the table for years. Six men, no women. One widower, one single, and four married with kids. All of them had worked for her directly at one point or another in their time at the foundry. *Mostly good guys. Out a little too long after work today?*

She caught the eye of Shawn Adams – the widower – across the table. "Hey, Kelly," he acknowledged, tipping his glass in greeting. "How you holdin' up?"

"Oh, fine, I guess," she said. She looked from side to side and asked, "Who's a girl gotta blow to get a drink in this place?"

71

Shawn chuckled. He waved for the attention of a server standing by the bar and pointed at Kelly. Shortly, a gin and tonic with the expected heavy pour was delivered to her, and Shawn paid.

"To Eric," she reached her glass across the table to toast with Shawn.

"Yeah, to Eric," he clinked with her.

After a few moments, Shawn moved around the table to sit next to Kelly, looked straight at her, and spoke just loud enough to not be heard by anyone else – just above a whisper.

"Don't it piss you off? Those jerks are comin' in sayin' the explosion is because we don't have our shit together. We never had an explosion before they started pokin' their noses in!

"Now – all of us have to take these tests that are just bogus! They ain't nothin' about foundry science. Psycho-babble is all. It was an explosion – dammit – not a friggin' schoolyard fight!

"I'm tellin' you, Kelly. If it weren't for you, I'd just quit and head out to the country somewhere. Maybe I can find someplace where those Thelite jerks don't care about."

Kelly knew that Shawn was impulsive and influential. She was humbled by his allegiance to her. She adopted her professional role: advisor, leader, mentor for employees in service of the foundry.

"I know how you feel, Shawn. But you know I wouldn't ask you to do anything on my behalf. You should do things that you know to be right, and hopefully that are right for you.

"You're right. My job would be harder if you left," she continued. "And we'd struggle to replace what you know. But you know what? That's life. We'll make it. I don't want you workin' for me. I want you workin' for the foundry. As long as you can contribute and feel rewarded. Otherwise, what's the point?"

"That's what everyone loves about you," Shawn said. "No bullshit. But I'm serious! There's towns around that aren't gonna take kindly to being conscripted, and maybe I'd fit better there. I ain't givin' it away anymore if I don't have to. I'm not beholden to anyone here anymore – unless it's you. Things at the foundry ain't gonna get better."

"Well, um," Kelly stumbled over her words, trying to be truthful. "My role is to make sure everyone at the foundry is equipped to make the best castings we know how to make, safely, every day, and all the time," she recited. "But a lot of what you're talking about, I can't do anything about. I mean – Junior is just like Eric. They let them pricks in. All I can do is my best, but that don't seem to count for much anymore.

"My point is, don't stay because of me. I can't make it different. Stay if you think it's good for you. I'll be sorry to see you go, if you do, but what the hell – I won't think any worse of you," she finished.

Shawn sat back and took a sip of his drink. Everyone else at the table was still watching the contest, low energy, with their chins in their hands. Conversations occurred in snippets of two or three sentences and then died. It was mostly commentary on the dartist's performance or other similarly mindless topics. Shawn and Kelly joined them for a few minutes just to blend.

Somebody won. The whole bar seemed to exhale. A murmur of conversation picked up as people discussed the outcome and reordered their drinks.

Kelly turned back to Shawn, who was standing to leave.

"Well, Kelly," Shawn said. "I been thinkin' about this for a while – even before the explosion. I think I'm outta here. Don't expect to see me in the morning." He extended his hand and Kelly shook it. "You know, you oughtta think about it, too." Then he turned and walked out the door.

Kelly sipped her drink. It was now mostly water from the ice melting, but with enough gin and lime left to give it some flavor. She swirled the ice and tipped the glass to her lips to drain it. She looked around the bar: the sorry reminder of what was left of her career and life.

"Ah, shit," she said to herself. She slipped off the stool and followed Shawn.

-10-
The Founders' Canon

2084

Finally, in the seclusion of her CosmoPod, Julianna shrugged aside any prep for her next game and considered how to learn more about proles.

Why was her uncle – assuming he really was her uncle – still a prole when her father was a Thelite? Why was she so comfortable with her uncle and Delores when they were proles that she had met only briefly? Had her father and uncle really communicated through dreams? Had her uncle really communicated with her through a dream?

It resonated as true to her, but she didn't recall any specifics of her dream that night – just the notion.

Was that coincidence? Power of suggestion? That seemed like a stretch. But if it was true, why didn't Thelites communicate that way? More importantly, if it was true, why did the Bureau of Scientific Truth conclude that it wasn't possible?

These enigmas conflicted with the core of Best Society principles. Julianna had always lived in unequivocal commitment to these principles and to the noble purpose of the Founders. The Founders' dedication to Safety, Equality, and Science in service to the whole of mankind were inspiring to all Thelites. She was disinclined to dismiss the tension without referencing the Canon.

The Founders' Canon was a NetSystem production that chronicled the history of the Best Society's formation. The Bureau of Historical Conclusions controlled the production, and it continuously incorporated the newest production features as well as the most recent outcomes of historical models. As base information for Social Awareness Training, it conveyed the entirety of relevant historical learning in ways that were unambiguously understandable by modern humans. All Thelites received the Canon through Social Awareness Training beginning with their earliest ability to communicate. When experienced from a CosmoPod, the Canon was incredibly descriptive and convincing, immersing the viewer in layers of holographic involvement, background images, animation, motion, and sound.

Thelites regularly used the Canon to center themselves or to resolve social difficulties. To experience the Canon in its entirety took months of commitment in a CosmoPod. After completing Social Awareness Training, most Thelites referred only to those sections relevant to their area of reflection.

Julianna's inquiries led to sections that directly addressed the relationship with proles. An impassioned exposition by one of the Founder's was informative.

"The new communities need to be exclusive to Thelite members whose education and commitment are sufficient to embody the Best Society model of structured happiness based on Safety, Equality, and Science. But while these initial steps focus on the living circumstances of Thelites, the welfare of the proles must be a central consideration. The Best Society must benefit the proles as well, but this can only happen if they participate and accept that the principles of the Best Society are superior to their *misguided beliefs*. This is best accomplished by demonstration over generations."

The content was coming to Julianna in full sensation through the CosmoPod. She could feel the presenter's pulse and anxieties as if she were with him – inside his head. She *knew* his vigor and commitment.

"In the existing states, Thelites have disproportionate influence. Thelites must enlighten those proles who are sophisticated and influential enough to assist. They must keep the broader population informed using the media and NetServices. Some proles will directly support the effort to convert the state, but most will simply come along passively. Most will lack the clarity of scientific comprehension to understand the vision. There is no way to make the step into Best Society principles without some division of the population along these lines."

Julianna took special note of the presenter's assertion that "some proles will directly support the effort to convert the state…" Even among Thelites her father was considered brilliant. If he started life as a prole, he could have been one of those who was "sophisticated and influential enough to assist." But the timing was off. Her father wasn't born until 2029. He would have been just a child when the first Thelite communities were established. Delores said something about how difficult it was for a prole to become a Thelite, but Julianna couldn't remember the exact words.

She was curious about the discussion of misguided beliefs. It seemed relevant, but she wasn't sure what to make of it. Julianna couldn't deny how comfortable the experience with her uncle and Delores was. *Were they misguided?*

To move between scenes and subjects in the CosmoPod, she simply had to think it. She followed the phrase "misguided beliefs" to a different point in the Canon and was struck by the argument of another Founder.

"At inception, the proles will be limited by their *intellectual constraints* and their *misguided beliefs*. Most will continue to live in relatively primitive circumstances based on their own preference – mostly the cities that Thelites will abandon. Some may even continue to live in the countryside. Wherever practical, Thelites must establish Hubs where Best Society Centers can provide goods and services directly to the proles in these locales with no requirement for consideration. Sustaining allocations of food, medicine, spirits, reproductive liberty, and repurposed goods must be commonly available. Opportunities must be provided for proles to serve in the Best Society Services in a variety of capacities, and that service should improve their allocations. Thelites must improve the living circumstances of the proles with every generation."

As she experienced the production, she found herself re-inspired by the Founder's genuine dedication to the proles. But she also took note of the words "…intellectual constraints…" Granted, she didn't know her uncle or Delores well, but those words certainly didn't match her first impression of them. Yet, they lived in the circumstance that was anticipated by this Founder.

Julianna followed the phrase "intellectual constraints" to another scene of the Canon. Soon, though, she became saturated with redundant material. It was overwhelming. There were hundreds of Founder presentations, dozens of which were specifically cited on these subjects. The important thing was the record of their personal risk and sacrifice in order to modify the structure of society away from disparate states and belief systems to a common Best Society. Overcoming the intellectual constraints of proles to rid them of misguided beliefs was a common and noble cause. Thelites were not the intended benefactors of this effort, but the workers who would take generations to bring it about. In fact, the word "Thelite" was a contraction of "The Elites." The Elites were those educated to consider the most difficult challenges of humanity and to work in direct service of society; they were those who shouldered the burden of ordering that society on the fragile planet.

For the next several hours, Julianna moved from the Canon to study NetGrams of current prole behavior. These were data-intensive reports with very little animation, so the CosmoPod kneaded her temples to assist her concentration and stimulated her tear ducts to keep her eyes moist. The NetGrams were studies from behavioral scientists and history specialists. They cross-referenced situations, geographies, and studies by other authors – but Julianna soon found herself frustrated again. The references circled her between perhaps a dozen original works. All of these were summaries lacking in specific details such as dates, names, or specific incidents. All references to original data were to a common and massive database of Deviation Reports that had been filed by Thelites who went off-grid. Those dated back for decades.

Julianna leafed through hundreds of original Deviation Reports just to see what they were like. The records' first purpose was to provide data to improve the performance of the Hub services and the BioGram neural network. Their secondary purpose was to capture data regarding prole behaviors. Julianna noted that very few recorded any details of prole contact. Those that did described erratic interactions, like her experience with

77

Winston at the People's Distribution Center. Nowhere in her brief search did she find a record of anything like her experience with Delores or her uncle.

Curiously, Julianna referenced the official NetGram on her father, Dr. Jacob 051729024. It was accurate as far as she could tell. His date of birth and death were the same as she understood, but again the biographical information was very superficial. There was no description of his childhood circumstance as a prole or even his career, as notable as it was. She could view productions of his most notable lectures, including those from his final event. Some of these were hours long, and she couldn't take time to listen to them completely. None of the recorded events predated his association with the optimum allocation model.

Before she knew it, the day was spent. Her normal routine upon leaving a CosmoPod included light calisthenics while experiencing the Centering Production of the Canon. Today's research was tedious, and she felt the routine would give her a lift.

"The Best Society will assure humankind happiness with abundant goods and social harmony. Scientific models will manage Earth's resources and living populations intelligently. Eliminate fear by guaranteeing safety. Eliminate jealousy by guaranteeing equality. Adjudicate everything with scientific truth. Immerse the whole of humanity into the service of improving that science and living in perpetual happiness."

All while the words Safety, Equality, and Science zoomed around her visual space, highlighted as they were mentioned in the production.

Physically refreshed, Julianna stepped out of her CosmoPod and considered what she had learned. Not much, unfortunately. Her only conclusion was that the specialists who reported on prole behaviors must have sources other than those she was reviewing. She was stuck. She wished she knew how to contact her uncle or Delores. *Hadn't Delores said it was possible for them to contact her?* Julianna realized that her effort to learn about proles would likely take a very long time. She had to be dutiful to life without her father in the interim.

-11-

I wonder why I don't go more

2084

Julianna walked away from her CosmoPod through the common area. As she proceeded toward the elevator, she was surprised to find Tim seated in the alcove. He stood when she approached.

"I've been waiting for you," he said. "I know you were upset with Ashley this morning. I hope you're OK moving on with the game."

"I'm fine," Julianna said. Using her voice for the first time in hours was refreshing, especially with someone as amiable as Tim. "I probably take the tests too seriously anyway. I guess it can't really do any harm." She offered the first authentic smile she had used in many days.

He returned it with sudden intensity. "Hey. I'm going to the Center tonight. I'd love it if you would go along. Interested?"

Julianna was interested. She hadn't been to the Center for Reproductive Liberty in many weeks. She usually enjoyed such visits on at least a weekly basis, but recent events had distracted her so much that she hadn't even missed it – until now. Tim's offer came at just the right moment. "Let's go now!" she said excitedly. "I've been cooped up too long today. This might be just what I need!"

They left the building together and walked the several blocks to the Center. While they walked, they BioGrammed the Center and reserved the rooms, partners, and appurtenances they would use. Upon arrival, they went into the reception bar to wait for their rooms. The bar was crowded and buzzing with couples, larger groups, and individuals. Each table had a dispenser for a special spirit that lowered inhibitions and heightened libido. An automatic system deposited glasses at their table.

They served themselves eagerly. Julianna quickly felt her inhibitions drop. She began flirting shamelessly with anyone who came near, causing Tim to laugh. He put his arm around her, and she let his hand rest on her breast, welcoming the stirrings it caused in her. At the Center, a person's consent was implicit, and such touching was considered appropriate. She molded herself to Tim's body and pulled away coquettishly when he attempted to hold her there. People came into and out of her field of view laughing, touching, and disappearing just to be replaced by others. Everybody was happy, beautiful, and sexy, which made her feel sexy as well. She loved this feeling and treasured the release it provided.

After about a half an hour, their BioGrams hailed them to their rooms. They each set their BioGrams to *solo-sensory* mode, which dedicated their BioGrams to privately share real time sensations with each other. Julianna made sure that she brushed Tim's crotch teasingly as they separated. She walked to her own room with giddy expectation.

Her partner was already in her room. Naked, chiseled, unashamed, and smiling – absolutely gorgeous. He was also sexually servile and aware of exactly what she loved. He moved toward her deliberately but without hurry, his penis semi-erect – exciting her even more. Standing in front of her, he massaged her shoulders, her neck, her back, her buttocks, and eventually her breasts. He disrobed her slowly and expertly. As her last item of clothing was removed, she felt completely liberated.

Adding to her pleasure, her BioGram's solo-sensory mode was allowing her to not just hear Tim, but to *feel* everything he was feeling in his own mind, in his own room, and with his own partner. Sharing his ecstasy magnified her own. Every sensation that he was feeling gave her a shadow sensation and vice versa. And little "what's next?" teases went back and forth between them, answered by the expertise of each of their partners.

Julianna's partner was caressing her body confidently and with perfect tempo, kneading her skin with scented oils, using his mouth and hands, doing everything right, heightening every sensation. Tim's partner was doing the same. It was synchronized. It was symphonic. The spirits, the expert partners, and the thrills she shared with Tim were making her dizzy. As the minutes ticked by and climax moved closer, Julianna was overjoyed with the sensations and wonder at how lucky she was to live now and have this. And she could feel Tim's joy and wonder as well, which took her ecstasy to unfathomable levels.

She sensed Tim's orgasm a moment before her own, and it caused an explosive sensation that was many times more intense than what she would have had with only her partner. Climax squared. She thrusted toward her partner in continuing pleasure. Almost crying, wracking her body and trembling with the combined release of Tim's climax and her own. She contorted almost uncontrollably for several more orgasms with her partner, even after sensing Tim's excitement and energy wane.

In their exhausted aftermath, Tim and Julianna teased each other as they rested briefly in the arms of their partners. It was one thing to witness another person's pleasure physically. It was completely meteoric to experience the actual sensations they were having simultaneously. *How could any person not want as much of this as they could get?*

Julianna napped momentarily and awoke alone, still naked but under a rich, soft sheet. Her clothes were laid out conveniently, clean and fresh smelling. She dressed languorously, making small talk with Tim through the open channel on their BioGram. They arranged to walk home.

They met outside and started toward their building. For the first time in her life, Julianna took notice of their changes once outside the Center. They greeted each other, but they didn't touch, they didn't hold hands, and they didn't think to. They kept the respectful distance that they had been taught to observe. Julianna recalled Delores' farewell kiss and wondered why that sensation had been so pleasing.

The sun had set, but their walkway was pleasantly lit and the signage to their building was clear. The evening air was just losing the day's heat. Everything was quiet but for their footsteps. Their conversation was more formal now, lacking any remnants of the intimacy and excitement in their ecstasy just moments ago.

"Thanks for inviting me," Julianna said. "I don't know why I stayed away so long."

"Every time I go, I wonder why I don't go more," Tim replied. "I think it's more fun to go with somebody. I don't usually go if I'm by myself."

"Really?" Julianna asked. "I go by myself quite a bit. But you're right. It's more fun with somebody else. Have you ever gone with a group?"

"Oh, yes," he said. "That can be a real blast. Some people I know only go in groups. But I find it a little confusing. I usually just focus on one other person as the session goes on."

He was quiet for a few seconds. They turned a corner and lost the last wisps of daylight in the shadows of buildings. There were fewer people, so their footsteps echoed more on this street. "Have you ever had sex outside of the Center?"

"No," Julianna answered. "I don't know why anybody would."

"I've never tried it either. The partners at the Center just know so much. Some guys I know can't even do it without the right spirits and the right partners."

"That doesn't surprise me," she said. "There are always more women than men at the Center anyway. I suppose women are just better at it," she teased.

"Nope, not in my case," Tim protested, sticking his chest out in jest. "But I know people who do it outside the Center. I've been trying to figure out what the big attraction is."

"Really?" Julianna asked. "That doesn't make sense to me at all. Who do you know?"

"Well – Ashley, for one," he answered.

"Ashley!? I never would have expected that. Who does she do it with?"

"I'm not sure. One time both she and I were invited as part of a group. We both showed up, but she left early with a guy I didn't know. You could tell by the way they were acting what they were going to do…"

"She left the Center to have sex somewhere else? Is she nuts?"

"I don't get it either," Tim said. "But," he added, returning to his normal flippancy, "to each his own. Or her own. Or their own, I guess." Then they were quiet until they reached their building. It was late. The secondary effects of the spirits she had consumed were kicking in, and Julianna was looking forward to a restful night.

-12-

Keaton, somewhere in what used to be Ohio

2073

Keaton had an especially bad week. He had been caught stealing again. Stealing was easy for him. He was thin with red, curly hair and freckles, giving him the innocent, boy-next-door look that he knew how to use to his advantage. He was unobtrusive. He could come and go with little notice. He could look an adult right in the eye while he lied.

He hadn't been caught by the police. That might be better. His mom and his older brother caught him. They had suspected what he was up to and warned him several times already. But this time his brother lost his temper. With only minor objections from his mom, his looming 17-year-old brother beat him horribly. Keaton was just a skinny 14-year-old. He had abrasions all over his arms and face where his brother had pressed him to the filthy concrete outside of the shantytown they were sleeping in now.

The shantytown was no more a home than the other dozen places they had bunked in the last few years. A place to sleep. No need for a table because there were never meals. His mom and older brother – they were nuts. Didn't want Dad to find them, whoever he was, if he was even looking. Keep moving. Stay together. Don't get noticed.

So, he ran away – miles this time. Not just around the block, but deeper into the city. He wasn't going back. Mom, his brother, and the two other little kids could fend for themselves. It never made sense to Keaton why begging was better than stealing. It took longer and there was less certainty. But his mom wouldn't submit to stealing. Never. She would work if someone would pay her. But never for long. She insisted that Keaton and his brother work whenever they could, but only for coin, which Mom would take. They had no identification. She believed in the compassion of her neighbors. And how many times had she just given away the goods that Keaton brought back? This life didn't make sense, and it wasn't going to.

He stopped to examine his reflection in a glass storefront. He wiped his face off with his sleeve. It didn't make much difference. He looked like hell. Probably best to get out of sight. He needed to watch the neighborhood and figure out his options. He spied a narrow alley between two commercial buildings. It was paved with uneven bricks. There were a couple older delivery vehicles and some dumpsters. Perfect. It was evening and he just wanted a place to hole up. He sat against a wall deep in the alley, hidden by the shadows of the buildings and equipment, but with a pretty good view of the street.

He watched the movements of the neighborhood for the remainder of daylight, an hour or two. Once darkness descended, he fell into a restless sleep sorely needed. As dawn approached, he awoke with a start, sensing the loss of a sweet dreamscape as he did so.

He smelled food. Bread. Deeper in the alley, a rattletrap exhaust fan in the side of a building filled the alley with an appetizing aroma. Keaton sidled in the direction of that building staying as hidden as he could.

Just beyond the exhaust fan, a door slammed open and a man and woman, talking loudly, carried out boxes of bread. Keaton ducked. The man and woman pushed the boxes into the sliding side door of a rickety delivery van. Empty-handed, they went back in the building. A minute later, they came out again with more boxes. Keaton sensed the tempo of their work and his instincts kicked in. Immediately after they went back into the building, he ran to the van and grabbed a random package from one of the closer boxes before running down the alley and hiding behind a dumpster.

The timing worked well. It was at least a minute before the door opened again, and by that time Keaton had eaten three of the spongy-soft, warm rolls that he extracted from the featherlite cellophane bag. His stomach rumbled a welcome.

Soon, he heard the van door slide closed, the engine start, and the van head out of the alley toward the main street. They drove right by Keaton. He doubted the driver even noticed him, or that they even missed the bag of rolls.

This is good. I've got my mark.

Keaton spent the remainder of the day exploring the labyrinth of alleys between buildings. He salvaged what he could for clothing, bedding, and other treasures from the dumpsters and junk heaps.

He used the same formula for several days: pinched bread in the morning and dumpster prizes in the afternoon. But the nights were getting colder. The walls in the alleys offered no protection from the advancing chill. One night he woke frigid and shivering. He carried what bedding materials he had toward the main street, seeking anyplace he might find for protection.

He soon found a tidy recess in the entry to a trinket shop. There was just enough room for him to huddle against the glass security door, where he was protected from the wind and warmed by what little air escaped from around the door sill. Not great, still outside – but survivable for now. He just needed to wake in time to steal food from the bakery van.

And he did. This time, just inside the sliding door was a sandwich, an apple, a roll, and two hard-boiled eggs on a paper plate covered in cellophane. *Somebody's lunch?* It was so appetizing that he grabbed it and ran to his hiding spot to devour it.

Now he was worried. The bakery people would miss the lunch and watch for him. He spent that day looking unsuccessfully for another mark. He would have to be very careful the next day with the bakers.

After darkness fell and the streets cleared, he again carried his belongings to the entry of the trinket shop. As he settled in, he noticed more warm air escaping the door than he had expected. On closer examination, the door was slightly ajar, caught on a pebble that kept it from latching. He opened the door and found himself inside a security alcove. The inner door was still locked. He couldn't enter the shop, but he was out of the wind and comfortably warm. He slept better than he had since leaving his family.

At dawn, he stayed further back from the van watching for signs of suspicion. He saw none. Once he was comfortable with the tempo of the couple, he ran in with more urgency. There was another lunch – identical – in the same spot in the van. He took the plate again.

Keaton couldn't believe his luck. There was a meal in the van every day. There was a warm place to sleep every night. But he was concerned that it would change, so he spent his days wandering the neighborhood seeking alternatives just in case.

He was returning from one of these sojourns near midday when he passed the doorway where he slept. Just then, a middle-aged lady stepped out carrying two over-stuffed bags, obviously too heavy for her. She walked clumsily down the sidewalk. As she met Keaton, one of the bags started to slip out of her grasp. She looked at him with pleading eyes. "Please?" she asked.

He stepped forward and took the bag that was slipping, allowing her to take better purchase on the other.

"Oh, thank you, young man!" she said pleasantly. "Could you please help me back inside? I need to repack these."

"Sure," Keaton said, following her in. A bell on the inner door tinkled welcome as they went through. The shop was quaint and colorful with an eerily familiar feel to Keaton. It smelled of lemony cleaning solutions mixed with a nasal cacophony of herbs – eucalyptus, jasmine, mint, and others. It was filled with all kinds of knick-knacks for cooking, decorating, and entertaining. The counter case contained dozens of transparent containers of different leafy products whose labels made no sense to Keaton.

The woman set her bag on a counter and stepped back so he could set his down as well. "Thank you, again," she said. "I don't know what I would've done. Silly me! Always putting ten where I should put five!"

"That's OK," Keaton replied.

He was anxious to leave. He knew he looked ragged and smelled. But there was something about the lady's demeanor that made him wait, like he shouldn't leave until she dismissed him.

She held out her hand. "Where are my manners? Hi, my name is Delores," she said.

He shook her hand. "Keaton."

"Keaton, it is an honor to meet you. Could I interest you in a cup of tea?"

"That's OK," he said. "I don't want you to be late."

"Oh, no. That's quite alright. An old lady like me has all day to do everything. You just have a seat there at the counter, and I'll make us a cuppa." She appeared delighted to have someone to serve.

He sat, still uncomfortable. "I, uh, sorry if I look, you know, like I don't want to keep your customers from comin' in."

She laughed. "Hush, Keaton. We'll have none of that. Everyone is welcome in my shop! Now you just relax and I'll be right back." She walked through a swinging door into a kitchenette in the rear.

His first inclination was just to bolt. He was embarrassed. But he could hear her puttering with things and humming to herself. For some reason, he felt it was right to stay. He kept trying to think of things to say to her, hoping he wouldn't make a fool of himself.

Sooner than he expected, she came back with two cups of tea and a plate of pastries. "Here we go," she said. His stomach growled audibly at the sight. They both ignored it.

"It's nice to have tea with somebody," she said. "Thank you so much for staying. Please, have a pastry." She put one of the pastries on a napkin and set it in front of him.

"Thank you," he said. He made every effort not to bite into it too quickly, but feared he didn't succeed.

"Now, Keaton," she said. "You seem uncomfortable to me, but you don't have to be. We all have our circumstances."

"I'm sorry," he replied. "It's just, I haven't cleaned up today. I know I don't look, you know, right."

"Don't let it bother you. Lots of workers come in here and look just like you do right now. Some of my best customers."

They both took a long sip of the warm tea. It was magnificent. Just the simple act of drinking it with her made Keaton less self-conscious.

"Now that we've met, I wonder if you could help me with some things. You see that I'm getting up there, but I still need to move things around and whatnot to run my shop. I'm sure you're busy, but would you have any time later in the day to stop back? I can pay you fairly."

She was older, but Delores' face was so open and welcoming that it was magnetic, and the tea did something indescribable to him. Somehow, Keaton could tell she knew more about him than she was letting on.

"Coin?" he asked. He didn't have to tell her he had no identity for allocations.

"Sure, coin is fine," she said. "Now, it's going to take a couple of hours. And I always like to visit with handsome young men. I don't want you planning to run right off unless you have to. Can I count on you?"

"Sure," he said, smiling at a person for the first time in – *how long?* It felt good. "Miss Delores, I'd be happy to help you."

He was surprised to find he actually meant it.

"Oh, good," she said with relief. "You can just call me Delores, though, and thank you, thank you, thank you! You just show up when you're ready. I'll be here all afternoon and evening. And please, take another pastry. I don't want them to go stale."

Keaton left the shop feeling lighter than he had felt in a long time. Delores seemed like a real friend. He killed some time half-heartedly looking for more marks. He used a public restroom and, for the first time in many days, sacrificed some of his rags to a sponge-bath. After a plausible amount of time, really just a couple of hours, he went back to Delores' shop.

"Good afternoon, Keaton," she said as soon as he walked in. "I hope you brought your muscles!"

"Sure did! What can I do for you?" he asked.

He could tell it was mostly make-work. He carried some old bins from the front to the back and some new goods from the back to the front. He set out some new products and rearranged some of the items on the higher shelves. He washed the windows, which weren't really dirty. All the while listening to Delores' appreciative banter and trying to use nice words in reply. He wasn't familiar with the joy that Delores seemed to experience regarding her shop and his company. After about three hours, it was obvious that she was spent trying to find things for him to do. She paid him generously with coin – more than he had ever received before in his life.

Evening was upon them and once paid, Keaton sensed that he should probably leave. He felt odd knowing that in a couple of hours, he would be sneaking back to sleep in her alcove and hoping he wasn't discovered. He started making his clumsy apologies. Delores interrupted him.

"Now Keaton, we all have our circumstances. I have some clothing left by an old boarder, and I'm sure they're your size. I live in the apartment upstairs, but I have a backroom here with a cot and a shower. Don't you think you would be comfortable cleaning up in there? I wish you would, because I have a nice meal that I would love to share."

"Um, sure," Keaton said. "I'd love to clean up."

He went into the back room. It was appointed sparsely with old furnishings. A full set of clothing was laid out on a simple-frame bed. The clothing was clearly used, the bed linens were threadbare, but everything looked incredibly comfortable. Keaton hadn't showered for months. He luxuriated in the process. Then he presented himself to Delores in the little kitchenette where she was setting out a meal.

"Now don't you look and feel so much better?" she exclaimed. "What a handsome young man! Hungry?"

"I sure am. Everything smells great."

"There's plenty!" she said. "Please eat up."

Keaton ate with unapologetic gusto. Delores served him generously. He split a roll in half and took a bite. He recognized immediately that the roll was from the bakery he had pilfered. He felt like he should tell her, but when he lifted his face to look at her, he could tell she already knew. He could also see that without words, he was already forgiven.

How did she do that?

Keaton woke only as the sun rose high enough to splash across his face lying on the bed in Delores's back room. He languished there as his dream-visions eroded. He was ecstatic at his new situation, regardless of how temporary it might be.

Through the door he could hear people moving around and talking. There was a man's level baritone interspersed with Delores' cheery morning voice.

He rose from the cot in a comfort that was entirely unfamiliar. He was warm. He was clean. He wasn't starving. He wasn't sure how to act. He rinsed his face in the sink and ran his hands through his unkempt hair to make it presentable. He put on the same clothing from the prior evening that Delores had given him. He stepped tentatively through the door to see what was going on.

Delores was sitting at the table in the kitchenette with a trim man in his mid-forties dressed in clean, functional clothing, like a workman who hadn't been to work yet. "There he is! Good morning, Keaton," she said. She turned to the man. "This is the young man I've been telling you about."

"Good morning," Keaton said, curiously.

"Good morning, Keaton. I'm David Sanderson," the man stood, shaking Keaton's hand. "It's nice to meet you. Thank you for helping out my friend Delores. If you hadn't done it, I would've had to!"

"Nice to meet you, Mr. Sanderson," Keaton said, returning the handshake and recalling as many ways to be polite as he could. He was never really taught. "I'm happy to help."

"Sit, sit," Delores said. "Let's have some breakfast. Toast OK?" she said to Keaton as he took a chair.

"Sure. Thank you."

David sat down across from him, and Delores moved around the room efficiently making toast and setting utensils, jam, and a coffee urn on the table.

Keaton was interested in David. When he wasn't speaking, he would frequently tap his fingers and wiggle his legs – not impatiently, but with nervous energy. Keaton sensed a frank intelligence, good will, and a sense of humor. These were not common in the men from Keaton's past. Most of them were mean, addled, or demented. David was a new character.

"So, Keaton, I'd like to know you a little better. Will you answer some questions for me?" David said.

"What do you want to know?" Keaton asked a little warily.

"Well, we've seen you around for the last couple of weeks. We don't know much about you other than you seem to try to stay out of sight. Are you on your own? Do you need help?"

"I'm on my own, yeah, but I don't think I need help. I do fine."

"That's what I thought," David said. "Have you been to school?"

If anyone else had asked him that, Keaton would be mad. Of course, he hadn't been to school but a couple days in his life. *How could he?* But for some reason, David's questioning didn't seem threatening. It seemed like part of a script they both knew. "No," he said.

"But you can read?" David asked.

"Yes, I can," Keaton said. "I taught myself."

"Impressive," David acknowledged. He was quiet then while he focused on folding his napkin in a precise way. After a few moments, he produced an origami bird. "Did you see me do that?"

"Yes," Keaton said.

"Can you do it?" David asked.

92

Keaton took his own napkin and, with very few missteps, reproduced the same bird that David had just made. Keaton was impressed with his own unexpected performance.

"I've never done that before," Keaton said.

"Very good," David said. "You have a talent."

"Thanks," Keaton said.

"OK, Keaton. You probably like straight talk. Right now, I suspect you're just doing what you have to do every day to survive. I respect that. But I think we can help each other if you can agree to some terms. Are you interested?" David said with a knowing, paternal smile.

"I, um, think so," Keaton answered. "What do you mean by terms?"

"I mean that if we are going to work together, you'll have to commit to your best effort, and to respect our guidance."

Keaton was shocked. "Are you offering me a job?"

"I'm offering you a situation, but yes, it includes work. For the time being, you can live in the back room here with Delores and help her as she needs. You will be provided with all the essentials: food, clothing, and whatever entertainment is convenient. In return, you need to agree to be educated."

Keaton liked the first part of the offer. "Well, um, I don't know what level I would be in school or anything. I'm probably way behind."

"Probably, but that won't matter," David explained. "Delores and I will see to your education personally. You'll see. It will be much easier than you think. You just need to agree to it. I'm certain that you will find it quite exciting, just like making that bird. Assuming you perform as I expect, I'm certain to have work for you along the way. All you have to do is agree to try."

Keaton thought about this last day compared to his life up to that point. He would have food. He would be warm this winter. He couldn't believe his luck.

"Sure," he said, sooner than he expected to. Then he looked both Delores and David in the eye and said, "I agree. I'd like to try." And for one of the few times in his life, he wasn't lying to the adults.

-13-
How can it be wrong?

2084

Julianna arrived at her work floor the next morning ready to focus on the next game. As she walked to her usual meeting with Ashley and Tim, she was struck by a buzz of anxiety among the workers she passed.

"Our game will be delayed," Ashley reported. "All discretionary computational resources are being redirected. We can't be certain for how long."

"What?!" Tim and Julianna exclaimed in unison. This type of disruption was unprecedented.

"It's an emergency," Ashley explained. "An earthquake off the west coast of Africa caused a tsunami overnight, and several hundred proles were killed. There were even a couple of Thelites in the area who might be dead as well. There was no warning. There has never been a significant quake recorded in that area. None of the models predicted anything in that region."

"Wow." Julianna was struck by the enormity of the event, an occurrence with near nil probability according to the model – and the scale of death.

"Yeah," Ashley agreed soberly. She gestured toward the other people in the area. "A lot of these people are with the geological model. That model has never been very good. Their catastrophic risk in the next century is still almost one percent. This event will require a major retooling. It will take hundreds of games. The High Council has directed that every geological game takes immediate priority, and there is quite a backlog building. In the meantime, all we can do is track the correlations of our model."

"I can focus on designing experiments on the boson-cannon with the other developers," Tim said. "But at some point, I'm going to need a CosmoPod."

"Understood, but that may have to wait. Do what you can." Ashley acknowledged and turned to Julianna. "Julianna, just keep up with your correlations. We can stay current on the NetGrams, but we can't start game prep until the Geological Team releases capacity."

They separated. Julianna quickly set up automatic correlation reports. She reviewed the results from the last day. There were a few deviations but nothing out of the ordinary.

Reviewing NetGrams did not keep Julianna's mind occupied. She felt some filial sense of duty to explore her father's message, but the shallow knowledge she had gleaned about proles from the Canon was not satisfying. She expected that her situation was unique. Few Thelites had interacted with proles as she had. *Perhaps the only way to learn more is to go there!*

She had misgivings. Interacting with proles was not prohibited, but researching prole behaviors was not Julianna's role. But protocols for those interactions focused on safety, not avoidance. *Weren't Hubs designed for that? Didn't Best Society Services employ proles directly?* Yet the Canon provided no guidance on relating to individual proles.

How can it be wrong to use my spare days, and possibly weeks, to better understand these people whom the Best Society is dedicated to serve? Julianna resolved to try. But she felt it best not to share her intent with others.

How could she contact Delores or her uncle? Could she find Delores' shop and get back without needing to file a deviation report? One hour didn't seem like enough time to learn much. Maybe she could use a short visit to arrange a longer visit in the Hub area, assuming Delores had any interest. It occurred to her that the free time and opportunity would never likely be better. She relinquished her CosmoPod and left the building, anxious to take this step.

When she stepped out of the driverless in the Hub of People's Village #179, she tried to recall the route that Delores had used to escort her just several days ago. She walked several blocks from the Hub looking for familiar surroundings, always keeping the Hub at an accessible distance and direction. If it didn't feel right and her BioGram sounded a connectivity alarm, she returned to the Hub to try another route. After an hour of back and forth, she entered a neighborhood that, while no specific store or street had names she could recall, seemed to possess the same character as Delores' shop. With a resolute breath, she continued her wander away from the Hub – outside of the reach of her BioGram.

People of varying sizes, ethnicities, and clothing styles crowded the chaotic streets. The size and tempo of the crowd grew the farther she went. Just navigating it became an effort. People were going in and out of shop doors, chattering, touching, arguing, and squeezing around each other to continue on their routes. Cyclists swerved through the crowd while vehicles of all shapes and sizes jockeyed for space on the streets causing a background din of bells, horns, squeals, and shouts.

The self-centeredness of it was disorienting, but Julianna bravely adapted. She stepped quickly between two crossing people only to find someone else in her path. She almost lost her footing on the unrepaired galling of a sidewalk. She shunted to the side of some bystanders and re-entered the fray beyond the knot of people. She gradually acclimated to the random order within the disorder. She moved forward steadily, gaining confidence, paying only casual attention to the lines, signs, and lights designed to control traffic.

After several blocks, Julianna turned a corner and ducked under the awning of a storefront to catch her breath. A big man with a dark complexion stood nearby smoking and staring toward the street. He was at least a foot taller than Julianna. They nodded to each other but said nothing. Julianna felt a little uneasy with him there and was relieved that he was quiet.

Just outside the entryway, the dazzling motion was like watching a loud, action-adventure film from a too-close seat. She glanced left, right, and across the street, looking for familiar landmarks to locate Delores' shop. Nothing helped. She hadn't gone that far, but she had been off-grid for at least twenty minutes.

Grudgingly, she resolved that it was best to return to the Hub and regroup. She inhaled and squared her body to start back against the crowd. She stepped out of the entryway and turned toward the corner. Coming from what seemed to be nowhere, a speeding bicycle veered hard to avoid her, and the rider tumbled into the street, separating from his bike with a racket. People scattered and cars squealed to a stop, but a sharp scraping sound made it clear that the bike had been hit and was badly damaged. The rider stood up, brushed himself off, nursed some scrapes, and shook his limbs as if to assure himself they all still worked. He was somewhat older than Julianna, but slim and bony with a sharp, mean face. His face darkened, and he marched threateningly toward her with a steely look in his eye.

"Jackass!" he spat as he approached. "What the hell are you doing here, anyway? Everything's fine, and then one of you Thelite creeps show up and all of a sudden, I've got no bike! Whatchya gonna do about it?"

Some people had slowed their pace to watch the altercation. The man standing in front of her was no bigger than her, but Julianna had never experienced his level of ferocity. She felt alone and foreign. For the first time in her life, Julianna felt real fear.

His confidence seemed to build when he saw that she was intimidated. "Well?" he shouted. "Aren't you going to say anything? You owe me one hundred coin for a new bike."

Julianna's sharp intake of breath alerted the man that he was onto something. Julianna knew that "coin" was a hard currency used by proles as a means of exchange. They were really tokens with no intrinsic value, a leftover custom from earlier state-centric societies. Coin was given value by the fact that prole communities would accept them to discharge taxes and penalties, and that those same communities would pay for the services they purchased with them. What Julianna also knew but had failed to consider until this moment was that in most prole communities, it was a crime to be caught without a certain amount of coin in your possession.

Trembling and confused, she responded meekly. "I'm sorry, I don't have any coin, sir. Please excuse me, but this was just an accident."

"No coin!" he screamed immediately in feigned disbelief. "Why would you walk around here with no coin? What are you here for? To steal things?" He gestured to the crowd, trying to incense them as much as he was. Some people murmured, but Julianna couldn't tell if they supported him or not. "I suppose you got something else that might do, though!" he said, stepping forward and grabbing her arm sharply to pull her down the street.

Just as he grabbed her, a large hand landed calmly on his shoulder and a deep, authoritative voice followed. "That's enough, now," said the man who had been standing in the entryway. "Move along, sir. This wasn't the young lady's fault. You've got no dispute with her."

The bicyclist turned his truculence on the man. "This is none of your business!" But if he expected to intimidate the man, he was soon disappointed.

"I see you ride by here like you're going to a fire every night," the man said, slowly and clearly. "You crowd people and scare people and expect everyone to get out of your way. It was only a matter of time before someone was going to get hurt. You're the one in the wrong here, sir. This unfortunate young lady was just leaving my store when you bulldozed by again. Nothing she coulda done." The crowd murmured again, but Julianna still couldn't determine their sentiments.

"But she's got no coin! What's she doing in your store with no coin, anyway?" the bicyclist complained, sensing that he was losing momentum. "These Thelites come here disrupting things – ruined my bike – and get away with it. And no coin! It ain't right!"

Things were calming down, and the crowd was starting to lose interest and move again. The bicyclist and the other man stood apart from each other for a few more moments. Finally, the bicyclist grumbled, turned away, and picked up his ruined bike. He moved off down the sidewalk with what Julianna presumed was an undignified gesture to the other man. The other man just watched.

When the bicyclist was out of sight, the man turned to Julianna. "Ma'am, you should probably get back to the Hub before you get yourself in real trouble." Then he turned and disappeared inside the entryway that he had been standing in.

The crowds were diminishing as she made her way back to the Hub. She was profoundly relieved when her BioGram reconnected. The confrontation with the bicyclist had caused depths of fear and heights of relief with more intensity than she'd ever experienced in her life. Her shoulder hurt, and her arm was bruised where he had grabbed her. No person had ever injured Julianna before.

She walked the perimeter of the Hub looking for more promising routes, but her heart wasn't in it. She had no more idea where Delores' shop was than when she started. She had no idea if it would be open or if Delores would even be there. Besides, she had no way to acquire coin and felt unsafe venturing back without it.

Discouraged, she meandered back to the transportation center and sat on the bench she had shared with Delores. *Was it really just three days ago?* She tried to recall the specifics of their conversation. Delores had said it might be dangerous for Julianna to try to contact her. After her recent experience, Julianna had to agree. *But hadn't Delores also said that she might be able to contact Julianna? How was that supposed to work?*

A thought donned on her. Supposedly, she had been contacted by her uncle through her dreams. That must be what Delores had meant. *But how did that work?* After some moments of recollection, she had an inspiration. *Maybe!* Anxiously, she stood up and hailed a driverless to return home. She knew what to investigate next.

Julianna unpacked her BioGrams as she traveled. There were notices regarding deviations on the correlations of some of her models – more than she expected – but nothing alarming. A note from Ashley confirming that there was little reason to go to their CosmoPods until further notice. She returned a BioGram from Mark which was seeking to know if she wanted company tonight. She didn't.

She arrived at her apartment and quickly performed her protocols for hygiene and nutrition. Finished and ready to settle in for the evening, she opened the drawer to examine the envelope Delores had given her.

"Tea?" she wondered. *Why had Delores given her this? What was she supposed to do with it?* She had no idea how to prepare it as Delores had. A pleasant aroma wafted out as she opened the envelope. Being careful not to spill the crushed leaves, she examined the envelope, looking for writing or a note, but there was nothing. She took a deep, slow whiff of the contents and closed her eyes to enjoy the heady smell. She started feeling groggy. It had been a long and eventful day. It was probably best to sleep and explore the envelope later.

Julianna's sleep was restless. She dreamt that she was a student in a class that her father was lecturing. Her father was much younger – younger than she was right now – but she was her current age. The lecture was entitled "The Nature of Truth." In the strange way that only dreams could be, her father was also an antagonistic student in the class. He was both student and teacher, and he was having a passionate argument with himself over the class title, which her student-father thought should have been "The Truth of Nature." She kept trying to get their attention to ask a question, but whenever they looked at her, she couldn't recall the question. Then they would pick up their loud discussion where they had left off until she thought of the question and got their attention again. "What is your question?" they asked in unison. Then she was confused and, again, couldn't remember the question. This loop played over and over, seemingly interminably, until she awoke briefly. She was frustrated as she recalled the dream and noticed that she had been asleep less than an hour.

She shifted to a more comfortable position and drifted back to sleep. It was morning when she woke again. As her dream-fog cleared, misty messages floated around her consciousness. They were not like a note or video, but rather mere feelings, shadowy inclinations that had somehow been registered through her sleep. They were clear to her in her semi-awakened state but hard to put into words.

Somehow, she knew that Delores loved her and was thinking about her and that Delores shared her grief for her father. Delores' very human warmth had been extended through the ether of her dreams. To what purpose, she had no idea, but it was an inexplicably pleasant state of mind to know that the sentiments existed.

Another perception was that her uncle was curious about what she had learned. This was an odd perception. *Learned? About what? Her father's message? If it were regarding proles, wouldn't he be the one to inform her? And if she had learned anything, how was she supposed to answer him?* A very simple, open-ended, but hard to answer question: what have you

101

learned? She was compelled to try to answer it, if for no other reason than to catalog her own thoughts.

There were jumbles of other perceptions, but she couldn't get them to materialize out of the dream-fog. They were seemingly lost as she became fully awake. Once awake, she closed her eyes again to try to recapture dream images.

"Father, what were you thinking?" she whispered desperately to herself. "What do I need to know?"

-14-
Kelly, somewhere in what used to be Ohio

2078

Kelly parked the junk-heap van she'd acquired behind the small, brick mortuary-cum-chapel. She felt ashamed of her relief to finally be attending Sandy's funeral. Sandy had suffered too long, but the end had still come too quickly.

Kelly entered and was directed to the family gathering area. Aunt Delores was there comforting Abby and Meghan. Her brother-in-law, the new widower, sat silently several feet away and showed no emotion. *Creepy guy.* The girls begged him to have a funeral, against his wishes. She gave him a brief hug before approaching the girls.

They took turns giving her long hugs, their bodies trembling with a fresh round of sobs for the newcomer. Kelly held each of them hard, whispering whatever small comforts she could. When they released, she turned to Delores and received an embrace and a tender kiss on the cheek. "Kelly," she said. "It's been too long. You look nice."

Kelly got the mid-length, black dress she wore just this morning from a second-hand shop. She was lucky that most clothes fit her small body without alterations. "It's nice to see you. I feel so bad for the girls," Kelly said. Meghan and Abby had sat down next to each other, holding hands, with their foreheads touching, but several chairs separated them from their father. His stoicism seemed out of place. "They're too young for this."

"There is no right time. They will find peace," Delores always had soothing words.

"Things must have happened quickly," Kelly said.

"Yes. He…" Delores nodded to their father, "…moved her to the Hub hospital about ten days ago. It was getting too hard to tend to her at home. It didn't take long after that. Abby is very bitter."

Kelly looked sympathetically at her nieces. Her visits over the last few years had made her feel especially drawn to Abby, now fifteen. As Sandy's respiratory illness slowly debilitated her, Abby tended to her mother as much as she was able. And she mothered Meghan. Kelly helped with what little she could when she was around, but her brother-in-law made it obvious she wasn't welcome. Abby had grown into a serious young lady who did little to make her plainness into anything more.

Meghan had barely understood her mother's illness and vied for attention. She was sweet, and she did everything she could to draw positive notice. It would have been cute if not for the circumstance. Now only twelve, she was poised, flirty, and flighty – everybody's friend. As she grew to understand her mother's condition, she relied on Abby. The sisters' devotion to each other was poignant.

But Kelly's protective instincts toward them were thwarted by their father. *It's probably best. I'm not the right person for them anymore.*

They were summoned to a row of chairs in front of about twenty-five attendees. The officiant spoke in a monotone, "Sandy Brooks. Devoted wife. Loving mother. Loyal sister…"

Kelly found the accolades trite, and her thoughts rambled. The service was faithless. Kelly didn't recall she and Sandy ever renouncing their Christian upbringing. It just happened. In her own case, she preferred a lascivious lifestyle and didn't care to repent. *But Sandy? Huh. Did she just adopt her husband's disdain for faith?* She looked askance at the family members who shared her row. Her non-descript brother-in-law stared apathetically into space. Her faithful Aunt Delores was attentive to the service. *Hadn't she always encouraged them to dream?* Meghan and Abby, who she was seated next to, wept openly. *Did the girls dream?* Kelly didn't know. *But Sandy? Did she dream?* Again, she didn't know. She just knew that *she* didn't. Such ethereal ideas seemed impractical to Kelly.

104

"…and we bid farewell to our sister, Sandy." The service ended.

The reception following was interminable. People tried to smile but weren't happy. They picked at snacks. They talked either too softly or too loudly. Kelly avoided her nieces as much as she could without being obvious. She didn't want to mislead with a promise to be around. A promise she knew she would break.

Kelly left as soon as she could. Sentimentally, she guided the rattletrap vehicle along a familiar route that would take her by the foundry. *Would this be the last time? Probably.* She remembered driving the same route in racier vehicles when she was younger and more prosperous. Her spur-of-the-moment decision to leave with Shawn over a decade earlier had surely cost her.

No regrets! Living among renegades suited her. Her scruffy group adopted her leadership. They moved around. They lived for the day. They protested conscriptions at every opportunity. And she'd had dozens of gay lovers, most of whom had no concerns with fickle loyalties. *So far, I've had more of what makes me happy and less of what pisses me off.*

But they were planning more daring changes.

She recognized the plumes of smoke from the foundry a mile before reaching it. She passed without slowing and scowled at the slogan – "Safely Serving the Best Society" – on a billboard at the entry. Several miles later, she stopped at an asphalt drive that exited toward the river. The Brunson mansion was set back about a quarter mile down that lane. She had been there many times, but now her view was blocked by trees and overgrown hedges.

On a whim, she turned in. Potholes jostled the squeaky suspension of her cheap vehicle. The trees lining the lane were untrimmed, and the grounds needed mowing. *What happened? This used to be so majestic!* As she approached the stately residence, things improved very little. There were no people around, just a lone worker on a ladder repairing something on the house and another unloading supplies from a truck. Self-consciously, she steered her van around the circular drive to an entry archway. She stepped out and slammed the tinny door, noticing immediately that the fountain was not running and the only other vehicle looked in need of some care. *Times must have changed!* Nobody noticed her.

She rang the chime next to the huge, wooden door. She waited nearly a minute and was ready to ring again when the door opened. A lanky, polite adolescent boy greeted her. "Yes? May I help you?"

"Chad?" Kelly guessed.

"Yes, I'm Chad. Who are you?"

"My name is Kelly. I used to work with your father, Junior. Is he around?"

"Kelly!" Chad's face lit up. "Please come in. Dad just got back from the foundry. He'll be excited to see you!" He ushered her through the house, chattering incessantly. "Dad really missed you. All I ever hear is 'Kelly this' and 'Kelly that' and 'Kelly whatever.' It's nice to meet you in person. He still works all the time, even now…"

They stopped at a room that doubled as a library and office. She had met there many times with both Eric and Junior as they plotted improvements to the foundry. A picture window overlooked a meadow that carpeted the hillside as it descended to the river. Timeless accents included deep mahogany woodwork, a rustic conference table, a large globe, and shelf after shelf of books. *Still the same. And they still keep books.*

Chad excused himself to find Junior. Soon she heard two sets of footsteps.

"Kelly!" Junior boomed as he entered with Chad in tow. She stood and gladly received his bearhug. "Great to see you!"

"It's good to see you, too, Junior." Kelly turned to Chad. "This young man has sure grown up!"

"He's fourteen, now. Yeah. Time flies!"

Kelly raised a knowing eyebrow to Junior, communicating comfortably just as they used to, and mouthed: "Can I ask…?"

"Sure, Chad knows everything. Ask whatever you want." Junior gave Chad's shoulder an encouraging shake, and Chad returned an affectionate smile.

"Did she ever come back?" Kelly asked, referring to Chad's mother, who left him on the Brunson doorstep with a note when he was less than two weeks old.

"No. When Chad was about five, we found her in a rehab facility about a hundred miles away. I went back the next day to sponsor her recovery, but she was gone. We kind of gave up after that."

"Too bad," Kelly whispered.

"Probably for the best, though," Junior winked at Chad. "Chad's a blessing, and he wouldn't be here but for my, uh, *liaison* with his mother. Who knows if it could have been better? But she made the best decision for herself and Chad. You have to give her that."

Chad seemed unusually comfortable being the subject of that discussion. "I think everyone has something unique about them – and that's my something!" He said optimistically. Then he smiled at Kelly as if to put her at ease.

Impressed, Kelly returned his smile. "It's nice to know you, Chad, all grown up and full of charisma!"

When she looked back at Junior, he grabbed both her shoulders to face her squarely and look her up and down. "So, Kelly. What brings you around? You look great, but what's with the dress?"

"I was here for my sister's funeral – Sandy Brooks? As I was leaving, I passed your drive. I just wanted to stop and catch up."

"I'm sorry," Junior said somberly. "Did she have children?"

"Yes. Abby and Meghan. Chad, they're about your age. Do you know them?"

"I know who they are," Chad said. "I've seen them at community events and stuff, but I don't know them well. They seem awfully close."

"They've been through a lot," Kelly's mood darkened as she thought of them.

"It's too nice outside. Should we walk and talk?" Junior suggested. "Chad, let's show Kelly your project!"

Kelly followed them through wide hallways to a back door. She recalled the house being bright, immaculate, and full of activity. Now they passed no one. There were dust bunnies in corners and picture frames askew on walls of faded paint. Stepping outside, Chad ran ahead to prepare while Kelly and Junior strolled through the ankle-high grass.

"Junior, this place used to be so busy. Where is everybody?"

Junior glowered. "Just what you'd expect."

"What do you mean?"

"We used to employ a gardener, a housekeeper, a cook, a repairman, and a nanny. Now I have a lady come in once a week to help with cleaning and some meal prep. Once or twice a year, I have a service clean up the property and handle a list of repairs. But it's never like it was."

"What about the people?"

"That's what I miss the most," Junior acknowledged. "For generations there were aunts, uncles, cousins, and friends that practically lived here. Whole families visited for weeks in the summers. Neighbors were always around. When I was growing up, we sponsored camps for the kids in the community. We had goats and a horse; the kids loved it! But it's been years since we did any of that. Now it's rare to have anyone here at all."

The sun was lowering into late afternoon, and it shimmered off the river as they walked. They were silent as a cloud passed over. "So sad," Kelly remarked.

"You were smart to leave," Junior broke the ice.

"How do you mean? Is the foundry not doing well?"

Junior stopped walking to get her attention. "On the contrary, the foundry is doing great. All the business we can handle, and we ship more than we ever have. *But…*" he emphasized the word resentfully, "…but every time we have a problem, they invoke some heavy-handed protocol, people get frustrated and leave. Dozens of 'em, now. Some of the best foundrymen in the world!"

Kelly didn't acknowledge what she knew – that many of them had sought her out after leaving.

Junior started walking again. "Then, every time we have a problem, my allocations get reduced. So even though I'm working more than ever because of people leaving, I'm making less than I ever have."

So that's what's going on. The Brunsons had always been wealthy and generous. If the foundry did well, their community did well. The Brunsons saw to it. *Was that coming to an end?*

They approached a gazebo-like structure made of glass. Chad was inside tinkering with equipment and adjusting pots overflowing with leaves and vines. There were light strips and drip-tubes entangled in trellises, suspended buckets of chemicals, water pans, and electronic control panels.

"What am I looking at?" Kelly asked as Chad stepped out.

"This is my hydroponic garden!" he said excitedly. "I started building it two years ago. It's very productive, and we have fresh produce all year round!"

"Impressive!" Kelly remarked. "How do you know how to do this?"

"Mostly my own research. Dad helps some when he's not working."

"Some of it is innate. Chad is a dreamer," Junior offered. "I know you don't necessarily buy that, Kelly, but I've encouraged him."

"Whether I buy it or not, this is remarkable! Junior, I hope you're proud of him."

"Certainly am!" Junior acknowledged. "He built and operates this thing all by himself!"

Chad enthusiastically demonstrated his automated garden. As a capstone, he gave them each a plum tomato which they ate like an apple. "Delicious!" Kelly exclaimed.

Chad continued tinkering while Junior and Kelly returned to the house. Their long shadows walked in front of them as the sun began its final descent into the river.

"Junior, thanks for welcoming me. I should be going, though. I still have a couple hours to drive."

"I'm so glad you stopped. But I have to be honest, your being here reminds me of such better times. It makes me miserable to think about."

"There's only so much you can do," Kelly said wistfully. "At least your son has a bright outlook."

"True. But you have no idea how it feels to oversee the demise of this place." Junior spread his arms to indicate the entire estate. "Chad will never know how it could have been. And it didn't need to happen! This was taken from him, and nobody's better off for it!"

Dew moistened their shoes as they rounded the mansion to the parking area. Locusts had started their evening songs from the wooded lane. The workers had gone. They stood next to Kelly's beater and shuffled uneasily in parting.

"Junior, just so you know, I don't think I'll be back."

"I've heard rumblings."

"I hate what's happened to you. And to the foundry. The protests are just bullshit. Somebody has to do more!"

Junior shook his head and looked off into the distance. "It shouldn't be that way. Can't we just do our good work without those assholes trying to own us?"

"Clearly not," Kelly said, remembering why she left. She followed his gaze silently, as if looking back toward the foundry. She stepped forward and pecked his cheek. "See ya, Junior."

"Be safe," he said.

-15-
A closer look

It was midmorning when Julianna received Mark's BioGram to meet. She agreed, but she didn't feel like meeting at her apartment. The last time had seemed odd. So, they met at her conference floor.

She arrived early and reviewed her correlations. Some of her bodies had deviated slightly out of the modeled patterns. Small errors weren't unusual relative to short-term predictions, and the degree of error was not yet alarming. Nevertheless, she BioGram'd Ashley a note to review the last games they had run whose effects on the bodies were most significant. It might be necessary to adjust remediation plans if the nonconformity continued to grow.

Mark arrived just as she completed the note.

"Good morning, Julianna. How are you?" Typical of Mark, his words were friendly but his expression was flat. She restrained her signs of grief as much as she could when she talked to him.

"Fine, thank you," she replied. "It's nice to see you. Is your group shut down for the geological games, too?"

"No," he answered. "Our systems are essential services, and they run continuously. Since we installed the new model a couple of years ago, we haven't had to improve it much, so we don't run the number of games that the science bureaus do."

"Oh," she said. "I thought you and father were always discussing new features and tests."

"Yes, we were." Mark folded his arms over his chest uncomfortably and answered as if he didn't like the question. "Ever since starting the new model,

112

we've been designing new tests. Your father had lots of ideas. But we weren't actually running any, yet. That's a big investment. Now we are reprioritizing things under new technical leadership. I'm sure it will change."

"Hmm," Julianna responded. She recalled that her father had conveyed some urgency that Mark didn't appear to share. "So how do you have the time to meet like this?"

"It's no big deal for me," he explained. "I have a lot of latitude in my role."

"Why is that?" Julianna asked. "It seemed like my father was always held to rigid schedules."

"Much of my work is spent on the Bureau's organizational issues. You remember how your father and I used to talk about that?" When Julianna nodded, he continued. "In fact, I am overseeing preparations for a ceremony. Representatives from the High Council will be at our Bureau to commend the staff for the model's success so far." Julianna noticed that he straightened somewhat as he spoke about the Bureau and the event.

"Congratulations," she offered, hoping he would get to the point.

He nodded modestly. "I'm really glad we're not in the geological group, though. No telling what is going to happen over there. Have you seen the NetGram about the earthquake?"

"No," she said, genuinely curious. "I'll call it up." She BioGram'd the NetServices terminal in the conference floor, and the NetGram came up immediately. They reviewed it together.

"At 2115 hours Universal Time, an earthquake of magnitude 7.9 on the Richter scale occurred along a previously unknown geological fault line. The epicenter was 60 miles off the southwest coast of Africa. The earthquake caused a tsunami of 25 feet at high tide, overwhelming communities along several hundred miles of the African coast.

"The affected area includes a newly-developed outreach community occupied by proles living in the standards of the Best Society. The death toll is likely to exceed 3,000. Among the presumed dead are 5 Thelite behavioral scientists who were studying the capacity of such communities to participate in Best Society governance.

"This event was not predicted by the geological model, which has never achieved the targeted safety boundary. All available resources are being deployed to reconstruct, improve, and test a new model based on knowledge gained from this anomalistic event. This is the largest scientific effort in the history of the Best Society."

The NetGram described details of the new model, who was in charge, quotes from members of the High Council, and other related information.

"Wow," Julianna whispered. "It's a lot worse than they first thought, isn't it?"

"Yes. It's pretty bad. But that model has never worked well, and this event might be telling us why. It will be a ton of work, but now we might have what we need to make it better."

"I meant the three thousand people. At first, I heard it was several hundred," Julianna clarified.

"Yes, I agree," said Mark. He uncrossed his arms and leaned toward her. "I wanted to meet to invite you to the ceremony I mentioned. Next week. As my guest. Your father had a lot to do with this, and I thought you might appreciate it."

The invitation and mention of her father's recognition caught her a little off guard. "Oh! Thank you. Maybe I would."

"I'd like to convince you," he said. "It's an important event."

Just then, Tim walked by and stopped when he noticed Julianna. "Hey, Julianna. I didn't expect to see you here. What's going on?"

"Nothing really work related," she answered. "I just needed a place to meet Mark. Mark, this is Tim-127, my co-worker. Tim, this is Mark-057, one of my father's co-workers."

"Greetings, Thelite partner," they said simultaneously. Tim looked Mark over and asked, "Have we met before?"

114

"I don't recall," Mark answered. "We may have passed by each other in this building. I spent a lot of time here with Julianna and her father."

"That's probably it," Tim mused for a moment. Then he turned back to tease Julianna as usual, "I'm just here to see if I can steal a CosmoPod for some estimates on the boson-cannon experiments. Any great ideas?"

The levity felt good. "Nope," she teased back. "But I wish you'd hurry up. I might need it if my correlations don't start improving!"

"Later this afternoon!" he exclaimed, pointing toward the ceiling. "I'm on it!" Then, he quick-stepped away with feigned urgency.

They watched him until he was out of earshot. Mark smiled a little and turned back to her. "Why don't you meet me at the Bureau of Optimum Allocation next Tuesday at about 2000 Universal Time? The ceremony will start at 2030, and I can introduce you to some representatives from the High Council. It might be good for you to know them."

"Ok," Julianna agreed, but she had no idea why it would be good for her to meet these people. Mark said it as if it should have been obvious. "But that's in the afternoon. If we have resources by that time, I will probably have to be in my CosmoPod."

"I doubt it, but it won't be a problem. I can make sure that this is scheduled for you so there won't be any concerns," he said with self-assurance. "I'll see you there." He stood and she nodded to affirm. Mark nodded back and left.

With no work to do, Julianna was again at loose ends regarding her uncle's message. *What had she learned? Very little. What was it that her father feared for her? Was that even true? How could she learn more?*

Julianna felt a compulsion to go for a walk. She left the building and followed the groomed walkway that skirted the urban buildings around her own. Compared to her venture into the prole community, everything was clean and sensible. There was a distinct order to the neighborhood. The buildings were in perfect repair. The walkways were level, and handholds were available for any steps up or down. Signs pointed to local destinations and clarified any restrictions. The few people around were all compliant with the protocols regarding the use of the path and grounds.

It had been many months since she had last walked this neighborhood during the day with no destination. Julianna was content to just continue walking and note the changes that were in progress around the community. She was impressed.

New greenspaces were frequent and colorful. Playgrounds were filled with groups of youth frolicking under the supervision of trained leaders. All the children were healthy and genetically optimized. Outside amphitheaters hosted Social Awareness Training groups. Water and nutritional outlets were plentiful. Public gathering areas had all the newest amenities, and they always functioned according to set standards. Nobody she met was even slightly deformed, infirm, or demented with age. Everything was perfect. *It was called the Best Society for good reason*. It was hard to imagine better.

Eventually she came to a construction site where a building was being disassembled to be replaced. In Thelite communities, if a building was over 25 years old, it would be torn down and its materials repurposed. Those buildings were replaced with new buildings with the most recently developed technical features offered in the Best Society. Thus, Thelite communities were systematically and continuously improved.

The site was fenced to limit access, but workers and equipment were in constant motion everywhere. A continuous stream of vehicles carrying materials came and went through a gate at the site, following a thoroughfare that led straight out of the city.

Julianna sat on a bench to watch the activity. A sign at the entry gate read "Safely Serving the Best Society." This was the slogan for Best Society Services: the organization that managed manufacturing, construction, and all other services that were performed by proles. She watched curiously, trying to understand the hierarchy of the different people she saw. From this distance, everything seemed orderly. The muffled din of machinery and workers voicing commands left her with the sense of progress each moment.

Soon, a Thelite lady came and stood near her. She had several devices with her that she trained toward people in the construction site, taking readings and recording them. They eyed each other briefly.

"Greetings," she said to the lady.

"Greetings, fellow Thelite," said the lady. "It looks like you are enjoying your day."

"Oh, yes. I'd like to be at my CosmoPod, but all of our resources are being used to update the geological model," Julianna explained. "I've never been this close to a construction site before. Do you have something to do with it?"

"Yes," she said. "I'm with the Bureau of Optimum Allocation. My job is to take a census of the proles who work in service of the Best Society. The census ensures that each of them receives their premium allocations from the People's Distribution Center."

"How interesting," Julianna said. "So, you record each prole as they come and go?"

"No," the lady responded. "It is a statistical sampling. Best Society Services arranges the work crews and determines who will show up and how fast the work will get done. There are other people who measure the progress of the work. If the target work gets done and the statistical sample of attendance correlates, then the individual proles can retrieve their allocations. It's very efficient and very similar to how the factories work."

"How is the work supervised? Are there Thelites who oversee it?"

"Sometimes yes, sometimes no. In this case, it is a pretty basic structure. This prole work group has built many of them. There is no reason to provide direct supervision, just general monitoring. On more complex structures, there would be a Thelite team on site overseeing the details."

With nagging inspiration, Julianna asked, "Can I look closer?"

117

"Possibly," the lady said. "It's not up to me, but it's OK to check in at the gate and ask. There are strict safety protocols, but Thelites are usually welcome to view the work sites."

"Thank you. I think I'll do that." Julianna stood up to leave as the lady resumed her work.

Julianna walked to the entry gate. Just being closer made the motion around the work site seem more haphazard. Muffled voices turned into urgent shouts. The hum of machinery turned into clanks of metal treads and thumps as large objects pounded against each other. There was smoke and sparks in the air and mud on the ground. There were people stepping around and through these hazards that she had not noticed but that now scared her. The workers wore protective gear that looked uncomfortably hot for this season. Julianna wondered how people could thrive in this environment day after day.

A small structure to the side of the gate housed site management. Relieved, she opened the door and entered. When the door closed, the hubbub of construction dimmed into the background. Immediately inside, a young man, obviously a prole, was seated at a desk with a sign labelled "Site Host." He was busily punching on an ancient electronic device and raised his eyes while he finished a task. He eyed her with a pleasant expression on his face.

"Greetings," Julianna said. "I am Julianna-119. Can I get a closer look at this construction site?"

"Greetings to you," the young man said, politely. "My name is Keaton. Sure, I can give you a closer look. First you will need to review the safety NetGram for this site. You can use the holograph in that conference room." He directed her to a door on the side of the entry foyer. She entered the room and stopped dead. Uncle David was looking expectantly at her from his seat at the conference table.

-16-
The cosmos doesn't need a language

2084

"Hello, Julianna," her Uncle David seemed comfortable with the clatter that made its way through the walls and windows. After he spoke, there was a shout followed by a loud bump that even shook the office a little. He didn't flinch. "Did you know I was going to be here?"

"I think I did, somehow," she replied. "Was it from my dreams last night?"

"Yes, it was. Last night is the first time I've been able to get through to you since we met."

"Have you been trying?" she asked.

"Every night."

As they spoke, Julianna was able to tune out more of the noises, or just simply got used to them. "Last night I sniffed some tea leaves that Delores gave me. Is that why you were able to get through?" she asked.

"The tea isn't necessary. If all you did was smell it, it probably didn't help much. But if you drink it, it can make the messages clearer and improve your recollection."

"I just smelled it. So how come we were able to communicate?"

"Did you have any spirits last night?" he asked.

She thought for a moment. "No," she answered. "The smell of the tea made me sleepy, so I just went to sleep without spirits."

"That's why," he explained. "The spirits are formulated in a way to specifically inhibit dreams. When you have spirits, you have no dreams. And when you have no dreams, you can't communicate that way."

119

"But couldn't spirits be formulated to allow dreams?"

"Sure. But preventing dreams is one of the reasons that Thelites are encouraged to drink spirits."

"I don't understand. Why aren't Thelites supposed to have dreams? And how do you know all this?"

He studied her for a moment. "Let me answer the second question first, because it's easier. Prole communities have varieties of teas and other substances like spirits that affect your state of mind, as well as mental and physical performance. But none of them are as regulated or purposeful as the spirits you are used to.

"I have advanced training in several fields. One of those fields is medicine, and I specialized in nutrition. In my early career, I actually developed some formulations for spirits to enhance mental acuity. I am very familiar with spirits and how they work."

She interrupted. "Delores said you were brilliant."

"People say so," he acknowledged without modesty. "But I'm still just a prole."

He was reflective for a few moments, and Julianna was patient. Now the noises floating in from the site were kind of comfortable, filling in silence gaps as Uncle David considered what to say next.

"Your first question has no direct answer. Why do *you* think Thelites aren't supposed to have dreams? What have you learned?"

"That is a very annoying question," Julianna snapped. "I can't seem to learn anything about proles or dreaming or my father's roots. Everything is a dead end. There is plenty written about proles – but it is all very general. Reports-on-surveys kinds of topics. There is no description of anybody like you or Delores. Nothing."

"But doesn't that teach you something?"

"Oh," she said, surprising herself. "I see. Perhaps I've learned that I'm not supposed to know anything about specific proles?"

120

"So far, so good. But not just you," he said.

"It is not intended for *Thelites* to know anything about specific proles?" she restated her guess.

"That's one thing. Have you learned anything else?" he asked.

She reflected desperately for a moment. "A cataclysm in Africa killed about three-thousand proles in an outreach community."

Her uncle nodded sadly. "Yes. It's horrible. What else do you know about that?"

"The geological model never correlated well. The Bureau of Scientific Truth is putting all available resources toward upgrading it," she said. "This event should help perfect the model."

"Then the model will be perfect?" he asked.

"The initial goal of all models is to demonstrate less than .01% probability of an un-remediated event over the next one hundred years and improve from there. That's critical to how the Best Society guarantees safety. The geological model only achieved about 1%."

"And yet safety is guaranteed?" he asked. "Was safety guaranteed to the proles in that community?"

"It was an outreach community. It was built for the proles that lived there, to see if they could adopt the Best Society principles of Safety, Equality, and Science and subsist with them perpetually. So, yes, I expect their safety was guaranteed."

"And yet about three thousand of them died," he said. "As well as several Thelites."

"But that's why it's such a big deal to use the event to improve the models," she responded, a little defensively. "The guarantee is the goal. Once the models are perfected, safety will be assured. Thelites work very hard at this. We all know that this could take several generations."

"Did the proles that died know that? If they hadn't moved to that community, they would probably still be alive."

"The safety of Thelites has improved each year that the Best Society has existed, and continues to improve. Thelites are serious about improving the lives of proles in the same way. My father was adamant about this. The Canon demonstrates how committed the Founders were. And so is the High Council. This event is unfortunate, but it can only further inform the models to improve safety forever," she continued with conviction. "Thelites dedicate their entire lives to this. The data are clear. Proles die every day for all kinds of reasons that Best Society principles could prevent!"

He was looking at her with a calm, friendly face, twitching with his characteristic pent-up energy. She felt somewhat embarrassed by her defensiveness. She focused on the question she was trying to answer: *what have I learned?* Julianna remembered when Delores told her that she just didn't care to work in service of the Best Society. She challenged him with her observation. "One thing I'm learning is that it seems that proles either can't or won't accept the truth."

"I suppose you are right, to some degree." He paused and continued looking at her, his visage open and gentle. "At least, you are on the right line of thought."

From somewhere outside, a heavy clunk followed by a muffled cry caused her to jerk. Shouts of others in response followed quickly. Despite this, her Uncle David remained placid.

Then, he told her the story of her father's life.

"Your father and I were twins. Fraternal, though. Not identical. I was about ten minutes older than he was. We were born in a small town – a prole community near what is now People's Village #471. But it was before that, shortly after the founding of the Best Society. Our parents were builders and caretakers of buildings in our community. They were modest, but reasonably well-off. We were their only children.

122

"Your father and I shared a gift. We were incredibly strong readers, and we always tested well above our age levels in any academic topic. We were educated at home. Our nanny was Delores, and she served as a live-in teacher. She and our parents would lay out lessons every day. Our reference materials were mostly books, which even then were becoming rare."

Books had been discussed in Social Awareness Training, so Julianna was aware that prior generations had used them as archives, entertainment, and for educational purposes. She also knew that books were incredibly inefficient and potentially confusing due to the inexactness of written words, depending on the author's native language, perspective, and biases. The Best Society had replaced books with multi-sensory media which conveyed truths with modeled outcomes based on expert scientific consensus. It was eye-opening to know that her father had been educated with books. He had never mentioned it.

But then, he had never mentioned any of this.

"We were very competitive with each other – at least intellectually. Both of us tested in the top one-hundredth percent of the population. Relative to each other, on rare occasions, I would outperform your father on a test, but for the most part he always had the edge.

"We were still in our mid-teens when we enrolled in our local college. Local colleges emphasized mathematics, physics, and hard sciences, which we both breezed through. Although we both did well, your father was actually the first person in history to turn in perfect scores on some of the standard tests. That caught the attention of the Thelite authorities, and he was invited to attend a Thelite school where he continued his education in philosophy, political science, and economics."

Julianna was fascinated with the story. "So what did you do? Were you jealous?"

"I continued in the local college and completed degrees in engineering, medicine, chemistry, and history. I was jealous at first, just because it seemed like an awfully big opportunity for him and no opportunity for me, even though our academic credentials were almost identical. I don't know whether it was that jealousy or just personal differences that drove us apart."

123

"Drove you apart?" Julianna asked.

"We went down different paths. I completed my training early and started working in Best Society Services almost immediately. I lived in the same community as our parents. But your father always had another research grant or fellowship that kept him away. He would come home several times each year, but we always ended up in some type of conflict.

"Our parents were faithful Christians. Neither your father nor I really followed the faith. But your father would argue that they should give up their faith and acknowledge science as the only way to know truth."

"Really!" Julianna blurted. Social Awareness Training had discussed the different religions that permeated human history and that persisted in some communities. But she had never imagined that her father was from a religious family. The idea was disorienting.

He continued. "I couldn't really agree with either of them. Their arguments were so ambiguous, and their positions on them were so intractable. The conflicts were respectful at first, but he resented that I wouldn't take his side. Between each of his visits, our personal viewpoints grew farther apart. It was obvious that his training was taking him one way, while my experiences were taking me another. Eventually, the arguments became vicious. Each time he would leave, it was like a relief, but then he would come home again, and we would pick up where we left off – arguing. Finally, something dramatic happened. And it involved you."

"Me?" Julianna quizzed. "I couldn't even have been around!"

"Well," he said, taking time to assemble his next words. "Another reason that your father kept coming home is that he was in love with a girl named Julia. She was a playmate from our neighborhood. Almost from the time they knew each other's name, we could tell they had a very special relationship. As we grew up, your father grew close to her – much closer than to me, actually. She was also from a Christian family. She was very smart, but very loyal to her family and her community, less adventuresome than your father.

"We all expected that your father would return after his training and marry Julia. There was a time when he might have. But a series of things happened that tore everything apart. First, through his university your father was invited to join a Thelite work group to improve the optimum allocation model. One of the benefits of the offer was the opportunity to move into the Thelite community – to become a Thelite. The idea appealed to him intellectually, but he was conflicted. Julia wasn't invited and couldn't go. Only Thelites are allowed to live in Thelite communities." Her uncle went quiet and looked at the floor.

Julianna was prickly with anticipation. "What else?"

He gave it a moment before raising his eyes. "Julia was pregnant. She was due just as your father received the Thelite invitation."

Having grown up in a Thelite community, Julianna had never really questioned her heritage. It was disquieting to discover at nearly thirty years of age that she was the product of prole parents from Christian families. She felt like she was looking at herself from a distance and seeing someone she didn't really know.

"So, I have a mother?" she asked meekly.

"No," he whispered. "Your mother died from complications of your birth."

They were both quiet, and she was unsure what to ask next. The noise from the construction site seemed to be dying off as the day aged. Less frequent shouts, fewer machines moving. After a few moments, her uncle took the burden.

"After she died, your father was mad with sorrow and rage, and he directed it toward us, his family, and Julia's. During her pregnancy, Julia had attended to herself and her unborn child – you – at the local clinic. Your father was encouraging her to move to his community, which was near a Thelite Hub. She was reluctant to move, especially knowing that when he became a Thelite they wouldn't be able to be married and have a typical family life. At least, not one that was typical for Christian proles."

He considered his words closely again. "Your father was positive that if Julia had used a Hub facility with better medical technology, she would have lived. He was probably right. He blamed us for not supporting him. He blamed her family linkage – thinking that if it weren't for those loyalties, she would have followed him and lived. And he blamed our parents and Julia's parents for persisting in Christian beliefs. Even though religion had nothing to do with what happened, in his mind, those beliefs held Julia back from accepting Thelite orthodoxies regarding the benefits of science."

"But you said he was probably right. It seems to me like he *was* right," Julianna observed.

"Probably so, as far as that goes," he replied. Quiet again. The rumbles from outside were getting more distant. The shouts had softened to just loud voices.

"So what did he do?"

"He accepted the Thelite invitation, took you, and left. I never heard from him again until his visit to my dream."

"Did you dream when you were growing up?" she asked.

"Yes – but it didn't seem like a big deal to us. People may not know it, but most have some ability to communicate that way. Some people use it without knowing, some people never develop it, and some people can develop real expertise. Your father and I used dreams to articulate thoughts to each other that are too difficult for words. You know – where you have an impression of a truth, but no words can describe the impression? Dreams are perfect for that because they communicate at a level *beyond* words. The cosmos doesn't need a language. And it isn't just us. Delores was a great teacher for us because she could do it, too. We were all good at it."

They shared a long, thoughtful pause. It was now totally quiet outside. "OK," Julianna said, recalling her earlier question. "Then why is it intended for Thelites to have no dreams?"

"Because science can't explain them," he answered.

-17-

Abby and Keaton, somewhere in what used to be Ohio

2082

Still sniffling from a vicious argument with her father, Abby knocked on Keaton's apartment door. She carried a backpack with some items she had gathered. Clothing and toiletries, plus some materials, compounds, and ointments from her classes.

Keaton answered the door. "Abby?" he said, surprised. "What's wrong?"

"I'm sorry, I tried to call," she said. "I—I…" She trailed off, crying.

"Come in, come in," he said urgently. "I've been unplugged all evening. Is something wrong? Are you OK?"

She stumbled inside. "I'm sorry, Keaton, but I didn't know where else to go. You're the only person I know with an apartment, and my Dad kicked me out!"

"Kicked you out! What for?" he quizzed, trying to get a sense of her situation.

"Because I won't quit the trade college and go to his school!" she spat. "It finally came to a head tonight. If I'm going to keep going to this school, I can't live at home!"

"Wow," Keaton gasped. "That's serious. I had no idea what was going on with you." A moment later, he remembered himself. "Here, let me help you with that." He took the pack from her shoulders and set it in the corner.

"So, can I stay here? Do you have room?" she asked timidly.

"Of course, of course," he said. "No problem – it's small, but it's enough. Stay as long as you need!"

Abby sighed in gratitude. "I can't help with expenses yet, but I can help pick up and stuff," she offered, still tentative.

"Abby, we can figure that out later. Let's just make sure you're safe and - - should we call your dad or something?" he said.

"I'll just let Meghan know. She'll tell dad. I don't want to talk to him at all," she replied, gaining some confidence.

"Here, sit," he said, offering a chair at a bar-height dining counter that divided the kitchen from a cozy common room. "Can I get you a drink?"

She sat, feeling more comfortable. "What do you have?"

"Well, not much, now that you ask," he said, opening the refrigerator and some cabinet doors to investigate. "I have some beer and some tea. So, I have whatever you want, as long as it's beer or tea!" he continued, trying out some light humor with her.

She smiled through what remained of her tears. "Well then," she said, "I'll have whatever your having!"

"We'll have tea, then," he said.

She inspected the apartment from her perch as he prepared the tea. It was small, but neat and comfortable. It was typically male, totally lacking in decorations, plants, or wall-hangings. A sofa table that doubled as a desk was in front of an easy chair. There was a scatter of various electronic and lab devices on and around the table. It appeared he was tinkering with these when she knocked.

"Looks like you were working," she said. "I'm sorry I interrupted."

He eyed her from across the counter where he was setting up cups. "It's all good," he said. "I'm just working on a new presentation for Dr. Sanderson."

"Figures," she said. "You guys do a great job."

In addition to his role as a manager in Best Society Services Construction, Dr. David Sanderson was a regular guest lecturer at the trade college. He didn't teach a class, and he wasn't employed by the college. He was commissioned by certain professors to present supplementary materials in a wide variety of technical disciplines.

Keaton was Dr. Sanderson's assistant. Among other things, he developed materials, graphics, and live demonstrations as props for the lectures – one of the reasons Dr. Sanderson was sought so frequently. The lectures had developed a reputation of their own. They were regularly attended by a growing group of students regardless of their subject.

"It's easy with him," Keaton acknowledged. "He knows so much about so many things. Very practical. Plus he has so many resources in his lab. There's always something new to show."

He set a cup of tea in front of her from across the counter. He carried his around and sat close to her because the counter was small. She was comfortable with him close. They clinked their teacups as if in toast, but nothing was said other than with their eyes.

"So," Keaton clumsily tried to start a conversation. He was several years older than Abby. He didn't know her well, just that she attended the lectures. She was among a small group of students who stayed after to discuss the material and socialize. "What's your dad's problem with the trade college?"

"He says that the trade college is going to hold me back." She rolled her eyes. "He's convinced that the only path to premium allocations is to attend the Thelite school in the Hub. Something about its focus on educational protocols of the Best Society – I don't completely understand it – but that's what he says."

"I probably agree with him on that," Keaton said. "I think we are all destined for a role in Best Society Services. At least our children are. I can't imagine premium allocations being available without that type of education. What's your argument with that?"

"They don't teach anything I want to know!" she rebutted. "When my mom was sick, all I wanted was to heal her, or at least get her to breath better with less pain. People would come to our house, and they could make her feel better for a little while. They had salves and potions and they knew how to touch her in a way…I could see it made her feel better. I wanted to be like them. To know how to make her feel better, so that I could do it when they weren't there." She paused to search for words. She wanted him to understand her conflict.

"But just that person – that one-on-one thing – the person who is looking right at you, needing you," she explained. "That's what's important! And that's a trade school thing. The protocols they teach at the Thelite school – they're all about using the algorithms and models that they use in the Best Society. It's not the same thing and it's not what I want." She looked at Keaton, deliberately doe-eyed, hoping that he understood her like she thought he would.

"That makes sense to me," Keaton agreed. "That's exactly the difference between the schools. I'm surprised that it's causing such a rift. Why would he kick you out?"

"Well," Abby admitted. "He didn't exactly kick me out for that. But I can't stand to be there with him fighting about it all the time. Every night we're together I get the same lecture. I'm selling myself short. I'm ignoring his advice. I'm rebellious. But when we listened to him and sent Mom to the Hub hospital? Sure – they made her feel better! For about a week! Then she died. How smart does that make him? I told him that if I had to listen to that all the time, I was going to leave – and he said 'fine.'"

"That happened tonight?" Keaton asked.

"Yes. It was a big blow up," she answered sadly. "I probably shouldn't have brought up Mom. But it's been coming for a while."

"I'm sorry," he said. "I didn't mean to make you relive it. I'm surprised you thought to come here, though. You seem so close to your classmates, especially Chad. Don't you know them better?"

Abby hadn't completely admitted her motives to herself. "They all still live at home," she excused. "I'm sure Chad's family has a lot of room – I guess they're very well off – but don't you think it would be uncomfortable explaining this to someone else's father? It was hard enough knocking on your door," she said with just enough self-pity to be convincing.

"Oh. Don't give it another thought. I'm glad you did," he said. "OK," he continued, now businesslike. "I'm not here a lot. If you're going to stay for a while, you'll need the access codes. If you need something that's here, you're welcome to it – but I don't keep a lot of stuff around. If you want the bathroom to be anything other than a guy's bathroom, you'll have to do it yourself. Feel free to open any cabinet door or drawer you're curious about. If you need something that's not here, you'll have to figure it out or we can go get it when I'm here. Between our allocations and coin, we'll make do."

"I'm so sorry to put you out like this," she said earnestly.

"Please stop that!" he said. "I understand! And it's not the first time in the history of humanity that something like this has happened!" He laughed, recalling his own situation. "Also, you are going to take my room. I'm a night owl. I tinker on these presentations all night long sometimes. I'll just bring my sleeping roll out here for when I get tired," he said. "No arguments!" he emphasized just as Abby started to object. "You know it's the best alternative."

Keaton made quick work of all the adjustments, carrying her bag and tidying his room a little for her benefit. When he was ready to settle back to his easy chair, she faced him shyly just inside his bedroom door.

"Sweet dreams," he said.

"Thank you. You, too," she whispered.

He pulled the door closed leaving her alone. She tiptoed around the room, checking the closets and bureau drawers just like he knew she would. No pictures. No frilly clothing. No makeup kits. No female paraphernalia whatsoever.

Abby was overjoyed at Keaton's welcome. It seemed that her intuition had been right. Maybe he was even glad she was there. She casually undressed, put on her night clothes, and snuggled into his male-smelling sheets.

No girlfriend. A fraternal sleeping situation. Two things that she dreamed would change in short order.

-18-
Science can't explain them

2084

In the days following Julianna's conversation with her uncle, his words *"science can't explain them"* rattled her. *Was it true?* Adding to her distraction, the bodies she monitored were diverging with ever-more error. *Why weren't the games' predictions accurate?* In what little CosmoPod time she could arrange, she tested explanations but found no clarity. She needed help. So, she met with Ashley in the conference area to diagram her concerns using the robust NetSystem interface.

"I wouldn't be so worried about these deviations," Ashley said, impatiently sweeping aside the screen on the NetSystem display – and countless hours of Julianna's preparation. "The only meaningful data is long cycle, and these are very short-cycle measurements."

"I understand that," Julianna countered passionately. Others in the areas between CosmoPods were glancing her way uncomfortably. "But these are pretty dramatic short-cycle deviations," she emphasized. "It's almost like the remediation plans are having the exact wrong effect. Either that or there is a higher order disturbance that wasn't considered in our models. Shouldn't we re-run some games based on these variations and see what the new outcomes are?"

"Even if I agreed, we still don't have access to the computational tools." Ashley emphasized each word of "don't have access" with a light tap on the screen. "And once we do, we have a backlog of higher priority games to originate."

"What makes them higher priority?" Julianna asked. "If the remediation strategies aren't working as we expect, shouldn't we understand it before wasting the resources on other games?"

Ashley looked away, breathed deeply, and looked back. "You're overreacting, Julianna," she said levelly. "Nothing is imminent. The bodies that you are studying aren't even high risk – probably not even significant."

Julianna closed her eyes and exhaled, just to let Ashley know she was also making a thoughtful point. "I understand. My concern isn't about these bodies specifically. It is about the function of the model. Either the remedies aren't working as expected, or the model isn't accurate. Don't you think we should figure that out? If those things are wrong, the entire output of the system almost has to be wrong!"

"This is a little discrepancy inside of a very big, complex system. The model is statistically validated on a holistic basis more or less continuously," Ashley explained. "In my judgment, it is just not significant enough to change our plans."

"Shouldn't we highlight the issue to administration? I know these bodies aren't particularly risky, but they aren't moving as predicted. It's our job to monitor correlation."

"And we have," Ashley argued. "The recordings of this body's movement are fed back into the system and considered in all subsequent planning and games. This isn't the worst deviation I've seen. Disturbances like this are digested by the model's algorithms, and the model self-calibrates over time. In the worst case, the body comes back up on the risk scale, and we play more games with it later. Our direct monitoring is just a third or fourth level validation. Relax. You've done your job. Trust the model."

Julianna was out of arguments, out of options, and out of her authority. But she was still troubled. She monitored dozens of bodies involved with her history of games, but these were unique. *And why was she monitoring them if deviations were ignored?* Nevertheless, she felt forced to concede. She dropped her eyes and leaned back.

With the discussion over, there was little more for them to discuss. Resources were still prioritized for the geological model. Anxious to move on, Ashley changed the subject. "The schedule says you have an appointment at the Bureau of Optimum Allocation this afternoon. What's up with that?"

"There's a ceremony to commend the staff for implementing the new optimum allocation model. It was just a couple years ago, and it's been a big success. One of my father's co-workers invited me. Since my father worked so hard on it, he thought I should come."

"Really? Lucky! I'd heard about that, and I was hoping to attend as a representative of our group. I guess it's good that someone gets to go. Who is the co-worker?"

"Mark-057. We used to spend several evenings a week together at my father's apartment. I've known him my whole life."

"Oh." A cloud seemed to pass over Ashley's face. Her next words were snappy. "Well, you may as well go and enjoy it. We've got nothing more to do here, and I have no idea when we'll get resources for a new game." She stood, then turned on her heel and left abruptly.

"Bye…" Julianna said, looking toward Ashley's retreating form, aware that she wasn't heard.

With several hours until the ceremony, Julianna poked at the NetSystem. The improvements to the geological model were making good progress, according to a NetGram. The most recent games had significantly improved correlations to history. Another round of games was planned in the coming weeks. If things went as expected, adoption of the new model was expected quickly thereafter.

There was an announcement that a new People's Village was established in her metro-plex – People's Village #3742. People's Villages were being established at an increasing rate all over the planet. This one was the hundredth this year. The announcement described the features of the new Hub, the Centers bringing Best Society services directly to the proles, and the celebration that was planned by the new leadership council of the village. There were images of throngs of proles cheering and smiling officials waving. *So noble!* According to the announcement, 650,000 more proles would now live better lives because of Thelites' work.

135

Eventually, she BioGram'd a driverless and left for the ceremony. When she arrived at the Bureau, she took the lift to the event center on the top floor. She wound her way through pods of associates to the station where Mark was waiting. He was engaged in conversation with dignitaries whom Julianna immediately recognized as members of the High Council. He greeted her with uncharacteristic animation. To lead her through introductions, Mark took her gently by the elbow. Julianna found this odd. *Was there some protocol that she wasn't familiar with that explained this touch?* Rather than make an uncomfortable objection, she allowed it.

"This is Julianna-119, my escort for this event. Julianna, this is The Honorable Malik, The Honorable Christina, and The Honorable Oleg – all from the High Council – here for today's ceremony."

"Greetings, fellow Thelites," they all said, simultaneously, with slight nods.

Members of the High Council were well known. When appointed to the Council, members were given first names that were unique among the members. The appointments were for life, and thereafter, they were always addressed as "The Honorable," without a numerical last name.

Julianna knew all the Council Members' names and titles, as did all Thelites. She was astonished, having expected to meet an emissary or two from the Council, not actual Council members. The Council Members didn't reside in her metro-plex, so they must have traveled, which meant the ceremony was much higher profile than she was aware.

Mark acted like a different person than she ever knew him to be. He was charming, almost gregarious. He moved expertly from group to group, introducing Julianna variously as his "escort" or an "associate from the Bureau of Scientific Truth." Her father was never mentioned.

Spirits were available from automatic dispensers throughout the room. Servers expertly navigated the groups offering choice snacks to everyone. As the afternoon wore on, the event area grew crowded. Most of the people she met were new to Julianna, and she answered many inquiries about her occupation. The spirits did their work, and she found herself enjoying the banter.

The sun was descending, shining through the arc of windows that made up the back side of the room. They looked over top the secretive Behavioral Science Research buildings to the city's edge and beyond into the countryside. The sun's glare was dimmed automatically by the photochromatic shading on the windows. Tinted red-orange with the coming of evening, the muted orb provided a perfect backdrop to a low stage centered in the arc of the windows. A brief program was announced, led by the Honorable Christina. Standing with her on the stage were the other members of the High Council, Mark, and several associates from the Bureau of Optimum Allocation.

"Greetings, fellow Thelites," Christina started. "There is no higher honor for a council member than to acknowledge the contributions of your work to the goals of the Best Society. This is especially true concerning the optimum allocation model.

"For many years, the progress of the Best Society was constrained by the capacity of this model to assimilate the needs of many of the world's proles. The scale of the demands required refinements in production and distribution models, and the new version is significantly improved. But the breakthrough innovation is its treatment of behavioral science. In this model, social constructs are no longer just inputs, but outputs – so that happiness itself can be managed and maximized. Higher levels of happiness can be achieved, even with the same goods and services. So far, the evidence is convincing. *People have more of everything that makes them happy, and everyone is happier with what they have.*"

That sentence inspired the audience. Julianna joined them, interrupting Christina with enthusiastic cheers. She knew more than anyone how much of their lives this group, and her father, had given to the effort. Christina took control by raising a hand and speaking over them.

"Since its implementation, the model has equipped us to establish People's Villages much faster, bringing the Best Society's benefits to more proles every year. Today, we marked the hundredth People's Village established this year – earlier in the year than any time in history. At the current rate of establishment, within the next two generations our goal will be achieved. The whole planet will share the benefits of Safety, Equality, and

Science. Your effort to implement this new, innovative model has accelerated this achievement. Thank you. Please, give yourself a round of applause."

The audience of over a hundred made committed applause for almost a minute. As it waned, Christina gestured to Mark who stepped forward with her. Julianna anxiously awaited his words.

"In closing," she began, "I take this opportunity to announce that the Senior Administrator of this section of the Bureau of Optimum Allocation – Mark-057 – has been appointed to the position of a High Council trustee. Trustees are not Council members, but they are important to perpetuate the Council. Not only will Mark advise the Council in areas of his expertise, he will also prepare to assume the duties of a Council member, in the event of future necessity. Please give Mark a round of applause."

Again, the audience applauded politely for a long time. There were hoots of recognition from some of Mark's closer associates. Mark smiled broadly and nodded to different sections of the crowd and stepped back without speaking as the applause ended.

"Thank you for coming. Please enjoy the rest of your evening," Christina concluded.

As Christina and the others stepped away from the stage, Julianna felt a pang of confusion. *Why was her father not recognized during the ceremony? Wasn't that why she was there?* She watched Mark work his way toward her through groups of his associates, stopping to accept congratulations and exchange pleasantries along the way. The difference in his demeanor was stark. She had never expected him to be this socially adept. *Was this how he behaved normally? Had he expected her father to be recognized?*

When he arrived, he took her by the elbow again and continued to work the crowd. As the afternoon turned into evening and the crowd began to subside, they joined several others who were in tight, mid-conversation with the Honorable Oleg. Julianna soon realized she was with other High Council Trustees, like Mark, who had held their positions for some time.

"The casualties at establishment are also going down," one of them was saying, as they all nodded.

"Yes," Oleg said. "It is much more humane now, but we must continue to improve. Any casualty is too many. Right now, we are down to about a point zero five percent rate. We need to get to zero."

"What causes the casualties?" Julianna asked before she could stop herself, drawing more attention to herself than she cared to.

Oleg turned to her with a patient smile and explained. "Prole communities have fairly high concentrations of people with character disorders which can manifest as violence. These people often band together and use violence to try to stop progress. It makes no sense, but it happens. It seems to be more prevalent in this metro-plex over the last several years."

"But how could they stop it? What could they even do?" Julianna asked.

Mark answered for Oleg, as if seeking notice. "They can't stop it, and they *know* they can't stop it. But they put themselves at risk anyway, which defines their disorder. Roving groups that sabotage supply transports are especially disruptive. We're focusing on that right now."

Oleg nodded in agreement. "Once we get that under control, it's just managing the protests at the conscription sites. If the work crews need to defend themselves, there can be casualties. Lowering the casualty rate is one of the primary concerns of the High Council, and we are certainly trending in the right direction. The new optimum allocation model has been a great help. Many of the behavioral tools are pre-positioned in the community to prepare the population, so there is less resistance."

Julianna did some quick math. "At that rate, isn't it about three hundred and twenty-five casualties for the newest People's Village?"

"Yes, it is," Oleg said, still kindly. "But they are all disordered proles from the former community, so it doesn't amount to much. There were several casualties among the work crew, but even they are mostly proles helping with the establishment. There have been no Thelite casualties establishing a People's Village in many years."

One of the trustees chimed in. "That's what we were just talking about. We now set up Hub infrastructures in less than a month. Casualties are going down while the rate of establishment is going up. The proles are happier with all they're getting – all because this new model is so effective!" He raised his glass. "To Safety, Equality, and Science!" They toasted each other with the last of their spirits, Julianna included.

It was late as the last people began to disperse, and she walked toward the exit with Mark. He was unusually charming. "Julianna, thank you for being here for the best evening of my life!"

"Congratulations, Mark. I had no idea! But wasn't there supposed to be some recognition of my father?"

"Everyone here already knows how important your father was! Many of them told me how happy they were that you came. But what good does it do to celebrate someone who isn't even here? A waste of good will. Gone is gone. It is up to the living to celebrate life!" he exclaimed.

Julianna shrugged in acknowledgement. She couldn't disagree. Mark's words could have come straight from the Canon. And the spirits had worked their usual wonders, helping Julianna control her reactions and even appreciate the discussion.

"Speaking of celebrating life," he continued. "Julianna, I've had a great night. And you've met some very important people – so you've had a great night. Don't you think we should enjoy a visit to the Center with each other?"

What? So she wasn't misreading him some weeks ago! "It's a little late," she demurred almost automatically, wondering why she did. After all, there was no harm in his suggestion.

"Late? C'mon," he laughed. "We may never have another night like this! Let's make it perfect!"

I guess, if it makes it perfect for him, what's the harm? "OK. Perfect it is, Mark. Let's go."

She had a pleasant time as always with her partner. Somehow, though, with Mark she never sensed the joyful, solo-sensory abandon she treasured from her other companions. It left her a little hollow as they bid each other polite good nights afterwards on the sidewalk.

When she awoke after sound and dreamless sleep the next morning and reflected on the evening, she felt like a fake. She had toasted Safety, Equality, and Science with a High Council member and several trustees. A once-in-a-lifetime experience for most Thelites. She should feel honored. But she had never been aware of the casualties, and she suspected they weren't typically reported through the NetSystem. In truth, she couldn't help being troubled by her mental image of 325 proles dying in a month to establish a Thelite Hub in a People's Village. The hundredth Hub established so far this year.

-19-
Should I ask?

2084

"Primary Audience:

Administrative Services Staff

    Task Group for Extra-Terrestrial Threat Remediation

Department of Cosmological and Astronomical Observation Unification

Bureau of Scientific Truth

Secondary Audience:

    N/A – Not for General Publication

With reference to Stellar Threat Section 692016

Greetings, Fellow Thelites…"

Julianna had found an unoccupied CosmoPod by going at an unusual hour. The area was nearly vacant. She stepped into the nearest cylinder and BioGram'd her intent to engage. She was comfortable – but anxious. She loved being in the CosmoPod. She closed her eyes to avoid distraction, directing her thoughts to assemble what she hoped was a compelling NetGram production.

For weeks the bodies that Julianna monitored behaved at odds with the predictions of the model. She poured over the results, recreating and testing different scenarios that might explain it, but to no avail. She argued vehemently several times with Ashley and even with Tim. Both were clinical regarding her observations, yet completely biased to the virtues of the model. This increasingly frustrated Julianna who became more emotional with each interaction.

But she learned from her father, and her father had been bold. She knew her concerns were important. Rather than risking an outburst, she decided to elevate the issue on her own. Surely the senior administrative staff of her section would be interested that one of their scientists had reason to believe the model was unreliable.

Composing on the NetSystem with a CosmoPod was incredible. As she completed or modified a thought, the NetSystem suggested representative information from her archive of work, animating it for effect as background to the message. As audience members were added, the NetSystem would dynamically adjust the production to use media techniques that were best received by that member. So, in composing it only once, the NetSystem created as many versions of the production as there were members receiving it.

The CosmoPod was subtly kneading and cooling her temples, simultaneously providing massage pressure to large muscles all over her body. In this condition and with her eyes closed, thought clarity was easy to achieve.

"This NetGram includes datasets describing unpredicted and non-uniform deviations from the modeled outcomes for certain bodies within Stellar Threat Section 692016.

These bodies have demonstrated uncorrelated motion relative to the predictive models. This condition persists even after exhaustive reconstruction of all applicable remediation techniques…"

The NetGram continued outlining details of the specific remediation methodologies. She also included a compilation of her prior experiences and the uniqueness of what she was witnessing. Her stress level increased the

143

more she composed, but the CosmoPod compensated by lightly supporting her shoulder and neck areas and providing positive pressure for her entire upper torso. The result was better focus as she made her arguments.

"These particular bodies do not represent a significant holistic threat. The concern is that these errors may indicate a deficiency in the model's general predictions which are used to guarantee safety from all such threats.

Please consider the information and advise how I may best assist in further investigation."

The NetGram was only ten minutes long. It was complete, but not yet published. *Should I publish?* Instead, she activated a brief callisthenic routine from the CosmoPod to clear her head. Then a series of cooldown stretches lasting about five minutes. Finally, several minutes of quiet reflection…

Should I include Ashley and Tim on the audience list? No. They might obstruct. Should I ask Mark's advice?

Ever since the ceremony at the Bureau of Optimum Allocation, Mark contacted her much more frequently, sometimes several times per day. His endless invitations – which seemed more and more like demands – to meet or attend events were a constant distraction. Julianna was wholly consumed with her pursuit, and because Mark seemed to have no interest in discussing it, like Tim and Ashley, she had kept her research largely to herself. Besides, today he had left on a trip associated with his new role as a trustee.

No. Mark will defer to the hierarchy. At least, that was her excuse for not asking him. Julianna was also looking forward to a break from his attention.

What bad can come from publishing this? What is the worst outcome? After several moments of concentration, she answered herself. *The worst outcome was that she was wrong, and someone would discover how. And that outcome was actually good, because it would mean that the model was likely reliable.*

She sat through the production yet another time to ensure that her work questioned just the model, not the hierarchy. Finally, Julianna considered her father's posthumous warning. Somebody was corrupting science. *But who?*

144

Wasn't her situation the classic symptom? Was that what he was trying to warn her about? Wouldn't ignoring this problem be the biggest danger to both society and her career?

She was resolved. She knew what her father would do. She closed her eyes and nodded her head to confirm.

"Publish." It was done. A few more stretches to put her at ease. Then she exited the CosmoPod.

-20-
It's good that you know the truth

To Julianna's surprise, by the next morning her NetGram elicited action. An Inquisition Team was named and put out immediate calls for unending amounts of detailed reporting. The pace was challenging, and every question answered inspired new questions. It sometimes took their whole team long hours to thoroughly answer just one of the questions, and all questions were characterized as urgent. Julianna was afraid she may have alienated Ashley, but she did not seem upset. She assisted answering the ever-more-intrusive inquiries with professional detachment.

Julianna was satisfied that the issue was getting the attention it deserved. From what she had seen, once she got beyond her little circle of associates, the scientific method was proving sound. Perhaps she had figured out her father's warning and done the right thing.

The exhaustive pace continued for several weeks. Access to CosmoPods was still difficult, so when they were available the days were long and the nights were short for the whole team. When the intensity of the inquiries finally diminished, Julianna had only to wait on the report from the Inquisition Team. Unusually, she was in her apartment at a reasonable hour, satisfyingly tired and reflective, and with no morning tasks to prepare for. Resources for their next games were still unavailable.

Relaxing in her apartment, her professional drama slipped into the background, and she ruminated on the prospect of her prole heritage. With weeks of removal, it seemed like fantasy. But she couldn't dismiss that her father's message, delivered by her uncle and Delores, may have guided her.

She retrieved the envelope Delores had given her from her drawer. The pleasant smell of the contents relaxed her. She decided to try making the tea.

She put a pinch of the leaves in a cup of water and swirled it for a few moments. Then, she scooped out the leaves and took some sips.

Immediately she felt her mind unfurl. And yet, she was fully in the moment, seeing the objects in her apartment with new clarity and almost sensing her own breath. She had a delightful sense of peace and attachment, but to what she couldn't guess. She felt as if the universe was trying to send her innumerable messages and she just needed to figure out how to receive them. And in this condition, she lay on her bed and let fatigue have its way.

Her dreams were as vivid as they were surreal. She watched a young Delores crying, whispering comforting words to a newborn baby. At the same time, an older Delores was speaking to Julianna in the present, "I love you. I'm so sad about your father. I wish I had known you better." Simultaneously, Julianna could hear the young Delores whisper to the baby, "I love you. I'm so sad about your mother. I wish you didn't have to go away."

But more than hearing what Delores was saying, she felt what Delores was feeling. Her intense faith, commitment, and surprising intelligence overlaid everything. Julianna sensed that Delores could answer any question she could ask. Like her last dream, Julianna couldn't articulate questions. Yet Delores comforted her, saying, "It's OK, it will come." And she saw Delores as if through the eyes of the infant, and she wanted to say, "I love you, too" – but couldn't – but somehow knew that Delores knew it anyway.

These scenes and sensations revolved through clarity and mist, interminably repeating, yet simultaneous; this continued until the young Delores handed the child to Julianna's father, whose face was troubled and yet determined. She sensed a deep, deep sadness and an even deeper resolve from her father. She sensed love from her father – but a different kind of love. Resolute. Protective. Not warm, like Delores, but not cold. The infant felt safe in his arms.

Julianna awoke. She had been asleep less than an hour. Sensing more to come, she settled into her pillow and quickly fell into dream-disrupted sleep.

147

"Thank you for coming," Julianna sensed Delores through an opaque dream mist with no images. "It's good that you know the truth."

"Why?" Julianna asked. "What good comes from me knowing the truth?"

"Finally," her uncle, now superimposed over Delores, said in response. "Is that your question?"

"Yes, that's my question." Once said, she realized that was the question she could never quite find.

Her dream mist morphed to a classroom setting. The teacher was her uncle. There were many seats in the room, but she wasn't in any of them. She stood beside her uncle at the front of the room as if on display. A crowd of college-aged students bombarded her uncle with questions. One would ask a question, and the others would repeat and restate it in a challenging melee until another question was asked, after which followed another raucous round of inquisitive confusion.

Everything seemed to be said all at once. "What difference does it make if Julianna was born a prole?"; "What difference does it make if Julianna's mother was a Christian?"; "Why do people die to stop the Hubs?"; "What did Julianna's father mean about science being corrupted?"; "Do other Thelites dream?"

And on, and on, and on…

Every question highlighted some point of her own confusion. Her uncle didn't even attempt to answer the questions. He just kept saying "good question" to each new exclamation from the students. Eventually, after what seemed like hours, one of the students asked, "Why was Julianna's father worried about her safety?"

Everyone went quiet. Her uncle knitted his brow. "I don't know," he admitted. "He wasn't clear. But he thought it was important. I hope she figures it out."

Julianna awoke again. It was deep in the night. She consciously registered both dreams, then continued her slumber. She dreamt more, but without conscious recollection, and managed to sleep continuously until morning.

148

Upon waking, Julianna was immediately compelled to walk again to the construction site where she had met her uncle earlier. The site was less chaotic. In the intervening weeks, the new building had taken its final form. The mud was gone, replaced with gravel and concrete. The huge equipment for excavation and handling big parts had been replaced by smaller pieces doing lighter work, manlifts and skid-steers. There were more workers doing more disparate tasks like painting, wiring, and landscaping.

She walked past a disturbingly loud generator and entered the trailer a few feet beyond. When she closed the door, the noise became a gentle rumble that seemed to come from everywhere. Keaton familiarly waved her past with only a glance. When she entered the conference room and saw her Uncle David, it was clear he had been waiting for her. He was seated on the conference table facing the door with his legs splayed, feet planted, arms crossed, bearing his welcoming grin.

"This is weird," she stood very near him so they could talk over the sound of the generator vibrating the walls. "Were you in my dream last night?"

"Yes," he said. "Last night was the most interaction that we've had. You must have had some of the tea."

"I did," she acknowledged. "How does it work? How did I know to come here today?"

"Nobody knows how it works from the aspect of biology, chemistry, or physics," he explained. "For those of us who know how to use it, it is the most thorough way to communicate anything complex. Dreams allow cognition both consciously and unconsciously. When you first met me in the People's Village, you were responding to a compulsion that I conveyed to you in a dream. That's also why you're here now. You clearly have the capacity to communicate this way."

"It doesn't seem like a skill," she reflected. "I don't do anything. It just seems to happen."

"Being aware and letting it happen is a big part. There's so much you're going to learn!" He continued, "Dreams can transmit whole sensory experiences. For example, if I described my dinner to you through a dream, you would recognize how the food tasted, how it smelled, and its texture, even if you'd never had it before."

"Really?" she murmured, disbelieving.

"Yes, really. What did you notice?" he asked.

The generator sputtered, then renewed its rumble at a higher pitch, causing the windows to rattle lightly in their frames. She moved even closer to answer. "I noticed how everything seemed to happen at once. It wasn't a linear dialogue, like this conversation. It was this jumble of words and emotions that somehow I just understood after the dream was done."

"Yes," he said. "That's typical. Dreams reduce information to impressions. They can convey intuition and wisdom accumulated from generations of experiences. People who dream might have some of these benefits and not even know it. Dreamers can accumulate very specific knowledge and capability in incredible depth. Mathematics, art, music, and craft know how. Whether they realize it or not, most people who are identified as prodigies are dreamers."

Julianna considered what he said. It was hard to believe, but harder not to believe given what she had experienced the last several weeks.

"And sometimes dreams have nothing to do with communication. It's like you are just interacting with this big cosmological community." He looked pensive as he finished.

"What is the tea for?" she asked.

"The tea encourages dreams and improves recollection. Without the tea, you would likely have fewer dreams, and your recollection of the dreams would be less vivid," he explained. "Most people who dream just accept the idea that dreams are rare and hard to recall – mostly subconscious impressions. They may not even be aware that they are communicating."

"This all seems kind of, well...*spiritual*, doesn't it?"

150

"Interesting question." David was taken by Julianna's insight. "Yes, it's linked. In ancient times, people slept and dreamed more. Prophets had visions and recorded them. Shaman walked in the spirit world through meditation. Omens and signs of fortune were divined from these experiences and nature's other messengers. But as humans became better at explaining nature through science, we relied less and less on these bygone practices. But that doesn't mean they didn't exist, and it doesn't mean that they're gone. They just lack a scientific explanation."

The generator slowed smoothly to a lower, less-imposing pitch. "Shouldn't it just be accepted for what it is? Something that hasn't been explained, yet?" Julianna asked.

"You'd hope so. Centuries ago, spiritual believers would defy scientific discovery based on ridiculously strict interpretations of an ancient tome, or just the proclamation of religious leaders. Sometimes under penalty of death. This made no sense, other than to preserve social power for those leaders," he explained. "Over time those tables have turned. Now, to chastise science has gotten dangerous. People still dream, but to acknowledge that it is more than hallucination is to deny science. This makes no sense either, but it's part of the human psyche."

Julianna had never heard the historic twist he described. She still didn't understand what he meant by dangerous. "But nobody can do anything about it, can they? If people dream, they dream – even if other people don't believe it. Right?" Julianna reasoned.

"For many years including my childhood, Thelites worked to purge communities of spiritual leaders and dreamers. They identified them as 'disordered.' They would turn neighbors against neighbors to find them and send them to research centers. None of them ever came back. This still goes on during conscriptions.

"Now, 'dreaming' has been stigmatized out of self-preservation, like other mental health issues. It's kind of an open secret. People dream, but they hide it. Very few people ever speak of it. In fact, other than with you, I never speak of dreaming to anyone."

Julianna was troubled by the idea of Thelites "purging people." She didn't want to believe it. But just as she was forming her questions, he interrupted.

"Do you recall telling me that it seems proles either can't or won't accept the truth?" he asked.

"Yes. It was in our last meeting."

"You're right, you know, but there is some nuance you should understand," he said.

"I'm right?" she asked, surprised. She had said those words earlier out of frustration, not because of any particular insight.

"Each prole has unique beliefs and experiences that create their individual sense of truth. But each one is different. In a way, your comment is less about the word 'truth' than it is about the phrase '*knowing the truth.*'"

"But there can't be more than one truth!" Julianna retorted. "If two plus two equals four, it always equals four, and it never equals anything else. That is the nature of truth."

"Do Thelites know *the* truth?" he asked.

"Thelites accept that all matters of truth must be based on provable, scientific facts and replicable models. If there is ambiguity, the Bureau of Scientific Truth investigates and publishes their findings. That is the only way the Best Society can establish the common truth. It works better than anything humanity has ever done in the past."

"Do you believe that?" he asked.

"Absolutely," she answered. "So did my father. Best Society principals of Safety, Equality, and Science have improved human happiness dramatically. Thelites are living with this blessing for the first time in history. They are working hard to bring those benefits to the proles, so all of humanity can experience optimum happiness."

Even as she said it, she felt like she was a walking billboard, shallowly advertising the Best Society concepts. The generator slowed to an idle, now just a background hum. She stepped back a comfortable distance. When

David spoke in a normal tone, it seemed like a whisper. "No matter how many they have to kill to get it done?" he asked, rhetorically.

"What choice do they have?" Julianna retorted defensively. "This is the problem with proles. The benefits of Best Society principles are so obvious, proles should simply accept them. But they don't! How else can these benefits be shared without overcoming proles who would use violence to stop it?"

He knitted his brow. "Your question is *how*. Many proles might assert that it should be *why*."

"But most of them must agree," she argued. "Many proles are helping! And fewer and fewer of them are fighting the establishment of new Hubs."

"Maybe that just means they don't want to fight."

Having less competition from the generator, Julianna tried to continue the conversation in a more level tone, opening her hands and arms in reasoned appeal. "It all seems so simple. If proles would just accept what we know to be true, everyone would be better off. Happier. Isn't that what we should all want? Just accepting scientific truths seems straightforward and like the best answer."

"Your father and I had similar arguments before he left," he admitted. "He dismissed any belief concept other than provable science, too. But he was stymied by his own dreams. Whatever mechanisms dreamers use to communicate frustrated the researchers. Various studies came up empty. Thelites are not receptive dreamers to begin with. So, they were content just to medicate them away completely – that's what spirits do – in the name of healthy rest. The same way they might treat an allergy or some physical disorder. Now they even use genetic science to disrupt them. When nobody dreams, then there is no reason to *ever* explain them."

That's good information, if true. Julianna wasn't ready to concede any points, but it reinforced her emerging concern to be cautious with what she was learning. *If I discuss dreams, nobody will even understand what I'm talking about!* "Is that why father never brought it up?" she asked.

"Probably. Your father was satisfied that scientific explanations would emerge. He accepted the compromise that if science couldn't explain something now, then that thing should be negated until it could be explained – later. That was the only way for him to assist the development of the Best Society. Those were the last things we discussed before he left. I never heard from him again until he was dying."

Just when he stopped speaking, the rumble of the generator stopped completely. It was a relief, but the stifling silence portended an end to their conversation. David continued.

"Julianna, I enjoy getting to know you – even when we argue. But this building is almost complete. Now that we can communicate through dreams, we should avoid meeting in person. Now that you understand how, it is much easier to communicate these complex concepts through dreams, because the concepts themselves sometimes defy words."

"Okay, I suppose," she said. She surprised herself by being a little disappointed. "How will I know when?"

"It won't matter," he said. "Any time you don't drink spirits, you are receptive. Any time you drink the tea, you can expect more clarity. I'm sure to be there whenever." He stood. She noticed a wetness in his eyes, and he stepped toward her and gave her an enormous hug. "Please be safe," he said, with more raw emotion than she could understand.

-21-
Doing important work

2084

The geological model was complete, and computational tools were once again available. Julianna was relieved to return to her normal work schedule. She spent the entire first week enveloped in her CosmoPod following up on suggestions from the Inquisition Team regarding her correlations. She made adjustments, played abbreviated games, and modeled a myriad of assumed disruptions to demonstrate the issues. Based on her work, she was more and more convinced that there were problems with the model, but it was taking forever for the Inquisition Team to fully assemble a redevelopment plan.

As demanding as that was, the effort invigorated her. She marveled at the CosmoPod's incredible comfort, and the sense of productive power that it conveyed to its user. You simply had to think a thought or feel a curiosity, and it was immediately sated with multisensory action or response, strings of information, and experiments that you could follow interminably and inexhaustibly. All in perfect physical comfort – temperature, muscle stress, stretch and motion – all exactly tuned to you. Each day she felt that perfectly satisfying combination of fatigue and exhilaration that comes from a productive day of hard mental work. And evening spirits induced much-needed, perfect rest.

In these moments, her own strange history receded as a share of her conscious concerns. The tempo of her life didn't allow it. Besides, she was doing important work. She logged each of the trials and the results. She forwarded everything immediately to the Inquisition Team, confident that her concerns were comprehensively described.

Engrossed in these trials, she had ignored all her non-essential BioGrams until late in the week. When she finally stepped free of the CosmoPod with some idle time, she reviewed her backlog. Most were routine, several from

Mark. He suggested with increasing urgency that they should meet, and his most recent proposal was for this evening. She was wary, but had no excuses to offer. Resigned, she walked toward the exit and ran into Ashley and Tim who were headed in the same direction.

"Good to be back, isn't it?" Tim said. "Up for some 'recreation' before going home?"

"I don't think so," Ashley said. "I just turned fifty, and I need to report to the Center for Health Solutions for my exam tomorrow morning. I'll probably just stay in tonight."

"Sorry, I can't go either," Julianna said – although she wanted nothing more. "I have to go see Mark. He says he has something urgent to discuss, but I can't imagine what it is."

"Mark-057, again?" Ashley asked pointedly.

"Yes," Julianna answered. "I'm tired, but he is really insistent."

"Huh," Ashley spat. She looked down for a moment, then looked up quickly and said, "Oh well, see you sometime tomorrow." Then, she hurried away without looking back.

Tim and Julianna watched in confusion as she disappeared around a corner. "That was unusual," Tim remarked.

"I know," Julianna said. "That's happened a couple times now. I'm not sure what's going on with her."

They made small talk for a few minutes when Julianna excused herself to go meet Mark.

"Where is the meeting?" Tim asked.

"In his flat above the Bureau of Optimum Allocation where he works," she said. "I've never been there before. I can't imagine what he thinks is so urgent."

Tim looked uncharacteristically reflective for a moment. Then, quickly returning to his jocular self, he smiled broadly.

"Well, I expect to have spirits galore at the Good-Time Center. Wish you could come, but I understand the importance of 'trustee' business. Enjoy. We'll talk tomorrow!" He was whistling as he walked away.

Anxious to get the meeting over, Julianna hailed a driverless to Mark's place. When she arrived, she was taken with the ornate quality of the floors, walls, and decorative items that greeted her. She noted that there were doors for only two flats off of the common area. Based on the size of the building, she expected there would be ten or twelve. She presented herself to his door and BioGram'd her arrival. The door was opened by a woman in a uniform who escorted her inside. *Mark has an assistant?*

The flat was amazing. The rooms were huge with ceilings at least fifteen feet high. All the surfaces had rich, elegant finishes, which converted to vivid electronic scenery, geometric patterns, and art depictions depending on the purpose of the visit or the mood of the occupants. There were holographs in abundance portraying notable historic events of the Best Society. There was a CosmoPod dedicated to the flat. Spirit dispensers were in alcoves throughout. There were floor-to-ceiling windows arcing around an outside foyer, which was itself a huge and comfortable space, with doors into different rooms. Everything was completely out of proportion to the utilitarian apartments that she and her father had occupied.

The windows were photochromatic and programmed to shade or lighten the foyer. The view was breathtaking, looking out over the tops of the many well-ordered municipal buildings just beginning to light up at nightfall. That bright urban scene was disrupted by the darker buildings and dimmer lights of the expansive Behavioral Science Research Center at the city border as it gave way to the countryside.

The assistant scanned Julianna with an instrument she didn't recognize. *Security protocols? Really?* The assistant said nothing, but Julianna sensed it would be inappropriate to move about freely.

She heard voices emerging from within the flat that got louder as the speakers drew nearer. Soon Mark appeared with another man, finishing what had apparently been a meaty conversation. Mark's demeanor was not the gregarious socialite of the ceremonial events, nor was it the stiff, emotionless,

157

mild-spoken Mark that she remembered growing up. He asserted confidence she didn't remember him having and behaved as someone used to being in a position of authority. Mark nodded to Julianna as he finished his conversation with the man and bid him farewell.

"Thank you, Alexa," he said to the assistant. She stepped into an office to the side of the entryway, leaving them alone.

"Hello, Julianna," he said, smiling broadly. "Thank you for coming."

"You were so insistent," Julianna said. "What is so important?"

"Come back to my meeting area so we can discuss it more comfortably," he said, beginning to move back into the complex of rooms making up the apartment. She followed.

"You have a CosmoPod and a meeting room in your apartment?" she asked. "I had no idea. And an assistant?"

"I didn't get all of that until recently," he acknowledged. "My old flat wasn't this nice, but I've taken on substantial accountabilities for the High Council that they value. We've been quite successful. They insist this is properly allocated to my use."

He walked to the end of the foyer and opened a door into a comfortably appointed sitting room. Julianna sat in a chair near the window to look out. He went immediately to the spirit dispenser and brought them both a glass.

"Please," he said. They both took healthy sips, and she felt the tensions of the day start slipping away, even more quickly than usual.

"You're in trouble, Julianna. I want to help you."

"What?" Julianna spat, caught off guard. "What kind of trouble?"

He studied her, then said, "Your emotional reactions are probably contributing."

Julianna took another drink and tried to relax and steady her voice. "What do you mean by I'm 'in trouble'? I can't imagine that I've done anything wrong."

"There is a complaint that you are trying to subordinate the credibility of the model that quantifies the risk of extra-terrestrial threats. And associated with that, exhibiting behaviors viewed as being outside of expected norms."

Julianna felt her anger rising and quickly sipped more spirits to help her control it. It was helping faster than usual. She forced herself to a controlled silence. When she spoke again, it was without the high emotion that she felt. "What is the process for following up on the complaint?"

"Well, from your standpoint, nothing. In fact, you're not even supposed to know there is a complaint."

"How do you know about it?" she asked.

"I stay informed on all of your professional activities," he said. "The way you acted after your father's transition, I was afraid something like this was going to happen. I have that privilege in my position. I knew your father well, and I'm sure he would have wanted me to."

Julianna wondered why he thought so, but didn't ask. "So what happens next?"

"It has been turned over to the Behavioral Science Group to investigate. They will interview people, track your diet, exercise, hygiene, work performance, and social activities. They will consider whether there are problems with the behavioral model, but that is unlikely. This model is quite mature."

"So, if the model is good and I am outside of the norms, what then?" she asked, taking a huge gulp of spirits to keep her fear under control.

"In the best case, you will simply be monitored to ensure that your behaviors are consistent and harmless. In the worst case, you could be sent to a clinic for correction," he said. "You don't want that to happen. Once you are in the clinic, there's not much anyone can do."

"Why? What will they do in the clinic?" she asked.

"It is hard to know. I just know that sometimes it works and sometimes it doesn't. Either way, you don't want it." He waivered for a moment, then said,

"The best way I can help is by giving favorable input for you when they interview me. They are going to interview a lot of people, and who knows what others are going to say? I am very credible and have known you for a long time, so my input should help to steer the decisions to the best outcome."

The spirits she drank had put Julianna in the right frame of mind to have the conversation. She was getting more internally focused, and she found herself as curious as she was fearful.

"Isn't that interfering with the process, though? If you give information to try to steer the decision, how will the behavioral group get the best information to test or improve their model?"

Mark examined her with a look of pitiable concern. "This is one of your problems, Julianna. All the benefits that the Best Society provides, and you want to question their correctness. You refuse to just be happy. That's what got you into this jam," he said.

"That's not true. I am happy! I love the benefits of the Best Society! I'm just doing my job!"

"Julianna," he began sternly. "You need to know something. In the grand scheme of things, your job only has a tiny impact. It doesn't really matter that much. The models are intelligent. What matters is that you do it, and that you behave as a happy person."

"I realize that my specific job might have little direct impact. But everyone that does what I do needs to do it honestly and well," she objected. She drank the rest of her spirits and looked at him. "We use the models and gather information on their performance. The Best Society can't function if the models aren't optimized."

"No," he said. "The Best Society needs people to *believe* that the models are accurate and to behave as happy people. If you disrupt the *belief* in the models, you disrupt the whole foundation. It is the belief that matters, not the function."

"But how can people believe in something that doesn't function well?" she asked.

"If nothing bad happens, the models' function doesn't even matter. People just believe it. If something does happen, we improve the model and claim it as a benefit for all humankind. That's what happened with the geological model. That's the newest innovation of the Best Society. It's about happiness first, not function. The models are just a tool. But, Julianna - you keep calling yours into question. That promotes fear. And calls attention to you. That's why you're in trouble right now."

"So, I'm supposed to just be quiet, even if I know that the model isn't working in reality?"

"Reality isn't the issue," he explained calmly. "The issue is that we maintain conditions that maximize happiness. You can't really know if the modelled outcome is true or not, and it doesn't matter. How do you even know someone will put your remediation methods in place fifty years from now? But it needs to be believed. The Best Society maximizes happiness by eliminating fear and jealousy. People can live the entirety of their lives in extreme happiness even if the models are completely wrong."

Mark stood and took their glasses, refilled them, and brought them back. They both sipped for a moment, letting the spirits do their thing. For having just received such bad news, Julianna was now very much in control of herself. She was concerned for her future, but felt that it was good to have Mark in her corner. Each drink she took made her less argumentative. She was able to internalize her situation; she was sharp and prepared to address it.

"At this point, I guess the complaint is registered," she acknowledged. "There's nothing I can really do about that. What do you think the best course of action is for me, now? Is there some way you can help more directly?"

He smiled. "I think I can manage this to a happy outcome. You can count on it. But first things first. Come with me please," he asked.

Uncharacteristically, he offered his hand. She stood and took it, confused, and let him lead her across the room and through another door into a huge, beautifully appointed bedroom. One wall was an extension of the arched floor-to-ceiling window looking out over the inner-city scape, now well-lit for the night. She was curious that the view, the lights, the scents, and the

161

background music were all very sexually suggestive and exactly to her taste. When Mark put his hand on her shoulder, she realized that he was inviting her to bed with him.

This didn't offend Julianna. She had no moral objection. But it did make her curious. She looked at him and arched an eyebrow. "Why wouldn't we just go to the Center again?" she asked.

"This is permitted," he answered. "And I think it's more fun."

"I've never done this," she said. The spirits had made her receptive, but in the further recesses of her mind, she would have been happier with the Center.

"Well then, it's about time. I'm here to help," he answered.

Julianna relinquished, and he led on. But compared to her partners at the Center, Julianna found him boorishly amateur. He went through his rituals energetically but paid little attention to her experience or preferences. Once he was spent, he quickly nodded off to sleep. Becalmed but still awake, Julianna acknowledged that she enjoyed very little of their encounter. She went to sleep wondering why anybody would prefer this to the Center.

-22-
Falsehoods are the guideposts

2084

Julianna awoke alone after a restful sleep. The morning light was perfectly tuned through the smart windows of Mark's bedroom. The room had been tidied up, and the appurtenances for her hygiene were neatly ordered in the washroom. A new set of fashionable clothing hung invitingly in the dressing area. All the items were of unusually high quality. Julianna examined them tentatively, reluctant to use any of it until Alexa entered the room and reassured her. All these things were for her comfort. Mark was already down at the Bureau.

She prepared for her day quickly and took a driverless back to her building. Out of habit, she went to her CosmoPod and engaged with it, but found herself at loose ends. She had been focused on documenting the deficiencies of the model and now knew that was getting her in trouble. She poked at the most recent game for most of the day without enthusiasm. She disengaged a little earlier than usual, hoping to avoid Ashley as she left. As she walked through the common area, Tim was waiting for her and seemed anxious to talk.

"Hey," he greeted her. "I figured out something interesting last night after you left. Do you remember introducing me to Mark-057 a couple of weeks ago right here?"

"Yes," she acknowledged.

"Well, I finally figured out why he seemed familiar. He was with one of the groups that I went with to the Center a while ago, and he is the one who left with Ashley! I'm pretty sure he's the one Ashley has sex with instead of going to the Center!"

"Really," Julianna's curiosity was piqued. "So that's why she acts so unusual every time I mention Mark?"

"I bet it is," he admitted. "It's weird."

"It *is* weird," she said. "She's acting so weird that I wanted to get out of here before I ran into her again."

"Oh, don't worry. She's not here. She isn't back from the Center for Health Solutions, yet," he replied. "We were supposed to meet this afternoon, but they sent a notice that they needed to run some tests, so she's still there."

Julianna was quietly alarmed. "Wow. I hope everything is OK."

"I'm sure it is. They know what they're doing over there. Those health models are about as good as they get," he said with confidence.

"Thanks for letting me know," Julianna said, dismissing herself.

She returned to her apartment. With nothing pressing to do, she took some extra time to think about her situation. *Who would have complained about her? Ashley? Tim? The administrators?*

Now resigned to her last week's work being fruitless, her interests wandered back to her uncle and Delores. She deliberately avoided spirits, and instead prepared another tea. She noted how different the sensations were when drinking the tea compared to spirits. Spirits created a sense of internal control, focus, power, and heightened the pleasant sensations of socializing. The tea opened your mind, giving you a sense that your liberated soul could freely travel the awesome, infinite, incomprehensible universe, and connecting you to other souls on their own journeys. With this realization Julianna submitted herself to sleep.

She was back in the classroom with her much younger father as the instructor. Actually, she was somehow back in two classrooms at the same time, because she was also in a classroom where her much younger uncle was an instructor. In both classrooms, she was the subject, standing in front and watching the class talk about her question.

Some of the people in the classes were the same as her prior dreams. But there were many more. Some were recognizable, but others weren't, like apparitions. Faceless shadows in the periphery of her senses.

"What was your question?" both instructors asked her at once.

"What good comes from me knowing the truth?" she stated, and it came from her mouth in both classrooms at the same time. Somehow, she was able to clearly perceive both jumbled discussions that occurred at the same time.

"Truth," said her father to his class, "is a human invention. Reactions?"

"Truth," said her uncle to his class. "Is unknowable by humans. Reactions?"

Then all at once from the classes: "Without humans, there is no relevance to truth!"; "Truth serves no purpose *other* than human understanding!"; "Belief is truth!"; "Truth doesn't matter!"; "Science is truth!"; "Five senses are *not enough* to know truth!"; and other dogmatic claims were zealously repeated in a cacophony of responses, but she managed to hear every word.

Both classes were called back to order. Her father and her uncle began lectures at the same time.

"Truth," said her uncle, "drives the universe in ways that humans can never completely understand. Humans observe the universe and explain it as best they can based on some combination of science, experience, and faith. But our explanations and models are bounded by our perceptivity and intellectual range. We sense only an infinitesimal fraction of what is, like trying to discern the origin of the earth by closely examining a grain of sand. Humble submission to unknowable truth is the essence of the human condition."

"Truth," said her father, "is purely a manifestation of human curiosity. Truth is relevant only as it explains the universe to humanity. Aside from what is provable with science, there is no use for truth, and there is no relevance to truth without provable science. Science, and the advancement of science to describe truths more exactly, is the best use of human effort."

165

"Truth," her uncle continued, "must explain the entirety of the universe and human experience, or it isn't truth. Yet humanity is incapable of comprehending the full dimension and nuance of even the simplest truth. Science, experience, and faith provide humanity with only superficial context. To claim to know truth, or to assert control of truth, is a denial of its infinite complexity."

"Truth," continued her father, "is acknowledged when human experience equals scientific explanation. To sustain humanity, it is important to ensure that science and experience support each other. Science and experience must be kept in lockstep as science continues to advance."

The dream morphed from its classroom setting to a debate setting, with her father and uncle speaking from behind lecterns. The class members became a silent audience. Julianna sat as a frustrated moderator while her father and her uncle talked over each other in declaratory platitudes. They weren't angry, but each of them spoke as if the other one wasn't there.

The pace of their lectures quickened to an imperceptible speed. They just spoke faster and louder and in higher pitches, soon becoming piercing screeches. She understood both of them, somehow, but was frustrated that her question wasn't being addressed. After a few moments, she shouted, "Hey! Hey! Why is any of this important to me? Why do I care about this?"

Suddenly, there was total silence. Her uncle and her father stood silent, blinking at her quizzically. Everyone in the audience was looking at her; their foreheads were wrinkled in thought. One by one, they started raising their hands, anxiously, as if hoping to be called on first. They started tittering, "Ooh, ooh"; "I know, I know"; "Call on me!" Until all of them were bobbing and shouting with their hands up, hoping to be selected. She was getting ready to just pick one of them, but when she raised her arm to point, they all disappeared. She was so frustrated that she almost cried.

She looked back at the lecterns, but now there was only a small table, and Delores was seated behind it. Her father and uncle were no longer there. Without saying a word, with just her simple, tolerant facial expression, Delores settled Julianna. She relaxed. Even in the silence, Julianna sensed that Delores was asking her to answer her own question. Julianna sensed that she could say anything, and somehow Delores would cause it to be correct.

Even without knowing what she was going to say, Julianna started talking.

"I think," she began tentatively, "that understanding 'truth' is just a noisy, academic exercise. There might not be an answer, or there might be many answers." Delores nodded, encouraging Julianna on. "But humanity can only improve its condition by understanding truth more clearly, regardless of its form."

Julianna continued, inspired by the clarity of her own understanding. Somewhere from deep inside her, a new understanding was emerging that she only realized as she put it into words. "Falsehoods are declarations that are generally thought to be true, but aren't. They occur naturally as rationalizations of human interests and incomplete perceptions."

She paused, impressed with what she had said. She continued with more confidence, even though she had no idea what she was going to say next.

"Falsehood is not the opposite of truth. Falsehoods are the guideposts for humanity on the interminable path to truth. Recognizing falsehoods is a necessary process in truth-seeking."

She stopped again. She sensed that anything she said would create new insights, but not before she said it. Twice she opened her mouth to speak, but stopped short. No words would come. She looked at Delores in confusion and shrugged. Finally, she said, "I don't know what to say next."

"What's next is what makes this important," Delores said.

"Can't you just tell me?" Julianna asked.

"We are," Delores said. "Since you've been dreaming, we have shared many, many impressions into your subconscious. Believe it or not, much of it was there already. These impressions are at the root of your curiosity. But it will only be useful to you as you learn how to access it."

And then, Julianna woke up.

-23-
Meghan and Chad

2084

Meghan flipped her short, blonde bob as she turned in a wide circle on the sidewalk with her arms spread. Everything was so beautiful and orderly. The buildings were neat and square. The landscaping was edged perfectly, and all the bushes were trimmed to their most picturesque shape. There was never any yucky stuff in the streets; there were no smelly things, no ugly or destitute structures. Even by herself she wanted to dance every time she came to the college in the Hub of People's Village #471. Just being here made her feel pretty. Her Dad was right. This was what life was supposed to be.

Today would be even better than most. She would finally spend time alone with Chad Brunson in person. And he had asked! She was sure he was going to sometime, but there was still such joy to relish when it actually happened. Here she was, going to a spirit bar on a gorgeous day in the beauty of the Hub to meet Chad Brunson! Her sunny disposition was even sunnier than normal this afternoon.

About a half block before the bar, she collected herself. She checked how her colorful dress was draped across her body. The hem fell mid-thigh, an inch higher than her Dad would approve of, but an inch lower than she wanted. The flimsy fabric lay gently across her breasts, suggesting without showing their youthful contours, and the collar was cut just low enough to tease without offering anything lewd. With her eyebrows that never needed plucking and a splash of freckles across her small nose, Meghan was used to people noticing her face. Today, though, she wanted to be an attractive young lady, not a cute little girl.

She walked by the plate glass window of the bar and noticed her transparent reflection was superimposed over Chad inside the bar, sitting at a high-top table looking out. He noticed her and mouthed a greeting. She waved gaily back and walked in to join him.

"Hey, Meghan," he said with a broad smile as he stood. "Thank you for suggesting this place. It's nice!"

"Oh, I hope you enjoy it!" she said, returning his smile. She took his hands in greeting and hefted herself onto the bar-height stool. "I never would have believed how fun spirits are. And thanks for inviting me out! Isn't it a beautiful day?"

"Yes, it is," he affirmed, taking his own seat directly across from her. "I've wanted to hang out with you for a long time. But once Abby got it in her head that we should meet, she was relentless. I ran out of excuses, not that I wanted any," he laughed.

She faked a pout. "C'mon. I'm not exactly a blind date, am I?"

"If you were, you'd be the best one I've ever had. Isn't it weird? We've been in the same community our whole lives. Who'd think it would take us twenty years to hang out?"

"Eighteen, thank you," she corrected. "Old man!"

"Shit," he said. "I never thought I'd turn out to be a cradle robber!"

He looked around inquisitively at the sparse midafternoon crowd. "So, how does this work?"

"It's really easy. You just tell them the flavor of your favorite drink, and they bring you spirits that taste just like it. But they're different. They make you feel great. You're going to love it!" she said.

"I'm really looking forward to it. My family rarely comes to the Hub. Just for their allocations. My Dad is kind of old-school about that stuff," he admitted.

"So, what's your flavor?" she asked.

"How about lemonade?"

"No problem. Mine is simple lime water." She poked a button on her communicator. Within seconds a robotic server brought two tall glasses to their table. They picked up their glasses and clinked.

"Here's to first dates," he offered.

"Here's to more dates!"

Chad raised his eyebrows in mock shock. They both took a healthy sip. Meghan looked at him expectantly until his eyes widened.

"Wow!" he said. "You're right! This is great! I feel, I don't know…smarter?"

"Yeah," she said. "It's hard to describe, isn't it?"

"It's way different than the tea we use at my house," he acknowledged.

"That's what I noticed, too," she said. "I try to come here whenever I can around school. I've been wanting to introduce it to someone else. I can't convince Abby to come. She just hangs out with Keaton, and neither of them seem to want to participate in all this," she gestured to the bar and the Hub area outside the window.

"Hey, now. I hang around with them, too, you know. It isn't so bad!" he said. "You should see it. Keaton and Dr. Sanderson do an incredible job with their lectures. Abby and I have seen dozens of them. They're really special, and our trade school is lucky to have them. And speaking of school, how do you like it?"

"I love it!" she said. "What I'm learning in the classes about the Best Society – it's amazing! It's so hard for me to believe that so many people try to stop the conscriptions. My Dad says a lot of people died trying to stop this from happening right here in our community! And just look at it now! Compared to my neighborhood and the house we live in? When I graduate, I'm going to find some way to work in Best Society Services and live here in the Hub somewhere."

"I can see why," Chad admitted, taking in the scene outside. "I still like my home, though. But I'm not going to school here or learning what you're learning. It would be hard to choose."

"Well, sure. But look at your house. I mean, you're a Brunson! Anybody would want to live in that house!" she teased. "How come you decided to go to the trade college and not the Hub college?"

"I don't have anything against the Hub college, if that's what you're getting at. I'm just more interested in building things and food production." He paused for a moment. "But honestly, I think my dad would throw a fit if I went to the Hub college. He doesn't say much about it, but I know he's still bitter about my grandfather. He died in that explosion at the foundry. Dad thinks the Best Society models were to blame."

"So, you're not going to work for the foundry?" she asked.

"No, I don't think so. Dad thinks it's a bad idea. I'm not that interested, either. I never spent the time there that my past family members did," he said. "Sometimes I wish my dad could find a way to move on. It seems like he prefers to live in the past, rather than moving forward and making the world better, if you know what I mean."

"I do. You remember my Aunt Kelly worked at the foundry, right? She was the same way! She quit and ran off to get away from it. I guess she protests conscriptions – even tries to stop them. None of that makes sense to me. If she would have come here and had some spirits, I wonder what she would have been like? It's so happy here!" She paused. "I wish I could get Abby and Keaton up to speed with all of this, too. They seem so suspicious, or something."

"Why are so many people that way?" Chad lowered his voice. "My dad thinks that people who don't dream are missing something."

Meghan was thoughtful for a moment. "I know what you mean. I think Abby and Keaton are the same way. Like they're suspicious of something. And everyone is so quiet about it."

"Why is that?" he asked.

171

"In my classes, dreaming hasn't specifically come up. But in the Canon, there is a historical conclusion that before the Best Society, there were a lot of destructive superstitions. Like dreaming, but not exactly, like religion, spiritualism, and stuff like that. I know some people still do that. But I don't really understand it. So much of that stuff was just based on stories. But they're not true! Science debunks that stuff really fast. Thelites are just anxious to get the proles beyond that."

"Yeah, I understand that," Chad acknowledged. "But dreams really happen, right? Just not for everyone? By the way, what's the Canon?"

"Sure. Dreams happen. Surely they'll figure *that* out," she said. "The Canon is the study of historical truth and explains the founding of the Best Society. It replaces billions of other recordings of history, so it is much more efficient. It's part of every class I take."

"Neat. It's gotta be better than the books Dad makes me use!" Chad said, rolling his eyes. The robot server delivered two more glasses of spirits to their table. "So, what do you hope to do in Best Society Services when you graduate?"

"Oh, man! I want to work in NetSystem production! I mean, it's one thing to have all this…" She pointed to the many surrounding surfaces – their tabletop, the walls, the floors – covered with colorful and lively animation for guidance or entertainment. "But with the holographs and CosmoPods and sensory interfaces that Thelites have! You can do so much! I'm just so anxious!"

"You know what, Meghan? It's fun to be around someone with such a cheery outlook. I'm really glad we got together this afternoon!" Chad admitted.

Meghan sat back, discreetly trying to give him a full view.

"Me, too," she giggled. "I just can't believe I'm lucky enough to be hanging with Chad Brunson!" she said with an exaggerated flirtatious tone.

"Oh, stop," he said. "I put my pants on one leg at a time, too, you know."

"You do?" she teased. "Well then, speaking of pants, there are other benefits of spirits that I've been wanting to explore…"

-24-
Kelly

2084

"Ready, Joe?" Kelly asked.

"Ready," answered a skinny, pock-faced man at least a decade junior to her. His nasal voice grated on her ears. But he was ingenious and didn't talk much – definitely worth tolerating.

"Shawn, all accounted for?" she said over her shoulder.

Shawn called the roll in the dark. "Manuel?"

"Aye."

"Franco?"

"Aye."

"Sid?"

"Aye."

"Danny?"

"Aye."

Kelly raised her head over the precipice of the ravine. In the late-night darkness, she was virtually invisible. She trained a set of field glasses on a line of transport buses parked in a dimly-lit motel lot about a hundred yards away. She saw no movement. "All clear. Go, Joe!" Kelly announced.

Joe pushed a button on a remote key fob. For a moment, nothing happened. Then, she noticed a slight red glow on the LP tank atop the first bus. That would be the wire heating up. About ten seconds later, the tank burst into flames with an impressive plume, and the bus started to burn. In just moments, the fire jumped from the first bus to the second. Shortly after that, the tank atop the second bus exploded. In less than five minutes, all six buses were aflame, their destruction assured.

"Perfect!" Kelly lowered the field glasses and clapped Joe on the back.

People were streaming out of the motel to view the carnage. Distant sirens announced the impending arrival of emergency crews. But Kelly was relaxed. No people had been hurt. They were well hidden. They had taken nothing to the site and taken nothing away but the key fob for the first vehicle.

Thelite arrogance. Kelly shook her head with a smirk. *That's always their mistake.* Kelly's ragtag group had driven by and noticed the buses less than an hour before. Kelly approved, so they investigated. Access to the buses through the ravine was fortuitous. It had taken Sid less than five minutes to find the fob stashed under a fender. Franco and Joe rigged the makeshift ignition source from the bus's own batteries and wires. They used the door lock circuit activated by the key fob as the detonator.

Joe smashed the fob between two rocks until it was nearly powder and buried it in the soft earth. The group backed away from the precipice and meandered through the shadowy ravine toward their van.

"That was great!" Shawn exclaimed triumphantly to the group. "It's been a while!" Mumbled acknowledgements from all commemorated the end of their dry spell. They did as much damage as they could to Thelite property. But Kelly insisted on being opportunistic. Follow no patterns. No concentrations of activity. And no harm to people.

Most of their sabotage was minutely disruptive to Thelite efforts. Loosening or removing lug nuts from tires, shorting out vehicle charging cables, filling engine compartments with quick-drying concrete, or placing metal riprap under vehicles to damage them when moved – anything to inconvenience their progress. Tonight was one of their best.

"You have to admit – Joe knows how to make fire!" Franco exclaimed. Joe had been a thermal technician, and Kelly suspected he was a pyromaniac. They were all ex-foundrymen who knew practical things about metal, chemistry, and electricity. They were skilled with tools but could improvise without them. Disillusioned with how the foundry operated under Thelite control, they had followed Shawn and Kelly into the countryside.

After trekking nearly a mile in the ravine, they retrieved their van from a utility easement. Danny drove them back to the highway and turned away from town. Twenty minutes later, four of the seven were snoring.

Crammed together in the dark back bench of the van, Shawn wriggled his shoulder against Kelly's. "You awake?"

"Yeah. Just thinking." Kelly glanced at Shawn's profile, in silhouette from the outside lights they passed. Shawn had grown more passionate over the years, and Kelly was concerned for him. "That one will get a lot of attention. Do you think it was worth it? They'll probably have new buses in a couple days."

"Probably. But our guys needed something. What're you thinking? I suppose you'll want to lay low for a bit?"

The tires whined beneath them as the van swayed gently around a long curve, comfortably pinning Kelly between Shawn and the side of the van. The snorers repositioned, snorted their disapproval, and then renewed their slumber songs.

"Do you think we'll ever actually stop a conscription?" Kelly asked, changing the subject.

"Nah. Not us. How? They'll murder people. We won't."

"Then why are we doing this, Shawn? I mean – we're pretty good at these little smash-n-goes. But how are we changing anything?"

"We're letting them know there's folks that don't want it! There's lots of people like us, you know. If enough of us do this, maybe they'll find a place for us and just let us be!"

Wishful thinking. The more protests Kelly witnessed, the more disheartened she became. Unbelievably to her, many proles supported the Best Society and welcomed conscriptions. Non-supporters were more frequently considered outcasts, and activists were considered rebels. *Rebels?!? Aren't we the ones being forced around against our will?*

"It's just – it feels like a game with no end. Like we need some kind of voice to make it different. Otherwise, what's the point?"

"Now you sound like Eric and Junior. *Just work with them until they understand*," Shawn mimicked. "Look, Kelly. You're great at leading these little raids and keeping us centered. But if you want out, that's fine. We'll keep going."

"That's not what I'm saying. Even this is better than just giving in. I just wish there was someone telling our side of the story, that's all."

The tires whined at a lower pitch as the van slowed for a traffic signal, bumping gently to a silent stop. For several moments, they were mesmerized by the eerie patterns of light from crossing traffic decorating the interior of the van. Then, the van turned a sharp corner, accelerating again until the whine returned to its familiar resonance.

"We'll be near home in a couple hours. Whaddya think? Lay low? Join a protest? Or do some damage?" Shawn asked hopefully.

"Let's hole up in that encampment outside of town. It's been over a year since we've been back. We can watch things for a few days and see what's up," Kelly decided. Soon, Shawn nodded off. Kelly was unable to sleep.

As the sky turned into a rosy dawn, Danny turned onto a huge lot of crumbling asphalt and pointed the van toward a group of dozens of vehicles several hundred yards in the distance. He familiarly avoided the potholes and concrete pillars that supported damaged utility poles as he went. Along the length of the lot were grouped, low buildings with decrepit fascia and boarded-up apertures declaring decades of neglect. The buildings had been gradually abandoned as civic life centered around the new Thelite communities and hubs.

Encampments like this had emerged over the years as groups of resentful proles spun out of regular society. They were usually on the outskirts of

People's Villages, and they served as host sites for nomadic groups like Kelly's. Kelly's group had stayed at dozens of them over the years, and this one, which sat outside of People's Village #471, more than most.

"Something's different," Shawn noticed as they approached. Kelly noticed, too. There were improvements. The lot was noticeably smoother as they got closer to the vehicles. The security lamps flickered off as the new sun hit their photo sensors. That was it. "Lights!" She observed.

Danny stopped the van at the first line of vehicles. Birds sang stridently to the few early risers moving about in the quiet of early dawn. All seven emerged from the van and stretched in the muted morning air. Several of the guys sidled discreetly out of site to relieve themselves.

Kelly and Shawn searched hungrily for the source of the coffee aroma they immediately detected. They located it behind a canvas flap that served as an entry to one of the buildings. They slipped through it and surprised a man and a woman huddled around a makeshift table sipping their fresh brew from an electric pot.

"Excuse me," Kelly said. "We've been traveling a while. We need to rest and get some food. Any problem if we hang here for a couple of days?"

The woman had sad, gray-streaked hair pulled back in a loose ponytail. She looked Shawn and Kelly up and down with serious, gray eyes. "Coin, I suppose?" she asked suspiciously.

"Sure, coin," Kelly answered, surprised by the question. "Is that OK?"

"It'll have to be, I guess," the woman turned to the man. His brown hair was also in a ponytail, and along with a matching goatee and steady gaze, it gave him a professorial air.

"Sure, we can still take coin," he said. "Not much longer, though. We prefer to share allocations if you have any to spare."

"Really? Any chance we can talk about it over a cup of that coffee?" Shawn invited himself to their table. Kelly was concerned that Shawn was overly brusque, put off by the cold welcome and the apparent reluctance to accept coin payment.

"Sure, have a seat," the woman offered a cup and a chair but no apology. Shawn sat down heavily and Kelly followed. They each took a sip before continuing.

Shawn looked levelly at his hosts. "Look. We've been here many times. I've never seen you before. And we've always made good with coin. What's going on here?"

He's too aggressive. "We have some unused allocations, if that works better," Kelly interjected diplomatically. "But that's new. We're confused."

The man and woman exchanged a slight nod with each other. Then the man spoke gently. "My wife and I are missionaries. We've watched in sorrow as disordered people fled conscriptions and refused the bounty of the Best Society. We've come to this encampment to deliver reconciliation."

"Reconciliation?" Shawn blurted. "What can you offer these people that reconciles what they've lost?"

"By providing them the things they had to gain, but refused," the man explained patiently. "Several months ago, we started working with Best Society Services. We electrified the camp with the abandoned wind generators and battery bank down the road. Now we have continuous electrical service. Then we pooled some of our allocations for materials to repair the lights and the grounds. And we've improved sanitation and general hygiene. All we had to do was work with them."

"That's not reconciliation!" Shawn argued intently. "You're just giving them back what was taken from them! At a minimum!"

Way too aggressive! She understood Shawn hated people who compromised with the Best Society. *But we have no place else to go if he alienates these people!* She touched him lightly on the arm. "We're just talking about a couple of days. I'm sure we can share some allocations to cover us, and maybe even a little more."

Shawn looked at her with disdain, then back at the man. "You have no right to forbid us from staying here, regardless. How we pay is up to us. We pay in coin!"

179

The man was unruffled. "As I said, we can accept coin for a while yet. But we are trying to get everyone identification and use their allocations. We're teaching people how simple and enjoyable life can be if we accept Best Society principles. Many are recovering. They are healthier and happier. Some are even taking roles in Best Society Services. If you stay, we want you to understand that message. We don't want you to interfere. That's all we ask."

Kelly now grabbed Shawn firmly, digging her fingernails into his arm to restrain him. He hadn't slept much, and he had a hair trigger temper to begin with. "We understand," she blurted to pre-empt Shawn. He didn't say anything, but his eyes told a vicious story. She continued, "Just a couple days, then we'll be out of your hair. Thanks for accepting our coin." She rose and tugged on Shawn who stood with her. They went back through the flap into the brightening morning.

"Disordered!" Shawn spat. Kelly's tightening grip on his arm barely kept him from yelling. "My ass! Missionaries? Bullshit! They're just fucking traitors! Coming out here and bribing these people with the very stuff they stole to begin with! I can't believe they fall for it!"

"Shawn, settle down! You're doing damage!" Kelly used her authoritative tone to reach him. "That's not our mission right now. We need rest and we need food while we figure out what to do next. Focus on the mission, damn it. We can't do it without you!" The call to a task helped, and Shawn started to visibly relax. "The last thing we need is to cause a scene. Where'd the guys go?"

She panned the lot until she saw several of them talking with a group of early risers, all now with cups of steaming coffee. Joe was clearly the subject of discussion as Danny and Franco re-enacted the explosions of the night before. *Too much talk. Need to lay low!* Normally it wouldn't matter, but she didn't trust this camp anymore.

"Hey, guys!" Kelly interrupted as she approached. "Looks like we'll be here a couple days. Let's get our gear." They broke away dutifully and started unpacking the van's sleeping tents, cooking gear, and other supplies. Camp chairs were quickly set up in their usual semi-circle centered around a small cook stove with a wood fire.

Once seated, Danny started the conversation. "This camp is more comfortable now. Hot showers and all. Can't we stick around for a bit?"

"Not sure we're as welcome as we used to be," Kelly poked at some embers with a stick to help the fire while she talked. "It looks like some outsiders have taken charge. They don't want us talking bad about Thelites." She waved her stick toward the other vehicles in the camp. "I have no idea what everyone here thinks – whether they like it or not. But we need to be careful."

Shawn shifted restlessly. "I got a bad feeling. We oughtta just get some food and rest and get out of here. It's only a couple hundred miles to a camp that ain't this fucked up."

Kelly had to agree with him. "OK, then. I was up all night. Danny and I will get some sleep. Shawn, you guys should go find some food and anything else we might need. Get cleaned up if you want. We'll hang here until evening and leave." The group groaned its reluctant acceptance and broke up. Kelly crept into her tent and dropped into an exhausted sleep.

"Pssst! Kelly!" Danny poked his head in her tent and whispered urgently.

Kelly's eyes flew open. "Wh..??" she tried to speak before Danny covered her mouth.

"Shhh! Something's going on!"

Kelly nodded and Danny removed his hand. She stumbled unsteadily to her feet outside the tent. It was already dark. She must have slept the whole day. It was eerily quiet where they stood, but the far end of the lot was alive with the movement of heavy trucks coming off the road and finding positions to park. Groups of campers were watching curiously from various spots around the property.

"Danny – what the hell?"

181

"I woke up about an hour ago when they started coming in," Danny waved toward the trucks. "It looks like a caravan of supplies for a new building or a hub or something. Shawn and the guys decided to go check it out – but they haven't come back yet."

"Shit! What do you think they're up to?" Kelly pulled on her boots and ran to catch Danny as he trotted toward the activity. "Hey, Danny. Stop! We should be careful!" Kelly warned, thinking quickly. Danny slowed to listen. "Let's not go charging right in there. Here, follow me."

Kelly led him to the eaves of the nearest building where the darker shadows provided cover. They stole along the building toward the end of the lot staying hidden from view. Reaching the end of the building, they heard voices coming from around the corner. Still in shadow, they peaked around the corner to an isolated area behind the building. About a hundred feet out, a group of people stood in the bright headlights of several vehicles.

Joe and Franco were faced away from them with their hands in the air. Behind them were two public safety officers with guns drawn. A third was patting them down and applying restraints. Two other officers were facing off with Shawn, who stood in front of Manuel and Sid. Shawn's body was tensed, and the officers facing him had their hands on their sidearms as if ready for an attack. The missionary couple stood next to a senior officer aside the lit area.

Kelly and Danny heard Shawn growl, "…and I'm telling you, you ain't takin' them anywhere!"

"Sir," one of the officers said. "We are in apprehension protocol. These subjects were witnessed confessing to arson. A third subject who confessed has been seen in your company. If you know where he is, you must inform us."

"I been with these guys the whole time, so I don't know what arson you're talking about!" Shawn lied. "And you ain't got no right to arrest them! You ain't taking them anywhere!"

"Sir, we are in apprehension protocol. Be warned. If you attempt to stop this arrest, we will switch to defensive protocol."

Shawn kept his posture aggressive and started looking around as if sizing up his odds.

"I can't let this happen!" Danny stepped out. Before Kelly could react, he moved around the corner with his hands raised. "It was me. I give up!"

Not knowing what else to do, Kelly stayed behind the wall. Danny walked hesitantly forward toward the lighted area. Shawn turned and glared at him. "Danny – what the hell!" He turned toward Danny as if to stop him.

"Sir!" yelled one of the officers facing Shawn. "We are now in defensive protocol. Stand down!" That officer drew a sidearm, and the other officer drew an immobilizer unit.

"Shawn – just do what they say!" Danny said calmly. "Let's not get anybody hurt!" The officer who had restrained Joe and Franco grabbed Danny and roughly added him to the line. Danny yelled over his shoulder. "Shawn – just get out of here. We'll be fine."

Shawn almost vibrated with helpless outrage. *I should go to him. He's going to get himself hurt.* But just as she was about to step forward, the female missionary spoke to the senior officer, "There was a woman who seemed to be in charge." Kelly stopped.

"Where is she?" the senior officer asked.

"She left this shithole to find a better place. Shouldn't be hard." Shawn glared at the woman. "Bitch!"

The female missionary glared back. "I knew they were gonna be trouble. And those three bragged about the explosions right out loud!" She was pointing at Joe, Franco, and Danny, who were now in handcuffs.

The husband confirmed. "That's why we called. We figured when the caravan showed up something would happen. We just didn't want any trouble."

"We needed to be here, anyway," the officer affirmed. "There's been too much sabotage of these supply missions. Best Society Services needed a spot for these materials until new personnel transports get here. Probably a couple days. We can't let anything happen to them."

"We appreciate it," the husband responded. "The extra allocations just help our efforts here."

Joe, Franco, and Danny were frog-marched to a waiting transport. Manuel and Sid were whispering to Shawn and touching him gently, trying to settle him down. Slowly, he succumbed. His body relaxed into a posture of frustrated dejection: arms at his sides, shoulders slumped, head down. The tension of the altercation seemed to be over. Kelly was waiting until the officers left before showing herself.

Then, the officer holding the immobilizer asked his partner, "Did we declare defensive protocol?"

"Yes, we did," his partner answered evilly.

"Good!" He aimed his device at Shawn and activated it. Two wire tethers flew at Shawn and attached themselves to his body. Shawn screamed and contorted his body, flailing ineffectively at the wires, unable to control his muscles. He tried moving away but stumbled to the ground in a heap.

The partner kept the wide-eyed Manuel and Sid at bay with his gun. The officer holding the immobilizer kept it activated and stepped forward to look coolly down at Shawn as his body bucked and his screams pierced the night. Soon his voice became muffled through a gurgle of phlegm. His arms and legs jerked erratically, but with less frequency the longer the immobilizer was attached. His screams became choking coughs as his mouth foamed over with bubbles and he thrashed in his own vomit, now covering his hair and face. After interminable moments, his screams stopped, but his body still jerked unnaturally. The officer continued to look at Shawn impassively until all motion stopped. Then he deactivated the immobilizer.

They just killed him! Kelly put her own hand over her mouth and bit down to keep from screaming out loud. The smug looks on the missionary couple's faces - she hated these people!

The officer gathered up the tethers and checked Shawn's pulse. "Fully transitioned," he announced. "This jerk won't do any more damage." Then he stood and walked away. The officer holding the gun on Manuel and Sid backed up and nodded. Manuel and Sid ran to Shawn's body and futilely attempted to revive him.

The senior officer spoke into his watch, "A group of disordered proles attempted to interfere with a legal apprehension. Defensive protocols were announced. One prole was legally terminated according to protocol." Then he turned to the missionary couple. "Two officers will stay here in case anything else comes up. Let us know if you find the woman. We think we know who she is, and we need to bring her in."

"Thank you, Officer," the husband said. "And sorry for all the trouble."

Kelly backed stealthily away from the corner and ran lightly to the other end of the building. She avoided the small groups who were still watching the caravan arrange itself in the lot. When she reached the other end of the building, in blind terror, she snuck to the van and drove it out a back exit with the lights off.

-25-
It's just a normal transition

2084

"You know what doesn't make sense to me," Julianna said warily to Mark. "You and my father didn't just *believe* in the old optimum allocation model. You both knew that model needed improvement, and you both worked your whole careers on it."

"Yes, we did," he said. "And it works well, and it's necessary. We have learned that people need the things that they need."

It had been an unusual day so far. Ashley still wasn't at work in the morning, so Julianna and Tim were untethered from their routine. But Mark BioGram'd her first thing to meet for an update on her investigation. She went to his flat for an early lunch. He informed her that he had managed to have her investigation suspended. She needn't worry. He had taken care of it.

As grateful as she was, Julianna was annoyed when he suggested having sex in the middle of the day. Again, she had no moral objections, and Mark was being helpful. She just didn't enjoy sex with him. He clearly did enjoy it, and she felt a bothersome sense of obligation. Mark's preference for sex with her over sex at the Center – which was so good for everyone – puzzled her.

Now, afterwards, she was trying to make conversation, naked and uncomfortable under the sheet on his bed, while Mark puttered around the room getting ready for his afternoon. He looked at her reflection while primping himself in the mirror.

"Your father was brilliant at modelling supply and distribution with uniquely personalized baskets of goods and services. His undoing was taking it too far. His idea was that the structure, selection, and organization of Best

186

Society leaders, members, and staff should have been an output of the model, to optimize their capacity to provide. That is a step too far. The High Council reserves their right to organize themselves."

"What do you mean his 'undoing'?" she asked.

"That's what caused his value to diminish. Nobody had any interest in furthering the model toward his intent. He kept pressing the issue with the Bureau, and his behaviors were becoming erratic. When he went to the Center, his life wasn't worth continuing."

Julianna's skin suddenly felt prickly and chilled. She had been haunted with a sense of something unexplained, maybe sinister, about her father's death. His unlikely health crisis in the Center was deeply suspicious. *Was it known that he would die before he went to the Center? Is that what Mark was saying?* Mark's sterile delivery of such devastating news also seemed wrong. *Did Mark have something to do with it? Had he forgotten they were talking about her father?*

Gathering herself, Julianna took a deep, controlled breath. She stared intently at his eyes in the mirror, struggling to keep her voice emotionless. "Who makes that decision, Mark?"

"It's not a decision so much as an equation." Mark was back to his old, stoic self again. "A person's value is calculated from their individual performance history, the uniqueness of their competencies, the criticality of work assignments, the likelihood of completion, and lots of other things. These factors are processed through a hellishly complex behavioral science algorithm. The output, though, is simple. It is the probability that uniquely demanding and valuable work assignments will be completed within a person's reasonably sustainable lifespan."

"Uniquely demanding? Why just uniquely demanding?" Julianna was frustrated by Mark's blasé responses. *Damn him! Shouldn't I know this?*

"Because the only incremental value any person has over another person is the uniqueness of their competencies to move forward the Best Society," Mark explained. "If their competencies are readily substitutable, there is no relative value."

"But you always said my father was uniquely brilliant? That hadn't changed!" Julianna was getting emotional.

"No, it hadn't," Mark agreed. "But the value of his work was diminished because the optimum allocation model performed so well when it was launched. And there was no interest in the next features he proposed."

Mark turned to look at her directly. "Julianna, you certainly understand that all of us will someday reach a point where we are of no relative value to the Best Society. When that happens, the best outcome for society is a quick and orderly transition. It's necessary to sustain the abundance we all share. Your father knew this – it is a core feature in all of his allocation models."

"I know all that," she said, somewhat defensive now. "It's just that the suppositions seem arbitrary. I need to understand it better."

Mark eyed her coolly for a couple of seconds. "Julianna, I would caution you from calling them 'arbitrary.' Just like when you call the models into question, you are doing a disservice to the Best Society. I've just gotten you out of your last little scrape. You don't *need* to understand it; you *need* to get out of your own way and accept the correctness of the system." He straightened and opened his hands and arms in a posture of appeal. "Safety, Equality, and Science! Incredible models that provide so much to humanity! How can you live with all the benefits and still have such skepticism?"

"I'm not skeptical!" she countered, now very defensively. "I just think that the work to sustain the models needs to be done with integrity. I learned this from listening to you and my father for my whole life."

"Yes," Mark agreed. "The work needs to be done. But once accepted by the High Council, they need to be accepted by all Thelites. Without that belief, we are no better than proles."

Julianna managed to stay quiet and lay placidly as Mark made some minute adjustments to his appearance. Eventually he turned back to her, ready to leave.

"You've had a pretty good day," Mark said, as if fishing for a compliment on his sexual performance. Receiving none, he soon said, "I hope you can get beyond this now and just be happy." He grinned broadly and left.

After several minutes, Julianna rose, dressed, and hailed a driverless to return to her CosmoPod. She was emotionally drained and paid no attention to her BioGrams during the brief ride. When she arrived at the common area of her work floor, she was greeted immediately by Tim and a pleasant young woman she had never met.

"Greetings, fellow Thelite," the woman said eagerly. "You must be…Julianna?"

"Julianna, this is Petra 090762013," Tim said. "Petra is our new Game Coordinator. This is her first assignment in the Bureau."

"New Game Coordinator?" Julianna asked. "Isn't Ashley coming back?"

"You must not have checked your BioGrams," Tim answered. "Ashley has been moved to the Center for Transition Management. Evidently, her value crossed over. I guess we won't be seeing her anymore," he said with casualness that Julianna considered to be very much out of place.

"What!" Julianna cried, incredulous. "She was fine!"

Both Tim and Petra recoiled a little from Julianna's outburst.

"Whoa!" Tim said, trying to lighten the mood. "Rein it in, Julianna. It's just a normal transition. No big deal. We just won't see Ashley anymore, and we'll be working with Petra."

Julianna could not bear Tim's matter-of-fact acceptance of the imminent death of their co-worker. *Was she the only one affected this way by the finality of a life?* She had a sudden sensation of being weirdly out of sync with everyone around her, as if seeing the world's social norms in a convoluted carnival mirror. It made her almost dizzy. She excused herself and hurried away to her apartment, fleeing the confused gazes of Tim and Petra.

-26-
Doesn't seem very equal to me

2084

Grief again. That's all she could feel as she snuggled into her cozy chair, staring blankly out the window into the late afternoon shadows. First her father. Now Ashley. Grief and fatigue. She felt drained of any ability to direct her thoughts. Julianna had no idea how long she'd been sitting there when she felt her chin drop for the first time and jerked back awake. Sleepy and again, and again. She finally gave in.

When she next jumped awake, she was startled to see it was dark outside. With strange inspiration, she left her apartment, hailed a driverless, and directed it to a People's Village nearby – one she had never visited before.

The village was small, and the Hub reflected it. She left the transportation center and walked to the edge of the Hub. Immediately across a primary street was a large greenspace. It was a park with some half-lit sports fields and unpaved paths that crisscrossed between benches and untended landscaping features. She noticed more people than she expected at the late hour. The screams of children playing, the corrective commands of adults, and the laughter of gatherings rang intermittently through the night air, giving a sense of joyful vibrance. She found it inviting and crossed the street to see it more closely.

Opposite the Hub, the park was bordered by buildings, ramshackle taverns, eateries, apartments, and row houses in various states of repair and presentation. All of it was intermixed with abandoned structures of no obvious purpose. She walked around the outskirts of the park and noticed several young couples: holding hands, embracing, whispering to each other in the semidarkness. Nobody acknowledged her though, even when she felt intrusively close.

After circuiting to the side of the park, contrasting noises from two nearby homes caused her to pay closer attention. From one home, she heard a young woman weeping and a man mumbling with a dull, indecipherable voice. From the next home, she heard peals of laughter from what must have been a raucous gathering of men, women, and children. The doors of both homes faced the park and were open, covered by just their screens for fresh air, but allowing noise to travel freely.

Julianna walked up the stoop to the first home and peered curiously through the screen. Three people were sitting at a table in a well-lit kitchen. A young woman was crying, and her parents were speaking to her, somber and soft. The father faced Julianna, but he seemed to be looking right through her as she overheard them.

"I'm so scared," the young lady said between sobs. "I don't know what to do."

"There, there," the father mumbled. "You're not the first."

"But I'm so scared," she said again, as if frustrated with him. Sobbing more. He was holding her hand on top of the table.

"Hush now. You're not hurt."

But she continued sobbing. This went on for several minutes. Several times, the father looked imploringly at the mother, as if for help, but she said nothing, just some grunts as he offered his little comforts.

After a while, the mother finally interjected with a voice that was less sympathetic.

"Look, young lady. You will have some decisions to make pretty quickly." The girl sniffed to control her sobs and listen. "We certainly weren't planning for this, so we can't help as much as you think. But we'll do what we can if you decide to keep it. But this is your decision and your responsibility. And you need to tell him! I can't imagine what you were thinking!"

The girl continued to try to control her sobs. "But what should I do?" she asked through tears.

"We can't tell you," the mother said. "You have to figure it out."

The girl looked to her father, who looked terribly uncomfortable. Finally, he steeled himself and spoke. "Sweetheart, we will love you no matter what you do. And we will love your baby if you have it. I know it doesn't feel like it now, but there's worse things."

This seemed to calm the girl a little, but the mother rolled her eyes. "That's all true," she said. "But you've got to start making good decisions. We won't be around forever, you know. At some point you'll be on your own, and how are you going to get along with all this?"

And with those words, the girl started sobbing uncontrollably again, and the whole scene started replaying itself. Julianna backed quietly away from the door, feeling apologetic for her intrusion.

She turned her attention to the next home and the noise coming out of it. Again, she walked quietly up the stoop to look inside. Three young boys were sitting on the floor around some type of a game board. There were little pieces and papers sprinkled around them. One of the children was moving a piece, and the other two were screaming at him.

"No, no – you can't do that!" and "Mom, Mitchell is cheating again! Dad!" Then, one of them dashed all the pieces off the board. "Dog-pile on Mitchell!" one of them yelled, and they scrambled onto each other, rolling around like playful puppies.

Heavy footsteps hurried from another room, and a tall man appeared. He had an unlit pipe in his mouth and pleasant wrinkles around his eyes.

"Hey, hey, hey," he said. "If you're all so tough, I guess you should take me on, too!" The children all abandoned their scuffle and charged the man, screaming with vicious intent. They grabbed his legs and beat on him with little, ineffectual fists. The man feigned weakness and carefully found his way to the floor with a grunt, while the children jumped on his back and held on to his limbs in an enthusiastic attempt to render him helpless. He growled and rolled with them for several minutes – letting the children have their way – and then one at a time, he gathered them together under his strong arms like a mother hen, finally immobilizing them with his size and weight.

"Say uncle!" he said.

"Argh!," "Never!," "Ahh!" they yelled back, wriggling and giggling.

"Say uncle!" he laughed and let his weight settle onto all of them.

"Uncle, uncle, uncle!" they all shouted desperately. He let them go, and they all sprawled about breathlessly on the floor.

In another room, several women had been engaged in conversation, speaking and laughing loudly enough to be heard above the shenanigans. Their laughter broke up, and one of them walked into the room and stopped, folding her arms and aiming a stern look at the wrestlers. "Who is cleaning up this mess, may I ask?"

"Awww," the children groaned. But the man started picking up the game pieces, and the children immediately started to help. The lady turned back and walked right in front of Julianna's view through the screen door, inches away from her face, without even a glance. Soon, the women's conversation and laughter started again.

Julianna stepped back into the park, absorbing the irony of the two households. *How could these people expect good lives?* These things were so easily managed in the Best Society. The sadness of unwanted pregnancy was completely prehistoric. And happily encouraging children to engage in violence to resolve disputes was entirely outside of known protocols to Thelites. Everything seemed so amateur.

She continued her walk. The night air was still. The din and muffled echoes of life surrounding the park came to her continuously. As she approached another building, the rattle of silver and the clatter of glassware jumbled with the many voices in conversations, spilling from an open-air seating area into the park. It was inviting. Julianna walked curiously up to the barrier. She avoided the gaze of the bartender. She had no coin and didn't want any attention.

Two couples sat at a table immediately inside the bar. They appeared to be in their late thirties or forties with competent bearings. Julianna could hear their conversation clearly.

"That building ain't gonna last any longer than the last one. And there was just no reason to tear it down to begin with. Then they send us those second rate, used materials, and that's what we got to use for our school! Doesn't make any sense. It's a waste of effort if nothing else," one of the men was complaining.

"If we ever get to build our school," one of the ladies said. "I've been scheduling the Guild for new projects out for years, but nothing here. Even in the Hub, there's just some small stuff. I don't see when there's gonna be capacity to build the school anyway."

"I suppose it's good to have all the work, though," interjected the other man. "There's no stoppin' progress anyway. Sure beats fightin' it. Look what happened to Shawn!"

Everyone was quiet at the mention of Shawn. "Bad judgment or bad luck, I guess," the first man reflected. "I don't want to stop it. I just think we need to get our part of it. What's their motto? Safety, Equality, Science? Doesn't seem very equal to me!"

"C'mon, it isn't that bad," the other woman said diplomatically. "The Hub has a school, and it's free if we want to use it."

"What good is that? Them Thelite schools don't even teach construction, manufacturing, or agriculture! What are our kids gonna do without that training? It's almost all on-the-job already." Then he went silent and pensive. After a long moment, he continued. "Ah, shit. I guess there's no use overthinking it. I'm just glad you folks were all up for a drink!"

"On that note," the second man said, "I should get going. Gonna be a long day tomorrow. Night all!" All four stood, bid each other good night with hugs and handshakes, and went their separate ways.

They hadn't noticed Julianna, but she found their discussion fascinating. These people were intelligent and engaged. *Did they not understand that Thelite structures had to be a priority, as they housed the groups that perpetuated scientific models to guarantee safety?* Allocating materials to their highest purpose was one of the key features of her father's model. It baffled Julianna that this was not common knowledge to these people.

Or were there things she wasn't considering?

Some unique music had started coming from a large building toward the far end of the park. It was in turn clear and muffled as the doors to the building were opened and closed by people entering. She approached the building and noticed that the people were dressed conservatively and wore very solemn visage.

Something primal stirred in her as she watched for several minutes and was finally compelled to follow a small group as they entered. The music was resoundingly loud and echoey, but beautiful, emanating from a huge pipe organ on one wall. Tall windows of colored glass scenes lined the other wall. Massive arched beams supported the ceiling. An ornate cross dominated the other end of the building. The floor between was covered with simple benches and was sparsely populated, seating some of the people. The building was magnificent in its overall presence but showed the wear of time in its detail. Nicks and bad repairs scarred the woodwork. Water stains streaked the ceiling. The floor was faded and deformed in high traffic areas. There were cracks and loose panes in the windows.

This is a Christian church. The realization came suddenly, and Julianna was excited that she had identified it. *And these people are worshipping!*

She gawked around, trying to take it all in. She noticed people that entered were filing by a large box at the far end of the aisle before taking their seat. She followed them through the line and was shocked to find the box contained the body of a man.

She stared – she couldn't help it – and for some reason tears came to her eyes. *Was he old or young?* It was hard to tell through his pale complexion in death. *Did he have a story? A family?* Julianna couldn't understand why she was crying. She didn't know the man or anyone else in the church.

Behind the casket, Julianna witnessed the specter of a woman fade into view and flicker with translucence, floating above and keeping vigil on the body. Nobody else noticed, but Julianna couldn't stop watching. *Who was she? Why was she here?* She was small and wore a black dress. At first she looked young, but as she grew less transparent, Julianna saw the tell-tale wrinkles of age around her mouth, eyes, and forehead. Her eyes were puffy and her face was flushed red. If people drew close, she became nearly transparent, as if avoiding them, but she would move farther away and return to visibility. The otherworldly woman's eyes focused only on the body with obvious grief.

The hair on the back of Julianna's neck went up when the apparition's head snapped up. She had detected something. *She's looking for me!* The ghostly eyes moved over the crowd seeking something, someone. Julianna was terrified! She tried to shrink into the crowd to avoid notice, but she couldn't hide. The apparition floated, circled the group, searching, accusing. *Hunting!* When her eyes finally found Julianna, she focused on her with a hideous, malevolent glare. The face behind the eyes grew to a monstrous size, threatening to engulf Julianna into itself, a slathering, repulsive mask of hatefulness.

She was suddenly hot and claustrophobic. She panicked. *Escape! Run!* She jumped the line and lurched toward the exit but felt the phantom's stare following her. She slammed through the door to get outside and gulped in the clean, cool air. Someone touched her lightly on the shoulder from behind. She jerked in horrified realization that the ghost had caught her. But when she turned, she found Delores looking at her sympathetically. "My dear, are you OK?" she asked.

Breathless with the realization that she was safe, Julianna closed her eyes and let the tension and terror flow out of her. She opened her eyes, relieved to see Delores still there. "I am now. But, Delores, what are you doing here? Did you come for me?"

"I knew you would be here," Delores answered. "This is a memorial for Shawn Adams. My niece Kelly ran away with him some time ago. I wanted you to know about this."

"Oh, Delores, I'm so sorry!" Julianna said with deep and genuine emotion. "What happened to him?"

"He was killed trying to interfere with a conscription. May God rest his soul." Delores' deep sorrow was apparent, but so was her deep faith. It made Julianna want to cry again.

"I don't know what to say," Julianna murmured. "I didn't come here knowing about this – I'm sorry if I've interrupted!"

"It's perfectly OK, dear," Delores responded softly. She slowly put her hand up to Julianna's cheek. Julianna closed her eyes to enjoy the matronly touch as Delores cooed, "You need to see these things. You need to know these people."

"I have so much to ask you," Julianna whispered.

But then, she opened her eyes and woke up with a start – still in her cozy chair, with morning light streaming through the window of her apartment.

-27-

It has to change

2084

"Do you have any idea how dangerous that might be?" Keaton addressed Meghan. His voice was deliberately lowered.

Keaton and Abby had agreed to dine in the Hub with Meghan and Chad. It was a first for them. Keaton was holding Abby's hand beneath the table, but he felt ambushed.

"I think the danger is exaggerated," Meghan responded. "People are afraid of this, and they shouldn't be. Someday, it has to change, and somebody is going to have to start!" She was louder than Keaton would have liked.

Keaton clamped Abby's hand harder. She was quiet. Abby was unwaveringly loyal to him, but Keaton suspected she didn't want to argue with her sister. Keaton and Abby had been inseparable for years. To Keaton, it happened in an instant. One night she knocked on his door. A few months later, he couldn't imagine life without her. Now they were discussing starting a family. The last thing he wanted was to disrupt those plans with Meghan's half-baked idea. *Yes, everyone knew Meghan was smart. But she was not as grounded as her sister.*

"Shhh," Keaton cautioned. "You can't be so sure!"

Meghan was seated next to Chad, her new boyfriend, in a booth across from Keaton and Abby. Meghan and Chad were leaning toward Keaton, trying to emphasize their point. They had obviously already discussed the idea.

"Keaton," Chad said more quietly. "Don't shush her. You should hear what Meghan has to say. She's going to the Hub college, so she's really the only one here who can know both sides of the story."

198

At least he didn't shout! Somewhat relieved, Keaton sought clarity. "Ok, fine. Let's go through things in a little detail. Quietly! I can tell you I'm not thrilled with the idea."

All the dining booths had NetSystem terminals embedded, highlighting recent Thelite accomplishments. A window looked out over a thoroughfare where various driverless vehicles moved in ordered fashion, ferrying people and goods between Hub facilities.

Eventually, one of these vehicles would deliver their food. The food itself was prepared in different kitchens around the Hub, each of which was designed to deliver its specialty with automated precision. They could have dinner with each other without compromising on what anybody wanted to eat. Prole diners were not that way. Their kitchens were adjacent to their dining areas. When you ate there, you could only choose from what the kitchen could offer. Keaton, admittedly, enjoyed that. But he was skeptical about most of the other Hub amenities.

Meghan, however, was in awe of all the services offered in the Hub. Particularly spirits, which she understood were simple, general formulations. Someday, she longed to sample the individual formulations she had studied in her classes. *How much could it improve life? Not just spirits, but everything she was learning!*

The effect of even general spirits was better than intoxicating. She thought more clearly. She listened better, articulated better, and enjoyed each moment better. She loved finding occasions to share spirits with Chad. Tonight, she was finally introducing them to Keaton and Abby, too. Meghan had an ulterior motive, though. She wanted them to think about her proposal, and she knew the spirits would help.

But she had done things in the wrong order. They had only just ordered when Meghan started the conversation. *That was too early. They're not as familiar with all this. Slow down. They'll come around.*

"I'm sorry, I didn't mean to upset you, Keaton. We'll discuss it in a bit," she spoke quietly, beaming her cutesiest smile which she knew would disarm anyone. "Before we do, I would like you all to try this. I know you're going to like it."

She filled four small glasses from a dispenser at the edge of the table and set one in front of each of them. "Just sip," she said. She and Chad sipped; Keaton and Abby followed tentatively.

"Wow," Abby said. "That's...that's..."

"That's really something!" Keaton interrupted. "It should be illegal!" he declared in jest.

"My guess is you two are going to have one of the best nights you've ever had!" Chad offered. "We can vouch for it!" He pinched Meghan playfully on the waist.

"We'll see," said Abby with faked, schoolmarm stiffness. "We've had some pretty good nights already!"

"True!" Keaton agreed. "But this stuff – it's not how it tastes. It's how it makes you feel. Like Abby said, wow."

Meghan waited until they had finished their first glass before continuing. *Perfect.*

"Let me try this again." She put her hands on the table and sat straight to gain their full attention. She spoke deliberately, but quietly restrained, respecting Keaton's concerns, "We've all experienced these things. I know that I've had dreams that were more than dreams." She looked at Abby. "I know you and I have resolved many, many things in our life through our dreams. You've felt it, too."

"Oh, yes," said Abby without hesitation but with careful, sidelong glances at Keaton. "I know it. Most of the best decisions I've made in my life were guided by my dreams," she smiled knowingly at Keaton. Then turning to Meghan, she said, "Meghan, we talked about this when we were younger. We know each other so well, and it's not like we tell each other everything. We just know each other. How does that happen? I know that I've gone to sleep not knowing what's going on with you, but woken up with complete understanding. And I know I've heard your voice when I needed you."

Chad chimed in. "I agree, Abby. But to me it's more systematic than that. My Dad taught me to use tea. It helps with dreaming and interpreting. I know that I met Meghan first in a dream." Then looking at Meghan, "I knew you were Abby's sister, of course. And when Abby got us together in person, I already knew so many things about you. Sure, I'd heard your name and everything before, but the minute we met, I already knew what I could say to make you laugh. How you would feel if I did something wrong. It was more than a guess. It was something I knew! That's why I'm interested in this idea," he finished.

Much better! The spirits were doing their job. Looking at Abby, Meghan said, "I heard your voice, too. And I remember when Mom was dying – all the things we didn't know how to say to each other, or to her – somehow, we said them all in dreams. I remember Mom coming to me, teaching me about how you and Dad would need me, and figuring all that out. And I know we talked about this when we were younger, but it seemed – I don't know – not real? But how could it not be real? It happened!"

Meghan didn't want to push too hard, but Keaton still hadn't said anything. She refilled their glasses hospitably, and they all took another sip. She enlisted Chad with a nod to Keaton. "Chad, isn't there more?"

"Personally," he started, "I learn a lot in dreams. When I use the tea, my dreams are more…effective? Is that the right word? I know there's more to dreams than most people realize. There's a greater thing out there than people admit." He leaned toward Keaton directly across the table. "I'm curious, Keaton. Don't you feel this? Don't you think we know each other awfully well for as little time as we've spent together? I know Dr. Sanderson is a hero to you, but I'll bet you're skeptical about some of his approaches, aren't you? Somehow, I've seen it. We've shared it at a subconscious level. Even he knows it."

Keaton had to admit that truth, but he was not ready to relent. *We should be more afraid of this!* "Are you guys aware of the history of what you're talking about?" he questioned. "I've been lucky to spend a lot of time with Dr. Sanderson. I've learned. We're both aware of the capacity of dreaming, but we never, ever talk about it. There have been purges. Wars fought! Horrible human tragedy…century after century of people hating other people simply because of the differing nature of their beliefs. That's why so many proles have been shunned. It has to stop!"

He caught himself and checked around to see if he had been overheard. *Best to be rational. And quiet!* More cautiously, he lowered his voice. "Sure. I dream. And I've used the tea. But it has never been a condition that I sought to define my life. I am more inclined to repress dreams than to seek them. We have to live in this world – the way it is – not in some foggy, notional dream world."

He leaned aggressively toward Chad. "You're right, Chad. I'm a little skeptical. Dr. Sanderson thinks we can have it both ways. Live a waking life of torturous submission but a dream life of expansive joy. To me it doesn't add up!"

Keaton felt a little embarrassed by his minor outburst. Abby squeezed his hand a little harder. "Hey, sweetheart, don't be mad."

"I'm not mad." Indeed, he had recovered more easily than he expected. Now in control, he sat back. "You know, I wonder sometimes if dreaming isn't an addiction." He looked around the table at each of them, then said, "I confess, I enjoy dreaming. I use the tea a lot. I wish I could stop – but when I try, I just want it more. I just don't want to end up on the wrong side of something." He turned to Abby. "I want to live a happy, prosperous life with you, Abby. I don't want to be part of something that I have to hide, if you know what I mean. I've already lived that way."

"I know what you mean," Abby said softly. "But we all dream. We know that. That's probably how you learn things so fast. Why should you have to hide it?"

The discussion was interrupted when a port door opened at the end of the table and four meals were dispensed. They distributed their plates to each other as they had ordered. They ate quietly, mumbling expressions of satisfaction at their choices. But really, they were too preoccupied with their discussion to focus on the food. They had crossed a taboo line. Once their appetites were abated, Meghan served them all another glass of spirits.

After a brief toast, Keaton said calmly, "So, Meghan. What exactly is your idea, again? I want to make sure I understand it."

"OK. Let me explain first," she said while gathering everyone's plate and placing them back into the port for removal. She collected her thoughts and talked carefully. "The technology that the Thelites use is incredible. It's hard to understand if you aren't exposed to it yourself, like at the Hub university. They have virtual models for *everything*! And they have groups of researchers improving them all the time!"

"What do you mean by *everything*?" Keaton asked, genuinely curious.

"I mean everything that it takes to manage life on Earth and maybe beyond," she said. "You know the slogan: Safety, Equality, and Science? The virtual models are the scientific tools that the Best Society uses to guarantee safety and equality. I don't think most of us understand how genuinely Thelites intend to bring those benefits to all of humankind. That's what has become so apparent to me at school. There is so much to gain by helping to bring this about!"

"For example, just imagine if you knew you had been infected with a flu virus before you had symptoms and an antidote was delivered to you immediately – so you never got sick. You don't even need to go anywhere. That's how all Thelites live! Their biometrics are constantly monitored – each person – and the virtual model constantly compares them to their normal metrics and to the whole population. Anything suspicious and bang! You get cured. Once every five years you go to the Bureau of Health Solutions for re-imaging and an assessment – but that is mostly to help improve the models," she explained.

"There are so many other things, too. Climate, microbiology, genetics, history, geology – you can't name a field that isn't subject to modelling. Sexuality…" she said, batting her eyes at Chad. "Just wait 'til you guys try out the Center for Reproductive Liberty!" Chad smiled knowingly and nodded his head.

"And their optimum allocation model – it's amazing," she continued. "All Thelites have everything they expect that they should have! It just happens! They don't have to buy anything; they don't have to think about where to get it – it just shows up for them. They do their jobs every day, and they live their life happily. Like bees! That's it!"

Chad stiffened to an admission. "This was my heartburn, at first," he explained to Keaton. "My Dad is an important guy down at the foundry. The foundry was conscripted the same day this Hub was established almost twenty-five years ago. He *hates* that model! He thinks that bugs in that model caused an explosion that killed my grandfather. Almost everyone at the foundry thinks the same thing.

"But after Meghan's experience here, she and I talked about it a lot. *Maybe* it was a bug in the model that caused the explosion, but *probably* – it was because my grandfather never accepted the model and never really tried to make it work. He just came up with workarounds to get through the schedule. My father is the same way! He's not trying to make it work, either – and maybe that's the problem," he concluded.

"And since then, it's been greatly improved anyway," Meghan chimed in. "Even if it was imperfect before, it's been fixed by now. If people would just start to help, these things would happen faster. It would be good for everybody! That's what I'm learning. I can't wait to find a position in a Best Society Service at some point and experience it all for myself!" she exclaimed.

"Yes, but…" Keaton started, trying to bring her back to the issue. "So, your idea is that conscriptions are good things." After Meghan nodded, he admitted, "I have kind of always wondered about that. At least, I never understood why it was worth dying to stop them. Wouldn't it be better to try to integrate than to die?"

Abby chimed in for the first time. "I don't understand that, either. Aunt Kelly's friend Shawn just died in one of those stupid protests! And she's disappeared. Maybe dead! Why? What makes it worth it?" Abby was clearly upset. Keaton put his arm around her and pulled her closer. They gave her a few moments before recovering the conversation.

Keaton finally asked the question he most wanted to understand. "OK, Meghan. Why…you know…why is it about the dreaming to you?"

"OK. Here's why," she said. "To me, dreaming seems like a hot-button issue that nobody ever talks about. But why? Here we all sit, knowing that we all dream and that our dreams are more than hallucinations. But isn't that what science is about? Explaining experiences?

"In my classes, they claim the behavioral science model is one of the most advanced they have. Behavioral science researchers are the most capable in the world! And there has never been as many scientists collected to look at this singular subject in the entire history of humanity!

"Next to the optimum allocation model, it is the model that most impacts how fast communities can be conscripted. If the model worked perfectly on proles, there would be no resistance to conscription. In my dreams, I wish there was such a thing as 'self-conscripting,'" she paused, looking at each of them to see if the subtle irony of her last sentence registered.

After a couple of groans, she continued, "There is a new area of research dedicated to proles. It is called 'behaviors outside modeled norms.' Supposedly, the behavioral model works near perfectly on Thelites. But it doesn't work nearly as well on proles. It's really good – but it fails on just a small group. And some from that group try to stop conscriptions!

"My instructors never mention dreaming. And of course I've never brought it up. They've mentioned religion, spirituality, and mysticism when they discuss disorders of historic societies. They must think dreams fall into those categories. They treat them as if they don't exist. But to me, that explains why the model doesn't work. How can it work if it doesn't consider something that is so much a part of us?"

Abby looked at Meghan. "Have you talked to Dad about this?"

Meghan answered, "He's always bought into Best Society ideals. He does everything he can to act like a Thelite. He's never been big on dreaming, but I'm sure he would like the idea."

"What's the good idea, *exactly*?" Keaton asked.

"I think we should approach the administrators at the Hub college and offer to perform research to develop a behavioral model that accounts for dreaming," she summarized. "We are unique. We all know what our dream experiences are. Keaton – you've worked with Dr. Sanderson for years. He's brilliant! But we've all seen how he avoids this topic. Maybe we could get him to help? Nobody is doing this. But it should sync with this new work on behaviors outside modeled norms. Isn't that the point – to model behaviors that are currently outside of the model's capability? The Thelite scientists *must* be looking for people like us. How else are they going to do it? Maybe it could be a game changer! Maybe we could help a lot of people and save a lot of lives!"

Meghan sat back, looking satisfied. She looked at Abby. Abby met her gaze, then turned to look at Keaton. The spirits made him more receptive. *Yes, she is smart. And convincing!*

Keaton met Abby's gaze, then looked down into his lap. Chad and Meghan watched him process. Keaton felt everyone waiting for him to respond. Frustrated, he said, "I'm thinking!" And continued looking at his lap.

Meghan tried some encouragement. "Maybe – just maybe – if we do this, we could even be invited into a Thelite community."

Keaton had little interest in that, but he didn't say anything dismissive. He looked at Abby with pleading eyes, "Abby, what do you think? It's a big step. I still think it might be dangerous."

"Maybe we kept Mom at home too long," she thought out loud. "Maybe if we had just used the Hub hospital earlier, she might have been more comfortable. Why should she have had to suffer so much? She might have even lived! Chad's grandfather and Shawn both died, and maybe they didn't have to. Aunt Kelly could be with us now. And that's just our experience sitting at this table! Maybe we just put off doing these things too long.

"I admit I'm scared, but I think we should try," she concluded.

Keaton lifted his eyes and met hers. He would do it. *Anything for her.*

-28-
They only damage themselves

2084

Julianna did her best to be happy. At times, she felt she succeeded, but more often it seemed like pretending. The protocols to relieve her grief did little. She couldn't dismiss both her father's and Ashley's deaths in mere days. Time helped, but she felt very alone. Her associates didn't grieve. They all seemed happy. She resisted showing her grief lest she get reported again.

Tim sensed the change in her and kept his distance. With Petra around to receive his attention, he rarely reached out to Julianna to socialize. He was still playful, but there was very little of their former collegiality and intimacy.

And while she used to visit the Center when she could, Mark was consuming both her time and what was left of her libido. Growing up, she held Mark in the high regard otherwise due an attentive patron. After her father's death, he was helpful but increasingly annoying. Now, she almost resented him, even though she felt deeply in his debt. Tonight, Mark was insistent that she accompany him to one of his ever-more-frequent receptions.

Julianna found the receptions ever-more-*tedious*. There was always some celebratory purpose that seemed less significant the more she went. There were usually about fifty attendees. Six or seven High Council trustees like Mark were regulars along with their escorts. The remainder were Thelites associated with the reception's purpose. On rare occasions an actual member of the High Council would be in attendance, and these events were always larger. To Julianna, each event seemed like a repeat of the last event. Many of the same people expressed the same views with a self-congratulatory aspect that she found increasingly distasteful.

Tonight's reception was small, celebrating the completion of the building from the construction site where she had visited her uncle. As usual, spirits flowed generously throughout the event. As the evening was winding down,

Julianna again found herself in the company of several trustees and their escorts discussing the most recent progress of the Best Society.

"The density of CosmoPods in this building is thirty percent higher than the old one! And it consumes less than half the energy!" one of them was saying. "It's amazing how technology has improved in just a couple of decades. Now, we are fully equipped for the next modeling efforts. It feels great to be ahead of the game, doesn't it?"

"Absolutely," agreed another. "And we're finally making some progress with the supply problems. I'm glad to see Public Safety taking a harder line. Best Society Services has been struggling with that sabotage for a long time. I bet this building could have been done weeks earlier without those disruptions."

Another added, "What's silly is – you know the proles that do that crap? They only damage themselves! They slow everything down and force others to live in such privation. Who wants that?"

"Speaking of proles, did you hear what happened at People's Village #471? Supposedly, they've found a group of dreamers."

"Really?" several of them said at once, disbelieving. Others shook their heads and rolled their eyes. One of them made a follow up observation, "Are there really still proles hanging on to this lunacy? I mean, dreams, religion – it's madness! How can they be so, so…what's the word – stupid?" Everyone giggled.

Marlo-286 was standing quietly near the group and moved closer as she heard the discussion. Julianna recognized her from her father's final event. She was Julianna's height, but voluptuous with a deep East Indian complexion. She wore a formfitting, black outfit with bold emerald and red accents and a pencil skirt that highlighted athletic hips. Large, colorful costume jewelry perfectly adorned long, muscular arms. Her black hair was teased to perfection, allowing some early gray highlights to frame her face. *Striking more than beautiful, but either adjective would work.* But the feature that drew Julianna was her eyes. Piercing, deep black eyes that focused sharply on whoever she spoke with. Julianna had never seen her at a reception, yet she was someone who was impossible to miss or ignore.

Marlo interrupted with more meaningful information. "Interestingly, they volunteered. Three of them are students – one of whom attends the local Hub college. They approached the Thelite educational authorities with a research idea. They were genuinely looking to assist research into dream science."

"Really stupid," someone responded. "And wasteful. Why not faith science?" They all groaned. "Where are they now?" he asked.

"At the Behavioral Science Research Clinic, of course," Marlo answered. "This is a great opportunity to improve our models."

"Sure. On fanaticism!" Mark chimed in and laughed.

Julianna had never heard the term "dreamers" used this way. Tentatively, she asked, "I'm not familiar with 'dreamers.' What are they?"

Mark answered for the group. "Several generations ago, 'dreamers' claimed they had visions when they slept. They made all kinds of irrational claims about these 'dreams.' But there has never been any scientific explanation that validates these claims. Rather, it seems to be a disorder unique to some proles. Most likely hallucinations from mental derangement or some type of substance abuse."

Marlo added, "My group works on behavioral models to characterize these types of disorders. Similar disorders are common in proles who violently resist when the Best Society reaches out to new communities. We are working hard to minimize the effects of these disorders in future generations. That would be a tremendous benefit to the whole prole population."

Mark continued, "There's been great progress. Years ago, proles with spiritual tendencies, especially dreamers, were among our biggest problems with conscriptions. A lot of work was done to eradicate the disorder. These students are the first we've come across in a long time. Now that we have them, we can develop more modern and effective remedies. It's a good opportunity."

Julianna's pulse quickened at Mark's words: eradicate the disorder. *What word had her uncle used? 'Purge'?* Julianna steadied herself with a huge gulp of spirits. "What are the research protocols? How will you model these 'dreams'?"

Several people guffawed contemptuously, laughing quietly with each other. Mark shared a smirk with them before explaining. "None of their claims can be reproduced experimentally. Years of research was wasted on that. Dreamers just have a pervasive disorder. Any new research should be aimed at understanding the scope of the disorder so that it can be eliminated."

Marlo considered Mark's words soberly, then commented, "It's interesting how far we've come in understanding human happiness. Our behavioral models are just so good. Yet, there are still proles behaving outside the modeled norms in this regard. If we truly understood it, our models could revolutionize our approach to conscriptions."

Mark affirmed. "It *is* exciting! Deism, spiritualism, dreams – they are almost gone right now. We are so close to getting rid of them completely! The faster we can conscript their communities into the Best Society, the better off they are going to be. Who knows? We might be less than one generation away."

Marlo offered yet another observation. "The strange thing is that these students are young. They were actually *eager* to talk about dream science."

"Like it wasn't already settled!" Mark interrupted, with satisfying mirth for his audience.

"Anyway…" Marlo continued more seriously, "a lot to look into. There might be some genetic link to their condition."

"But what if…" Julianna checked herself. Everyone turned to her. *She wanted to ask: what if the dreamers' claims were real? But was that tenuous ground?* She clumsily redirected her question. "But what if there are more dreamers their age? Wouldn't that mean we're not as close as we think?"

"Yes," Marlo's eyes grabbed Julianna. "But this discovery is unusual. Like Mark said, a lot of work has already been done to eradicate the disorder. So we *assume* they are already very rare."

"And like Marlo said," Mark threw her a flattering smile. "The models are already really good. If we could account for these disorders, the models might even be perfect. This should be a great demonstration of the newest innovation in the Best Society. And it couldn't have come too soon. Thank goodness this generation of the High Council finally understands!"

"What's the innovation?" Julianna asked. "Aren't we just going to study them and refine the model like we always do?"

"Nope," Mark said, smiling smugly. "The innovation is that the High Council now accepts a two-prong approach to modeling. I've been working on this for years. Now that I'm a trustee, we will finally have the protocol! The first prong is to refine the models to capture more and more of the population's characteristics – which is what we've always done. The second prong is that at some point, after capturing those things that are reasonable to model, to eliminate extreme anomalies when they are destructive or too insignificant to waste the modeling effort. What good is it to make models account for all of the various extremes if they can simply be removed from the data set?"

Marlo was less excited. "In behavioral science, we call this 'behaviors outside modeled norms.' Now that we have these dreamers, we can directly explore the relevant social and genetic links to the disorder with specificity. Then we can explore remedies."

The dialogue turned celebratory and the evening went long. Spirits flowed liberally. Julianna kept up, noticing that Mark was fawning over Marlo. Their audience cheered them on as they toasted their successes. As it got late, people started drifting away. Eventually it was only Julianna and several others watching Mark's obvious pursuit of Marlo. Marlo had warmed to his attention, and they huddled close, ignoring everyone else.

Julianna caught the eye of the Marlo's escort, and they sidled away quietly to the entrance, leaving Marlo and Mark alone.

"Now that was a great reception!" Marlo's companion said once they were outside.

211

"Yes, very enjoyable," Julianna agreed. "But it looks like our hosts might have plans for later," she said, not hiding her relief.

"Seems like it," he laughed. "Good for them, though. I don't know Mark, but Marlo is an absolute beast. Always working. She is one of the most preeminent behavioral scientists at the Center. Maybe in the world. She rarely gets out to attend these things. I'm happy to see her enjoying the benefits however she sees fit."

"I didn't think I'd seen you two before," Julianna said, craning her neck a little to look up at him. He was nearly a full head taller than her, broad-shouldered and fit. A heavy brow covered friendly eyes that darted appraisingly between people and objects for only moments at a time. "Mark brings me to a lot of these things. He's not so hardcore, though. Maybe he just likes coming because it's new to him or something."

"He should watch out," he joked. "From what I know of Marlo, she doesn't get out much, but when she does? Whew! Marlo could chew him up and spit him out." They both laughed.

"How do you know Marlo?" she asked.

"I'm one of her assistants," he said, proudly. "With her schedule, she needs several. I am mostly in charge of her physical training and security – but all of us do what we have to."

They chatted idly for several more minutes, neither of them certain if they should hail a driverless and end the evening. Finally, he suggested hopefully, "Speaking of enjoying benefits, how would you like to spend the next couple hours at the Center?"

Julianna found him delightful company, and the evening's spirits had done their job. "Sounds like a great idea to me," she acquiesced. No Mark tonight – finally – and a trip to the Center! She enjoyed the remainder of the evening more than she had in a long time.

-29-
What good had he done?

2084

Dr. David Sanderson's shop was impressive, at least 10,000 square feet in the main room. It was a crowded playhouse of scientific toys used to entertain and educate. A cloud chamber demonstrated particle physics, a Jacob's ladder introduced electrical potential, and a fiber laser exhibited structured light. Simple chemistry applications like invisible ink and soda explosions were at the ready just as attention grabbers. Aisle after aisle, there were dozens more. A variety of special shop tools also had their places in support of his tinkering. As the sole heir of his parents' country home and business, he had sold their estate and invested in this lab. He continuously added or improved things to make it more interesting.

David managed construction projects for Best Society Services to sustain the staples of his life. Otherwise he applied his nervous energy here. He loved using science to help with real problems. Local companies frequently contacted him to troubleshoot or develop new processes. Trade schools contracted with him to give supplemental lectures. He built props to excite students by seeing and touching this scientific subject matter. He was personable, often staying for hours after a class in casual discussion, putting science into the context of history of who, when, and where it came from, the conflicts it caused, and what it replaced. How it both advanced and disrupted society in its time. It was a gratifying life.

So far.

He was turning a small metal part on his lathe when he heard someone enter and familiar footsteps approached. His assistant Keaton was walking toward him. Keaton had become the family that David had lost. His brother Jacob had disowned his family in preference for an opportunity as a Thelite. David never married. He stayed close with Delores, his childhood nanny. He socialized with the cadres of students flowing through his lectures and equipped them for occupations in his sphere of influence. But for the last decade, he interacted almost daily with Keaton. They made a great team.

Keaton appeared serious. "Hey, Dr. Sanderson. Do you have a moment?" he asked over the hum of the lathe, always respectful.

"Keaton! Sure, always. Great to see you!" David shut off the lathe, letting it wind down so he could pay attention.

"I need to let you know something. Abby and I are planning to participate in a new study for the Best Society with Chad and Meghan. It's Meghan's idea, and I think she has a point."

"What is the study about?" Suspicious now, David removed his safety goggles.

"According to Meghan, there is a new Thelite study named 'behaviors outside of modelled norms.' It is an effort to advance Thelites' behavioral model – they say to 'perfect' their model – so it can be applied more effectively to proles."

Jacob would have approved. He leaned on his work bench, tapping his fingers. "So how do you plan to participate?"

"We intend to offer ourselves as subjects of the study. All four of us have talents that fall outside of the norms for Thelites. You know..." he said.

David *did* know. David had cautioned Keaton for years not to broadly discuss dreaming. Best to keep to yourself and practice it without scrutiny. His reaction now was concern. "You know that Thelites feel threatened by those talents, right?"

"I don't think 'threatened' is the right word," Keaton explained. "I think they are more curious. Why else would they introduce a study to improve the model?"

David didn't have an answer, but he was leery. "Well, that's what they always say. They invest in the models to make them 'perfect' – until they're not; then they invest in them again. It seems that an unusual number of proles get killed in the discovery process!"

"I know what you mean. I had my suspicions, too. But Meghan makes a pretty good argument. They can only capture our talents in the model if they have subjects to study. If everybody is afraid to share their experiences, it *has* to fail. Why wouldn't we try to make it work instead of ignoring the opportunity?"

"I understand her logic," David answered. Young people enjoyed talking with David. He never dismissed someone who was thinking in good faith with sound logic – even if he disagreed. But his brother's warning to Julianna haunted him. "You know, my brother and I were pretty fair scientists in our day. And we had the same talent as you. We were never able to measure anything that could decode the experiences. Delores laughed at us for wasting our time. And we weren't the only ones. It's been tried many times in the past with nothing to show for it. The scientific community pretty much gave up on it."

"With all due respect Dr. Sanderson, that had to be thirty years ago," Keaton said, looking a little sheepish. "The instruments they have now to measure and model things at the sub-particle level and to visualize energy streams has advanced tremendously. How can you rule it out?"

"You're right," he agreed, reluctantly. "There are more tools, and I can't rule it out. It's just – I'm not sure if that is their genuine intent. My brother Jacob would have agreed with you. He thought the science just had to catch up. But for the study to be genuine – the scientists have to *believe* that it is happening. Do they? I know Jacob did, but…

"For example, if I told you there was an invisible, five-hundred-pound gorilla walking around this lab that I could see but you couldn't," he spread his arms and looked around, as if tracking the gorilla, "how much time would you spend trying to find it? Darn little, I bet."

Keaton chuckled. David loved to pepper his discussions with these fantastic challenges that could startle a person into new perspectives. "True," Keaton acknowledged. "But, if there were four people telling me that there was an invisible gorilla, and all four could describe it identically in a double-blind study, *then* I might spend that time. I think that's more what we're talking about."

David had always been impressed with Keaton's natural intelligence. "Well," he said, "I hope I'm describing my concerns right. I've never objected to pursuing new discovery. It's just, depending on who you were, you might try to find the gorilla. *Or*, you might try to prove that it wasn't there. And who's going to know other than the four people? After all, the gorilla is still invisible. That's my concern with any study like this."

"But the Thelites proposed the study," Keaton explained. "Why would they do that unless they were genuinely interested?"

They crossed their arms, taking each other in. David was proud of Keaton. Like a son. Keaton was grateful of David. But they both sensed a parting.

"It seems like you've convinced yourself," David finally said. "I have to be candid. My biggest problem is that a lot of proles get hurt while Thelites work so tirelessly for their supposed benefit. That's why I've always held back. Why not just coexist? We'll do our best with our tools and talents. And if that's good enough for us, why is this being done?"

"I know," Keaton said. "But that thinking would stop all progress and keep society divided. So, whose fault is it really that proles die?"

David didn't answer. He'd had vicious arguments on the same point with Jacob years ago. It was like going down a rabbit-hole. There was only one right answer, and it was always the perspective you'd started with.

"Well," he said eventually. "I truly wish you and Abby the best. I hope it works out how you expect."

They shook hands solemnly. Keaton was moving on. And he would be with Abby. It was natural.

Now, a week since Keaton's visit, David's dreams had been dark. Very dark. It wasn't working out as Keaton had expected. David sensed things coming to an end. Maybe today, maybe tomorrow, maybe next week, but soon.

And there was Julianna – David's only living relative. It made little sense that he cared for her as much as he did. Like her father, she was committed to the principles of the Best Society. But unlike her father, she would spend time in dream-space. She was rediscovering the things her father had chosen to discard. He could tell she was brilliant and curious – and confused.

He had been loyal. He had tried. *Should he have? What good had he done? What bad?* He had misgivings. *Why did she need to know? How did that help?* David feared for her. But time was passing, and things were happening. He couldn't stop it.

He was mostly thinking about Julianna while he mindlessly set a titration tube stand above a beaker for a new demo. There was a knock on his door.

Ah. It's now.

There were two Thelite Public Safety officers at the door. "Mr. Sanderson," one said. "Please come with us."

-30-
I am who I am

In the weeks following the last reception with Mark, Julianna deliberately drew less attention to herself. Like her father, she was predisposed to constructive disagreement as a way of life. But according to Mark, that may have compromised her father and had apparently concerned people who monitored her behavior.

Mark had not communicated with her since. She was grateful for the respite. She had restarted her old routines of fitness and visits to the Center.

Work was now just work. For each new project, she would run fifteen or sixteen tests and pick the best result, even if the tests were not to her satisfaction. As Mark had advised, she monitored and logged her correlations, but didn't even attempt to diagnose them. She assumed the models would reconcile the information.

But the conversation about dreamers at the reception troubled her, like the joy of progress was being gravely misplaced. Julianna's one risky behavior – dreaming – seemed simultaneously harmless and mutinous. But she couldn't stop doing it, like a drug. The longer she went without spirits, the more tangible the dreams were. She used the tea sparingly because she had so little. She fretted about how to acquire more if she ran out.

There was enormous variety in her dreams. Some were like her first dreams, where Delores, or her uncle, or others delivered lessons with some type of message. Some were exotic, some were fantastic, and some were unremarkable. Some dreams left her no specific memories but transmitted deep sensibilities about the cosmos. She started to know things that she'd never been taught. She started to question things that she had always considered unquestionable. And some dreams left her with nothing but unanswerable questions.

The more she dreamt, the more she felt that she shared dream space with hundreds, or maybe thousands, or maybe millions of other dreamers. The warm community was vast and seemed to be from everywhere. Some had names, some were just personalities, and some may have been totally notional. She could meet another dream participant for the first time and somehow know everything about them instantly. There were dreams where she feared resentment because she was a Thelite, like with the lady at Shawn's funeral. Excepting that, her dream associates welcomed and embraced her as if totally disinterested in who she was.

By this time, she'd had dozens of dreams, and she could sense new personalities who remained distant, as if suspicious of the experience. She suspected that some of these mystery dreamers might be other Thelites with a shared experience to hers, but so far, she had no certainty.

The week had been socially quiet for Julianna. Today was the second consecutive day she had avoided spirits. It was the first time in her adult life that this had ever happened. As her evening was ending, she indulged in a healthy helping of tea. She immediately went to bed.

As was typical upon falling asleep, warm sentiments flowed over her like a refreshing shower. She sensed the well wishes of many, many dreamers: some who were known to her like Delores, and some whom she knew of but didn't know personally, like the audience in her dream classes, and some who were total strangers. She released her own warmth into the dream ether – wishing well to whoever was there – and that release caused her such happiness that she wanted to keep doing it over and over…She sensed an immensely large space that she could move in, free of the constraints of her body and gravity, but she had no sense of where she might go or what she might seek. She simply drifted amid pleasant feelings until disappointingly, she felt herself wake up.

As she awoke, the warmth flowed away from her like stepping out of a bath into cool air. Surprisingly, she noticed she had been asleep only a few minutes. She turned to a more comfortable position and quickly went back to sleep. Then everything seemed to go blank.

The next thing she knew, she was looking down at herself sleeping. She was floating along the ceiling of her apartment. She saw her hair and nightgown and bed covers wrinkled and unkempt amid the unconcern of sleep. She saw ghostly reflections from a cloud-covered moon changing subtly through the windows. She saw various objects in the room from weird perspectives she had never experienced while awake. She started moving around the room, not feeling like she was in control of where, and not understanding if the walls would stop her or if she would bump them and wake up. She went through them instead and saw the other rooms in her apartment. She was anxious. *Was she dead? What was she supposed to do?*

Then a voice that wasn't really a voice spoke to her. "Come," it beckoned her outside. She willed herself in the direction of the voice and passed through the exterior of her building, then found herself far above her city. She was in the middle of a soft, luminous mist, and the mist was the body of something or someone whose voice she had responded to. The mist was moving like a radiant cloud over the night landscape, and Julianna was watching the countryside change as she moved with it. She recognized that she was no longer afraid.

"Hello?" Julianna tried to communicate with the mist.

"Hello," came the disembodied message back to her. She couldn't describe it as a voice. It was like someone transmitting to the auditory part of her brain but without using her ears. The message, the coolness of the mist, the motion, and the view of earth left her with a Zen-like sensation; she thought of nothing other than what she was experiencing in that moment. She felt relaxed, like she was part of something peaceful and eternal.

As the mist drifted over the landscape, she could see the curve of the earth on the horizon. Whole cities and towns would come into view and then disappear behind them. Julianna could see them closer just by looking. Focusing on them was like putting them under a magnifying glass. If she looked toward a new landmark, the mist would move toward it. But she couldn't see any people. All she saw were lights. Some areas had thousands of pinpoints of light with varying intensity, like looking at a starry sky, but with motion like the stars were vibrating. In other areas, the lights were sparse, like fireflies in an open field.

Moving over the earth this way, she sensed that the mist was showing her something, waiting for her. "What are those lights?" she finally asked.

"Each light is a soul seeking truth," the mist intoned in her brain.

"How do they seek truth?"

"By acknowledging that they don't know it," the mist responded. The non-voice was melodious – neither male nor female – and infinitely patient. If Julianna said nothing, the mist was quiet. If Julianna spoke, the mist would respond immediately with perfect clarity, kindly, but with no extra words.

As she continued watching the landscape, she noticed there were also points of shadows that moved among the lights. In areas where there were many lights, there were fewer shadows, and in areas where there were fewer lights, there were many shadows. Some of the shadows were darkly shaded while others were less dark. As she watched more closely, she saw that the intensity of any point varied, and a point might even switch from shade to light and vice versa.

"What are the shadows?" Julianna asked.

"They are souls who have stopped seeking truth," the mist answered.

"Is it important to know the truth?"

"It is important to seek the truth," the mist responded.

"Why?" Julianna asked.

"Seeking truth makes life better and adds light," the mist answered. "Not seeking truth, or knowing things that aren't true, makes life worse and adds darkness."

"What do you mean by 'knowing things that aren't true'?" Julianna asked.

"People stop seeking truth because they believe they know. But what they know is not truth."

Julianna was quiet and watched the drama of the lights unfold below her. Now, from a very distant perspective, the intensity of the light and darkness moved in ethereal waves across the globe, like the aurora borealis. But with passing time, the overall intensity was dimming, like a battery was slowly running down. Julianna sensed a thoughtfulness within the mist – almost a sadness – as they quietly watched.

"Will the lights go out?" Julianna whispered.

"They can," the mist responded.

Julianna was quiet. She was cool, yet warm enough. She felt no pains, no itches, no twitches, and no discomfort. She could see and hear with perfect clarity. No anxiety – just serene existence. She basked in it, hoping to hang on to the experience for as long as she could. The mist did nothing to interrupt.

"Who are you?" Julianna asked almost sleepily.

"I am the sum of all consciousness," the mist answered, then continued, "I am the source of all conscientiousness."

"Do you have a name?" Julianna pressed.

"I have many names, but they are unimportant. I am who I am."

Quiet again, Julianna closed her eyes. She felt perfect. When she was next aware, she was back in her bed, sleeping half-conscious yet comfortably. She had no concept of how long she'd been under.

Suddenly, she felt yanked into another dream – dramatically, almost violently. She felt as if she were lurching around a formless and crowded space where panicking people would bump her and recoil in terror. There was fear, screeching noises, and an incessant pounding. The only discreet thing she could identify was a voice crying out to her in delirium.

"Deny me!" it screamed. It was her uncle's voice.

"What do you mean?" she yelled back.

Then from a greater distance, it came again, "Deny me! Deny me!" Then it faded away, but the screeching and pounding continued and grew louder.

Her eyes flew open as she awoke in a panic. The screeching turned into her BioGram's emergency beacon hailing her to attend to an urgent message. The pounding turned into an insistent knocking at her door.

She arose quickly and unpacked her BioGram while she gathered herself to answer the door. It was a message from Mark telling her not to be afraid, but she was needed immediately at the Behavioral Science Research Clinic. Someone was being sent to escort her. When she answered the door, there were two women in security uniforms. Julianna recognized one of them as the assistant from Mark's flat and thought she remembered Mark calling her Alexa.

"Good morning," Alexa said. "Would you please come with us?" She wasn't unpleasant, but the question was intoned more as a statement.

"Certainly," Julianna answered. "Just let me gather some things…"

"That won't be necessary," Alexa said. "Everything you need will be provided for you. Please, just come along now." Then she reached in back of Julianna to pull the door closed and encouraged Julianna with a firm hand on the small of her back. The other woman took her position to the other side and walked slightly behind. They went down the elevator and outside to a waiting driverless which delivered them to the Behavioral Science Research Center in a matter of minutes.

-31-
You might not be aware that you are ill

2084

The Behavioral Science Research Center was a massive complex of unremarkable buildings on the edge of the city. There were few windows and very little traffic in or out. The buildings never served as host sites for public events. Behavioral science research was staffed with the crème de la crème of scientists. Their models were lauded as the standard of effectiveness in their import to sustaining the Best Society. Activities within the building were treated with inordinate discretion, so it operated inside a shroud of mystery.

Julianna was escorted to a room with utilitarian decor where she was provided a set of austere clothing and personal hygiene items. She was left alone and told to wait. She changed and freshened up. For only the second time in her life, she was truly afraid.

Soon, Julianna was attended to by brisk and efficient people. A Bio-Metric Technician recorded innumerable facts about her body. Another technician led her through a regimen in a specialized CosmoPod, measuring her physical acumen and reactions to stimuli such as pinpricks and slight electrical shocks. Yet another specialist used a CosmoPod that measured cognition and took brain scans while interviewing her with a series of puzzles and nonsensical questions.

The barrage of tests took until midafternoon. A dietician brought her a light, perfectly-balanced meal including several forms of spirits. She consumed it hungrily.

Now alone again, Julianna considered her situation. She sensed she was a prisoner and wondered what would happen if she tried to leave, but she was afraid to try. She closed her eyes and tried to recall how she felt during her dream last night. Peaceful. Safe. She tried to put herself in the same mindset but lost the battle every time she reopened her eyes.

After what seemed like hours, a woman came to her room with an assistant in tow. She knew the woman, Marlo, the trustee Mark had flirted with at their last reception, but she was with a different assistant. Marlo was a rumpled version of herself in this setting, but with the same dignity. She wore an open, pale-green medicinal smock which revealed a bland outfit underneath that hid her intimidating form. Her hair was pinned back. She wore no adornments other than shapeless eyeglasses with heavy frames and practical lenses that magnified her eyes. Emanating competence. She carried herself with the self-assurance of high rank.

Was she just forty or so? Wasn't she already a trustee? She must be highly thought of.

She sat down and considered Julianna with distant recognition.

"Greetings, Julianna-119. I am Marlo-286, Trustee to the High Council," she said.

"Greetings, fellow Thelite," Julianna mumbled out of habit.

"I am sure you are curious why you are here. I am here to answer those questions and lay out the process for your recovery."

"Recovery?" Julianna asked. "I'm not ill."

"You might not be aware that you are ill," Marlo answered. "Our models have identified that your behaviors indicate several disparities. We also have an anomalistic linkage that we need to research along with your recovery."

"What are you talking about?" Julianna asked. "I feel fine, and I've been attending to my fitness rigorously."

"The behavioral model continuously gathers data on the entire Thelite population. It measures where you go, what you do, the effectiveness of your work, how well you sleep, a lot of surface bio-metrics from your CosmoPod, the number of words you speak – many, many things. The model identifies

225

patterns within this data to flag risky behavioral and health situations before they develop to a point of being harmful.

"On the surface, your case is not particularly difficult. The diagnosis is quite distinct. We know the exact protocols to correct your behaviors. But we very recently identified an anomaly that makes you worthy of more research. It will take us longer than usual."

"Oh," Julianna said, anxious to get as much information as she could. "How long does this usually take?"

"Normally we expect the corrective protocols to take effect within a couple weeks."

"What are the protocols?"

"In your case, your response to separation anxiety resulted in imbalances in your diet and sleep patterns. This usually corrects itself over a few weeks, but in some cases, it can become a self-reinforcing spiral, resulting in a lack of systemic trust – fear – and a loss of happiness. That's what is happening to you. We can confirm from your tests that your diet has become unconventional. We also know that the enzymes accountable for your happiness are out of norm. We know your sleep patterns have been disrupted by analyzing your BioGram record. Beyond that, your brain scans and response mechanisms are normal.

"The protocols are to rebalance your diet, perhaps modifying your spirit formulations, and subsequently measure your sleep and monitor your brain scans and happiness enzymes. Part of rebalancing your diet is eliminating unregulated substances. Assuming everything responds as we expect, that's all there is. We keep you safe and comfortable here in this building while we do all of that, so that we can ensure the protocols are implemented exactly and that we can make adjustments and measure the effects in real time."

"Happiness enzymes? I don't understand that," Julianna said.

"Happiness is objectively measurable by the production of enzymes that optimize a person's sense of well-being. Diet, fitness, and regular socialization create the physical conditions to produce the enzymes. This can be adjusted over the course of a life, of course.

"There are things that can limit or counter the effect of those enzymes, such as fear and resentment. So, to maximize everyone's happiness, we need to not only produce the happiness enzymes but remove fear and resentment. Sometimes those can get out of balance as well, such as during periods of high emotional stress."

"So, basically, my diet and sleep got out of balance due to my grief response and need to be rebalanced so my happiness will return. And then I can go home?" Julianna asked.

"Normally, yes. But in your case, there is an anomaly that needs further study."

"What kind of anomaly?" Julianna asked, now suspicious.

"You couldn't have known this," Marlo said cautiously. "But you have a close genetic link to a prole, a leader in the prole community who we suspect is inciting destructive beliefs."

Julianna had no idea of the proper, expected response to this news. She assumed the person was her Uncle David. Evidently, he was considered a rebel.

Deny him. She remembered her dream last night. *Should she be shocked? Inquisitive? Sad?* She didn't know. She opted to deflect the conversation in the simplest way she could. "I don't understand," she said. "A genetic link?"

"I'm sure this was never mentioned to you. Your father would have agreed that family identities are destructive. It shouldn't matter to you, either. But to understand our work, you need to know that your father was born a prole and was assimilated into the Thelites about the time you were born. You were also born a prole. Neither you nor your father had the benefit of genetic optimization. But you have both been model Thelites. We have always been aware of your prole heritage, and there has never been any cause for concern," Marlo explained.

Julianna looked surprised. "I've been a Thelite my entire life!" she said with just a hint of defensiveness. Then, "And a scientist."

"This is a lot of information to digest," Marlo acknowledged. "Your father was among very few proles ever invited to become a Thelite, and the only one who brought along a natural child." Marlo was looking directly at Julianna as she finished her sentence. *Searching? Suspicious?*

Julianna did her best to just appear confused. "I'm not sure how to interpret what I'm hearing," Julianna said in her best scientific-inquiry voice. "Am I in some kind of trouble?"

"Not at all," Marlo answered. "Everything we are doing is strictly in conventional service of the Best Society. You may be the only Thelite in your generation without the benefit of genetic optimization. Proles have no protocols to optimize reproductive outcomes. If we are going to assimilate prole communities faster, we need to understand how to adjust our behavioral models to their less advanced genomes. Your genetics provide a perfect control point. It will take some time, but we intend to mesh this research with your recovery protocols. As a scientist, you can certainly recognize how unique this opportunity is.

"The combination of your genetic link, your scientific training, your Thelite upbringing – and frankly your general *lack* of disorders – makes you highly valuable right now to serve in this research," Marlo ticked off her points meticulously.

"So can I leave?" Julianna asked tentatively.

"No. That wouldn't make sense. We will be making many adjustments and measurements. We need to keep you in a perfectly controlled situation."

"So, I'm a prisoner?" Julianna asked, showing some irritation.

Marlo seemed a little shocked by the insinuation. "Of course not!" she responded. "You just have a different role to play in service of the Best Society for a few weeks. It's your duty. It's no different than if you had a new job. I can't even imagine you would want to leave."

Julianna was quiet, sensing she had overstepped – again. She looked around the room, avoiding Marlo's eyes long enough to notice the background hums and ticks emanating from the building's mechanical systems. When she finally looked back, she said, "Mark-057 contacted me this morning to tell me I was needed here. Will I be able to talk to him?"

"Your BioGram capabilities are unrestricted. You can hail or communicate with anyone you choose. Mark is a Trustee. He is here on High Council business occasionally. He can visit if he so chooses," Marlo said with a dismissive tone.

"What's next, then?" Julianna asked.

"For the next week or so, we will be varying your diet, regimenting your fitness and socialization, and measuring your bio-metrics more or less continuously. We will likely adjust the diet several times, focusing especially on refining your spirit formulations. You will be busy."

Without waiting for Julianna to acknowledge, Marlo stood and nodded to her crisply. "And now, I must attend to other matters." Then she and the assistant left.

Once in the hallway, Marlo dismissed her assistant and went straight to her private conference area. Mark was waiting for her as scheduled. She impatiently accepted a quick embrace, something that would never happen unless they were alone. Ever since their first tryst after the reception, Mark had been more attentive and familiar than she was comfortable with. They stood next to a NetSystem screen that was highlighting the performance of the recently improved geological model. They ignored it.

"What is Julianna's status?" he asked.

"Routine," she said. "If it weren't for her prole heritage, she might not even be here."

"Really?" he asked, sighing in relief. "I was afraid that her history of disruption would be a complication."

"Disruption?" she asked.

"In your position, I assumed you knew," Mark said, coyly. "She's the one who launched that horribly wasteful investigation into the model for extra-terrestrial threat remediation. Really a bad idea. Especially when the geological model needed so many resources at the same time. I mean, the last thing we needed was somebody making a big deal out of trivial concerns when we have so much going on," he explained.

"I don't have time to pay close attention to these other groups. Was it wasteful?" Marlo asked. "I understood it was just a temporary redirection of their regular work effort. Did they use any more CosmoPods or staff than before the investigation?"

"If that's all you measured, sure, it didn't take much," he answered. "But it spread more distrust than we were comfortable with. Definitely not the right time – again with the geological model in its state. One thing at a time. Focus gives us the best outcomes for the effort." He lowered his voice as if sharing a secret. "I worked directly with the High Council to keep that effort in check. They rely on me for a lot of those assessments. Julianna was lucky to keep her career intact."

She looked at him blankly for a moment, then redirected, "Well, anyway, we've seen lots of cases like Julianna's. The models indicate an extremely high likelihood that the recovery protocols will be effective. I'm more curious about whether she can be helpful in researching the dream phenomena or the fanaticism that supports it."

"That's why I brought her to your personal attention," Mark said enthusiastically. "Ever since I was assigned to Jacob-024, I was concerned that their prole heritage might be an issue. You know, like they don't really accept the Canon. Like they might question things that shouldn't be questioned."

"You seem to have some highly-developed concerns," she observed.

"I spent a lot of time with them. And finding this group of dreamers who identified Jacob's brother as their leader is pretty scary, isn't it? Like we think we are beyond those things that divide society, and then we find those very characteristics nearly in our midst?"

"Scary how? Wouldn't you rather know they are there?" she asked.

"Yes, I guess so, but the Canon is so descriptive of the history and so prescriptive of the best outcome. Differences in beliefs that defied science have caused unquantifiable carnage in society. Belief in dreaming is no different than belief in anything else. It's just another belief lacking scientific explanation. To allow it is to invite the threat of a divided society – even after all we've learned!"

"I agree with you in principle," Marlo said. "If they can't be scientifically explained, they eventually *will* disappear," she acknowledged. "According to the Canon, that is expected to happen naturally, as science is demonstrated over generations."

"The High Council now believes we can do this in our generation," he claimed. "We're almost there! My work with them has resulted in this new protocol, and they've asked me to stay involved with this effort to help speed things up. Does it cost society more to interminably improve the model? Or to sort the population? That's all we need to determine."

"Mark," she said, not quite sharing his excitement, "the behavioral model that we have right now has taken over forty years to develop. It's really good, but not yet perfect. To investigate and understand prole fanaticism in enough depth to model it will take some time. For the first time in my career, we have willing subjects, we have a fanatic, and we have a control subject. We can get some pretty good information from all of this and then make some decisions."

"Well," Mark replied, "I've spent a lot of effort advocating for this new protocol. It's up to you if you want to take the position with the High Council that we should take several more generations."

"I'm not taking that position yet," she said. "Let's just see where the evidence takes us."

"You sound so much like Jacob!" he teased, taking the edge off the conversation. "But it's your expertise."

"Yes, it is," she acknowledged.

Now done arguing, Mark stepped toward the door. "Marlo, can I expect to see you later this evening?"

She looked him up and down with a wry smirk. "I'm going to the Center tonight. That's where you can find me if you want."

"Oh, I will," he said with a too-wide smile and saw himself out.

Marlo shook her head. She still had work to do. She went to her office and recovered an envelope that had been found in Julianna's apartment. It contained a leafy residue that she didn't recognize. She headed to the lab to have it analyzed.

-32-
Never to lapse again

2084

While waiting for her first activity, Julianna packed off a series of BioGrams to Tim and Petra. A temporary assistant had been placed in Julianna's role to keep things moving. They would keep her updated. She sent an especially detailed BioGram to Mark, seeking an audience and some advice.

She was led to a CosmoPod where she spent several hours in an unusually long workout. The routines were all new, so she felt refreshingly stiff and sore afterwards. Her evening meal was perfectly balanced, and the spirit formulation had been tweaked, reducing her anxiety.

The next day after her sessions, she was introduced to small groups of people for conversation and competitive games. She was presented with a new partner for sexual recreation and found him capable and exciting. She was allowed some time alone in a CosmoPod to pursue her own entertainment as well.

She became increasingly comfortable with the recovery process and how tolerable it was for her. Each day after the scheduled sessions, her bio-metrics and psychological factors were measured and recorded. She had less anxiety during the day, and she was enjoying the social opportunities. Her diet, spirit consumption, and fitness regimens were stable, and she was finally able to be more clinical with herself. As the week went on, she even noticed her sleep improved little by little, although it still wasn't perfect. By the end of the week, the clinicians reported that her spirit formulations had been significantly adjusted, which could have been part of the problem to begin with.

She reflected on the fact that, for some reason, her response to separation anxiety had been extreme, and she hadn't been rigorous with the protocols for recovery. She now knew and acknowledged her weakness, and she committed to herself to leave all that anxiety behind and never to lapse again.

At least, that's what she wanted everyone to believe. Only she knew that upon her waking, she had indistinct, shadowed memories that lingered for a few moments. They would virtually disappear upon total wakefulness. Something had happened, but if it was a dream, she couldn't articulate what it had been about. But she *knew* it was best to hide it.

She never heard from Mark.

That changed when Mark and Marlo came to her room one afternoon. Julianna was finishing her midday meal when they marched in unannounced followed by an entourage. She knew both Mark and Marlo were continuously attended to by aides. The aides kept them aware of schedules and saw to any needs for personal comfort or security during their busy daily circuits. The aides were deferential – always a couple feet to the side or back of their charge – but always attentive. *Two trustees? So many assistants?* Julianna had the bewildering impression that very important people were scrutinizing her progress.

The group filed into the room quickly and stepped to the side of the door, standing. Marlo entered last and took a seat across from Julianna. Julianna hadn't seen Marlo since her first day in the Center. She looked at Julianna with an expressionless face. Mark, standing back, spoke first.

"Greetings, Julianna," he said familiarly. Today, he was the gregarious Mark.

"Greetings," Julianna replied, wearing the most clinical demeanor she could muster.

"It's too bad you ended up here, but you seem to be doing well. The High Council appreciates your contribution to the final developments of the behavioral model," he said.

"I haven't contributed anything," Julianna responded. "So far, it's just recovery protocols."

234

"That's just so far," Mark explained. "It is still informative to measure the efficacy of Best Society protocols." Julianna said nothing, so he continued. "The next phase will be interesting." Marlo just watched Julianna coolly during the dialogue.

"What is the next phase?" she asked, looking from Mark to Marlo and back.

Marlo took over the conversation. "Greetings, Julianna. Are you aware of the students from the prole community who approached us about dream research?"

Julianna had to think. "I heard about them at one of the receptions. But just what was talked about there. Why?"

"I assume you know that the current effort to improve the behavioral models is called Behaviors Outside of Modeled Norms – BOMN for short. It's a massive effort. We intend to improve the model to account for that small percentage of prole behaviors that have been beyond our scientific understanding," Marlo explained.

"Yes," Julianna nodded. "That's been broadly reported."

"These students offered themselves as subjects for dream research, which they view as part of the BOMN effort. They are the first 'dreamers' we have been aware of in decades," Marlo continued.

Mark interrupted. Marlo waited patiently while he expressed his pre-conception. "These students *expect* to research dream science. But we already know dreams are just beliefs – remnants of spiritualism. So, this research may be subject to our new protocols."

Marlo watched him with her normal detachment. After he finished, she turned back to Julianna. "These students are genetically unremarkable – exclusively prole heritage. They test as highly intelligent, but cling to an idea that they have, or have had, visions during sleep - dreams. To Mark's point, they characterize these hallucinations similarly to spiritualism."

Mark nodded emphatically in agreement.

"We know that in a fit, socially normalized, happy person, these phenomena don't exist. Look at Thelites as a group. What we don't understand is why they believe this thing that is demonstrably false? Is it fanaticism? Some other disorder? That is one subject of our research," Marlo concluded. She continued to examine Julianna with appraising eyes.

"Ok." Julianna summarized, "I understand that you have some prole students who claim to dream and who voluntarily came forward. So, what are you doing with them?"

Mark answered for Marlo, interrupting again. "We are researching what must be done to correct such disorders, if anything. To do this, we needed willing people with those beliefs, and now we have them!" Whenever Mark spoke, he added a level of excitement to the discussion that Marlo tolerated but didn't seem to share.

Marlo took over with some details. "There are two couples, males and females in committed relationships." When she said this, Mark shook his head and made a dismissive gesture with his eyes, as if it was unbelievable to him. She continued. "One of the couples has been kept in a tightly regulated regimen of diet and fitness, like what you are doing. The other couple has continued their regular living habits, not participating in Thelite regimens.

"To develop and optimize the formulations of spirits for the first couple, each of them has taken a lot of trials. Balancing their diet, fitness, and socialization regimens has taken some time. It's been a while now, and the results are telling.

"The enzymes of the first couple show they are happier, as expected. Their behaviors are normalizing, too. For example, to begin with, they had no interest in sexual recreation beyond their partner. Now, they both enjoy sex with expert consorts. They are less committed to each other and more committed to their rigors. Their sleep is less disturbed. They comply promptly with rules. This is real progress. In fact, with one exception, their behaviors are very similar to model Thelites.

"The second couple is continuing to live in the domestic style common to prole communities. They are not hostile. They are physically comfortable.

236

They are enlightened and curious about participation in the Best Society. But they are less objectively happy than the first couple. They seem a little regretful about their situation. The more time goes by, the more they seem exclusively committed to each other, as if they are fearing or judging the community around them and find comfort only with each other."

Julianna interrupted her curiously. "But what is the exception?"

"Exception?" Marlo asked.

"Yes," Julianna continued. "You said 'with one exception' the first couple behaved like Thelites. What exception?"

"Oh, yes," Marlo recalled. "The exception is that they won't dismiss the idea that they've had dream experiences. They cling to the delusion, even though they say they are no longer having them."

"That's so telling!" Mark interrupted – again – with exaggerated disbelief. He looked at the aides standing nearby, looking for acknowledgement. "Even when you prove with objective science and create the exact experience for them that science would predict, proles will not dismiss these archaic beliefs. It so highlights why Thelites need to accelerate their control of society." The aides appeared to acquiesce but remained silent.

Despite her reregulated, spirit-controlled diet and fitness, Julianna was uncomfortable. She wasn't registering new dreams right now, but she couldn't deny that she had. *Were they simply hallucinations?* That was the scientific explanation, and maybe the truth, but it seemed incomplete. She clearly couldn't discuss it here. She wished she had never dreamed at all, so she didn't have to wonder. And Marlo's tenacious, inquisitive eyes were always on her. *What was she looking for?*

Part of her father's warning was starting to make sense to her. *What words had he used? "Someone was corrupting science?" Was it right that when experience defied current science, that the experience should be held to question?* There – that's what she was uncomfortable with. *But should she raise the question?* She closed her eyes for a moment. When she did so, it was clear to her from her uncle's words. *Deny me!* She deflected instead.

"So, you're telling me we know we can create happiness, even in proles. But we can't eradicate a primary cause of unhappiness – at least not yet?" Julianna probed.

Marlo raised her hand to impolitely restrain Mark while she confirmed to Julianna, "Yes, that's it in summary. Now, we have the unique situation of having three test profiles from willing people with prole genetics. We have the first couple, who has been exposed to fanaticism but is following Thelite behavior-management protocols. We have the second couple, who has been exposed to fanaticism and is continuing to live without those protocols. And we have you, who has never been exposed to fanaticism and has lived your life inside of Thelite protocols.

"And the students who came forward were happy to identify a man whose ideas they follow closely. They refer to him as their teacher, but he appears to be somewhat of a hermit. So, there is evidence of influence by this person who is likely the fanatic. That man is your father's brother. We talked about him earlier – your genetic link."

When Marlo finished her explanation, she lowered her hand, allowing Mark to speak again. "Julianna, did you have any idea you were genetically close to a prole?" he asked.

Deny me! "No. It's weird," Julianna lied quickly. She looked at Mark with sudden curiosity. "Did you?"

"Of course, I did," he bragged. "At least, I knew your father was a prole and that you were born a prole. That's why I was assigned to him in the first place. A prole family couldn't just reside in a Thelite community without close scrutiny."

Julianna had to steady herself as she processed that news. There had been so many open doors in her mind that seemed to slam shut at the same moment. When she looked, Marlo's probing eyes made her queasy. *Could she say anything? No! But why did Mark ask that? Did her father know this? Was Julianna just part of a study, too? Deny me! Get back to the research!* "So, the students think we are researching dream science, but we're really not?" she asked, hoping to steer the discussion away.

238

Whenever Julianna looked directly at Marlo, she felt she was being judged. *Was that question Ok? Did it sound like she was accusing somebody of something?* But Marlo answered her questions without evasion. "Yes. Right now, it is a behavioral analysis. Studying your interactions with them will give us a trove of new data to help identify causes of behaviors outside of our modeled norms."

Mark and Marlo each took note of their aides, who were signaling that there was other business to attend to. Marlo stood. She looked at Mark and said, "Thank you for your interest in this effort, Mark." Mark nodded. He and his aides filed out.

Marlo looked at Julianna and said, "We are ready to proceed with the next phase. Thank you for contributing to this." She and her aides left, and a pair of research technicians came in and took charge.

Julianna was taken to a CosmoPod for background work. Once engaged, she was shown recorded snippets of each student while they did mundane, day-to-day tasks and interactions. She was asked to describe their activities and answer innumerable "why" questions about them. "Why do you think this student uses both hands for this task?" or "Why do you think this student looks down so much?" or "Why do you think this student cocks her head while listening?" She had to infer most of the answers, but she described her thoughts to the best of her ability. This went on for the rest of the afternoon.

She figured out that her characterization of the students was a force-fed, one-way, get-to-know-you session. And it was easy for her. She already knew them.

-33-
She already knew them

2084

She already knew them because they had been in her dreams. Chad, Meghan, Keaton, and Abby were among the students in her earliest dreams. They were in the audience of the debates between her uncle and her father. They had frequently been in her dream community ever since.

She studied them for several days in the CosmoPod. As she learned more about them, she found that she liked them. They were young and intelligent. They were curious and genuine. They believed that Best Society principles could make a better world, and they were anxious to join the effort. But they were also innocent. They believed passionately that dream science should be taken seriously by Thelites, and they offered themselves to that purpose.

She recognized that Keaton was her uncle's assistant from the construction site. But she had never met the others outside of her dreams. She didn't know what to expect. *Would they recognize her?* She couldn't deny to herself that she had met them during her 'hallucinations.' *How would that be interpreted by the behavioral scientists?* She didn't want to risk the appearance of damaging the research that Marlo was working so hard to complete. Until now, she had simply lived with a duality. But from now forward, she knew not to acknowledge any 'dream' familiarity with the students. Nothing could be scientifically proven – so that was her safest path.

After several days of study, Marlo and her aides came to her room. "Well, Julianna," she said, "are you ready to meet them?"

"Oh! Of course," Julianna feigned excitement.

They took an elevator to a higher floor in the building and walked down an interminably long series of airy corridors passing many apartments.

240

Amazed at its scale, Julianna asked, "Do people live in this building?"

"Mostly subjects," Marlo answered. "It is a tightly controlled facility, but very comfortable."

Julianna estimated the capacity for hundreds of subjects on this floor alone. The whole facility must have housed thousands. And this was just one of many regional centers. "Where do they come from?" she asked.

"Most are proles enlisted into research after they demonstrate disorderly reaction to conscriptions," Marlo explained. "Some of them are turned over by other proles out of safety concerns. Separating the disordered from the general population is one benefit the Best Society provides for proles."

Eventually they reached a door and BioGram'd the entry system to hail the occupants. Then they stepped in. They were met by Meghan and Chad, and Marlo introduced them.

"Greetings, Meghan and Chad. This is Julianna-119."

"Greetings," Julianna said, nodding her head.

"Greetings, Julianna," they said simultaneously. They looked at each other and smiled. "It's very nice to meet you," Meghan said brightly.

Marlo noticed the familiarity. "Do you know her?" she asked them, nodding toward Julianna.

"We're aware of Julianna," Chad said. "David is her uncle. But we've never met."

"That's interesting," Julianna faked, casting sidelong glances toward Marlo and her aides, trying to figure out what they were thinking. Marlo was watching her with interest. *Always watching.* "I only recently discovered I had an uncle. My father never said anything about it."

Marlo turned again to Chad and Meghan. "Julianna is a Thelite scientist, but she has prole heritage. Part of our research for BOMN is to monitor your interactions to identify behaviors that are explained by genetic or environmental factors unique to proles."

"Maybe she could be helpful in the dream research as well?" Meghan offered hopefully, to Julianna's distress.

"Perhaps. Work on that is already going on. Your brain scans and energy emissions are being sampled during your checkups and during your sleep. But a comprehensive study is going to take a lot of time. We're still piecing a lot of that together," Marlo explained.

Chad chimed in, "There's something about the environment here. It's very pleasant and we enjoy it. But for some reason, Meghan and I don't dream clearly now. It's unusual. We can't do any research or provide any structure to our ideas."

"That's what we need," Meghan said. "Some validation. We're sure our dreams happen, but there has never been a scientific explanation. We support the conscription of our communities. We think it is counterproductive for people to try to stop it. We hope to work with Thelite institutions to understand dreams and use the discovery to improve society. Maybe dreamers could even be helpful!"

"I hope you're right," Marlo said, subtly non-committal, balancing Meghan's infectious optimism.

Julianna wanted to move the discussion away from dreams. "You two seem like you're comfortable here," she observed.

"Oh, it's great!" Meghan answered. "We wish we could see our friends, of course. But geez, the spirits are awesome. I've never felt better!"

"Human happiness is the goal of the Best Society. Safety, Equality, and Science are fundamental," Julianna confirmed as she recited the familiar platitudes.

"We agree," Chad said. "We just wish we understood how to participate more directly in the research."

"Just be patient," Julianna counseled. "I know from experience that improving these models can be a very involved process. And waiting here certainly isn't a hard duty!" She looked to Marlo for some indication that her comments were appropriate. Marlo remained impassive.

They chatted for a few more minutes. After all their time in the Center, Julianna expected that Chad and Meghan would be discouraged or frustrated, but they weren't. They were enthusiastic about the chance that her introduction was part of the research.

At the prompting of one of her aides, Marlo ended the meeting. As they strode away, Marlo asked, "Any thoughts?"

"Except for their discussion about dreams, they could be like any Thelite."

"Yes," Marlo said. "With that exception, our models totally predict their behaviors. They are happy, fit, and socially acclimated, yet they can't dismiss their fanaticism." She stopped at the door of the lift. "The next couple is also informative."

They went to a different floor of the building and entered the flat of Keaton and Abby. The differences were stark. They didn't engage immediately. They looked tired and fearful, glancing inquisitively at each other before saying things or answering questions.

"Greetings, Keaton and Abby," Marlo said. "This is Julianna-119."

"Greetings," they said in response. Keaton's eyes bugged a little when he looked at Julianna, as if seeking some type of recognition or acknowledgement, but he didn't say anything.

Julianna broke the ice. "Are you comfortable here?" she asked.

"Yes, very comfortable," Abby answered. Then quiet.

Marlo took over. "Our BOMN project is moving along," she explained to them. "Julianna is here because she has prole heritage. She will spend some time with you in the coming weeks. Those interactions will help us understand if there are hereditary or environmental components to the un-modeled behaviors."

"When do you think we can begin the dream research?" Abby asked, suspiciously. "It's been a long time. We haven't had any contact with Meghan or Chad."

"Is he OK?" Keaton asked, looking hard at Julianna. He had a haunted look about him, as if expecting some horrible news. His demeanor alarmed Julianna. *Who did he mean? Was he worried about someone?*

"They're fine," Marlo answered instead. "We are already gathering some data on dreaming. Brain scans, energy emissions, and things like that. That is just one part of the research, and it takes some time."

Keaton and Abby looked at each other for a few moments and then turned back. "Thank you," Keaton said, unenthusiastically. "We look forward to getting this done. We're anxious to see the convergence with the Best Society accelerate and get on with our lives."

The meeting was very short. Julianna, Marlo, and the aides left. While they were walking, Julianna observed, "Keaton and Abby are afraid of something."

"They're proles," Marlo answered. "They may believe in Best Society principles, but they haven't experienced them. Spiritualism is highly correlated with fear and unhappiness. Safety, Equality, and Science are not. Since arriving, they haven't been immersed in Thelite rigors. Chad and Meghan have. It's clear they are not happy compared to Chad and Meghan, and that is the principle difference. In fact, they are less happy and more fearful now than when they arrived."

As they walked together with Marlo's aides trailing, a sense of disproportionality overcame Julianna. *With so many subjects, why was Marlo so interested in just her?* She needed to understand her role more completely. "Marlo, I feel kind of like a lab rat. If I'm going to be helpful, shouldn't I understand how you are learning anything by introducing me to them? What is your hypothesis?"

"Remember that earlier in the century there was more interaction between the prole and Thelite communities. Since then, Thelites have practiced genetic editing. Now Thelite characteristics are encoded in their genetic signature. That has helped Thelite communities advance rapidly to their current order, but it has increased the gulf between modern Thelites and proles. In theory, that genetic gulf exists within you," Marlo explained.

"What difference does that make?" Julianna asked. "It's not like I'm a Neanderthal!"

"A what?" Marlo asked, confused.

"You know, a Neanderthal. I'm human just like you and every other Thelite."

Marlo shook her head briefly, then proceeded in her normal, level tone. "That's not what I'm saying. Yes – we are all human. Proles are all humans.

"Right now, the biggest impediment to conscriptions is that so many proles exhibit regressive behavior. Even when communities are conscripted, these disruptive traditions continue, as if in defiance of the Best Society.

"We cannot rule out a genetic component to this behavior. And if we can break that destructive chain, we can significantly reduce the number of generations it will take for full assimilation."

Julianna was frustrated with the circular logic. She interrupted, "But what does that have to do with me? How can I help?"

Marlo sighed. "Julianna, we need you involved to assess the relative strength of the factors that make proles capable of dismissing objective reality. Your unedited genetics – closely linked to a known prole fanatic – are unique. Yet, you are a model Thelite. Your behaviors have been closely monitored your entire life and generally within the norms of our models. And you've never been exposed to the prole traditions.

"In exposing you to these subjects in a controlled environment, we expect to isolate differences in biometric responses and brain scan characteristics. If you are receptive to their power of suggestion, your brain scans will show identifying patterns that wouldn't be present in a modern Thelite. If we can identify those patterns, we should be able to model and identify behaviors in proles that will not comport with assimilation. Then we can just sort."

"But you've got a whole building full of proles with unedited genetics. Couldn't you just do a population study on them?" she challenged. "I'm a Thelite scientist with important work to do."

Marlo stopped and responded sternly, staring Julianna down.

"I'm starting to understand what Mark means about you! Stop challenging the process! Yes, you *are* a Thelite, serving the Best Society in your most unique capacity!" After several seconds, she softened her voice. "I understand this might trouble you. We appreciate your participation."

"I just want to know how to be helpful," Julianna demurred. "This is different from anything I've ever been involved with."

"And me," Marlo admitted. "I wasn't even personally aware of you until your father transitioned. Your history is fascinating. I intend to learn as much from it as I can."

They parted at the door of Julianna's apartment. Nothing in their discussion made Julianna feel less like a lab rat. Dismally, she recognized that Mark would be no help. *I have nobody!*

-34-
But not necessarily standard work

2084

"Wow!" Meghan exclaimed. "You are really lucky to be a Thelite, Julianna. Everything here is amazing! The facilities, the spirits, the sex! I just can't believe everything is so available. And so good!"

"I agree," Chad nodded. They were seated across from Julianna at a table in an outside, park-like court. The area was entirely enclosed by their building, but roomy and orderly. There were well-tended green spaces, walking paths, and dozens of semi-secluded gathering spots like the one they were using. It wasn't crowded, but several groups used the other amenities. Chad turned to Meghan, "And to think – we thought we had it so good before. Who knew?" Meghan just smiled dreamily.

Julianna really liked them. They were so genuinely excited by the experiences that Thelites took for granted. "Some of many benefits in the Best Society," she agreed. "It's a shame you don't have BioGrams."

"We can't wait," Meghan said excitedly. "We'd love to assimilate as soon as we can. Hopefully we can get these dream studies going soon!"

Julianna was always careful when dreams were mentioned. Her BioGram was continuously forwarding her conversations and base bio-metrics to a NetSystem record. She deflected discussions that might reveal her own experiences. But she was supposed to be providing information to guide behavioral research. So, she mostly just prompted them to talk, then feigned ignorance regarding her own recollections.

"Has anyone discussed how long the study might take?" Julianna asked.

"Nobody has talked to us about that," Chad answered. "All we know is that they are doing research and that it has something to do with you. That makes sense to us, since we believe you've been in so many of our dreams."

"I never know how to respond to that," Julianna evaded. "It's difficult to envision."

"Not for us it isn't," Chad answered. "You showed up a while ago. You were often in dream space with Dr. Sanderson. Sometimes you were even his subject. More recently, you have just been in dream space like a lot of us. Communicating. If you were an experienced dreamer, you would remember all of this."

"Can you tell me about Dr. Sanderson? How did you meet him?" Julianna tried to lead them in a different direction. She didn't want to get drawn into her own dream memories where she was a subject.

"Sure!" Chad acknowledged. "My dad knew him. They grew up close to each other. See, my family had a foundry until it was conscripted from my grandfather. My dad and grandfather worked together there until my grandfather was killed in an explosion. It was horrible. My dad saw it all, but then he had to take over the next day. I was just a toddler then, but he's still bitter.

"Dr. Sanderson was always very helpful at the foundry because he was so good with the science. He helped Dad figure out what caused the explosion. My dad says they did this while dreaming. They did a lot to advance foundry science but always kind of secretly. My dad and my grandfather never believed in the optimum allocation model to run the foundry. They didn't really try to make it work, and they weren't interested in sharing what they discovered with the Bureau. That never made sense to me."

"That's quite a story," Julianna said. "So you met Dr. Sanderson through your father, somehow?"

"Yes," Chad answered. "My father encouraged me to attend the trade college – not to work in the foundry business. Dr. Sanderson was a frequent lecturer at the college. We connected right away."

"What were his lecture topics?"

"Mostly technical – applied science in medicine, agriculture, construction, and manufacturing. For me it was great. I was doubling in agriculture and construction science. He's experienced and he's a really good teacher. He's great at figuring out real-world workarounds to flawed virtual models. The Best Society really needs that," Chad asserted.

Chad and Meghan looked at each other and nodded. "But," Chad said, "a lot like you, he never said anything about dreaming in person."

"What do you mean?" Julianna said, with internal alarm bells clanging. "I don't know what you're talking about!" she exclaimed.

"That's what we can't figure out. We interacted with Dr. Sanderson an awful lot in our dreams, and you were in our dreams," Meghan said, much too assuredly for Julianna's comfort. "But you don't acknowledge it in person. Everybody hides it. That's why we need this study!"

"This is why we've come forward," Chad explained. "My grandfather probably died because everyone at the foundry defied the Best Society principles. What a waste! My father and Dr. Sanderson blamed it all on the Best Society's models. But what if people like my father and grandfather were more open to Best Society principles, and our dreams were scientifically understood? Wouldn't that be the best of everything? Maybe conscriptions would be nonviolent!" Chad was passionate.

Julianna did not want to get dragged into a discussion of dream experiences. "So how did you two meet?" Julianna asked Meghan, clumsily attempting to divert the topic.

"Oh. Well, formally, Abby introduced us," Meghan answered. "But I knew who Chad was long before that. We all grew up in the same community. Chad and Abby were classmates at the college. I was two years behind.

"Abby wanted a trade education in medicine. When we were teenagers, our mom – Sandy – developed respiratory problems. She fought it for years using medical services available in our community. Eventually Dad admitted her to the Thelite hospital in the Hub. They made her a lot more comfortable, but she died within weeks. Abby always thought that if she could have made Mom more comfortable at home, that she might have lived more comfortably and longer. She wanted to learn those skills.

"Dad wasn't happy with Abby's choice. They fought, and she went to live with Keaton. When it was time for me – there was no question; I was going to the Thelite college. I'm training in NetSystem information models. We use the NetSystem to assemble information from all the various sources and create new productions. I actually got to use a CosmoPod last term! It was amazing…" Meghan beamed.

Julianna was fascinated with Meghan's experience. *Proles actually thought it was wise to select their own professions?*

"Chad," Julianna inquired. "How come you selected agriculture and construction science?"

"I enjoy science. I just find those topics interesting," he answered. "And," he added proudly, "I'm the top of my class!"

"What does that mean?" Julianna asked. She was confused by the idea of ranking within a common discipline. "Aren't all of you educated uniformly?"

"We all take the same subjects, yes," he said. "But we are given practical assessments, and our work is measured. For example, if the yield from my hydroponic growth center is greater than someone else's, I am ranked higher. Especially if that is consistent over time."

"Interesting," Julianna said. "But doesn't your growth center comport with the optimum allocation model? My father's model was supposed to be totally inclusive."

"Yes, it does. The allocation model also projects certain improvements in performance over time, based on history." Chad thought for a moment. "You know how centuries ago, agriculture took the bulk of humanity's labor and vast tracts of land to feed a much smaller population?" he asked.

"Yes," Julianna said. "As humans devolved from nomadic hunting and gathering to more stable communities," she recalled.

"And how over the years its practice became largely automated and industrialized but dangerously unsustainable for the ecosystem?" he asked again.

"Yes, I'm aware. And I know that those dangers were alleviated by new technologies. That trajectory of improvement is baked into my father's models," Julianna said. The intersection of her father's work and Chad's experience was compelling discussion.

"That is the role of trade education," Chad explained. "The allocation model doesn't direct how the improvements happen. It assumes them. But it also stipulates that those types of assets should be given over to the people who improve them the most. While it doesn't say how those improvements are realized, it apportions those assets to people who best apply their skills. It's the same with construction, foundry work, and everything else, I think."

"I hadn't thought of it that way before," Meghan had been listening intently. "These models are really important. But what if you didn't do those things? I mean the improvements. How could the model work?"

"Yes," Julianna recalled her own questions. "What if the models assume something that doesn't happen? Then what?"

"I don't know. I mean, my father seemed to quit trying at the foundry. I know he had ideas. I thought he didn't want the model to work. Maybe he just wasn't motivated?" Chad wondered aloud.

"Motivated?" Julianna was intrigued. "What should that have to do with it? Couldn't standard work improve things in sync with the models?"

"Maybe. I'm sure you could improve a little by complying with standards. But Dr. Sanderson taught that inspiration, know-how, and opportunity were the bases for innovation. Work, yes. But not necessarily standard work. Much human progress was made by renegades who *defied* the conventions of their time," Chad explained.

Julianna was fascinated. Mark expected her to *believe* in the models. *Did those words make sense? Was skepticism just as important?* She sensed that her uncle would have approved of her raising the questions on her own model. But those very actions got her in trouble.

"But why would anybody do that?" she asked. "What if they were wrong?"

251

"I suspect many of history's innovators were dreamers, too. So they were armed with some certainty as they did their work. That brings us back to this whole study! Why aren't we dreaming right now? I miss my dreams…" Meghan finished wistfully.

"How close are we to starting?" Chad asked. "We love it here, but it would be great to see the science developed! It would make everything so much better!"

"I see why you think that," Julianna answered. "I don't know the schedule. But I sure enjoy our visits."

"Well," Meghan said as she and Chad stood, "so do we. But we've planned some things this afternoon. Lots to do, here! We'll talk later, Julianna!"

"Bye," Julianna said as they strode away together. *Whew. That was close. Hopefully no damage!*

-35-
We'll be good parents

2084

"I think we might have made a big mistake," Keaton said, seated protectively close to Abby. He glanced at her guiltily. "If Dr. Sanderson were running this project, research would be moving by now."

"How well do you know Dr. Sanderson," Julianna asked. The three of them sat on comfortable couches around a coffee table in their apartment. The courtyard several floors below was visible through a large window at the end of the room. There was activity in the courtyard, but the room was quiet. Julianna sensed that Keaton and Abby rarely left.

"Very well," he said. "I've assisted him for many years. We created the most powerful lectures and demonstrations that you could imagine. Together. It was challenging work. Even a Thelite would be impressed." Keaton seemed proud, but his tone was stoic. "I also helped him as a construction manager for Best Society Services."

They avoided direct eye contact. *He knows to keep it secret!* Julianna felt relieved.

Abby took over. "We met at those lectures. I went to a lot of them – they were so good. Afterwards, we sat around discussing what we'd learned. It was fun. We didn't know each other well, but I could tell that Keaton and I would have a future together," she looked at him with a placating smile.

"Are you being treated all right?" Julianna probed.

"Oh, yes," Abby answered. "We get everything we need. People are very attentive. There's plenty to do if we want to do it. But there's no…no…people? You know what I mean? Everyone who talks to us, it's like their job. Not something they just want to do. It is taking a long time."

"Why do you think you've made a mistake, Keaton?" Julianna asked.

"It just doesn't feel right," he answered. "Developing an experimental trial shouldn't take this long. Dr. Sanderson and I did a lot of research together, and things just moved more quickly."

"And our dreams are different," Abby added.

"Abby!" Keaton cautioned.

"Please don't worry so much," she replied in a conciliatory tone, taking his hand. "This is why we decided to do this." She turned back to Julianna. "Our dreams have a different personality now. Our involvement with Meghan, Chad, Dr. Sanderson, even you – they're all, I don't know the word, distant? Like we're there, but they're lost? I don't know how to explain it. But I understand what Keaton is feeling. It's different and scary," she concluded.

Julianna was alarmed by Abby's reference to her in the dream. "I can't really understand," she said, turning to Keaton. "But who knows what to expect with such a new study?"

"This isn't how I thought it would go at all. Nobody has even asked about our dreams. We have these interviews, we do these exercises, we talk to you, and then we have these assessments. It's like we're being diagnosed – not studied. We don't have any tools to do our own modeling. I can't understand why they brought us here if this is all we're going to do," he explained.

"And I really miss Meghan," Abby moaned.

"Aren't there other opportunities to socialize?" Julianna asked. "Can't you go to the community rooms? Or the Center?"

Abby guffawed. "The Center!? Sure, it's been offered, but I would never..." she looked possessively at Keaton. "And neither would he!"

Julianna found their attentiveness to each other charming. "Oh? Why?" she asked, innocently.

"Julianna!" Abby was aghast. "Keaton and I are in love. We hope to start a family. It's the most important thing in our lives! I wouldn't give that up for anything!"

"I'm sorry," Julianna rebutted. "I wasn't aware. The Canon explains how 'families' used to work in prole culture. But I didn't know the idea was still so…common? Is that the right word?"

"Well it is!" Abby said. "Meghan and I grew up together with our parents. We did everything together. That's the way it's supposed to be."

Keaton interrupted. "I agree – that's the way it's best. It's the way I want our family to be. But it doesn't always work that way. Remember? I ran away from a crappy home on the streets. I was a mess until I met Delores. Now Delores and your Uncle David – they're my family – but I'm not related to either of them." He put his arm around Abby and pulled her closer. "But Abby and I hope to have children. We'll be good parents. We'll make a better home than I had."

Julianna was astounded by the disclosure. "Children? By yourselves? Isn't that dangerous?" Julianna aimed her last question at Abby. "Why would you put yourself through that?"

"It's just part of life. I want to have children with Keaton more than anything in the world," Abby admitted, nestling into Keaton's arm. "I want to care for them, to see them grow, and just be a normal family."

"Children are that important to you?" Julianna puzzled. "I had no idea how ingrained the idea of having a family was. I only knew my father. But he recently transitioned."

"Oh, Julianna. I'm so sorry," Abby wrestled free of Keaton's arm to grab her hand. The sympathy caught Julianna off guard. Holding Abby's hand gave her comfort that she didn't know she sought. "I know how you feel," Abby said softly. "Meghan and I lost our mother a few years ago. We still miss her." They shared a quiet connection with moist eyes.

Uncomfortable with the emotion, Keaton cleared his throat. "Julianna, just so you know, families can be pretty much anything. Abby and Meghan's was typical. Two parents in an exclusive relationship with two kids. Abby and I hope to be like that. But there are other situations. Some like mine – one parent who really wasn't a parent. Some parents have more than one partner. Some people live in communes where they don't even pair off. Prole families come in all shapes and sizes!"

Julianna released Abby's hand. "That sounds pretty random," she observed.

"True. It can be a mess!" Abby exclaimed brightly and snuggled back into Keaton. "But I still can't wait to meet our children!"

They laughed. Julianna felt she had helped them. They seemed less fearful as their conversation moved to lighter matters. Julianna reflected jealously that she wanted to feel the way Abby felt – about Keaton, Meghan, families, or anyone. Such complete connection. Since her father died, Julianna had none of that.

As the session ended, Abby called the question. "Julianna," she said earnestly, "you seem like the only one we can talk to. Surely you understand why we think dreaming can benefit the Best Society. We are anxious to get on with the study and get on with our lives. What can we do to move this along?"

Julianna was forced to lie. "Be patient," she said. "These studies take time."

-36-
Until now

2084

For the next few weeks, Julianna spent her days socializing with each couple. If a dream association was raised, Julianna asked them to describe it. She would offer none of her own recollections. After, she would submit to brain scans and psychological tests.

She enjoyed the more illustrative descriptions of dreams. "I remember Chad wasn't a person," Meghan said. "He was a personality! There was no body or face to him. There was just a hollow, gentle spot in space that was personable. It's hard to describe a dream-being, but I knew exactly who he was. I could tell that we were going to meet and that we would have a future."

"I beg to differ," Chad argued. "I met you in that dream! You had everything! Your sunny personality, your cute face, your lovely figure. I knew what you looked like. I knew what you were thinking – and, yes, I knew we would meet. I even knew what to say that would make you like me!"

But Julianna avoided comparing notes with them between her dreams and their descriptions. Keaton seemed to choose his words carefully, as if avoiding descriptions that might trap her. Julianna used that wiggle room to her advantage.

"It seemed like your personality just laid over the whole session like a big, clear blanket – not like a person who was *there*," Keaton told her. "And perhaps there were others there – not just you – like layers of blankets, and every blanket was another person. It seemed like a group of us just lying there, looking at the sky through the layers of blankets. But somehow, we might have been listening to Dr. Sanderson and your father meditating at the same time. No voices at all – just thoughts moving around."

"But I was like a moth or a butterfly," Abby recalled. "I would flutter from a bush to a flower to a leaf on a tree. Each of the things I landed on was an idea, or a person making a point. I would look for certain colors that were like points of view, and I could land more than one place at a time. I was able to explore and understand the arguments that were being made."

Their recounting of settings, durations, and conversations defied description – phantasmagorical – and they were different from each other's and from hers. There were common pieces, like ideas and lessons. She hadn't experienced the particulars of their dreams, even though she definitely shared many of the same experiences. *Dreams must be unique to the dreamer.*

They were attentive as she described life in a Thelite community. Chad and Meghan were increasingly enthusiastic. They talked about their future, how they might fit, and what they might enjoy the most. Keaton and Abby were reserved, sharing less detail with each session. They expected their future would be in a prole community, and they grieved the loss of connection with Chad and Meghan.

The more she learned about their life's experience, though, the more conflicted she was about the importance of Thelites' work. *Yes, their lives were uncertain.* They didn't know their future situation or that their work would be fairly rewarded. Their health may fail for an avoidable reason. But there were indescribable experiences she never had as a Thelite. Families. There wasn't just happiness. Proles grieved, but found comfort; they feared, but found relief; they were sad, but found joy.

Julianna also harbored deep suspicion that she, too, was a subject of the research. Marlo didn't treat her like a peer engaged in a common project. On the rare occasions that she saw Marlo, Julianna sensed that she was scheduled precisely between "cases" – and that she was just another one. Marlo always seemed to look *through* Julianna, not *at* her. Julianna constantly worried that she wasn't successfully hiding what needed to be hidden.

The duality exhausted her. She couldn't lapse back into dreaming. The only antidote was to devote herself to her Thelite cause. Her very survival depended on sustaining her Thelite rigors.

258

When she had access to a CosmoPod, she spent hours digesting the recent progress of the Best Society. NetGrams reported new emphasis on the identification of spiritual leaders and their propensity to seed disorder among proles. She was left wondering if there was still violent resistance and death.

She noticed the acronym BOMN (Behaviors Outside Modeled Norms) became a common descriptor for prole subjects who participated in nonconforming behaviors. BOMN disorder, BOMN candidate, BOMN interference – the word was everywhere. "Centering Prole Behaviors" became a multi-bureau cause and a primary objective of the High Council. Segments of Social Awareness Training had been improved, informing young Thelites how eradicating BOMN disorder served the health and happiness of all humanity. Marlo's work was frequently cited, but Mark was constantly referenced as a champion of increasing the pace of the effort.

One day Marlo and her aides came to Julianna's room unexpectedly. "Julianna, there is someone you need to see," Marlo announced.

"Oh. Someone new?" she asked.

"Yes," Marlo answered, but she didn't elaborate. Marlo led her out of the room to the lift and down to a subterranean floor. They didn't speak. The only noises were the footsteps of the group as they echoed while walking through the interminable bowels of the building. Julianna had weird premonitions of peril but followed docilely. *Why must I always feel so helpless?*

Marlo stopped to open a door and beckoned Julianna to enter the room, then followed her in.

The tiny space was filled with a spaghetti of tubes and wires that were connected to the body of a man. The body was on a gurney and mostly covered with a sheet, but some features were distantly familiar to Julianna.

Be still. This seems dangerous.

There were machines clicking and hissing among the tubes. The walls were covered with panels and charts graphing biological functions that were being controlled or measured in the body. The panels and the room itself seemed too cluttered, like there was no way to move without disrupting one of the wires or machines and no way to know which ones were most important.

Marlo was watching her closely. "When your father came to his role here as a Thelite, he brought you along. But he left a family behind, including his brother," she stated. "This is Dr. David Sanderson, your father's brother, your uncle."

The body was limp and lifeless and almost unrecognizable to her. Unkempt gray hairs hung loose from his scalp. His clammy, mushroom-colored skin wrinkled grossly where his muscles should have been taught. There were deep, streaky discolorations where needles had penetrated his veins. His feet protruded from the sheet with yellowed, misshapen nails. A tube that went down his throat was taped to his face, twisting his mouth into an ugly sneer. The odor in the room was a combination of bleach and body odor. The room was chilly.

Julianna felt faint, uncoordinated, and claustrophobic all at once. *This couldn't be David! Where were his mirthful eyes? His nervous twitches? His voice? What monster could do this to him?*

He was so vital. Just like my father. So smart...so good...why? She was outraged. *Were my father's last moments like this?*

She wanted to cry or strike somebody. But she remembered David's words: *"Deny me!"* She had to concentrate. *Am I safe? Just keep your eyes focused.* She struggled to keep her composure when she looked at Marlo. "I don't..." she stumbled. "I don't know...him," she lied. "What is wrong with him?"

"We brought him here after the students identified him. We intended to structure his living regimen to Thelite protocols. We planned to have you get to know him – an actual fanatic." Marlo spoke just as if there wasn't a horrifying body laying right in front of her, whose chest only rose and fell in time with some machines' ticks and buzzes. Cold.

"But like so many proles, the benefit was lost on him. He refused. He didn't eat or drink for three days. So, we anesthetized him. He receives nutrition intravenously. Unfortunately, our studies won't be conclusive. Nutrition alone can't create the same enzyme affect as the synchronization of diet, fitness, and socialization. Hopefully he will regain consciousness, and you can meet him," Marlo concluded. Somehow, Marlo could look right at him with no distaste.

Julianna was disturbed by the word "hopefully." She tried to remove herself from what she was feeling. "I'm not sure what you expect from me," she said. "Is there something I'm supposed to do or say about him?"

"No," Marlo answered. "We just thought you should see him and understand your relationship. A real person. A prole. How do you react to knowing that you were born a close relative of this prole?"

Julianna hoped she wasn't shaking. *Is my voice quavering? Don't let it!* "I don't feel anything," Julianna said. But she did. She was barely succeeding to control her breathing and heart rate. "I feel the same. I've never had any second thoughts about Best Society principles." *Until now.*

Julianna felt faint. She felt on the verge of her knees buckling when at last, just in time, Marlo opened the door and steered her out of the room. While walking back to Julianna's room, Marlo said, "You should attend to your nutrition and fitness now. Then we'll get some final brain scans." That was her first indication that her work was nearly done. *What did she mean by "final"?*

-37-
You've been very helpful

The following morning Julianna was summoned to a meeting area. Marlo, Mark, their aides, and several behavioral scientists were gathered at a NetSystem surface. They were examining images of colorful data streams, like plasma rainbows crisscrossing each other on the floor they stood on. They were pointing out and discussing the tendencies of the streams to change speed, bend, and vary in color and intensity, hypothesizing explanations.

Mark spoke first. "Well, Julianna. Your sessions are complete. Thank you for your help."

"Complete?" Julianna questioned. "Really? I thought this would take longer. What did we learn?"

"We are still characterizing the details," said another scientist. "The brain scans and bio-metrics of both couples – and yours – are indistinct. We were unable to identify a specific signature for spiritual propensities. We expected a different outcome. But that's why we do studies."

One of the other scientists further explained, "We attempted to decode brain scans and energy emissions of Keaton and Abby, who still claimed to dream. No patterns in the data correlated to their recollections or distinguished them from any other prole, claiming dreams or not. It was an entirely unremarkable outcome."

"Ah," Julianna responded. "So, this was a waste of time?" she asked, looking directly at Marlo, who looked back unwaveringly but said nothing.

"Not really. Even the lack of explanation gives us information," the first person continued. "In the absence of specific signatures, we conclude that spiritual behaviors are unable to be modeled."

The second person continued. "Evidently, once a prole has adopted spiritual practices, they are impossible to displace. This is based on observations more than anything, both now and historically. Explaining the lack of evidence doesn't affect them. Demonstrating the science-based alternatives doesn't either. Even though they otherwise act rationally. It appears to be a permanent disorder that affects some population of proles."

Mark interrupted. "And, if it's impossible to model, it can't be allowed. That's the new protocol. Now we can focus on alternatives to eradicate them. It's going to take some effort, but it's clearly the right path. And hopefully faster than improving the model."

Julianna watched Marlo as Marlo watched each person speak. Always with her haunting gaze. No nods of approval no shaking her head – just watching. No hint of her thoughts. Nothing. Her impassiveness seemed sociopathic. Now she was looking at Julianna.

It was chilling.

To Marlo, Julianna asked the question she didn't want to know the answer to. "And the students?"

Mark answered without hesitation, drawing Julianna's attention away from Marlo. "We've discovered what we can from the students. And Dr. Sanderson. Marlo has been directed to send them to the Center for Transition Management."

Julianna digested the news with terror. *"Deny me!"* she heard again inside her head. *Don't show it! Don't care about this!* Looking at Mark, she struggled self-consciously to control her face. *Was her chin quavering?* She sought her next words for interminable moments before Marlo saved her.

"So again, thank you, Julianna. You've been very helpful," Marlo said, drawing Julianna's eyes back to her. Marlo's dead eyes looked back, unblinking. *What was she seeing?*

Julianna was quiet for a moment as she came to understand that she was being dismissed. "So I can go?" she asked.

"Soon," Marlo said. "Your recovery is complete. We are processing the details of all your brain scans. Nothing was learned from Dr. Sanderson, your genetic link. So you're done here."

"Soon?" Julianna asked. "What more is there?"

Mark answered, "You remember your thirtieth birthday is this week? It's time for your quint-annual check-in. Before you go, we will update your overall health status based on the protocols at the Center for Health Solutions. That will also validate that your recovery has been appropriately managed."

Mark was looking at her with his matter-of-fact face. More than she saw them, she felt several of the aides moving toward her, as if to prevent her from running. But she couldn't move her feet, even if she wanted to. *And where would she go?* She looked from face to face to face of each person: all blank. No sorrow. No outrage. It seemed inhuman. Out of the corner of her eye, she sensed Alexa step to her side and grab her gently on her upper arm. She felt a slight pinch on her arm where Alexa was holding her. The last thing she remembered before losing consciousness was sinking into the endless depth of Marlo's hollow eyes.

-38-
Can you go back?

2084

Julianna's dreamscape was a dark hurricane of noisy, terrifying forms. Strange apparitions screeched around the space like screaming, violently colored, air-born jellyfish. She was there a long time, sensing but not registering, feeling but not knowing. Sentences came out of her as erratic jumbles; thoughts were not connected; she tried to make herself understood to the cosmos that was impatiently trying to ignore her. Forces like magnets were trying to pull different parts of her into the raging confusion that was all around her, jerking and deforming her in weird ways as she tried to hold herself still in the torrent, knowing that she couldn't let it take her.

A horrible moan was coming from nowhere and everywhere at the same time. It would get louder as it went through her, then softer as it went away, but then it would come back like an audible pendulum. She spun in place trying to follow it, bracing herself in place with tremendous effort. The moan kept centering closer to her, then it focused itself on an apparition that took the form of her Uncle David, but not like a regular body. The moan didn't come from his mouth. It came from his whole being. His body was like a phantom blowing in the tempest; parts of his body were beating and tearing into other parts while his eyes were still, staring at her in horrific delirium and torturous pain.

"Ooooooooh! You shouldn't be here," his body shrieked. "I was wrong! So wrong!" Then he blew away and appeared again on another side of her. She struggled against the forces while she turned to him. "What do you mean?" she attempted to say. *Could he hear her?* "Don't you see? Ooooooooh! It was me! Forgive me! Forgive me!" He blew away again to another side. "What are you talking about?" she cried, no longer trying to turn, working so very hard to hold her place. Now he was blowing all around her, momentarily in

265

front of her, then gone, then back. "You shouldn't be here! Oh, it was me! It was me! I am your danger! You didn't need to know! Oooooooh!"

Julianna let the forces twist her for a moment until she regained stability. *Where was he? Where was she?* Then she heard his scream from afar, somewhere she couldn't see. "Oooooooh! Go back! Can you go back? Forgive me!" She twisted to follow the voice, but she couldn't. "Go back where?" she yelled. But he was disappearing. "Forgive me!" his voice kept repeating, simultaneously with his haunting moan, over and over, more softly until she couldn't hear it at all over the tumult.

Then she gave up. She was exhausted. The forces took her, like a giant roller coaster inside of a tornado. She was rocked, thrown, pummeled, struck, turned upside down, and twisted with no breath to scream. Then she sensed that she was squirted out of the melee into a peaceful sky where she fell, far and freely to familiar earth, and landed softly, as if she was set there by a gentle hand. Now quiet. The storm was gone.

She stood, shocked that she was unharmed. She looked around and noticed Delores sitting on a bench. She was peaceful, alone, and somehow notable against the landscape – as if she was a faded black-and-white character in the middle of a bright, colorful photograph. She was looking straight at Julianna and beckoning her toward her without moving or saying anything.

Julianna walked hesitantly toward the bench. She didn't know what to expect from Delores. *Would she be hostile...disappointed? Lonely?* Julianna wasn't afraid; she just didn't know how to act.

As she approached, Delores spoke, "Hello, Julianna. I've missed you."

"Missed me?" Julianna asked with confusion. "We've only met once!"

Delores was unfazed and looked at Julianna with a face that somehow transmitted welcome, peace, forgiveness, and warmth without changing.

"I'm sorry," Julianna said, piqued by Delores' disarming visage. "Greetings, Delores. It's nice to see you again," she said solemnly. Without being asked in any way other than the invitation on Delores' face, Julianna sat next to her. They were quiet for a long, long time.

"I miss them," Delores finally said.

"Them?" Julianna asked.

"Sandy. Your father," Delores clarified. "Your uncle."

"Why don't you miss the students?" Julianna asked with emotionless curiosity. "Because they betrayed my uncle?"

"They meant well," she said. "They couldn't know what would happen."

Quiet again. They watched the peaceful world as if from inside a bubble.

"Would you like to come to my shop?" Delores finally asked.

"No, thank you," Julianna said. "I've recovered now. I'm afraid I would relapse if I went with you."

Delores nodded. After a moment, she said, "I've been trying to see you for weeks. I'm glad you finally hear me."

"Hear you?" Julianna asked.

"Yes. You can never stop hearing, really. Many of us hear you, too, and send you blessings," Delores said.

"Hallucinations," Julianna clarified. "They're like drugs. When I started, I couldn't stop – even though it was endangering me. Now that I'm recovered, I need to be disciplined." Then, after a moment, she said, "Though I am glad to see you here."

"I see," Delores responded. Then she waited quietly.

"What are you going to do?" Julianna asked.

"I'm old and my work is done. I will pass soon and leave the world to my friends." Delores said this without remorse or second-guessing. "There are still a lot of people like me, happy with our humble lives."

"Happy, really?" Julianna challenged. "That defies scientific proof."

"I know," Delores said. "I've heard it all before. Your father was a great debater."

They were quiet again, neither wanting to argue the point.

"There are lots of people like you, too, Julianna. Good people. Capable people. Thinking but not certain people," she said, confusing Julianna, who simply nodded.

After a moment, Delores offered, "I've brought you a gift." She handed an envelope to Julianna. "Please take it."

Julianna took it, assuming it was more tea. "Thank you," she said, but she didn't mean it. She didn't want to offend Delores, but she planned to throw it away as soon as they separated.

"What are you going to do now?" Delores asked, as if she had read Julianna's mind.

"Oh," Julianna recalled, surprising herself. "I'm thirty! I need to check in at the Center for Health Solutions."

Delores looked at her with deep compassion. She took Julianna's hands in her own. "Please don't go. Please come to my shop instead."

"No," Julianna said softly. "I'm happy now, and I don't want to be unhappy again."

Delores nodded, reluctantly ending her plea.

Something was pulling on Julianna again. Her body was being compelled away, like a light suction. She resisted, but the pull kept growing stronger. She finally spoke, "I think I have to go now."

"I understand," Delores said. The look on her face was still serene. She tightened her grip on Julianna's hands. "Your father and your uncle," she said, "they were different. But they were truth-seekers. You are, too. There are others. You need to know that."

Then, she kissed Julianna's cheek, stood, and walked away. Julianna struggled with the forces pulling on her as she watched her go, her body fading more the farther she went. After a few moments, she just disappeared completely in a dim flash of light.

The forces on her kept strengthening. She had to fight them more urgently now, seeking a refuse container. Spying one in the distance, she trudged toward it to discard the offending package. Bracing herself with her legs, she opened the lid with one hand, holding Delores' gift in her other hand. Then, confused about her own reactions, she stopped. *Was it subconscious inspiration she was feeling...or was it rationalized guilt?* She couldn't tell. But somehow, she knew it was right to just close the lid. She tucked Delores' gift under her arm and let the forces suck her away. Then nothing.

-39-
Not very believable

2084

"Do you believe them?" Marlo asked. At least, she thought it was Marlo. Julianna was afraid to answer. *Am I awake? How?* She mumbled something incoherent. *Why is it so dark? Oh, my eyes are closed. I will try to open them in a bit. When I have more energy.* Then she disappeared. She didn't know how long.

"Do you believe them?" Marlo asked again, patiently. *Yes. That's Marlo. What is she talking about?* She kept her eyes closed but felt herself awakening. *Conscious! Was she alive? Or was this something else?* She still said nothing. Too much effort.

"She's waking up," a voice announced. People moved around, things rolled, buttons clicked, fingers tapped on screens and tablets. *Busy things happened when people wake up.* Her thoughts seemed smudged, lazy. Her head hurt. Not like a headache. Like she had hit her head above and behind her left ear. *She must have fallen when, when, …when what?*

She tried her eyes. They opened, blinking rapidly for several seconds until the light quit hurting. She rocked her head slightly from side to side and moved her arms and legs just to see if she could. She could. She was not restrained. When she was convinced she was able, she turned her head in the direction of the activity in the room. Two attendants were fussing with complicated-looking gadgetry, tubes, and clear bags of liquid. Marlo was seated near her bed looking at her.

Over her shoulder, Marlo spoke to one of the attendants. "Is she ready?"

"Almost. Another minute or so."

Julianna felt her consciousness return steadily. Marlo was looking at her calmly. She dimly recalled her last conscious moment, when she was pulled into Marlo's eyes. Now she felt as if she was coming back out of them. They were familiar now. Less scary. Whatever was going to happen was going to happen.

"Can you hear me?" Marlo asked.

Julianna nodded slightly. Then she tried her voice. "Yes." It was rough. An attendant held a paper cup of water to her lips. She sipped and cleared her throat. "Yes," she tried again. Not perfect. But it would get better. She took more sips, and the attendant took the cup away.

"Can you give us some privacy, yet?" she asked the attendants.

"One moment," one of them answered. They made some final adjustments to the instruments that were taped on and plugged into Julianna, poked for several seconds on their tablets, and then left the room. Julianna had never been alone with Marlo before. She was intimidating.

"Where am I?" Julianna asked.

"In the wing of the Behavioral Science Research Center dedicated to transition management for research subjects," Marlo answered.

"Why?" Julianna asked.

"Once your help researching the student behaviors was completed, your value crossed over. According to the models. Evidently, your value is diminished by your disruptive behaviors. Awfully young for that," Marlo explained.

"So why am I...why am I not dead?"

"You were on your way. You've been in a coma for several days. I stopped the process."

She touched her scalp timidly. Julianna asked foggily, "But what happened to my head?"

"Your head is injured because your BioGram has been removed. They are always removed to avoid using them in the delirium of a coma," Marlo answered. Then she clarified, "I stopped the process because I need you to answer some questions."

"Questions?"

"Yes. Do you believe them?" Marlo asked.

"Who?"

"The students. Do you believe them? When they describe their dreams?" Marlo's probing eyes were on her again.

She knew she couldn't say yes. "I don't know what you mean," Julianna said. "What difference does it make if I believe something?"

Marlo poked on her tablet for a moment. "Who is Delores?" she asked. It was uncanny how Marlo trapped her with these questions. Watching her again.

"Delores?" *How could Marlo know about Delores? Where was this going? Was there any way to save her own life?* She was too drugged to think clearly, but she knew she just wanted to stay awake. Talk longer…

"Keaton talked about Delores to you one day. You never asked who she was. It was like you both knew her. Do you know her?"

"I was just letting him talk," Julianna said. "Delores is another prole I think."

"Inconsistent," Marlo shook her head and looked at her tablet, then back at Julianna. "What is a 'Neanderthal'?"

"A Neanderthal?" Julianna asked in confusion.

"You were talking to me one day, and you said you were not a 'Neanderthal,'" Marlo explained.

"You know. The subspecies of humans before they went extinct in ancient times. Neanderthals," she said slowly, making sure she pronounced it right.

"I don't know that," Marlo responded. "I've never heard that word. I've researched the entire Canon for references to it. The only references I found were archival, nothing that would ever be taught. The evolutionary path of humanity is described in models that no longer use those names – but you used it. How did you know it?"

"I don't know how I knew it. I just knew it. I thought everyone knew it. I must have stumbled on it in my own research," she lied. *How did she know it?*

"Hm," Marlo said, looking at her critically. "Not very believable."

Marlo poked at her tablet some more, then looked back up at Julianna. "How do you know so much about the history of agriculture?" she asked.

"History of agriculture?" Julianna asked again. "I don't know what you're talking about at all."

"Chad was discussing the history of agriculture with you. You were fluent in the specifics of the development of agriculture. But again, this topic is not part of Canonical teaching. Agricultural performance models don't require that knowledge of history. So how do you know it?"

"I don't know," Julianna said, frustrated. "I don't know how I know or why I know this stuff. I just know things. Why is it important how I know things?" she asked.

Marlo kept looking at her like she was trying to decide whether to answer. *If only I could read through those eyes, to know what she was thinking.*

"Don't you think it is important that behavioral science research should include an understanding of how people know things?" Marlo asked rhetorically.

Julianna was immediately attentive. *Was that her opening?* "Yes," she said carefully. "Now that you put it that way, I would think it is very important that you understand how people know things."

"I thought so," Marlo said. "So, do you believe them?"

"The students?" she asked.

"Yes. The students. Do you believe them?"

273

Julianna picked her words with caution. "I think the students believe themselves."

Marlo snapped in threatening exasperation. "Julianna, you are trying to control this conversation, but you can't. *I* am in charge. *I* stopped the process. *I* need to know these things. Quit being coy. Do you believe them?"

Julianna felt like every answer was a trap. "Why do you care so much if I believe them?" she nearly cried. "Why is it so important?"

Marlo sat back and, for the first time, softened her gaze. "It's important, Julianna, because *I* believe them."

-40-
Scientists need to do that

2084

"What…do you…believe about them, exactly?" Julianna asked, not completely certain where the conversation was going.

"I believe they are having the experiences they describe," Marlo acknowledged. "I also believe it is more than a mental disorder, that it is real. And that if we could understand it, it would be valuable to humanity."

Julianna felt herself relax. But not completely. She wanted to share her thoughts and experiences. *But was this a setup? Would an admission hurt her? No, don't admit anything. Yet.* Marlo's eyes were less cold, but they weren't warm. Still judgmental. *Go carefully.*

"Why do you believe them?" Julianna asked.

"Mostly by observing you when you interacted with them," Marlo said.

"Me?" Julianna was shocked. "What do I have to do with them?"

"You have empathy for them that can only be explained by shared perspectives, shared knowledge, or shared experiences," Marlo explained. "Even though I know from your BioGram record that you've never had the chance to interact or share physical space with them.

"The prevailing assumption among Thelite leadership is that proles are highly subject to uncontrollable mental disorder. If I assumed that they were disordered and you were disordered, I would simply dismiss my observations.

"And why would those students make these claims and offer themselves for this purpose? Naivety? Stupidity? A means of challenging us? Again, the assumption among Thelites right now is that it is consistent with their disorder.

"But, if I assume the opposite, that neither of you are disordered, everything becomes more explainable. How do you know what you know? How are you familiar with people you've never met? Why did the students come forward? It is all more explainable if you assume the truth of their statements.

"But Julianna, your deceptions have made my work harder," she finished.

"Deceptions?" Julianna asked, innocently.

"Julianna, let's not fool around. I am among the most accomplished behavioral research scientists alive. That's why I have such a high accountability at such a young age. That's why I was appointed to a trusteeship when I was just slightly older than you." Marlo said all of this with no apparent pride. Just facts.

"Julianna, it probably hasn't been disclosed to you, but your capacity to assimilate information and sequences is tremendous. But you have been shunned because of your heritage. You are far more inquisitive and suspicious than most Thelites are comfortable with."

Julianna thought hard for a few moments, and Marlo let her. *Her eyes!* Julianna finally understood. She had mischaracterized them out of fear. They weren't cold. They weren't passionless. They weren't mean. They were just extremely, extremely intelligent. She could look at them directly now with challenge, intellection, and camaraderie.

And she did. "Marlo?" she asked. "Do you dream?"

"No," she said. "I can't even conceive of it. It's beyond my ability to visualize. I experience only perfectly efficient and restful sleep."

"Then how can you believe them?"

"It doesn't matter whether I believe it or not. I'm a scientist. Science explains things. Part of explaining things is understanding when you don't understand. I am just saying that I am observing something I don't understand and that I believe what I'm observing. Scientists need to do that."

"Mark doesn't see it the same way," Julianna said.

"Mark's not a scientist," Marlo responded dismissively. "Mark's a toy."

"A toy?" Julianna asked.

"Yes. A toy. A thing for entertainment. After working with him these past few months, his role in the Best Society is not clear to me. He used your father to establish his own credentials. He used you to highlight his importance. He is attempting to use me to advance his causes, as misdirected as they are. His idea of science is absolutism. Unfortunately, he has an audience, so I need to be careful with him." She paused and looked at Julianna with those intelligent eyes. "But I know how to be careful," she concluded.

Julianna recalled her father's warning. *Aha. Thanks, Father.*

"Julianna," Marlo continued. "Do you dream?"

"Yes," she said. "I have."

"That explains a lot," Marlo said, not showing the excitement that Julianna expected. "And that's how you know so much – beyond what you have been taught?"

"Yes – I guess. I don't remember learning those things. But they had to come from somewhere."

"I had a lab examine an unregulated substance from your apartment. It seems to be a primitive hallucinogen. What was that all about?" Marlo was officiously tending to her tablet as they spoke.

"Tea," Julianna said. "It helps with dreaming."

"I suspected as much. In fact, that discovery was the key to my hypothesis." Marlo looked up from her notes. "So, you knew the students from your dreams, too?"

"Yes," Julianna said. She was terrified of what she wanted to ask. "But Marlo, if you believe the students, why did you…you know…kill them?"

Julianna was afraid she'd taken the familiarity too far. Marlo took just a little too long before saying, "I didn't."

"But I thought…I mean, Mark said…" she stammered.

"Mark said that 'Marlo has been directed to send them to the Center for Transition Management,'" Marlo finished for her. "That's really funny," Marlo said, smiling for the first time Julianna had ever seen. "Mark believed he could direct actions inside of the Center for Behavioral Research. Personalities like Mark's – they need to be researched as well! He even thinks it's done! I just did what I thought best."

"Are they still here?"

"Not for long. They were taken to the Center and held in comas. I had them transferred here, and now they are recovered. This interview confirms many of my hypotheses. It's tricky, but I have a plan to get them out of here tonight."

"You're letting them go?" Julianna asked.

"They are neither disordered nor dangerous. We're not ready, or frankly capable, of performing the study they sought. My opinion? Humanity needs more of them, not fewer. Yes, I'm letting them go."

Julianna felt uncannily satisfied with what was happening with the students behind Mark's back. "Marlo, I don't know how to say this. But I thought you and Mark were…together?"

"Collaborators? Co-conspirators? Sex partners?" Marlo wrinkled her eyes in muted merriment. "I'm sure he thinks so, too."

Then she turned serious. "Julianna, I can't know if you were close to your uncle. I somehow think you were. You should know, he transitioned. I directed to have him brought out of his coma. But there were unusual struggles with the process. His body didn't respond as it should have. Highly improbable. Ultimately it was unsuccessful."

Julianna felt her body giving way to weakness and fatigue. "Somehow, I already knew that," she whispered. "That's why I didn't ask." She looked around the room feeling very much like an invalid. "I'm not sure what I'm supposed to do now?" she asked Marlo.

"Your physical health will recover. It will take a couple of days. But your BioGram has been removed. Your value to the Best Society has crossed over. There is no home for you in the community," Marlo thought out loud. "You are a good Thelite scientist. I could use your help here discreetly as we examine subjects. Or…"

"Or, what?" Julianna asked.

-41-
I think I know how

2084

The orderly who brought his food said nothing. "Can't you tell me anything?" Keaton asked.

The technician who measured his vitals grunted. "Don't know anything. We're just treating you according to protocol."

The last thing Keaton recalled, he and Abby were in their apartment. Some attendants came for a check-in. The next thing he knew, he regained consciousness on a medical gurney, alone except for the attendants. When he was able, they moved him to this windowless holding cell.

That was two days ago. Someone brought him food and checked his vitals regularly. Otherwise, he saw nobody. He had fleeting thoughts of escape but had no idea where he was. There wasn't even a handle on the inside of the door.

He had dreamt that Abby, Chad, and Meghan were nearby, but equally isolated. He sensed they were in a similar state of deprivation, but safe. *But for how long?* He couldn't rationalize how this had anything to do with dream research. It was too sinister.

"Good night," the technician said as the door clicked shut. That was the only way he knew evening was approaching.

Keaton picked at his food. The lights in his cell dimmed slowly. Foreseeing another restless night, he lay down. The uncertainty and isolation nearly drove him mad.

Sometime later, half-conscious, he sensed someone standing over him. He jerked up, but the person touched his shoulder gently. A voice whispered. "Quiet. Get up. Let's go!"

Keaton saw no alternative. Once in the dimly lit hallway, he saw the person was Marlo, leading him quickly to the next cell. She opened the door and soon emerged with Chad, who looked as confused as Keaton felt.

They tip-toed to the next cell where Marlo stepped out with Abby. She fled immediately into Keaton's protective embrace, trembling but quiet.

They moved silently to the next cell expecting to retrieve Meghan. Marlo entered the cell, and the silence was soon broken when Meghan screamed, "Get the fuck away! This is bull…" Her voice turned into a gurgle; there were slaps and sounds of a scuffle. Chad leapt toward the cell just as Marlo fought Meghan out the door in a chokehold with a hand over her mouth. Meghan kicked violently and bit at Marlo's hand. Marlo flung her toward Chad and retreated, shaking the pain from her injured hand. "Get her to shut up if you want to live!" she whispered urgently.

Meghan clung to Chad, glaring viciously back at Marlo. "Go to hell!" she growled.

"Meghan," Keaton whispered. "Shhh. I think we're better off quiet." Meghan restrained herself after scrutinizing her companions.

Marlo cocked her head, listening for anything suspicious. Hearing none, she started down the hallway. "Okay. Follow me. Quiet!"

Keaton pushed his companions along from behind. At the end of the hallway, Marlo used a palm scanner to open a "staff only" door and held it while the four stepped through. The room was cold and reeked of antiseptic, but there was also a strange, putrid smell underneath. Hums, clicks, and rumbles signaled machinery running invisibly in the shadows beyond the lighted area where they were gathered. Marlo led them deeper into the room. Lights turned on in front of them and turned off behind them as they moved, keeping them in an eerie space without reference other than the noise and smells.

Keaton snuck up to Marlo and whispered, "What is this place?"

"This is your way out," Marlo kept walking but no longer whispered. "It's okay to talk now. There won't be anybody here."

"Good. But…what does this room do?" Keaton wanted to trust her, but he was wary of being lulled into danger. The humdrum beat of machinery was ceaseless from just beyond the shadows. "Why are we here? And what's that smell?"

"It's the safest way out. That's all you need to know."

"Bullshit!" Meghan objected to Marlo. "You're a liar. This could be another trap!" She jerked away from Chad and bolted toward the noises in the shadows. She had gone several steps when Marlo tackled her. Meghan fought, scratching and biting, while Marlo used her overpowering physique to immobilize her. When Meghan squealed in pain, both Chad and Keaton pulled Marlo off by her arms, but just long enough for Meghan to get back up. Marlo was so strong that she pulled them both to follow Meghan into the shadows toward the noises.

Just then, Meghan's motion triggered a bank of lights that illuminated the source of the noise. Meghan stopped short and put her hand over her mouth in horror. Keaton's stomach lurched at the sight. He turned back to grab Abby and point her away.

From a passage at one end of the room running a hundred yards to the other end, a conveyor was loaded with bodies. Dead. Naked. A ceaseless stream of pus-colored flesh. Some were on their back with their arms folded over their chest. Some were mutilated, the rotten black of congealed blood staining their wounds. Some were just piles of body parts. Some were splayed and contorted, their faces frozen in a final grimace. They were stacked on each other in horrific, pornographic intimacy.

Several times a minute, the conveyor would clunk, and the bodies would rumble forward about ten feet, then stop with another clunk. Hydraulic whines and whooshes of air pressure from the end of the building hinted at another machine.

The combatants stood with their arms slumped to their sides. Chad tried to turn Meghan away from the carnage, but she resisted. "Who are these people?" she whimpered. "Who could do this?"

"This is the feed system for the Post-Transition Processor," Marlo admitted. Indifferent to the sight, she pointed toward the far end of the building. "Bodies from Transition Management are deposited on the other side of that wall," she pointed to an escapement behind them. "This conveyor pushes them together and feeds them into the processor at the most efficient rate."

Abby and Meghan stared open-mouthed at Marlo. "How could you...?" Meghan started, then stopped. "Why would you bring us here?"

"This is the only unmonitored way out of the city. I didn't intend for you to see it. There is a maintenance tunnel at the end of this room. That's where we're going." Marlo started walking again.

"You're letting us go?" Keaton asked with sudden realization as they caught up.

"I'm trying to, yes. But I might reconsider if she bites or kicks me again!"

"But why bring us here? Why not just drop us back at our village?" Keaton persisted.

Marlo stopped walking and the group clustered around her. "Look. Proles are not allowed in this community without authorization. If I had done as directed, you would all be on that conveyor right now. The authorities want you dead. You were all in comas near transition."

The news that they had been nearly killed knocked the wind out of Keaton. Meghan and Abby gasped. Chad turned pale.

"But I had you revived to research near-death behavioral phenomena. So they think. Nobody would care if you died during that research. It happens a lot. If I'm to let you go, it has to be as if you're dead. And as I said, this is the only way out."

"Are we in danger?" Abby's voice trembled as she asked.

"You're not home free. Among other things, you could get caught in one of these machines!" Marlo peered at Meghan. "So do as I say!" She turned on her heel and started walking again.

283

They reached the far end of the room. The processor growled thunderously. Each time the conveyor stopped, a hydraulic plunger pushed the newly-arrived bodies into a set of serrated rolls that unceremoniously ripped them up and swallowed them. Bone, flesh, and entrails squished together with grotesque, mechanical disinterest. The growl intensified momentarily while the conveyor advanced again.

Marlo led them to a narrow hatchway adjacent to the processor. Everyone was gathered close, and she had to yell to be heard. "This is as far as I go." She pointed to the hatch. "That's where you're going."

Keaton recognized there were no choices. "Where does it take us?"

"You will go about thirty feet along the drive train of the machine. Be careful! There's not much light, and there's not much room. Hug the right-hand wall and walk straight. You will reach a ladder at the other end. Climb the ladder and push open the cover at the top."

"Here," Marlo held out face masks and goggles for each of them. "Put these on now. The cover is on the edge of an ash pile. Once you open it, soot will fall in. It gets in your eyes and nose – you could suffocate. You want to keep the mask on until you get away from the pile."

"Pile?" Keaton questioned.

"The city's refuse processors, including this one, feed a bank of gasifiers to recover energy. The ash discharges into the area behind this building. It floats around in the air until it settles into a soft pile, but it stirs up easily."

"How do we get away from the pile," Chad edged in, speaking for the first time.

"There is a service road used by Best Society Services. They spray the pile to keep it settled and remove it to a landfill every so often. If you walk straight away from the building, you will run into that road. Then you're out. But you're on your own."

"So we need to figure out how to get back to our village," Abby deduced. She looked at her companions confidently. "I think I know how."

"You need to get going. I need to get back. It's almost dawn." Marlo opened the hatch.

Light from the room illuminated several belts, pulleys, and gears spinning rapidly on the left side of the tunnel. The passage was only wide enough for one person to be clear of the mechanisms. They donned their masks and goggles. Keaton prepared to enter the tunnel, but Meghan shoved him back.

"I'm going first, Keaton. I got us into this mess! I'm going to lead us out!" she declared. She stepped into the tunnel before anyone could argue. Chad followed on her heels, then Abby, and last Keaton. Once inside the tunnel, he looked back to express gratitude to Marlo. She was already closing the hatch. Keaton was struck by the determination evident in her dark eyes, but she said nothing.

The hatch clicked shut and it went dark. The chill of the other room was replaced with oppressive heat. Keaton quickly broke into intense sweat. He pressed himself against the wall and grabbed Abby's shirttail to follow her. Moving carefully, they passed clacking contraptions and spinning shafts that whistled only inches away from their faces. Colored LED's flashed periodically, casting shadows of levers and cylinders moving with strobe-light weirdness. Valves clicked, emitting puffs of stifling hot air that smelled of ash and burnt rubber.

They crept forward with awkward restraint until Meghan reached the ladder. "I'm going up!" she yelled through her mask to Chad. "I'll see if I can get the cover off. Watch out for the soot!" Chad passed the message to Abby who passed it to Keaton.

It was only a few rungs until Meghan bumped the cover with her head. She raised her arms and pushed with all her strength. She was encouraged by a slight movement, but she needed more leverage. She stepped up another two rungs and hunched over, putting the back of her shoulders against the cover and pushing with her legs. It moved a little more. She took another breath, repositioned her shoulders, and pushed again. She felt it moving gently, and then it broke completely free.

Immediately, ash cascaded like water through the dislocated edges around the cover. Meghan was forced down and lost her footing, clinging to the top rung of the ladder with just her arms against the torrent. The masks were of little use against the particulate fog that now filled the tunnel. There was little air to breath. The ash piled quickly to their knees, but they couldn't move lest they get caught in the machinery.

Keaton resisted panic as he felt the ash deepen. He couldn't get his breath. Just when he thought he might die by drowning in ash, he felt cool, outside air against the top of his head. Sensing the flood waning, he stretched his neck upwards to the air. Wiping the dust from his goggles, he was able to see the half-moon hole of the dislocated cover, backed by a lightening sky. Meghan was already working to move the cover out of the way. Chad was several rungs up the ladder, supporting her.

Keaton felt Abby sagging, unconscious. He tried to lift her to the fresh air, but he couldn't kneel for leverage in the constrained space. He grabbed her hair to pull her head up and keep her from slumping into the ash. With his arm extended over Abby's head and his fist full of her hair, he pushed it toward Chad, touching his leg to get his attention. Chad saw what was happening and reached down to grab her hair from Keaton, helping to keep her up. Keaton let the hair go and put a hand under her arm pit to support her, but she wasn't breathing.

Meghan cleared the cover and climbed out. Chad climbed several more rungs and let go of Abby's hair to grab her arm and pull her up – but she was dead weight. Keaton pushed her forward and up toward the ladder, but he was wading in thigh-deep ash and unable to brace himself.

Chad saw the situation and came back down. Taking one of Abby's arms over his shoulder and holding it, he climbed the ladder with his other arm. Abby hung listless against his back. When he had raised her several rungs, Keaton was able to get under her and support her from the back of her thighs. Chad was able to reposition and raise her several more rungs until Meghan could reach down through the hole and take Abby's free arm. The three of them wrestled her up through the hole.

Keaton followed Chad out of the hole in dread. Meghan had dragged Abby about thirty feet to hard earth and was frantically compressing her chest. Flinging away the mask and goggles, he ran to assist. Just as he got there,

Abby coughed, spitting black goo from her nose and mouth and snorting it back. *But she was breathing!*

Abby hacked and spit until she mustered the breath to sit up. She spoke hoarsely, "I didn't think I was going to make it. That soot is so fluffy – it just goes everywhere! I couldn't get away from it!"

Keaton reached for Abby's hands. "Can you stand up?" he helped her and she stood unsteadily.

"I'll be okay. Now we need to find the road. Right?" Abby looked at him. "You should see yourself!"

They took stock of each other in the emerging light. They were totally gray except for their eyes. The soot stuck to their sweaty clothes and bodies like a coating of paint. Whenever they moved or tried to shake it off, they disturbed a layer of ash on the ground that would float up and settle on them again. Everything within several hundred yards was the same dismal gray as they were.

"We need to get going. We still need to figure out how to get to the village," Meghan trudged farther from the pile. "Can you walk, Abby? Didn't you have some idea how to get there?"

"I can walk, just not too fast. Marlo said to walk away from the building until we run into a road. If we find the road, I'm sure I know what to do."

They walked slowly to disrupt as little ash as possible and skirted the pile, heading away from the building. The machinery noises receded steadily the farther they went, and the landscape started to show some color. After about a half mile they entered a scrubby woodland, guiding themselves with the well-risen sun. They came to a hedgerow and squeezed through, crossing a shallow ditch before finding an isolated gravel road. They stomped and patted each other to shake off as much dust as they could.

"Follow me," Abby said, leading them down the road to the right. A mile along, the road veered to the left. As they rounded the corner, Abby yelped, "There it is!" She was still wheezing from her ordeal, but she trotted ahead of the rest of the group toward a rickety van parked on the side of the road.

She peered in the driver's window and smiled. The driver was reclined in the seat, asleep.

She pounded on the window and stepped back. Just as the rest of the group approached, the door opened and the driver stepped out. Abby squealed. Meghan stopped short. "Aunt Kelly!" they yelled together.

-42-
Can't we just ignore them?

2084

Kelly drove with the windows open, letting the fresh wind wash over their grimy bodies. They downed quarts of bottled water, smearing some on their hands and faces to little effect. They were exuberant.

"I knew you would be here!" Abby spoke over the wind from the front passenger seat. "But what made you come?"

"It's weird. I wasn't sure what to expect," Kelly mused. "I should take this stuff more seriously."

"What do you mean?"

"I've been on the run – alone – ever since Shawn died. Slept under the stars a bunch. It's hard to explain. Things that should have been mysterious weren't – like I was being led. I would wake up and somehow know where to find food. Like my dreams were guiding me. But this..." Kelly looked around the van, stumbling for words. "I knew to come here, but I don't know how!"

"I felt you," Abby acknowledged. "Same as I do with Meghan. Somehow I knew you were alone. And I knew you would be here!"

"Yeah. But how does it work?"

"I suspect we'll never know," Abby confessed.

"Hey, Aunt Kelly!" Meghan yelled over the wind from the second seat. "Where are we going?"

"Delores' shop is closest – about a half hour away. You can all clean up. Then we'll figure things out."

"Sure. Be nice to see her again! But we can't wear these clothes anymore," Meghan pinched the crusty material on Chad and Keaton's shoulders. They were seated on each of her sides.

"There's a box of clothes in the back from the group I used to run with. You can find something in there, at least for a while," Kelly offered, then changed the subject. "Hey, guys. I can get you to Delores. But then I need to leave. There's people – Thelites – looking for me. I'm safest in the countryside. Don't want to be near any Hubs."

"I hate Thelites," Meghan's face turned savage. "They lie, and they would have killed us for no reason!"

"Me, too," Kelly agreed.

"I guess I see why," Chad put his arm around Meghan. "Maybe my father and grandfather are right about them. But I don't think Dad *hates* anybody."

"Maybe he should!" Kelly admonished. "Chad, I love Junior. But he doesn't even fight them!"

"Neither does Dr. Sanderson," Keaton looked wistfully out the window. "I think he was in there with us. I hope he got out, too."

"I hope so, too," Kelly shook her head. "But those guys let things go too far! Somebody should have tried to stop all this."

"Maybe people just think about it too much," Abby contested. "If we make our own lives happy, does it matter that much? Can't we just ignore them?"

"Really, Abby?" Kelly was shocked by her innocence. "These people are not going to stop! They take what we build, and then they want us gone! I think they're evil!"

Abby looked back at her companions for support. "But Marlo got us out! Why would she do that?"

Keaton agreed. "I wanted to thank her, but there was no time. She saved us, and I'd love to know why."

Kelly had no interest in hearing about Marlo. She guided the van through the narrow streets of People's Village #179, avoiding any proximity to the Hub. She pulled into the alley behind Delores' shop. "You guys shouldn't go in looking like that. Just take the box of clothes up to her apartment and get cleaned up. I'll find Delores and let her know what's going on."

"I can show you where to go. I lived here for a while," Keaton grabbed the flimsy cardboard box of hand-me-downs and led them up an outside stairwell. They separated the pieces of apparel and flung them around the room to see what they had.

The warmth of their showers, the freedom, and the familiar confines renewed their spirits. They giggled as they tried on different garments, exchanging pieces with each other until they were clothed in functional but ill-fitting outfits. Chad and Keaton each wore jumpsuits with the insignia of the foundry above the pocket. Abby and Meghan were each in over-sized trousers with cuffs turned up and baggy shirts tied at their waists.

Clean and rosy-cheeked, giddy with conversation, they clambered down the stairwell. A back door led into the room where Keaton stayed when he lived with Delores. From there, a door opened into the kitchenette of Delores' shop. Excited to see her, they clomped noisily through the back room and entered the shop.

It took them a few moments to grasp the unexpected, somber scene. There were no sounds of appliances or clatter of dishware. The tea and spice aromas were secondary behind stale dust. The normally cluttered kitchenette was orderly, and the table was virtually barren.

Kelly was seated silently and looking across at Delores. Delores was seated with her hands in her lap and her eyes closed. On the table in front of her was a china cup and saucer half full of cold tea, a journal, and a pen. Both Kelly and Delores were ominously still.

Once they were quiet, Kelly turned to them and sniffed. "She's dead."

Slowly, Keaton stepped to Delores and bent to kiss her cold, stiff cheek. He rounded the table and sat next to Kelly. Each of his companions followed him until they were all seated.

"What happened to her? What do we do now?" Abby asked.

"I'm not sure." Kelly pointed to the journal. "I didn't know she kept a journal. Should we look at it?"

Keaton pulled the journal across the table. "She kept them her whole life, I guess. There's a box of them up in her apartment." He examined it for a moment and then read her last entry out loud.

"Sandy's gone. Jacob's gone. David's gone. My work is done. I'm happy. It is time for me to go." Keaton shook his head in heartbreaking acknowledgement, then repeated softly, looking at Abby, "David's gone. That's why our dreams were so dark." He slid the journal to Abby.

Meghan looked ready to burst into tears. "This is all my fault! If I hadn't…"

"Bullshit!" Kelly interrupted. "Meghan, I'm not gonna let you do that. I don't know how to say it like Aunt Delores would, but David and her would never blame anyone for what someone else did! Whatever happened to them happened to them, and you didn't do it!"

"But, but…" Meghan tried to continue.

"Kelly's right," Keaton said, trying to calm her down. "Grieve. Don't blame. That's what Delores might say."

Chad stood and put his arms around her from behind. "Honey, we tried to do something good. Don't do this to yourself." She leaned onto his arm, crying quietly, and accepted his comfort.

Seeing that her sister was well tended, Abby leafed curiously through the pages of the journal. Two folded papers slipped from inside the back cover, and Abby examined them. "Oh! These are Delores' and David's wills." She read the first paper, then handed it to Kelly. She read the second paper, then handed it to Keaton.

"What do they say?" Meghan asked.

"Delores' left everything to Aunt Kelly, including her shop. David left everything to Keaton, including his lab," Abby summarized.

292

"That makes sense," Meghan said, recovering her composure. "Aunt Kelly, do you need us to help with anything?"

Kelly shook her head. "I can't take it. I can't stay here. As far as I'm concerned, you and Abby can use it however you want."

"I guess…" Meghan looked at her sister and Kelly. "I'm not interested in going back to Dad. And I'm done with the hub college for sure. Can I stay here? At least for a while?"

"We'll need an income," Abby realized. "Sure, stay here, Meghan. Keaton and I can help you run the shop."

"I'll help, too," Chad said. "My family still has some resources, but I have to talk to my father to see what we can use."

They were tittering about the possibilities when Kelly rose abruptly. "Look, girls, this is all good. But I need to leave. Chad, it was nice to see you again. Keaton, it was nice to meet you." She went to Delores and put her hand on her cheek. "Safe travels, Aunt Delores. Thank you."

-43-
These were her people

2084

Moving around without her BioGram was tenuous freedom for Julianna. She couldn't have traveled to the Hub area of People's Village #179 on her own. Marlo smuggled her onto a transport for behavioral researchers who would observe proles. When they arrived at the Hub, Julianna simply walked away.

But the world no longer responded to her whims. Doors didn't just open; driverless cars didn't just show up; environments didn't just adjust to her presence. She couldn't order her thoughts and communications instantly. The lack of schedule reminders made her day haphazard. She just acted on her impulses as they occurred.

Pausing to look back from a block away, Julianna observed how the Hub worked like a precision machine. Each thing within it had a purpose. Walkways took people to specific places. People queued when they were supposed to. Nobody walked in the landscaping. Driverless devices on travelways had routes and protocols and priorities. Building corners were square, unless they weren't supposed to be. But they were always what they were supposed to be. Colorful surfaces were never chipped. All the glass was clean. Pristine. Julianna watched the machine work, accepting with bizarre removal that she was no longer one of its cogs.

It was easier to notice things. It was a pleasant fall day. Trees had more color. Birds had more voice. A cloud blocked the sun for a moment, and she heard the insects slow down. They sped up again when the cloud moved on. Having forfeited her Best Society uniform, her clothing was less accommodating. She could feel it on her body. The cool air crisped her exposed skin while the sun simultaneously warmed it. Her footwear was utilitarian. She might get a blister. Her bangs were too long and caught in her eyelashes.

Julianna knew instinctively where she needed to go. The route, so elusive earlier, was clear in her mind. The crowd was light and navigable as she left the Hub. The people were as nonconforming as she remembered, the routes as circuitous, the order as nonsensical. It suited her now.

She arrived at Delores' shop. The entry bell tinkled as she entered, triggering welcome reminiscences. She stopped just to take in the shop's aroma. So familiar. Homey. Standing behind the counter, Keaton looked up, smiling broadly. "Julianna! Welcome! We've been expecting you!" The announcement brought Chad, Meghan, and Abby from the kitchenette in an excited flurry. Hugs, kisses, tugs, rubs: they all felt so right as she was drawn to the back to sit with them. Chad made tea. Meghan and Abby made breathless conversation about their recent experiences. Keaton said little but attended to everyone, just happy to be of service.

The shared depth of sorrow for Delores and David was new and welcome to Julianna. The heights of joy in each other's company was, too. There was an uncertain future to think about. Plans for the tea shop. Plans for the lab. Things to be done. Possibilities to consider.

When there was a pause, Julianna reached for several of their hands to slow them down. She needed their attention, a pause. She had a thoughtful and important request. "I just want all of you to know, I'm so sorry about David. And Delores. They seem so…so…important? To all of us! It feels somehow wrong that we're here and they're not. And somehow, I think it was about me. My fault. Can you forgive me?"

They all looked at each other, sniffling a little, not knowing who should answer. Abby eventually wiped her eyes with her napkin to speak. "Julianna, Delores was our great aunt – Meghan and mine," she looked to Meghan, who was smiling around her runny nose and eyes. "She taught us so much. And your Uncle David was so good to her. But I think they wanted this. They wanted us all together. There's nothing to forgive. They loved you. We love you," she explained. Each of them nodded as she looked at them.

"I love you all, too," Julianna said. It was the first time in her life she had used those words. It was right. She could tell. These were her people.

The End

About the Author

Joel E. Lorentzen grew up on a small farm in eastern Iowa. Joel's family of seven lived the life of the rural working poor, saved by the stubborn resolve of parents who refused to give up. A scholarship permitted his Iowa State University education as an engineer, but his elective choices were literature and creative writing. He later obtained an MBA from the University of Iowa. Joel travelled the world extensively as an automation engineer for over 36 years. Along the way, he invested in a variety of private manufacturing companies which he continues to serve as a consultant, permitting his self-identified occupation as "semi-retired."

Long plane rides and airport layovers served his passion for reading and writing. His background provided a distinct sense of the travails and resilience of working people, those he recognizes as the ones whose efforts really make the world go.

Joel enjoys socializing with family, friends, and business associates of every background and culture, but prefers small groups where voices can be heard and reasoning fully explored. Joel avoids social media, sporting events, and concerts. He lives and loves a physically active lifestyle.

Joel shares his life with his wife, Ann. They have one daughter, Rebecca, all grown up and a mother herself. Ann and Joel reside in Rock Island, Illinois. They recreate at a second home in Lake of the Ozarks, Missouri where they enjoy boating, fishing, and hiking.

Learn more about <u>Proles</u> and the author at

www.prolesthebook.com

Made in the USA
Columbia, SC
12 February 2021